D1015839

ICEFALL

TOR BOOKS BY GILLIAN PHILIP

Firebrand
Bloodstone
Wolfsbane
Icefall

ICEFALL

REBEL ANGELS
BOOK FOUR

GILLIAN PHILIP

A TOM DOHERTY ASSOCIATES BOOK
NEW YORK

ICEFALL

Copyright © 2013 by Gillian Philip

All rights reserved.

Grateful acknowledgment is made for permission to reprint lines from "Love in Time's Despite" from *The Labyrinth* by Edwin Muir courtesy of the Estate of Edwin Muir and Faber & Faber Ltd.

A Tor Book
Published by Tom Doherty Associates, LLC
175 Fifth Avenue
New York, NY 10010

www.tor-forge.com

Tor® is a registered trademark of Tom Doherty Associates, LLC.

The Library of Congress Cataloging-in-Publication Data is available upon request.

ISBN 978-0-7653-3325-4 (hardcover)
ISBN 978-1-4299-6792-1 (e-book)

Tor books may be purchased for educational, business, or promotional use. For information on bulk purchases, please contact the Macmillan Corporate and Premium Sales Department at 1-800-221-7945, extension 5442, or write to specialmarkets@macmillan.com.

First published in Great Britain by Strident Publishing Limited

First U.S. Edition: March 2015

Printed in the United States of America

0 9 8 7 6 5 4 3 2 1

For Elizabeth Garrett, who gave the clann a home in exile.

And always for Lucy and Jamie Philip.

THE SITHE AND THE FULL-MORTALS

(THE STILL-HERE AND THE LONG-GONE)

Kate NicNiven: Queen of the Sithe, by consent

Seth MacGregor (Murlainn): Son of Griogair and Lilith; half brother to Conal

Jed Cameron (Cuilean): Full-mortal; half-brother to Rory

Rory MacSeth (Laochan): Seth's son and Jed's half-brother

Hannah Falconer MacConnell (Currac-sagairt): Conal Mac-Gregor's daughter

Iolaire MacEarchar: Once Kate's fighter, now Seth's; lover of Jed

Leonora Shiach: Witch, mother of Conal and bound lover of Griogair

Griogair MacLorcan (Fitheach): Father of Conal and Seth

Conal MacGregor (Cù Chaorach): Son of Griogair and Leonora

Lilith: Kate's right-hand woman; Seth's mother

Stella Shiach (Reultan): Half-sister to Conal; daughter of Leonora

Aonghas MacSorley: Bound lover of Stella/Reultan

Finn MacAngus (Caorann): Daughter to Stella and Aonghas

Eili MacNeil: Lover of Conal

Sionnach MacNeil: Eili's twin brother; Seth's best friend since childhood

Liath & Branndair: Wolf-familiars of Conal and Seth

Faramach: Raven-familiar of Finn

Gelert: Grian's hunting dog

Gocaman & Suil: Watchers at the otherworld watergates

Orach, Braon, Carraig, Sorcha, Fearna, Oscarach, Diorras, Sgarrag, Fraoch, Sulaire (cook), Grian (healer): Fighters of Seth's clann

Cluaran MacSeumas: Kate's Captain; Iolaire's foster father

Gealach, Alainn MacAleister: Two junior captains of Kate's clan

Glanadair: Clann Captain of Faragaig

Leoghar: Glanadair's lieutenant

Nils Laszlo: Full-mortal Captain of Kate's clann

Cuthag, Gealach, Darach, Raib MacRothe: Fighters of Kate's clann

Langfank: A Lammyr

Lauren Rooney: Hannah's Other Cousin

Sheena & Martin Rooney, Aileen Falconer, Shania & Darryl: Hannah's Other Family

Miss Emmeline Snow: A kindly stranger

The Wolf of Kilrevin: Not a very nice man

You who are given to me to time were given
Before through time I stretched my hand to catch
Yours in the flying race.

—Edwin Muir, "Love in Time's Despite"

On desperate ground, fight.

—Sun Tzu, *The Art of War*

A plague on both your houses.

—Shakespeare, *Romeo and Juliet*

ICEFALL

Prologue

He'd never slept well in the city. It was not the noise that kept him wakeful, the distant wail of a car alarm or the clatter and shriek of drunken students below the window. It was the light, the humming glow of streetlamps or the sudden fleeting glare of headlights across the thin curtains. Carraig flicked his half-smoked cigarette into the ashtray and flung his arm across his eyes, but the low-level orange glare leaked in no matter what he did.

I'll go back north, he thought. *Tomorrow.*

North is darker.

Streetlights and the city had to be better than the alternative, didn't they? Sometimes he wondered. Sometimes he wondered if no life might be better than half a life. Three years out of his hundreds, he'd spent this side of the Veil, and he knew he hadn't been missing a damn thing. The cigarettes he could live without; it was just that they passed the time.

Carraig lit another.

Tomorrow he had work to do, a minor rewiring job in that nursing home just out of the city. And that was another positive, wasn't it? He liked electricity; it had always felt to him like a kind of odd telepathy. He liked to sense it, feel the thrum of it as he worked with it. He'd taken to it straight away and learned it fast, fascinated by its invisible beauty and strength and the danger that lay in it. Predictable danger, if you knew it, but never to be toyed with, because treated with disrespect it became capricious. On the Veil's other side he'd always thought Murlainn's turbines and generators a frivolity. Now, if they ever returned—and yearning churned inside him at the thought—now, he'd happily take over the maintenance.

He needed to spend less time pining for home. Swinging his legs off the narrow hired bed, he walked to the window and pulled aside the thin curtain, then yanked on the sash frame. It stuck fast when the gap was no more than an inch wide.

Swearing under his breath, Carraig retrieved his dagger from his overnight bag, and prised out the rusty nail that restricted the window. He tossed it out onto the street and hoisted the window wide, letting icy air flood the room.

The smell of the October frost was tainted with beer and vomit. Leaning out, he gazed down at the kid throwing up in the hotel doorway. A shout, and the hotel owner was barging out to shove the youth away into the road, where a passing car braked and swerved and shrilled its horn. It narrowly missed Carraig's own car, parked below, feathers of thick frost settling on its roof.

North, he thought. North wasn't his true home but it felt closer to it. He missed his clann. He missed his Captain and he missed the boy he no longer referred to, even in his head, as *Bloodstone.* Because those days and hopes were gone and there was no point. Rory MacSeth was all the boy was; that and *Laochan,* though young champion he would never now have a chance to be.

Carraig's spine tensed instinctively and he lifted his gaze and frowned at the overground railway. A late train clattered across the arches, its grimy windows a long illuminated patchwork that faded, echoing, towards the central station. Shadows in this world were unreliable, but he could swear something had moved in the underpass, in the blackness of the central arch.

Carraig blew out a lungful of smoke and tossed his fag end to the street below. Its glowing tip shrivelled and died against the cold pavement. Going very still, Carraig leaned forward and reached out with his mind towards the darkness.

Nothing moved in the emptiness now, no hostile block scratched against his searching mind. How could he trust instincts that regularly lied to him in this alien place? It might have been rat, cat or homicidal enemy, but it was gone now. Spitting, he backed away from the window and shoved down the sash with an echoing clunk.

His Captain too was forced to skulk in this otherworld, and Carraig had no right to think himself worse off than Murlainn. He had no right to think he knew better than his Captain, or felt it more. Unless a wounded and bleeding soul took the edge off it, he thought sourly. More than three years Murlainn's soul had been slowly haemorrhaging, and Carraig could not help but wonder when it would be too late. Perhaps, for Murlainn, it already was, and that was why he had resigned himself to lifelong exile. Perhaps the man no longer cared. Perhaps his life was already reduced to nothing but the blood that throbbed in his veins.

Carraig shivered with pity. Sometimes he was glad he had no child, that there was no connection for a witch-queen to sever. Even though Murlainn was bound to another witch himself, there was nothing she could do about it, any more than the rest of them.

Still, Caorann's witchcraft might be negligible, but she had plenty of influence with Murlainn in other ways. Carraig grinned to himself. He liked Caorann. She knew how it felt to be on the sharp end of Murlainn's lousy moods. She wanted her lover safe, but she knew as well as the rest of them did that however safe the otherworld was for the clann, there was no safety for Murlainn, not with his soul bleeding and draining away.

If he spoke with the others, if they went together to Caorann, maybe she'd intercede. Maybe she'd talk sense into their Captain. The mere thought of it lightened Carraig's heart. Better to die fast in battle with the queen than rot slowly in exile, and surely Murlainn knew it in the depths of what was left of his soul.

Carraig stuffed his spare shirt and his iPod into his overnight bag, leaving only his wash kit and his car keys to grab in the morning. He found he was smiling. A half-decent night's sleep suddenly seemed a real possibility, and then one last job. And after that, a long drive north, to a sky with visible stars and to the sympathetic ear of his Captain's witch lover.

Caorann. We've had enough. Take us home.

She lifted her head, creasing her eyes against the silver glare off the sea. For long moments she held her breath, her heart slowing and thudding. But the voice was no more than a scratch against her consciousness; something overheard or half-imagined. There was no-one close enough to call out to her; if there was, she'd be dead by now.

With one more furtive glance over her shoulder, Finn relaxed. The broad white beach was deserted, but for the gulls and the skittering crabs and a single eagle, high up above the crags. She'd very much have liked to plunge right into the summer sea, but it would have felt unfair, like stealing an entire world for herself. She wasn't supposed to be in this one anyway. She'd go back soon.

Soon.

Kicking off her shoes, she walked into the sun-spangled waves. She wriggled her toes into the yielding sand. Sometimes the time-slip cheered her; summer was long dead on the other side of the Veil, yet here it lingered. Why would she be in a hurry to return to winter? Especially with the bone-deep chill still lingering in her marrow. The chill, and the tugging summons that had called her here.

She glanced back at the cave that was no more than a smear of shadow against the cliff. There was deeper shadow inside, darkness that the sun would never touch.

Finn shook off the memory of it. If she waited for the sun to penetrate as deep as the cold had gone, she'd never get home. And she had to go back.

Soon.

Sea-light caught dunlin-wings as a flock of them skittered onto the wet sand on the shoreline. Above the deeper, bluer sea, a gull rode the air current.

This isn't fair on the others.

There were birds here, and sky, and sunlit waves warming the skin of her feet. There was more to this world than the darkness in the caves.

I have to go back to the otherworld soon. But I'll tell the clann what's here.

Not everything. She couldn't tell everything about what she'd seen and what she'd done. Not ever.

But I'll tell Seth about the watergate. Maybe. At the right moment.

The sun beat warm on the nape of her neck, and the breeze smelt of salt and summer grasses. Above her the eagle circled higher into the shimmering blue, scanning a moor that she knew was empty for miles. She had time. Five minutes more, letting the horror drain from her bones, and she'd go back. And then she'd pick her moment to tell Seth. Tell him what she'd found, and perhaps half of what she'd done.

Soon.

The winter sun hadn't yet risen, but there was a paleness to the edge of the world that hinted at dawn. Carraig jerked the shabby hotel's door shut behind him and sidestepped the vomit of last night, then paused on the pavement, playing his car keys through his fingers.

On the brink of day it wasn't so bad, not if he closed his eyes. Even the city was freshened by the chill of the night just gone, and the hour before morning was sharp with smoky frost. The street lights were dimming as the strip of daylight pearl widened between the buildings.

Remembering his promise to himself, his gut twisted with longing and nerves. One last job, then, and after that: north. The roof and windscreen of his car were patterned thickly with ice but it was fine, he had time to warm it up and listen to the morning news as he waited.

The streets lay in such calm stillness, Carraig was almost reluctant to turn the key in the ignition. And it took him three tries before the engine coughed, and purred into life. He turned on the Today programme, the volume low, and sat back in the driver's seat, his breath clouding the inside of the windows.

One of the presenters laughed at a comment from the sports reporter. He'd missed it. Carraig leaned forward, turned up the volume. He glanced at his watch, impatient. He rubbed his palm across the condensation on the window. The sooner he got going, the sooner he fixed the wiring in that bloody Merrydale place, the sooner he'd be driving towards his clann.

He sighed, shook his head, and pressed his foot on the accelerator.

Carraig knew electricity. He had time to sense it now, and somewhere in his blood and bones he understood the gentle movement of the tilt switch, the moment of completion as the current closed.

He understood, he had time for that, but there was no time even to take a breath to scream. The fireball exploded with the speed of thought. Carraig's last moment was light and heat and a crushing blast wave, and a crystal rainstorm of shattered glass.

PART ONE

Hannah

The sound was so soft, I'd never have heard it if a breeze had stirred. The faintest whisper, like leaf against leaf, or steel against leather.

I hesitated, glancing behind me, hitching my backpack higher on my shoulder. I was probably imagining it. I had things to do, books to read, prospectuses to study. This was my final school year and I was impatient to know where my life was going. I didn't have time for getting spooked by shadows.

All the same.

Turning, I scanned the street. Broad autumn daylight. Cool and overcast, it was true, but weak shafts of sun filtered through onto cracked concrete and corrugated iron. This was the dingy end of town, the deserted end. No reason that alley between the warehouses should look so dark. No reason, except my imagination.

Except I was fairly sure that was a footstep.

Nothing moved. Shadow leaked out of the alleyway, pooled between a parked car and a lorry: so very dark, when there wasn't much sun. I couldn't even hear a gull. Late afternoon and even the shabby corner pubs were quiet. Weird. Like being sealed in a capsule of stillness and fear.

I shrugged. Sniffed. Walked on. Stopped again.

The silence wasn't empty. There was something inside it,

something that could think and hate, something that could move. Something that *would* move, when it chose to.

I stood quite still. I could feel the cold fear in my spine, now, trying to make me run. I mustn't run.

Too late to call Rory. And anyway, did I want to? If this was anything more sinister than some suicidally ill-judged piss-take from cousin Lauren and her pals, I might only draw him into a trap. He was the one they mustn't have. I was dispensable. In the long run.

Not that I thought much of that idea. In the short run.

I showed my teeth. There was still the chance this was only Lauren, and I didn't want to make a fool of myself. Didn't want to overreact or anything.

I didn't think it was Lauren.

'Come on, then.'

My words echoed off blank walls.

'I said come *on*. If you're hard enough.'

That was fine. That was fine, my voice had come out steady. It wouldn't do that again, not now that a figure had stepped out of the alleyway. A woman, I guessed from the silhouette moving forward: tall, and kind of elegant. Yes, a woman: pale hair twisted into a braid, mouth curved in an apologetic smile. Sword held lightly, almost casually, and now she flipped its hilt so that the blade was held high, and drew it to her face in salute.

Lovely, I thought. Honestly, very graceful. With luck she'd do the whole thing as beautifully as that. Fast and painless.

Of course, I'd rather she didn't do it at all. Letting my backpack slip from my shoulder, I swung it in a threatening arc.

'Hannah Falconer McConnell.' It wasn't a question.

'Yeah? And?'

'Come along, now,' said the pale-haired woman. 'Don't make a fuss.'

'I will, though.'

'Please don't make this any harder.'

'Uh-huh. Right.' I lashed the backpack at her.

Pathetic. The bag was heavy, the movement clumsy. Stepping neatly back, the woman swung her sword, severing the strap. Lunging, I snatched it as it fell and raised it like a shield. Even more pathetic, but I'd like to have heard a better suggestion.

'You're being very silly,' the woman told me.

I didn't dignify that with a reply. Anyway, I only had time to thrust the bag forward to catch the swinging blade. It thunked through canvas and into textbooks and notepads and glossy university brochures.

Homework has always had its uses.

Sucking her teeth in exasperation, the woman tugged her sword loose as she grabbed the backpack with her free hand and wrenched it from my grip.

'Now, shush. Let's get it done. Quickly, I promise.'

I stumbled back as my bag was flung to the ground. I don't know what was stronger, the disbelief or the terror. This had happened so fast. I'd been walking home, pissed off at the thought of having to study at the local redbrick next year because *you can't leave here, not on your own, you're not going out of our sight*. And now I was never going to take a degree anywhere, because I was going to die.

This was not how I'd planned my life or my evening. I'd have liked to run, but there didn't seem any point.

'Shush,' soothed the woman again, and drew back her blade on a line with my neck.

At the furthest point of her lazy backswing, she hesitated, and frowned, and glanced down.

My breathing was high-pitched, and my whole body was shaking, but I looked too. A sharp point of steel had appeared between the woman's ribs, just to the left of her sternum, and as she growled in astonishment, a sinewy arm went round her neck and jolted her backwards. The blade tip poked further out of her chest; I watched it, mesmerised.

Her shock had turned to rage, too late. As she tried to turn, the silver light in her eyes faded. She dropped to her knees, her sword scraped and then clanged on the pavement. With a last irritated look at me, she pitched forward onto her face and died.

The man who stood over the corpse tugged at his sword. It wouldn't come loose, and he had to put his foot on the woman's back and jerk it hard out of her ribs. It came out with a horrible sucking *thwick* that made me want to be sick. Nothing altruistic. I was thinking it would have made the same noise coming out of me.

My saviour raised an eyebrow.

~ *That'll teach her to keep an open mind.*

Someone was breathing hard and very fast. It wasn't the newcomer, the man with the neat goatee, the unruly black hair and the brutal facial scars. Presumably it wasn't the dead tart. Must be me, then.

Taking a deep breath, I smiled.

'Sionnach,' I said. 'Have you got nothing better to do than be my bodyguard?'

He shrugged, glanced down at the corpse. ~ *No.*

He frowned again.

~ *You okay?*

No, I'm about to fall over and I think I want to cry. 'I'm fine. Fine.' I let out a shuddering breath.

'You shouldn't walk home alone,' he said aloud. 'Where's Rory?'

'In the library. He's still got loads of catching up to do.'

'Well, we need him. Call him.'

Seeing as I'd been dying to, I did what I was told. Of course, Sionnach didn't give me time to catch my breath or rearrange my hair. When the love of my life appeared, running to my rescue, I was grunting and sweating from the effort of helping drag a corpse into a handy doorway. Sionnach let go of the woman's limp arm and straightened, eyeing Rory accusingly as he skidded to a halt.

'Sionnach.' He was out of breath.

Sionnach shook his head. 'Hannah was alone. Not again, hear?'

'No. Right. I know. God, Hannah, I'm sorry.'

I pushed a damp rat-tail of hair behind my ear and smiled, trying to look cool, so glad to see him the fear of death was already slipping off me like snakeskin. I liked that tight knot of love in my gut. It let me know I was still a human being, and being hunted down in an alleyway wasn't all there was to it.

Rory's face split in a grin. It was pretty funny that he still got bossed around by Sionnach, now that he was an inch taller than him. Tall, feral, and full of mischief: an overgrown Lost Boy. His bright hair had darkened in the last couple of years, his face had grown thinner and harder, and his grey eyes had the shadowy glint of his father's. But he still had the elfish beauty I'd fallen for on the most chaotic day of my life. Best of all, he still loved me. I hoped he always would. My Rory Bhan. My one-time lover. My cousin.

Sionnach coughed. 'When you're quite ready.'

Rory looked abruptly away, and I forced a pout to stop myself laughing too. I liked to hear Sionnach being sarcastic. There hadn't been much of the old Sionnach in the last three years. Not since he lost the other half of himself, not since Alasdair Kilrevin put a sword blade through his twin.

He went still, raising his head. 'Someone's coming. Do it now.'

Shocked, Rory said, 'What?'

~ *Do it.*

Obediently Rory reached for thin air and the fragile thing that was hidden in it. Sionnach's nerves were contagious. My own heart, which I reckoned had stopped five minutes ago when it got stuck in my throat, crashed back into my chest and into overdrive. Delayed shock, maybe, but it made my head spin. The fear was becoming panic, because I knew Sionnach was right—he always was—but Rory was struggling with the Veil. Beyond the defences of a Sithe fortress, that was unheard of.

'Rory. What's wrong?'

Rory's fingertips scrabbled, like he was trying to grab glass. He swore. I could feel his panic growing.

'I thought it was thinning,' I hissed.

'It is. It was!'

'Come *on*. Veil or no Veil, somebody's going to notice a *corpse*.'

'Yeah, no *kidding*.'

Sionnach said nothing, only stared into the shadows.

This was stupid. It was meant to be withering, but the Veil had picked a fine time to get its strength back. Rory was getting no grip on it at all. For an instant he looked completely bewildered, but he clenched his fists, and his face darkened.

He had that cold look of his father's now. Flattening his fingers he thrust them forward like a blade, snatching hold of something I couldn't see.

Sionnach took a step towards the alleyway. ~ *Whoever it is, they're close.*

With a growl, Rory hauled on his handful of Veil, and it began to give: like tearing oilcloth. He put his other hand to the rip, dragged it remorselessly wider. The sinews stood out on his wrist with the effort.

He grunted as the gash widened at last. Let go, and stood up. He froze.

Then he stumbled back, and would have fallen on his backside if he hadn't crashed into me.

'Rory . . .' I began.

A tremor ran through his skin, and he'd gone very cold. I looked up and past him, towards the tear in the Veil. Something oozed from the gash, all chill and black fear. Instinctively I shuffled backwards away from it, dragging Rory.

For a moment he let himself be tugged away, then his muscles hardened and he wriggled out of my grip. On all fours he crawled back towards the hole, then clambered to his feet and seized the Veil's torn edges in both hands. Even Sionnach was staring at Rory now, the intruder forgotten.

'What's that?' he said. There was fear in his hoarse voice.

Rory couldn't spare him an answer. The gap in the Veil couldn't be more than a metre long, but I could just make out its distorted shadow where the weak sunlight caught it. It sagged inwards, bulging, like it was going to rip further.

I'd never felt anything like it, not in all the many times it had given way to Rory. It *always* obeyed him, but now I had a feeling the Veil had rebelled for the first time. You'd almost think that at its heart, caught in the membrane, there was a trapped darkness that wanted out.

I'd never been afraid of the Veil between the worlds, never. Even the first time Rory tore it for me, four summers ago that felt like decades, I'd been only gobsmacked, and mistrustful, and rationally angry. I'd never felt this lump of fear in my belly. Whatever the darkness was, it didn't fascinate me. I only wanted it gone, but I was terribly afraid it *wouldn't* go. The gap yawed, sagged further, stretched like a living thing.

We'd taken it by surprise. The Veil, I mean. The thought struck me, unexpected and bizarre. We'd woken something that hadn't expected to wake; it had been disturbed unawares, but it wasn't ready to explode from its restraining membrane.

And just as well, was my instinctive thought.

Rory dragged the edges together and stood rigid, clutching the gap shut. I couldn't so much see that it was closed as sense it, because the strange coldness was gone like a sigh.

It seemed an age before Rory loosened his fingers and stepped back.

I took a breath to say *And what are we going to do with the dead tart now,* but I never got the chance. Rory reached out, almost thoughtlessly, and tore the Veil again.

It ripped like gossamer. He used a light forefinger and he didn't even have to take a breath.

I gaped at him, but Sionnach wasn't struck dumb. He grabbed the dead woman's arm and hauled her to the new rip in the Veil, bundling and shoving her through. Getting a hold of myself, I helped him, pushing the woman's dangling foot through the gap as Sionnach threw her sword after her. With no fuss at all, Rory clasped the Veil's edges and sealed it, and she was gone.

The three of us were panting for breath, staring at the space she'd filled, when the air was shattered by a tinny blast of unidentifiable R&B.

Sionnach turned. The music died abruptly; a phone clattered to the paving stones. As we gaped, a manicured hand shot round the corner to grab for it.

Nonchalantly Sionnach took a pace closer and trod hard on the hand. There was a yelp of angry pain as he bent to pick up the phone, turning it in his hand, thumbing the touchscreen with interest.

'Come out,' he said. 'Lauren.' He tilted an eyebrow at me.

'Aw, hell,' muttered Rory. I swore more creatively.

She stumbled to her feet, clutching her bruised hand, glaring at all three of us. Not a muscle of Sionnach's face moved now, and I thought: *Uh-oh.* When his hand went to the hilt of the short sword hidden inside his leather jacket, Rory put a hand on the man's arm. Sionnach scowled.

I forced a smile. 'Hi, Lauren.'

Rory's breath sighed out of him. 'Sionnach, watch where you're putting your feet. Y'okay, Lauren?'

'Fine,' she spat.

'What did you just see, Lauren?' asked Sionnach.

'Nothing. Like I'd be interested. I wasn't even looking.'

'Really?'

'You broke my best nail.' She folded her arms aggressively. 'Although that's nothing compared to you dragging that wom—'

This time Rory had to shove in front of Sionnach, seize his jacket, and pull it back across the emerging blade. He gave Lauren a tight smile. 'The drunk one?'

'The—'

'Drunk one,' I said.

'She didn't look drunk to—'

Sidestepping Rory, Sionnach offered Lauren her phone back, his lips tightening in an almost-smile. The girl just stood there, glowering nervously.

Sionnach's unconvincing smirk stayed in place as he thrust the phone forward again. I knew he was still wondering if he ought to kill Lauren, so this time I shouldered him sideways. Now Rory and I together were blocking him quite efficiently, but I knew the man could snake past us fast enough if he felt like it.

'In the middle of the afternoon and all,' said Rory. 'Dead. Drunk.'

Lauren eyed us, mistrust fairly oozing out of her. 'Where did she go?'

'I dunno.' Rory shrugged and pointed hopefully at the grubby stained-glass window of the nearest pub. 'In there? Gosh, I hope she doesn't come back!'

Oh, very convincing. Not. I gave Lauren my sweetest smile. 'I'm sure she won't be back.'

I knew fine Lauren wasn't even half-convinced, but Sionnach hadn't taken his eyes off her. Working on the girl's brain, just like Rory. Between the pair of them, Lauren didn't stand a chance. At last she rolled her eyes and blew out a sigh.

'Stupid drunk.' She nibbled crossly at her ragged nail. 'She made me break my best—'

'Well,' said Rory. 'All over. Want to come back with us? Have a go on my Xbox?'

~ *Rory*. Sionnach had stiffened, and he was giving him the kind of glower that used to be reserved for when Rory was a young brat and had a habit of running away.

~ *Sionnach*, said Rory, glaring back. ~ *It's not a problem*.

~ *Yes. It is.*

I'd have backed Sionnach up, but I was unnerved. ~ *Sionnach, she saw something. We can't just let her*—

~ *Live?*

~ *Sionnach!*

But Lauren heard none of that. She was still watching Rory with narrowed eyes. 'Have you got *Grand Theft Auto*?'

'No, but he's got the latest *Call of Duty*.' I back-kicked Sionnach's ankle. 'Yeah, come on back with us.'

'Well, that's a first.' Lauren almost grinned at me. 'Thanks.'

Sionnach's anger was coming off him in radioactive waves, but it was an offer Lauren couldn't refuse and I wasn't about to withdraw it. She was my cousin, even if not the one I was in love and lust with, and it was undeniably odd that I'd never invited her back to my new place. After all, I hadn't bitten her face for at least three years, and she hadn't gouged my eyeballs. Maybe we were both older and wiser; maybe it was just that we didn't have to share a bathroom any more, or indeed a house.

I lived with my real family now, with my uncle and the exiled clann he captained, and I was happy. Probably happier than any of them, since I was the only one who wasn't dislocated and homesick. My life would be pretty much perfect, in fact, if it wasn't for college applications, and the high chance of being hunted down and murdered.

~ *Get rid of Lauren as soon as you can,* Sionnach told me. ~ *This is a mistake.*

~ *It'll be fine.*

~ *We're all going to regret it.*

Within about ten seconds, I already did. At school Lauren was inclined to eye Rory a little too closely and too long, and now, as we headed home through the deserted streets, she might have been surgically attached to his flank. Rory was way too polite and naive to tell her where to go, and Sionnach dropped back about fifty metres.

It pissed me off, and funnily enough it wasn't jealousy. It was just that Sionnach belonged with us more than Lauren ever would. Nobody had the right to take his place.

I glanced over my shoulder, and Sionnach gave me one of his most beautiful grins.

~ *It's okay.*

Well. He might not mind, but I did.

Nobody could say we lived in the best part of the city, but it was certainly the oldest. Half the old warren called Fishertown— 'town' must have been a bit of stretch from day one—had been flattened to make way for warehouses and factory units and offices. What was left, when the heritage charities finally got their act together, was huddled on the far side of the industrial estate, cut off from the rest of the city: a few cobbled streets and low terraced cottages with quaint streetlights that I suspected weren't the originals. Some Victorian shipowner had built a big house to the south, right up on the cliffs, overlooking his fiefdom. It was ramshackle now, dilapidated and unloved and unsold because the sea was eating at its foundations. Frankly I didn't like to walk out on the headland and look back at the cliffs, riddled with tunnels and caves. At two in the morning, waking with a start, I could imagine the whole house collapsing into one of those holes.

Rory's stepmother had found the house, or it had found her: love and real-estate lust at first sight. It had no name and they didn't give it one; my friend Orach once told me that if you named something, you tied it to you, and it would tie you right back. Old and huge, unrenovated so that its rooms and halls were a warren of secret places, the house was set at the end of a dark winding drive in more than two acres of wild rhododendron-haunted garden. And there we all lived, and when I say *all*, I mean all. The place was treated as an open house by what seemed like an entire exiled race. I never knew who I'd find when I got home from school.

As Rory trudged up the drive with Lauren, I hung back under the untrimmed laurels and waited for Sionnach. He gave a soundless laugh as he caught up and put an arm round my shoulder, and together we negotiated the stuff piled in the hall. Motorbike helmets, mountain bikes, two pairs of muddy hillwalking boots, a sack of dry dog food. A case of empty wine bottles put out for recycling. Snowboards, waiting to be cleaned and waxed for the oncoming winter. I swore as I tripped on someone's laptop bag. Minus laptop, and just as well, since I kicked it hard.

I'd never altogether get my head round the Sithe's gregarious ways. They just didn't seem capable of living in nice little nuclear units. Always had to be in great sprawling anthills of humanity, and the more the merrier, but somehow, if you wanted space and solitude, you could find it. You could even find peace and quiet.

At least, you could find a moment's peace when Rory's father and stepmother weren't tearing verbal strips off each other. As we caught up with Rory and Lauren, waiting in the hall, my heart sank. The kitchen door was shut but we could hear every word.

'You conceited ARROGANT stubborn UP-YOURSELF FAERY! *What makes you think you know better than me?*'

'Yeah, it's not like *I've* had more *experience* of life. It's not like I would know better because I've seen about a *thousand percent more* and know *ten thousand* times more than you do because I've been *around a bit longer.*'

Rory had his hand on the kitchen door but he paused. If he walked in now, Seth and Finn might shut up, but then again they might not, and that would be even more embarrassing. He raised an eyebrow at me, and I shook my head. Sionnach sighed—half exasperated, half sorrowful—then edged past me and out towards the back garden and his workshop.

Smiling brightly, Rory and I looked at Lauren, and Rory said. 'Sorry about this. Let's go upstairs.'

Lauren stared at the kitchen door. 'For God's sake. Is he violent?'

'Hoo!' I laughed. 'In his dreams. Take no notice.'

'Wait till they make it up.' Rory rolled his eyes. 'That's when it gets *really* embarrassing.'

'I'll prove it to you! I'll show you what I saw, if you've got the guts to look!'

'Don't bother. You were hallucinating. I don't want to share your hallucinations.'

'Sometimes I could just SLAP YOU, SETH MACGREGOR!'

'Well, why don't you? It's NOT LIKE YOU USUALLY HOLD BACK.'

The total hideous silence was broken after a few seconds by a snort of laughter. A clatter of crockery falling to the floor, the scrape of a table. A growl and more laughter.

'If I didn't love you so much I'd have to kill you.'

'Yeah, yeah. I'd like to see you try. Shut up and kiss me, woman.'

'Oh, for crying out loud,' I said. 'Let's get out of here.'

'If my mum called my dad a fairy, he'd kill her,' said Lauren as we climbed the stairs. 'I'm amazed Doctor Evil puts up with it.'

Rory stiffened, one foot on the top step and a dangerous look in his eye. 'What did you call my father?'

'Sorry.' Lauren shrugged. 'Thought everybody did.'

I felt a surge of violent resentment go through Rory. 'Not in front of me they don't. All right?'

I gave him a mental nudge. ~ *Calm down, there, Laochan.*

~ *Like hell I will. Like any of them have been through what he's been through. You don't get scars if you spend your whole life on your fat backside, do you?*

~ *Your dad thinks it's funny, you know.* I glanced at Lauren, who was watching us both as if we were mad. ~ *He doesn't mind.*

~ *Well, I do.* But he shrugged. 'Come on, Lauren, forget it. My room's up here.'

Actually I wasn't telling the truth, there. Seth did mind. He was still self-conscious, and he was never going to have a perfect face again, but I reckoned he looked more beautiful now, as if life had given him a good slapping and he'd bounced back stronger and a whole lot wiser. The beatings he'd taken from the Wolf of Kilrevin had knocked his features slightly out of symmetry, and his right eyelid didn't open as far as the left one since a deep vertical scar had been drawn down his face with a knife, but his eyes got a sort of mournful beauty from the aching homesickness. Ironic. Or maybe his non-existent gods just had a terrible sense of humour.

I got bored fast with Rory's new game, since I couldn't get near it. It was no great thrill watching him and Lauren sprawl on the bed and hog the controllers, so when I stood up and stretched, I was easily distracted by a black scrap in the sky. Opening the window I leaned on the sill and watched the raven soar and dive and loop impossible loops. That'd be Faramach. For all the mob of birds that hung around the cliffs, there wasn't another one that took quite such delight in showing off.

Finn was with him. She stood right on the edge of the cliff, arms folded, watching him fly. Either the squabble with Seth was over or she'd stormed out: wouldn't be the first time. But I reckoned they'd made it up, because she looked perfectly happy. Her hair whipped crazily in the breeze, but even out there on the bleak cliff-top she didn't look cold.

She spent a lot of time out there—especially when Seth was working away from home—though it was barely more than wind-scoured grass and whin, and any fence must have crumbled away as the rock face did. All that was left of a formal garden was the mass of laurel and rhododendron that hugged the house and blocked the light from the downstairs rooms. I used to wonder why the clann didn't cut the bushes back to get the view, but I'd worked it out now. It was the wrong sea, that was all. They loved it but they didn't want the permanent aching reminder of the right one. No islands at the horizon here, just a fusion of sky and water.

Finn liked the cliffs, though. Sooner her than me. As I watched, she sat down on the cliff-edge, dangling her legs over, then leaned forward to follow Faramach's aerobatics as he spiralled lower. My stomach lurched just watching her.

Faramach wheeled upwards again, but Finn went on staring down. There must be something else at the foot of those insane cliffs that fascinated her.

The sea had turned silver-blue, glittering and popping like a million flashbulbs, so brilliant it hurt my eyes. I didn't want to spend any more of an afternoon like this with a couple of Xbox bores, and they hadn't even started the game proper: they were still choosing weapons from a ridiculously massive arsenal. Boys would be boys and some girls would be boys too, and Finn would be much better company.

Unfortunately, though I stalked off unnoticed, I didn't get far. To the left of the staircase the door of the TV room stood open, and Grian was leaning on the newel post glaring up at me, blocking my way through the hall. I glanced past him at the darkened space within. The volume on the TV was so high I could follow every word of the dialogue.

I eyed Grian again. Big and blond and a trueborn healer, and I didn't know which of those gave him his permanent air of superiority.

'Get in here,' he said. 'We want a word.'

With a very bad grace I stomped down the remaining stairs and barged past him into the room. *We* didn't seem to want a word at all. The rest of them, about a dozen or so, were slouched across sofas and armchairs, feet on the upholstery, drinking beer out of bottles and watching *Blackadder* on DVD.

Boys, I thought for the second time in a minute, would be boys.

'You bunch of slobs,' I said. 'It's a gorgeous day. At least open the curtains.'

'Hi Hannah.'

'Hey, Hannah.'

'Shut the door, girl.' Sprawled across Iolaire's lap, Jed waggled his fingers by way of greeting.

'Somebody better pick up those peanuts,' I told them, nudging the spilt bowl with my foot, 'before Finn gets here.'

'She's busy.' Fearna sniggered.

'They're not still fighting?' Iolaire glanced across.

'Nah,' I said, and ate a peanut.

A suggestive sigh drifted round the room.

'Leave them alone.' Braon appeared from behind me with a platter of chicken wings and a bottle of hot sauce. Not like her to do the cooking for this lot; she must have been really peckish. 'Seth has to go back to work tomorrow. Course they're fighting.'

'Aye,' said Iolaire. 'It's an excuse to make up.'

'He shouldn't go away,' snapped Grian, flicking his hand across my scalp. 'His place is here. It should be Seth keeping the lid on you and Rory, not me.'

'He has to work, Gri,' said Braon mildly. 'We all have to eat.'

'He can live off us.'

Braon gave him a *you-can-tell-that-to-Seth* look.

Grian clicked the mute on the remote. 'Can I get some backup here?'

Iolaire helped himself to two wings, feeding one to the flat-out Jed and wagging the other at the huge flatscreen TV. 'Leave her alone, Gri. There's no harm in it.'

'There could be.' Grian wouldn't let it go. 'Would you slobs focus? You know what the little cat's dragged in.'

'Cheers, mate,' I growled.

'What was Sionnach thinking, letting you do that? And where is he anyway? I want a word.'

I sighed, and nodded towards the garden and Sionnach's joinery workshop.

Braon hesitated, took her teeth out of a wing. 'Is he okay?'

'Okay as ever,' I said. 'We had a . . . bit of an incident. On the way home. *That's* why we had to bring home the only witness, as it happens.'

Grian stiffened, folding his arms as if his point was made. His lazy grin fading, Jed pushed Iolaire's chicken wing away and levered himself up.

'What kind of an incident?' he said.

I bit my nails. 'Oh, a woman. Darach, Sionnach said she was. He, um . . . he dealt with her. It's okay.'

'Darach,' spat Iolaire. 'I know her.'

'You knew her,' I said dryly.

There was a silence.

'Did anyone get hurt?' asked Jed sharply.

I shook my head. As an embarrassed afterthought, I added, 'Except Darach.'

'Gods,' said Iolaire.

'Sionnach should have killed the girl,' said Grian.

'*The girl* is seventeen years old.' I felt my cheekbones redden with anger.

'*The girl* is a nosy cow. We could feel it as soon as she walked in. You and Rory are idiots.'

'You can take that and stick it—'

'*Suicidal* fecking idiots.' Grian was yelling now. 'Have you ever heard of keeping your heads down?'

'Anybody for *Big Bang Theory*?' Iolaire interrupted brightly. 'I don't think the Witchsmeller's that funny.'

'That's 'cause it isn't comedy, it's history,' muttered Diorras. 'Christ, I should know.'

'Less of the funny, more of the news,' snapped Grian. He fired the remote at the TV as if he wanted it to shatter, and yanked his phone from his pocket. 'I checked the BBC website a minute ago. Want to see?'

'No,' said Sorcha, lifting a beer bottle to her lips.

'I do.' Iolaire sat forward, dislodging Jed's head and provoking a grunt of protest.

'Watch,' said Grian, and everybody did.

'*They kept themselves to themselves,*' a woman was telling a fuzzy microphone. Her hair blustered in the breeze across her pale face, and she combed it away then re-folded her arms. Behind her stood the shell of a council house, the neighbouring walls smeared with black smoke. *'Very quiet and reserved. They seemed a nice couple. It's a nice area.'*

The recording cut back to the balding reporter, swaddled in a dark overcoat, his face solemn. *'The bodies were found in an upstairs room, and reports indicate the room may have been barricaded from the inside,'* his brow furrowed, *'and that items of weaponry were found with the couple. The police are not commenting at this stage. For Reporting Scotland, this is . . .'*

Grian clicked the mute button. The silence, for a moment, was so oppressive I thought it would smother the lot of us.

'Sgarrag and Fraoch, in case you were wondering. Because they buggered off to live by themselves.' Grian rapped the back of my skull with the remote. 'Still fancy Durham University, do you, Hannah?'

'Shit,' breathed Sorcha.

'I hope,' said Braon, and cleared her throat. 'I hope they were dead before the house was fired.'

'They wouldn't *burn* them to death,' said Iolaire, not very convincingly. 'They wouldn't.'

Nobody said anything. I guess nobody wanted to think about it too hard.

Sgarrag and Fraoch didn't account for many on-screen seconds. The newsreader was doing the final-item funny now. I didn't have to hear it to get the story: yet another sighting of the Beast of Ben Vreckan. The Beast itself featured in a uselessly blurry mobile-phone photo above the presenter's right shoulder. *Aye, sure* said her cynically tilted eyebrow.

'Hannah,' said Iolaire, a pleading look in his eye. 'Try not to bring strangers home, 'kay?'

His thumb was caressing Jed's close-shaved hair, and my anger melted away. Jed had shut his eyes, but I could tell from the tight set of his mouth that he wasn't asleep. He was unhappy, that was all, possibly unhappier than anyone, and Rory's reckless invitation to Lauren had put the already-distant prospect of home just that little bit further away.

'Okay,' I grunted. 'But it's only my cousin Lauren.'

'I'm sure it is.' Grian's attempt at conciliation came out through gritted teeth. 'This time.'

I turned to leave. 'And next time,' I said, 'you can take it up with Rory. He's the one that invited her.'

'Or maybe Seth can do some parenting instead of me, for a change.'

'You've got a lot to tell him to his face,' I said spitefully. 'Good luck with that.'

Rory

The thump of a car stereo beyond the window was enough to wake him from a restless sleep. Rory opened his eyes and stared at the wall.

They'd tried to kill Hannah. He'd thought he was ready for the possibility, but the fear was colder and more hideous than he'd expected. He wanted her here with him, in his own room, so he could never let her out of his sight. It wasn't as if they were even under-age any more. But Hannah had to be alone, and so did he. She was his first cousin, unremoved, and he couldn't have her. It was forbidden: by the clann, by his father, by his brother.

As if Jed was some model of moral rectitude.

Rory kicked off the duvet and swung his legs off the bed, glad to feel the cold floor beneath the soles of his feet. The air chilled his skin, since he was wearing only sweatpants, but at least it took his mind off his resentment. Not for long. Pacing to the window, he glared down onto the darkened drive, at his brother climbing awkwardly out of the Saab's passenger seat. As Jed straightened, giggling at something Iolaire said, he swayed slightly and had to grab the car's door frame.

Rory blinked. The rage was an acid ache, and he knew he wouldn't sleep again for a long time. Grabbing a t-shirt, pulling it over his naked torso, he went out onto the landing and peered over the banister. When he heard the door clunk shut, he padded down to the next flight and sat on the stair, blocking their way.

Iolaire, catching sight of his shadow before Jed did, swayed to a halt, one arm round Jed's shoulders. It wasn't just affection, thought Rory. He was holding Jed up.

Iolaire's smile was a little uncertain. 'Rory. Hi.'

'Hi, Iolaire. Pissed again, bruv?'

Jed gave him a red-eyed glare.

'Leave him alone, Rory,' said Iolaire softly.

'Nah,' grinned Jed. 'Let him have a go, the wee hard man.'

'Stop it, Jed. And you, Rory. It's too late for this. Talk tomorrow when you both feel better.' Iolaire pushed past, dragging Jed on.

The reek of whisky was enough to make Rory's throat catch. 'They tried to kill Hannah today,' he snapped.

'Yeah, I know—'

'Oh, okay. I thought you might have forgotten.'

Iolaire's glare was uncharacteristically cold. 'I. Said. Tomorrow.'

'Rory?' Jed half-turned to face him. 'Hey, listen. Nobody's going to hurt her. Promise, m'kay?'

Rory stared up at him. His lip curled, he couldn't help it.

'Promise again when you're sober,' he said. 'Bruv.'

As soon as it was out of his mouth he felt bad, but he was still too angry to go after Jed and take it back. Iolaire was muttering some half-hearted reassurance: at least he had the brains to stay semi-sober and in charge. Rory heard the door of their room open and close before the silence closed in on him, frigid and lonely. For the briefest of instants he felt like crying. But what was the point of that? It was late. Jed was hammered, and no use. He'd check on Hannah himself, and to hell with Jed and Iolaire.

Stealthily he padded along the corridor towards her room. Keeping quiet wasn't a problem. He didn't want to be Seen, but Finn was the danger there, not his father. He was as invisible to Seth's mind as Seth was to his.

He should be used to this: it was more than three years since Kate NicNiven had cut their link, had split his mind from his father's. Worse for Seth, whose soul was left leaking through a wound that wouldn't heal. But that had been life for so long. It shouldn't bother him so much. It was the lousy, frightening day that had made his nerves raw, that was all.

It seemed there was no danger of being found out: Finn wasn't paying attention. Rory could hear the pair of them squabbling, their venom muffled by the old panelled door. Despite himself, he hesitated.

'You are not going back to the army,' he heard Finn snarl. 'You are not going to fight somebody's else's war!'

'You are not going to tell me what to do. And it's not someone else's war.' His father's voice was low, the way it was when he was truly furious. 'It's ours. On this side.'

'Semantics.'

'Damn it, Finn. Don't you dare—'

'It's not like it was. When were you last in a war over here? It's not the same.'

'It's what I'm built for. But if I take my clann home, I could get every one of *them* killed, and I'm *afraid*. So let me fight here! You want me to rot?' he spat. *'I'm rotting already!'*

'No!' she yelled. 'No! I know it hurts, *I know*. But you can't give it to her. You *can't*.'

'Who says I have a choice?'

'Kate can't take your soul, not even now, not ever. Not unless you *give it up*.'

'And *fighting* is my bloody soul! It's what I've always done!'

'You won't survive. Not this time.'

'I'll adapt!'

'You'll die!' she shouted. 'You can't throw your life away on somebody else's war.'

'I'm a lucky bastard, Finn. I'll live. But I *need* to fight. It's all I can *do!*'

'That's not true! You think death would be better than what you're going through now? Easier?'

'Than losing my soul? *Yes.*'

'You can't risk your neck, you're our Captain!'

'Not here, I'm not.'

'*Yes!* And you're Rory's father! You're Hannah's uncle!'

'And a fine role model I make,' he sneered, 'doing work I hate in a place I hate for people I despise.'

'And you're my lover,' she said. 'Murlainn. You're the love of my heart. Don't go.'

The silence fell again and this time it wasn't broken. The hostility dissipated like a mist in hot sun, and Rory backed away from the door, half embarrassed and half touched. And scared, now, of being detected.

Forget this idea. Hannah would be fine, and she probably wouldn't thank him for waking her up. He was being irrational, and there was more than enough of that around here already. Turning, he crept back towards his own room. He'd see Hannah in the morning. She'd be fine. *Fine.*

He'd got as far as the head of the stairs when he heard Finn scream.

Racing back, he flung open the door but by that time she was curled in his father's arms, rigid, her eyes febrile. Footsteps thudded along the corridor, doors were crashing open, sleep-blurred voices yelled questions.

'It burns,' Finn howled suddenly, striking at Seth with her arms. '*It burns.*'

Seth ignored the blows, clutching her and stroking her hair. Rory was shoved aside by Grian, and was caught in Fearna's grip as he stumbled. Braon burst into the room behind them, her blade bared. The raven on the headboard flexed its black wings and shrieked harshly at the intruders, and Seth's head jerked up to glare at them.

'What?' As the rest of them came to a halt, breathing hard, Grian took a step forward and stared at Finn. 'What happened?'

'Carraig's dead,' said Seth, and then again, with a note of disbelief: 'Carraig's dead.'

'He what?' Something like a cold fist constricted Rory's throat. Finn was shaking uncontrollably now, and his stomach twisted with pity.

Eyes wide and horrified, Braon sheathed her sword. 'She didn't—Seth, she didn't . . .'

Seth wasn't listening; his lips were at Finn's ear, murmuring something.

'Shit. Did she see him?' whispered Rory. 'A fetch? Can't we . . . is there time to . . .'

'Felt him. *Felt it.*' Shaking his head, Seth didn't even look up. 'He's dead already.'

A stranger, thought Rory, walking in on one of their endless scraps, might have thought Seth and Finn couldn't stand each other. A stranger might think they were incompatible souls who regretted their impetuous binding more than three years ago. Then there were times like this, when it was clear how it really was. Their jagged pride and quarrelsomeness would be shucked off, like a scratchy but comfortable old coat that had grown too warm, so you could almost see their souls slide and fit together like two halves of a complex puzzle.

'This isn't right,' whispered Grian. He couldn't take his eyes off Finn.

Ignoring him, Seth kissed his lover's hair, stroking it back from her temples.

'Seth,' said Grian more loudly. 'This isn't—'

'Get out,' Seth murmured.

'Dad, is she—'

His eyes blazed silver. 'All of you. *Get out.*'

Grian gripped Rory's shoulder and pulled him with him, the rest backing out behind them. Reaching for the door handle, he hesitated.

'This conversation isn't over, Murlainn.'

Seth did not answer. Softly, regretfully, Grian clicked the door shut.

Kate

She did not like to see the sky. The crisp frostbitten blue pierced her with slivers like shattered glass. She felt that deep inside her, where there should be no way for her to feel anything but the ever-gnawing hunger. What was the sky after all but an atmospheric trick? There was no sky. There was a film of reflected light, and beyond it only darkness, black matter stretching to infinity.

The thought reassured her. Thin-lipped, she smiled at the illusion of sky.

You're nothing to the darkness, she thought. *A delusional skin for those who can't face the endless night.*

All the same, she put her heels to her mare's flanks to hurry it. Dusk could not come fast enough for her, not even in this fast-approaching winter, and the precipice was close. Already she could make out wheeling birds, and the cliff-edge fringed with pink and yellow flowers, with stiffly rustling sea-grass; the edge that looked like the furthest tip of the world itself.

But you're not the limit of my world or any other. There are worlds beyond you, and you can't contain me.

The mare halted, and Kate slipped from its back, pricking her bare soles on stunted whin. Far below her the sea boomed against black rock, shattering into spray. For a fanciful moment she imagined falling, leaping into space and that eternity that was hers by right, only to break on the stones. They said that heights like these could bewitch a man, compel him to take the last step.

But she was no man, and she was more than woman.

~ *And more than queen. Do they know it yet?*

She smiled at the voice of the darkness. ~ *Ah. Still here, then?*

~ *Where else would I go?* Laughter inside her skull. ~ *How well do you climb, Nameless Queen?*

Very well indeed, was the answer, and she took a perverse joy in descending without the aid of her mind's strength. The towering basalt columns jutted sheer from the sea like the instrument of a god, but they offered her handholds and paths that she wouldn't have expected. She'd never have climbed in this way if her clann had been with her, but the indignity of it amused her: the only person who could inflict this on her was herself. And it gave her a new insight into Murlainn, if ever she needed one. To delight in this fragility and peril: it was so prosaic, so oddly pathetic, so . . . human.

And so very male, she thought with an inward laugh. It was almost like a death wish.

Well, she'd indulge him. *I shall be your fairy god-mother, Murlainn. I shall grant you three death wishes.*

~ *Let's not get ahead of ourselves, shall we?* The voice was scolding.

~ *Indeed not. I apologise for the presumption.* Not that she'd have to apologise to anyone or anything in the future. Not even to the thing in the dark.

Oh, her future: so close, she could smell it like ice on the north wind.

Swiping her hands to rid them of stone-dust, she gazed at the maw of the cavern. Salt spray hung in the air around her but the waves did not reach this part of the rock, hadn't for millennia. Something sighed from the cavern. Kate took a deep breath that tasted of night, and walked into the gap.

The passageway was short: who but she herself would ever dare come here? It wasn't as if the thing had to hide. The cave seemed blacker than she remembered, but she didn't fear that, and she didn't have to see; she felt the space open around her when she stepped into its vast inner chamber.

She waited.

The breath of the Darkfall was around her; Kate felt it whisper across her skin. Still she waited, not speaking, until at last a faint light sparked, and grew, and threw shadows that she wouldn't look at too directly.

The child had been dead for years. Centuries. The light was cupped in its hands. Cross-legged in its alcove in the cavern wall, the child lifted its head and gazed at her with eyeless sockets. It opened its mouth.

~ *How does it feel?*

Kate smiled. The voice was not that of the child; it was like the voice of the basalt, hell-deep notes wrung from the pipes of a prehistoric organ.

~ *It doesn't feel*, she told it. ~ *And nor do I.*

Strange how that resonant echo in her head could still sound amused. ~ *Good answer. But not true, not yet.*

~ *It will be true. I won't disappoint you.*

~ *I can't be disappointed. So no, you won't.*

She laughed. Then she disliked how that sounded in the vastness of the cavern, so she stopped.

~ *You've spared the boy*, it teased.

~ *The boy needs his soul, for my purposes.* Kate clenched her jaw. ~ *If I have to rip it from him at the end, that's how I'll do it.*

~ *You can't be sure little Rory will let you have it.* Again, the undercurrent of laughter. It scraped against her spine.

~ *No.* Through gritted teeth. ~ *So yes, Laochan can keep his soul. I have need of it.*

~ That's not all that's kept the boy safe, is it? Go on, admit it.

~ No. Alistair never told me that drawback to the spell, but perhaps he never knew it. Kate seethed inwardly.

~ No. He didn't. There was smugness in the voice of the Darkfall. *~ A child's wound heals in the end. A parent's never does.*

And how could I have known that? thought Kate irritably. *~ So Rory's soul is intact. It doesn't matter. It works for me.*

~ Oh, but how it must rankle! The thing chuckled in her head. *~ Is that why you toy so with Rory's father? Poor Murlainn!*

Was it? Was that why she kept the charm with her always? Was that why she played endlessly with the spell, turning it on and off like a recalcitrant switch? She withdrew it from the pocket of her silk coat: the falcon that nestled in the palm of her hand was carved from obsidian, with a dry and faded strand of once-golden hair twisted round its neck. Oh, Alasdair's spell was a tricksy and a pretty one. She wanted Murlainn to last, and she liked to merge herself with him, take a moment here and a moment there; take a piece or two of his essence to amuse herself. The Darkfall was right about that. It salved the pain of having to leave Laochan his soul entire.

But for that small vanity of hers, Murlainn would have been soulless long since, and probably dead. He ought to be grateful. Kate released her grip on the charmed falcon, let it rise into the space above her hand; she made it turn in the air, then sent it smashing down. Just before it hit the rock, she jerked it to a hovering halt in mid-air.

She drew a breath, coming to her senses. The charm mustn't break. Tilting her palm, she brought it back to her, and her fingers closed around its smooth coolness.

~ That looked to me like passion. The thing invaded her thoughts again. *~ Are you sure you're ready for what I have to give?*

~ *More than ready.* She felt her skin pale with the old anger. ~ *The otherworld is ready for me. I've practiced till it hurts.*

~ *You mean till the otherworlders hurt.*

~ *Yes, yes.*

~ *You may not kill them. It's forbidden. You made a deal with me.*

Could she hear a grin in that echo? ~ *Silly of me. To think you made that condition out of benevolence.*

~ *Come now. You knew better when you made your vow; in the depths of what was left of your heart you did. And your contortions have pleased me these last centuries; you've showed some cleverness along with the ruthlessness. Who needs to kill when they can cajole others into it? Don't deny it's been amusing. For both of us. And my, you've had plenty of souls out of your cats-paws. As have I.*

Resentment seethed inside Kate, and she knew the Darkfall knew it. ~ *Well, I don't harm the otherworlders. Not physically. Stop playing with me, Soul-Eater. It's themselves they hurt in the end. And it won't always be so.*

She had taken the souls of priests and charlatans, of artists and dreamers, of politicians and tyrants and warlords. Rarely could she use her witch's sucking touch on them as they died—even if they had powers worth the taking—but their souls she could take while they lived. She felt them, she warmed her innards on their souls' dying moments, she knew them better than they knew themselves. She knew what they desired, she knew how to make that godforsaken world of theirs perfect for them. Indeed, she knew how the godforsaken needed gods. They would not always hurt; at least, only a few of them.

Kate knew how to be loved. It was something she'd always known. ~ *That fool Carraig might have discovered something worthwhile if he'd reached his destination, but he's dead now.*

Something like invisible feathers touched her cheek, though

the child didn't move and its gape-mouthed expression did not change. ~ *Carraig's death was hardly necessary. Who'd have believed him, even if he had seen Merrydale and understood it?*

~ *You have other daughters, other sons. I never forget that. They would listen, they would know. They would oppose me. Look at Leonora! Had she not fallen in love and bound herself to Griogair, she would have done what I have done. She might even have beaten me.*

~ *But she kept her Name, and loved.* The voice grew silky. ~ *Like Lilith.*

And look what happened to her, thought Kate. ~ *Lilith was weak, like Leonora. But others may not be. What strong witch wants another to have power over them? Does any strong witch want the rule of a god? If you keep our bargain, your other children have to die. All your witch-children, and you know it.* She shrugged lightly. ~ *All but one, perhaps.*

~ *Yes, I know it. That was our bargain.* A drifting sensation on her neck, like a cobweb. ~ *Oh, you are good.*

~ *Yes. Yes, I am. But I'm also impatient.*

~ *It will come. Patience and the long game, Nameless Queen.*

~ *But the boy is untouchable.* Her rage seethed upwards in her gullet. ~ *I need the boy!*

~ *The boy will follow what he always follows.* The child's mouth closed softly, and its head bowed into shadow. ~ *Lead him.*

Rory

Rory sat very still on the sofa in the darkness, some unrecognised film flickering at him from the screen. A soldier screamed in silence; another fell backwards in a spray of blood. Rory turned the remote in his right hand, finger twitching on the volume button, then creeping towards the channel changer. He clicked that instead. Full-mortal Christmas, and the schedules were full of films. *Alien Resurrection.* Another click. *Casablanca.* People standing in a bar, singing with fierce soundless pride to muted fuming Nazis at the piano.

Rory had assumed Carraig's death would seem unreal. He'd thought the pain would be dulled because he hadn't seen so much of Carraig in the last couple of years. The man travelled a lot for his job, and he'd be gone for months at a time. If Rory had expected anything, it was the soft regretful ache of grief for a half-forgotten friend. As it turned out, the pain was a savage throb of loss under his breastbone, and a brutally empty void in his mind where once there had been Carraig.

Dawn was greying the gap in the heavy curtains, but it was dark enough in here. Maybe he'd sleep tomorrow.

Your father hated Carraig, a long time ago, and Carraig hated your father. True.

He tied your father's wrists so the clann could flog him for Conal's death. True.

He stayed at your father's side and gripped his hand while it was done. Also true.

When Rory was smaller he'd fitted easily on Carraig's shoulders. *Your father is coming home. No, he won't die. Your father is always lucky, he's coming home. I'll take you up to the parapet and we'll watch for him. You can see forever from the parapet.*

Did you cut your head open again, you short-arsed bastard? Come on, I have chocolate if you don't cry while Grian fixes it.

Awake again? Don't you go wandering, little shit. Fearna and I are bored and the fire's still warm. Which story do you want tonight? Haven't we told you them all?

We have? Well, brat, we can always start again. The endings change anyway, when Fearna tells them. That's not down to his addled old brain, no. That's the good thing about stories, little bastard. The ending can always change.

A racking surge of grief brought Rory to his feet. Stumbling, he yanked open the curtains to let pale light soak the room. Light wasn't enough, so he unlocked the French windows and shoved them wide. The rush of air was singed with frost, and made him catch his breath.

Out on the cliffs, the weather suited his mood. As he trudged towards the edge he could make out the water below, but only just: a surly heaving tide churned into a lace of foam on the rocks. As minutes passed and the mist sank lower, the sea vanished. It was as if the rocks below him were pillowed with cloud, as if you could take one step out and float gently down.

Stay back from that cliff, bastard boy. You don't want the mermaids to sing you down, do you? Oh, did I not mention the mermaids? If you get up here on my horse I'll tell you all about them. I'll take you back to the dun and I won't tell your father you were on the cliff. Do we have a deal?

Rory gave his blurred eyes a vicious swipe with a fist. Blinking them open, he thought for a second that the sun was breaking through, but it was only defiant clumps of early whin, glowing as if bits of sunlight clung to the earth. But the morning mist must be dissipating, a little. Otherwise he wouldn't have caught sight of Finn.

She was sitting below the cliff edge, on a narrow ridge of sandstone, hugging her knees. Beside her, on the ledge, the raven stretched its wings; they were both staring down at the foot of the precipice. Something down there fascinated Finn, but her hair hung across her face in the stillness, and Rory couldn't see her expression. The raven hopped up and across her knees, then took flight, but she didn't watch it swoop out into the grey mist. She stood up, edged along and down the ledge of rock, manoeuvred carefully round an outcrop and was gone.

It could be worse, thought Rory: at least he didn't have to see Carraig's last sight, like Finn had. And Carraig had been nothing like in range; he'd been nearly two hundred miles away when his car exploded. How by all the gods had Finn felt that? She wasn't related to Carraig. She hadn't even seen his fetch; she'd felt his actual *death*. Finn always Saw more than most, felt more than most, but this was ridiculous.

'Not ridiculous,' said a voice behind him. 'Not even amusing.'

He jumped. 'Grian, quit that. You scared me.'

'Scary is not me, Laochan, it's your father's lover.'

'She doesn't mean it, Grian. It's not her fault.'

'That scares me even more.'

Sighing with aggravation, Rory turned on his heel and glared. 'Leave her alone. Why do you have to go on about it?'

Grian rubbed his bare arm, staring down into the cushion of mist that hid Finn. 'Believe me,' he said, 'I'm blocking. I wouldn't want to get on her wrong side. Doesn't that tell you anything?'

'If you're seriously implying she can't be trusted,' said Rory silkily, 'you'd better back away from that cliff.'

'I'm saying no such thing. I'm saying it might not be her choice in the end. Witches are the children of the Darkfall, Laochan. Every one of them.'

'There is just *so much* you've got to break to my father face to face, isn't there?'

'Seth barely qualifies as a witch,' said Grian brusquely. 'He keeps a handle on it. He hasn't got the skill or the inclination.'

The power of speech, Rory realised, had temporarily deserted him. He opened his mouth, shut it again. At last he cleared his throat. 'And you're telling me this because . . .'

'Look, there's a lot of it about. Fine. You've got it too, of course, more than your father.'

'Gods' sake, it's all relative. We can all throw mind-bolts, and the full-mortals would think that was witchy.'

'Which is why nobody does it, unless they're trying to hurt someone. You're proving my point.'

Rory shook his head, exasperated. 'Grian, there's people who'd call your healing witchcraft.'

'Not on our side of the Veil, they wouldn't.' A dangerous light sparked in Grian's eye, but it didn't take Rory long to stare him down. The man shook his head in frustration. 'Look, I'm not name-calling. I'm just saying we need to be careful around her. Something's changed. She's stronger than she knows and she doesn't care. She doesn't control it and I don't know if that's because she can't, or she *can't be bothered.*'

Rory began to turn away. 'You're talking to the wrong—'

'She should not have felt Carraig die!' barked Grian.

A single angry step, and Rory shoved his face into Grian's, seizing his shirt collar. 'I'm pretty sure,' he hissed, 'that she didn't want to.'

Grian did not back off. 'She didn't want to, and she didn't mean to. I'm damn sure of that myself.' His breath was hot on Rory's skin. '*That's what worries me.*'

Rory released him sharply and strode away, shaking his head. If he didn't, he thought, he really might shove Grian two metres backwards. All the same, the man's low voice followed him through the closing fog.

'There's only one other witch who ever felt a man's mind at that distance. And she spends her endless, pointless, godforsaken days eating souls.'

Lauren

She knew she was irritating Hannah, and that was a bit of a shame when they were getting on better these days, but if Rory was willing to share Xbox time or anything else, Lauren wasn't about to stand on her dignity and stop going round to the house on the cliff. She was pretty sure Rory didn't fancy her, and she was well aware he was off-limits, but a girl had to have a respectable excuse for spending so much time away from her own home.

Anyway, there was no question that Hannah's new set-up was interesting. Lauren wasn't entirely sure what the deal was—commune or simply very large and long-lasting house party—but the blokes were easy on the eye and the women were bearable. Okay, the big blond guy actively detested her, oozing distaste every time Lauren was near him. And she went out of her way to avoid Rory's parents: the frosty stepmother, and the father who had the air of a man clinging to a cliff-edge by his fingernails. Rory had an older brother: a shaven-headed brute with beautiful eyes that glinted with the hot light of alcohol. But she'd twigged fairly quickly that he wasn't an alternative, and it wasn't as if he was threatening. It was even ironically amusing, being around a big thuggish guy who had absolutely no interest in cornering her at random moments.

Sometimes she wished Hannah had never moved out.

Twelve Dunnockvale was in darkness when she got home. The television was on but the muted screen was obscured by a message about standby mode. Even as Lauren watched, the screen blinked dark, and until her eyes adjusted, the only light in the room was the tiny red glow of a phone charger on the side table.

She could feel a headache threatening, so she rubbed the bridge of her nose hard. She heard a small grunting snore, and when she blinked open her eyes, they had adjusted enough for her to make out the sprawled shape of her mother on the sofa.

Lauren stood over her, undecided. If she didn't wake her up to go to bed, Sheena would be in a filthy mood in the morning. On the other hand, she seemed to have escaped into a particularly nice dream for once. A tiny smile twitched her mother's mouth as Lauren watched, and a mumbling sound escaped along with a sliver of drool.

Okay. Leave her here, then. Lauren turned away to tiptoe out of the room, and straight into a dark bulky shape. She yelped.

'Where have you been all night?' asked her father.

Lauren backed off. There always seemed to be five times less space in the room when her father was in it. He took up much more than his actual body size.

''S only midnight.'

'Half past. Where you been, love?'

'With Hannah.'

That unpleasant expression flitted across his face. She knew he didn't like it that Hannah didn't live here any more. 'Good for you.'

'I'm away to bed.'

His tongue touched the corner of his lip and his eyes flickered to the sofa. 'I'll see you up.'

Lauren sidestepped.

'Don't wake Mum,' she said. She picked up the remote and aimed it threateningly at the TV.

Marty looked back at her, his eyes creasing a little. There was a smell of beer off him, but it wasn't strong. 'Are you tired, love?'

'I'm really tired. I've got school in the morning.'

Marty shifted awkwardly, glanced at the TV, flicked imaginary dust off his knuckles. 'Away to bed and get some sleep, then.'

Lauren nodded at her mother's unconscious form. 'Don't let her chuck up and choke in her sleep, will you?'

'I'll look after her. Don't I look after you both? Night, love.'

Lauren's headache was back, but once she was in her room she didn't want to go back to the bathroom for the paracetamol. She shunted a chair against the door handle and sat down on the bed, and wondered why the hell Hannah had ever had to move out, and whether she could ever follow if it meant her mother would be stuck here alone with Marty.

She couldn't be bothered undressing. She just kicked off her trainers, then huddled under the duvet and pulled the pillow over her head. Why did she have to be the last one left?

Sometimes I hate you, Hannah Falconer.

Finn

I heard the door bang, rattling in its warped frame, and a moment later Seth came into the kitchen and chucked his leather jacket down on a chair. He stood there, lost and angry, and I glanced over my shoulder, my fingers cold and bloody from cleaning pheasants.

Oh, he was impossible. Refusing to go home, hating where we were, racked with irrational guilt for the clann's exile. If we weren't in exile we'd be *dead*, everyone told him so, but still Seth brooded and raged. I wished he'd snap out of it. I wished he'd tell me what was wrong now, but I waited in silence. I knew he'd tell me in the end.

At last he shoved his hair out of his eyes, put his arms round my waist and kissed my neck, a little brusquely.

'I had to talk your little boyfriend out of a cell. Again.'

'Oh,' I said.

That explained the mood. My little boyfriend? He still called Jed that sometimes, but only when he was very cross with him and wanted me to take some responsibility.

'What's he done now?' I wiped my hands on a damp towel and glanced reluctantly at the half-gutted bird on the drainer. I hated this job but interrupting it was worse.

'Same old,' said Seth.

I turned and threaded my cold fingers into his hair, warming them on his scalp. I felt a tiny shiver run across it.

'Are you okay?' I asked him.

He nodded.

'Just mad?'

He nodded again, rested his arms on my shoulders and kissed me, then laid his forehead against mine. ~ *Not at you.*

~ *I know.*

~ *Caorann,* he said. ~ *When did we get to fight so much?*

Tears started to my eyes, heaven knows why. His arms closed round my shoulders and he buried his face in my neck. His melancholy was so physical it stung; I didn't even have to be in his head to feel it. It wasn't like him. It made me afraid.

'We always fought,' I murmured into his hair.

'Oh yeah.' He drew back, grinning his old laconic grin.

I smiled. 'I'll talk to Jed, okay?'

'Again.'

'Uh-huh.' I kissed his nose. 'Watch this.'

'Watch what?'

'This.'

I twisted in his arms to face my half-gutted pheasant. Its feathers lifted and ruffled, though there wasn't any breeze. Seth's hands were locked together round my waist, and now they tightened. I put my own hands over them—just to prove it wasn't a trick—and the pheasant's left claw lifted. Curled and uncurled.

Waved at Seth.

'Stop that.' He was rigid behind me.

'No. Look.' I laughed. The claw pointed at Seth, and waved again.

He shook my hands away, reached forward and slapped the moving claw to the work surface, hard. He held it down, as if afraid of it, but his other arm stayed tight around me.

'Spoilsport,' I told him.

'Finn, don't. You shouldn't do that.'

I angled my head round to kiss his jaw. 'Don't be such an old woman.'

'Don't be such a witch.' He lifted his hand, hesitantly, but the pheasant's claw stayed where it was, dead and still. He flicked it with a finger. 'Clever, though.'

'I know I am,' I said smugly.

'So when did you start that?'

'Been practising for a while. I'd a feeling I'd be able to. Leonie could, you know. I saw her at it, in her workshop.'

'Why am I not surprised?' he muttered. He eyed Faramach, perched dozily on the windowsill with his black eyes half-closed, the old faker. 'That creature's been mighty quiet. Does he help you?'

'A bit.' I reached to tickle the bird's throat. 'Not that I can get in his mind, but he gets in *mine*. I thought you'd be happy he doesn't talk so much any more. Why don't you like him?'

'He's smarter than I am,' growled Seth.

'My dear. Is that why you hate half the human race?'

'Grr.' He nibbled my ear, a little too hard. 'Know what bugs me? Branndair thinks he's human. Faramach knows he isn't, and he thinks he's better than everybody.'

I rolled my eyes. 'Speaking of Branndair, you're going to have to do something before he gets shot. You know fine he's the Beast of Ben Vreckan.'

'Aw, Finn, he barely eats. He's never touched a sheep and the deer need culling. What d'you want me to do? Put him in kennels?'

'I'm just saying, that's all.' I sighed. 'You're not even trying to settle here, Seth. You say we have to stay here; you're the one who made Rory go to school. You're the one who told him and Hannah they had to get lives. You've got to try and have one yourself.'

'I go out,' he said sullenly. 'I meet people.'

'Have you ever met one you tried to *like?*'

'No,' he mumbled.

'My love, I rest my case. As for your bingeing, brawling blood brother—' Exasperated, I prised his hands off my waist. 'Where is he, then?'

He only pointed at the TV room, but he had the grace to look shamefaced.

With a sigh, I went through to find Jed on the sofa. He hadn't taken off his jacket, but was staring unseeing at a morning quiz show, arms defiantly folded. I picked up the remote and clicked the screen blank, then sat down beside him.

'It's been a while, Jed.' I tweaked his earlobe. 'You can stop being a delinquent now.'

He didn't unfold his arms but after a moment he pressed his head apologetically into the hollow of my shoulder. I put an arm round him and we huddled in comfortable silence.

'What did you do?' I asked at last. 'Another fight?'

He licked his lips nervously.

'See if *I* wasn't *me*, Finn. And if Iolaire wasn't Iolaire . . .'

'I know.'

'They'd have kicked our heads in. They might even have killed us. And they get the shit kicked out of them instead, because they deserved it. And who gets arrested? Us.'

'I know.' I didn't know what else to say.

'I didn't start it, Finn!'

'Jed,' I said hesitantly. 'You're not a Sithe. You can't get away with this stuff like they do. What happened to Iolaire?'

'He stuck with me. He could have got away but he stayed.' Jed gave me a belligerent look. 'So the polis kept us in the cells all night. Not the neds, *us*. Seth came down and talked us out of there, but Iolaire had to go straight to work. He'll probably get sacked. What are we supposed to do, just lie down and take it?'

'Course not.' Though they were, of course. You weren't supposed to fight back. You were supposed to wait for the police, if
they arrived before your skull crumpled. 'Jed, I'm sure they won't
take it further. They let you off with a caution last time.'

Silent, he looked back at the blank TV. There was a gash on his
temple, held together with steri-strips, and a black smear of bruise
under his left eye. Not much damage, then. Not to him.

I licked my lips. 'It's worse this time?'

'Much,' he said. He couldn't stifle a tiny smile.

'Oh, God, Jed. You didn't actually—'

'Course not,' he scoffed. 'Assault to severe injury, the guy at the
desk called it . . .'

'*Jed*—'

'They tried to kill us, Finn.'

I almost didn't dare say it, but I risked a smile. 'People have
tried to do that before.'

'For being rebels. For being at war. Not for just being us.' He was
the closest I'd seen him to tears since he was seventeen years old. 'I
need to be back where I belong, Finn. I need to be where I exist.'

'We all do,' I reminded him.

'You all have plenty of time. I don't.'

I said nothing. Nor did Jed, for a long time.

'The polis won't let this one go. It was too serious, they won't
forget. And when they find out I'm not who Seth says I am?'

It worried me too. 'It'll be okay. Seth'll think of something.
Just try and stay out of trouble, Jed, please.'

'I'm born for trouble,' he said bitterly. '*That's* who I am.'

I nipped my tongue, suddenly angry. I took his fist, uncurled it,
touched my fingers to the white scar that ran from the base of his
thumb to his little finger. His blood-brother scar. 'That's who you're
like,' I said, running my finger hard along it. 'Him and nobody
else. And sometimes I could throttle the pair of you.'

Jed laughed. 'I'd like to see you try, gorgeous.'

I linked my fingers with his and squeezed them. 'Lay off the juice, Jed?'

'I'll try.'

That was a lie and we both knew it. He drank for the same reason he got into brawls: that stupid death wish of his. Ironic, when he was doomed to die before the rest of us anyway, but perhaps that had something to do with it. He knew he'd go on into death alone, long before any of his friends. He knew he was going to get old, he was going to lose his strength and his beauty and his sense of humour before any of us looked thirty-five. Even his own brother, half-Sithe, would outlive him by centuries. Perhaps that knowledge would get to anyone after a while.

It was more than that, though. He hadn't been the same since he'd killed Nils Laszlo. He'd lived for that for so long, *too* long, and something changed in Jed the moment he did it.

Of course I'd been all but killed myself, on the same day, so I didn't see it happen. I only know that when I came back to the world, Jed was different. We were all too busy to deal with it, too busy fighting to stay alive, too certain we would all die anyway. And I'd been wrapped up in feeling sorry for myself, frantic with fear for Seth and sure I'd never see him again, that he'd die with his son far away from me.

By the time life was back to what passed for normal, the sickness had set into Jed's soul. It had set into his body, too, but he'd recovered from that. Just. He still had a gaunt look, his eye sockets more shadowed than ever since infection had ravaged his body from the arrow wound he took at the dun siege. Physically he'd recovered. Somewhere inside him, he never had.

Jed should have died. Coming back to his native otherworld had saved him, because the Sithe needed no antibiotics and had none. The unsettling thing was that Jed knew it, and had known it at the time, but if he hadn't been driven back here, he'd never have come. He'd *rather* have died. He'd have kept quiet till it was too late. And I still wasn't sure why, only that it coincided with the killing of Laszlo.

But we'd come here, and he'd lived, and now it was being here that ailed him. He was more than homesick, he was heartsick, and that was what was killing him.

And that was what I told Seth, and that was why he lost his temper, and it turned into one more pointless, victorless fight.

It ended the way it always did, which is why neither of us ever won an argument. It ended in exhausted stalemate, with the pair of us entangled on the rug in front of the sputtering gas fire, the wind sighing and whining in the blocked-up chimney behind it. The day had darkened to a last twilight; the curtains hadn't been closed, but the laurels were thick outside the window and the small room was in dusk but for the glow of the hissing fire. A chair was jammed hard against the door handle.

Propping himself up on one elbow, Seth stroked my hair behind my ear. His fingers traced the line of my ear, every kink and curl of flesh, sending small currents through my body all over again. I pushed his hand away: I needed to talk intelligibly and I wanted him capable of the same. Thwarted, he drew back. I saw the smouldering glow of his eyes, like silver embers, but then he smiled.

'Three people have tried to get into this room,' he said.

'Did they? I didn't notice.' I gave him a contented smirk.

He laughed.

I ran my hand across his shoulder. Scars and muscle and blood and flesh and sinew. I pulled him back down so I could inhale his scent. He gave a confused murmur as his body stirred against me.

Love of my heart, love of my soul, love of my body. All I needed. Suddenly I was furiously resentful of his unhappiness.

'Well?'

He combed his fingers obsessively through my hair, slid his hand down to my breast. 'Well what?'

Desire collided with rage, and I shoved him back from me once more. 'Did I make you feel alive?'

'Finn?'

My voice hardened, I couldn't help it. 'Did I? Was it half as big a thrill as killing?'

'Listen to me, Finn . . .'

'Go on. I need to know.'

'What difference does it make?' His voice had a coldness now too. 'We're bound.'

Sitting up I tried to slap him, but he curled swiftly upright and caught my wrist. He pulled my clenched fist to his mouth and kissed it brusquely. 'This is what you signed up for. We both did.'

'If you signed up for anything you signed up to stay at my side!'

'You know that isn't true.'

I wanted to weep with anger and frustration. 'You want a war? You want to die? Why not just go back and die in your own home with us at your side?'

'This isn't about the rest of you. It's about nobody but me, understand?'

'Nobody but you? There's no such thing any more! You selfish *tosser*. You're bound to me! You're as good as bound to your whole bloody clann!'

His eyes were just aflame now. 'I'd rather die with my soul intact. But it isn't, it isn't in one sodding piece any more, and I need to keep what's left, and fighting's part of who I am, and it keeps the scraps of what's left of me burning, and I have to do it somewhere. And I don't know why she hasn't killed me yet but if I go back to that other place she'll take the rest of my soul and there'll be nothing left of me and *you KNOW ALL THIS.*'

I took a breath, gathered the scraps of my lost temper. I couldn't speak, because he was right. But the way he spoke about *that other place* reminded me of no-one so much as my mother.

'You think Conal would go back?' he hissed now. 'You think he'd have the guts to fight her? My dun is held by *Lammyr!* I can't lead my people to certain death because your boyfriend's homesick. But you think maybe Conal would do that for Jed?' He struck his chest viciously. 'My brother nearly lost his soul to her once, but he never came half as close as *this.*'

Oh, the lowness of the blow. I'd never say that name that hung between us, but he would throw it at me.

I glared at him. 'You're as bad as Jed. You're as homesick as he is. It's so terrible you'll go to a stranger's war just to take your mind off it. And because you're *bored!* Where's the sense in that?'

'Boredom is the least of it.'

'I know. I *know.* But you're alive, Seth. You're still alive.'

'Don't you damn well lecture me, Finn MacAngus. Yes, we're both alive. So put up with it! And tell your little boyfriend he can do the same. I'm not going back, not now.'

'I didn't ask you to!'

He blinked, gave me a look that made my heart turn over.

'So what are we fighting about, Caorann?'

I slipped my arm around his waist, pressed my face to his chest. His fingers raked through my hair.

'I love you,' he said hoarsely.

~ *I love you,* I told him back. ~ *I don't want you to go away. Please don't go.*

Just when my lover had thought his exile was over, it had begun again, and now it seemed permanent. And even that couldn't hurt like the tortuously slow loss of his soul. Oh, I wished I had the power to do something about Kate. I wished I could do something *to* her.

'Finn,' he said, 'Caorann.'

I placed my palm against his shoulder blade, explored the muscles around it with my fingertips. They were hard like bowstrings.

'The Veil's dying, Finn. Has been for centuries.' His fingers were so tight on my shoulder he was hurting me, but I didn't let on, because I wanted to keep him there. 'There's no reason for us to go back. Rory can't fix the Veil. We know that, *she* knows that. He's no threat to her.' He rubbed his eyes. 'Oh, I dunno. Kate plays a long game, right? Maybe she's just waiting till it dies. It and me. Maybe she's not interested in Rory any more.'

I wriggled from his tight grip, then ran my hands into his hair and drew his head closer to mine. 'Oh, you're a vain bugger, Seth MacGregor.'

He tilted my chin so he could look into my eyes. His mouth twitched and he laughed.

'I wish you could be happy,' I said.

'You make me happy,' he said. 'That's the truth. You make me happier than I've any right to be.'

And there he went again. 'Stop that,' I said.

He pulled me gently down so that we lay side by side and face to face. My fingertips found and followed the ridges and furrows of his back, his lacerated back that was once half-flayed by his own clann. I remembered the first time I held him naked against me, remembered stroking those scars. My eyes had filled with tears, so that quietly he said *Don't touch them if they upset you.* And I'd said *They don't upset me. They're part of you and I'm proud of them and I'm proud of you and that's why I'm crying.*

He'd smiled and kissed me, but I'd held him back for a moment. With my hand flat against his chest, his heart beating against my palm, I'd looked into his dark dilated eyes and said *But I will kill the next person who hurts you like that.*

I hadn't, of course. Someone had indeed hurt him, hurt him badly, but I hadn't been given the chance to do anything about it. Not yet. But I still held that promise in my head, a promise I hadn't given lightly. I did nothing lightly that long-ago night, unless you count touching his skin. I did not lightly throw my soul into his keeping, I did not lightly consign my love to what could only be a brief flaring fire.

I'd meant that angry promise. But I hadn't kept it.

It rankled.

Kate

'She's still a threat to me.' Kate's mouth tightened as she paced from one time-eroded pillar to the next. Almost without willing it she swept her hand across a horizontal slab of rock, sending the lantern tumbling. Glass splintered, flame guttered and died on the damp grass, and shadows crept closer to the centre of the stone circle.

Cluaran eyed the outer darkness beyond the stones, his grip tightening on the bridles of the two horses. She noticed him suppress a shiver; and him such a powerfully-built brute. Her lip curled.

'Pay attention, dear. I've checked for monsters.'

Even in the moonless night she saw a blush sting his face. 'Sorry, Kate.'

And when did the old traditions die out anyway: *Your Grace, Your Majesty, My Glorious Queen?* Time for a return to the old values, in Kate's opinion. She swept back her long silk coat and gave Cluaran a filthy sidelong glance, then turned back to the tallest of the stones and laid her palm against its silvery coolness.

'Do you know, Cluaran, what lies under my feet?'

He looked down, startled. 'No, Kate.'

She smiled benevolently. 'Of course you don't. Murlainn told no-one where he put them. Not even the full-mortal who couldn't keep them alive in her feeble belly.'

Cluaran's eyes widened in shock. He couldn't tear his eyes from the flattened grass and the scraped mud at her feet. 'Murlainn put his children in the *ground*?'

'For the sake of the scrawny bitch's beliefs.' Kate smirked. 'It nearly killed him all over again, giving his sons to the worms instead of the eagles.'

Cluaran was watching her with nervous respect, she was glad to note. 'You know that, of course.'

'You can't begin to imagine how much I know now.' Kate pressed a fingertip to her temple. 'It's bliss, it's delicious, and yet it's sadly pathetic.'

He hesitated. 'And that's why we're here?'

Kate turned, surprised, then laughed. 'What do you think, Cluaran? That I'm going to dig up sad little bones and make voodoo?'

'I'm sure you wouldn't—'

'Oh, I would, believe me, if there was anything worth digging up. But it would only be for my own satisfaction. I don't need them, and there's nothing of them left anyway.' She sniffed, and kicked at the ground with the heel of her boot. 'It's a pity, in some ways. Had these brats lived, everything might have been resolved centuries ago. But they didn't, and he couldn't spawn another for four hundred years. It's just as well I've the patience of angels.'

Cluaran grinned, reluctantly. She knew he'd found that last remark funny, but she didn't mind. He was solid, Cluaran was, and dependable: her strongest captain and the one whose motives sprang from a relatively pure heart. He was better for her sense of perspective than the oily Cuthag, who'd do anything, quite literally, to please her, and enjoy himself while he did it. That kind of faithfulness too had value, but she had to admit Cluaran was more amiable company than Cuthag. And she quite liked to prod and provoke Cluaran, to see just how many of her means he'd tolerate in the pursuit of her noble ends.

Pretty much all of them, so far. She bestowed a special smile on him. 'You're waiting for me to finish my sentence, Cluaran dear. Go ahead, ask.'

His grin came easier this time. 'All right, Kate. Who's a threat to you?'

'I thought you'd never ask. That embryonic witch.' She frowned. 'Far away she might be, but she's tied to me by bonds she can't even recognise. I'll see her again; I don't have to torture a sooth-sayer to know *that*.' She wiggled her eyebrows at Cluaran's scowl of disapproval. *Prod! Provoke! Tease! Oh Cluaran, you lovely man, I do adore you.* 'She has so much potential, that witch, and I know she'll develop it. I *want* her back here, I positively do. And if she won't give me her loyalty, I'll have her damn soul.'

Cluaran couldn't hide his scepticism. 'She'll never be on your side, Kate, and I wouldn't borrow gold against the prospect of her soul.'

'Oh well, then. Her soul, her death. Whichever.' Kate shrugged lightly. 'In the meantime, let's talk about Raib MacRothe. That's why I brought you out alone, after all.'

'Yes,' said Cluaran, his distaste seeping through his words. 'Raib MacRothe.'

'Now, dear. I owe the man twice over. If it wasn't for him I'd have lost a fine source of souls in the otherworld. You've no idea how close Carraig came to exposing me.'

'I don't see what he or Murlainn could have done about it, even if he had discovered you.'

'I wasn't about to take *that* chance, dear. It was an unfortunate happenstance that Merrydale employed Carraig, but he'd have known as soon as he looked at those people. He'd know decrepitude and senility from a dead soul, even the fool Carraig would know that. And would he have kept his mouth shut? I've never known a single member of Murlainn's clann who could, except for Sionnach.'

'The otherworlders wouldn't have listened. At least,' he added hastily, 'they wouldn't have believed.'

'Some full-mortals will believe anything, take my highly experienced word for it. And that place is virtually a farm . . . no, an *abattoir* of souls. Carraig and Murlainn could have taken that away from me, and then what would I have done? Turned on my own people? There aren't enough of y–us. My enemies are few—'

'And fewer by the day,' put in Cluaran loyally.

'Exactly. And I'm not about to eat at my own support base, dear. I need the otherworld and I need it *now*.'

'Kate.' Cluaran stared at the reins in his hand. He'd twisted them round his fist, making it hard for Kate's mare to rip at the grass, and the animal was baring her teeth and tossing her head in irritation. The man had barely noticed. 'Kate, if you'll still permit me to advise you?'

Not for much longer, dear. 'Of course, Cluaran. You're my Captain. It's what you're for.'

'You're concerned about discovery. You almost lost your . . .'

'My livestock.'

'Your, ah . . . livestock.' He swallowed. 'But you didn't, because Raib was loyal and he dealt with Carraig. You will always have loyal fighters. Go on just as you are. Take the otherworld by stealth, until the Veil dies of its own age. Even then, you could continue forever without detection; you have the subtlety.'

'I'm glad you think so, dear,' she said tartly.

'I didn't mean to offend you, Kate,' he mumbled.

'No indeed. But you miss the point, Cluaran, you *miss the point*.' For a few seconds she had to link her fingers and clench them tightly, just to stop herself slapping him. *Destroy the Veil, and the NicNiven will have all she desires; let it die or survive, and nothing will be hers.* The Veil could not die before she killed it, *could not.* But what did Cluaran understand of prophecies? His head didn't work that way.

And besides: 'What's the point in skulking for eternity? Why *should I?*'

'That's not what I—'

Kate smiled, breathing evenly again, and brushed her fingers through her shining hair. 'Do you know what a soul is without love, Cluaran?'

'No . . .'

'Of course not. But *I do.* I've tasted enough of them. I've sucked enough of them dry. Men who don't give a damn for their own souls. No empathy, no compassion. Men and women who fear me so much they'll give up their souls to me like a shot, all shrivelled and sour and rotten. For such bitter reward it's *hard work,* Cluaran.'

'The others . . .'

'Them? Easy to take, certainly. So easy, I think I'll take that manager woman who was stupid enough to let me in. But they're souls in weak and dying bodies. Half-demented, lost and un-awares. They don't know who I am and they don't know what they're giving me!' She tightened her fists at her sides once more. 'They love me no more than the thieves and the killers and the cowards do! Oh, sour it is, Cluaran. Do you seriously think that is *all I deserve?*'

Mutely, he shook his head.

'Oh, I've had souls that loved, and they're richer by a country mile, Cluaran. That's what I want. Complete, entire, and willing. Loving souls! They'll want to give themselves to me because they *love me.*' Her voice was so high and shrill, she was afraid she might break into weeping. 'To love me, they have to know me! To know me, they must know I'm there! You think they can love a god who skulks in the shadows like the Darkfall?'

Cluaran's double take was almost comical. 'A what?'

'A queen. A monarch.' Kate put her hand to her throat, struggling to calm her panicking heart. *Careful, Kate.* 'A queen who skulks, Cluaran: what kind of queen is that? Not one you'd gift with your soul and your self. Not one to love!'

'Kate. Kate, I'm sorry.' His hand was on her bare arm. The horses pranced loose, shaking their necks. *Don't touch me. Don't you dare touch me.*

She closed her eyes. Laying her palm across the harsh hand that caressed her skin, she pressed it closer still, bore its abominable warmth.

'I'll give them everything, Cluaran. Peace and perfection and love, and all I ask in return is a soul or two. I gave up my own, all so that I can give *them* everything. Everything they never knew they wanted, and in exchange a bright flame now and then to warm my poor cold heart. Such a small price, and they'll pay it with love in their hearts.'

He clasped her wrist, bent his shaven head to kiss her hand and press it to his forehead. 'Of course they will. I didn't mean to doubt you. Forgive me.'

'There's nothing to forgive. You only do your duty.' She loosened her fingers from his grip and rubbed her temples. *Gods' sake, Kate, don't ever lose control like that again.*

'What are your orders, Kate?'

'I need to reward Raib; that's my first priority. He's done me two favours that he did not need to do. When you find such loyalty, you do not piss on it. Find him a captaincy in my personal guard.'

Cluaran rubbed at the gold torque on his neck. 'You've brought us such peace these last years, Kate. There's no captaincy vacant.'

'There will be,' she said with a dismissive wave of her hand. 'I can always find one if I want to. That's nothing but . . . administration. Let's assume it's done, shall we?'

'Of course.' He bowed his head.

'Far more to the point: There are three things I want right now, Cluaran. I want Rory. I want the witch back, to give her one last chance. And of course, I want Murlainn destroyed.'

'Consider it in hand.'

'It won't be properly in hand till they're back on this side of the Veil.'

'Murlainn's clann won't return easily.'

'I didn't say they had to do it easily.' The temperature of her voice dropped a few degrees. 'That's quite enough duty of advice, Captain.'

Turning her back on him, she seized her mare's reins; Cluaran knelt and cupped his hands. *Good.* In these circumstances and after such a conversation, it was best to mount with some regal elegance, if not actual divine grace.

'I've trusted you with my life and my future tonight, Cluaran, and we've shared more than enough words. I've one final test for Rory; when it's done and he passes it, I want him in my hands immediately. A boy, not the promise of one.'

And my damned tongue will not slip again till you bring him to me.

Jed

He loved the buzz of the razor against his skull. Every image that plagued him, every memory that stung, they were all soothed away for a while like hurt muscles. Leaning forward on the bed-covers, he wrapped his arms round his knees, shut his eyes and felt the tingle of pleasure creep down his spine and spread across his shoulders. Iolaire's hand pressed his head forward and the razor purred against the nape of his neck.

'When I see how much you like this,' said Iolaire, 'I'm tempted to let you shave mine, too.'

Jed gave a growling laugh, his eyes still closed. 'You leave your hair where it is. If you want a neck rub I'm here for you.'

'It's the easiest thrill I ever had to give,' said Iolaire. 'You're such a cheap turn-on.' He clicked off the razor.

Jed rolled over and pinned him against the sheets. 'But it *is* a turn-on.'

'No you don't.' Iolaire shoved him off. 'We need to talk.'

'*Right now?*'

'Right now. Caorann insists.' Iolaire tilted a rueful eyebrow.

Jed grunted. 'Finn MacAngus can kiss my arse.'

'Oh no, she can't.' Iolaire gave him a sweet smile. 'But we'll get to that later.'

Jed flopped back, defeated. 'What, then?'

'She's worried about you.' Iolaire traced a fingertip across his temple. 'We all are,' he added before Jed could fire back a retort.

'I'm fine.'

'No,' said Iolaire, 'you're not. I was there, Jed. I watched what you did to that thug the other night.'

'There's your operative word.' Jed swung down off the bed and examined his shaved head in the mirrored wardrobe. 'The *thug.* He asked for what he got.'

'That's not the point. The point is, you gave it to him.'

'That's right. And he won't be doing it to anyone else. Not ever.'

'And I'm glad.' Standing up, Iolaire put his arms round Jed's waist and watched his eyes in the mirror. 'But the look on your face, Jed. I saw that, too.'

You saw it. Well, mate, I felt it. That rictus of elated joy, like a mask that had melted onto his skin and fused with his flesh. And the best and worst of it was, he wasn't even sorry. He'd watched the blood spurt from the stump of a wrist and he'd felt no shock and no horror. More like hunger.

'Jed. It's not only a witch that can take your soul. Don't give yours to Laszlo.'

'He's already got it.'

'That isn't true . . .'

'It might as well be. And he's dead, so he ain't giving it back any time soon.' He turned into Iolaire's arms and cupped the man's face in his hands. 'I'm joking.'

'Some of your jokes I do not like.' The corner of Iolaire's mouth twitched effortfully. 'Jed.'

'Uh-huh.'

'There's something you've never told me.'

Christ. He knew what was coming. He was surprised it hadn't come sooner, except that he'd been lulled into thinking it was long ago now, that no-one could possibly care. He knew he didn't. He turned in his lover's arms to face the mirror again.

'I'm sure there's lots of things I never told you. Uh. I stole a bottle of blond hair dye one time, and I—'

'Jed. What did Laszlo say to you?' Iolaire stroked his shoulder lightly, staring at his spine. Jed felt the vertebrae tense and contract under his lover's gaze.

Jed raised his eyebrows at Iolaire's reflection. 'Does it matter?'

'It seems to. What did he say as he died? Just tell me. Please.'

Jed coughed a laugh. 'It was nothing. *Nothing.*'

'No, it wasn't.'

'All right.' Jed shrugged. 'He said, "Welcome to my world."'

'Is that it?' Iolaire took a step back, frowning. He bit his lip. 'Look, Laszlo was winding you up. He knew your weak spots. He knew how much Skinshanks riled you, he knew how you felt about that. He was just trying to—'

'I know what he was trying to do. I'm not stupid.' Jed shook his head. As if that bothered him any more. It almost amused him to remember the angst he'd suffered, knowing the Lammyr had a soft spot for him, knowing Skinshanks had seen something in him worth nurturing. Knowing that every Sithe thought him Lammyr-turned and evil.

And sure, as Laszlo had bled out in his arms, as the life in him had drained out down Jed's blade, the man had said what he'd said in the hope of sending another poisoned dart into him. Jed knew perfectly well what Laszlo had intended by that remark. What a waste of a man's last breath, when there was so much more to be said.

Iolaire was watching his face, bewildered. 'I wish you'd let me in your head.'

'I know.' Jed sighed, then drew his lover close to kiss him gently.

Iolaire gave him a wry grin as he pulled away. 'Sometimes I could kick Seth hard in the balls for what he did to you. Messing with your brain. You'll never trust any of us again, will you?'

'Of course I will. I do. And I don't think, you know . . .' Jed chewed his lip. 'I don't think that was entirely Seth's fault.'

'Say *what*? Catch me before I fall.'

'It's as much to do with me, I think. I don't think Seth planned it. It just happened. 'Cause he could feel my mind without even trying, really. He's told me so.'

Iolaire shrugged. 'So you have a little Sithe blood. Who doesn't?'

'Not much. Maybe a little bit, way, way back.'

'And even then, Seth had no business screwing up your mind.' Iolaire's brow creased. '*What*?'

Jed blew out a breath and slumped onto the edge of the bed. 'Can I make a confession?'

Iolaire sat down beside him, silent.

'I might have *asked for it*,' Jed told him, avoiding his eyes. 'Seth always said my mind was sort of . . . leaky. He said he could hardly help what he did.'

'Aye. Excuses. Sometimes Seth makes me—'

'You don't get it.' Jed shook his head sharply.

'No, I don't, and I never truly will, because you won't let me near your head. So, you know, that kind of makes it your responsibility.' Iolaire spoke through his teeth. 'To fucking *tell me*.'

He could have said nothing better suited to making this a hundred times worse. Jed put his head in his hands. 'The times Seth was in my head. The times I was in his. That wasn't the last . . . it's not the last time my mind's gone, uh . . . walkabout.'

Iolaire turned. There was a light of unbearable hurt in his eyes and Jed wished he hadn't been the one to put it there.

'Not deliberately. That's the thing. It's a bit, kind of, out of control. Just once in a while. Like when—'

'Oh Jesus,' said Iolaire, paling. 'No. Not him. Not *him*, Jed, when you won't let me—'

'Like when Laszlo died.' Jed raised his voice, drowning out Iolaire's intolerable hurt. When Iolaire subsided into silence, Jed could only stare rigidly at the cheap print on the wall. It was a cheap and boringly common old etching you saw everywhere in town: the ruined local cathedral. 'Laszlo, he kind of . . . fell into me. Or vice versa. I lost control of my own head. *Again.* I couldn't help it. That's what happened.'

Iolaire was studying the print now, too. 'No wonder you didn't want to tell me.'

'Are you angry?'

'How can I be angry?' Iolaire's tone was clipped. 'It's not your fault, you said so.'

'It hasn't happened since. I don't go around seeing people's minds, I promise. Nobody sees mine. Honest.'

'It's okay. I understand. *Honest.*' Iolaire managed a smile. 'So you've been in Laszlo's mind when you've never been in mine. I mean, so what?'

'I really am sorry.'

'Don't apologise. *Goddammit.* No. Don't.' Iolaire took his hand and threaded his fingers through Jed's.

'I'm sor—'

'Damn it, god *damn it.*'

Jed shut up. The perspective was all wrong in that print, and the eighteenth-century sightseers in the foreground looked stiff, their faces drawn with childish crudeness. He inspected it till he thought he must be able to replicate every line and shading. It seemed a long time before Iolaire's hand tightened on his.

'So, Laszlo's swansong.' said Iolaire at last. 'You see anything worth seeing?' He was smiling. Just.

Jed's heart constricted in his ribcage, and for a moment his breath ached, but he grinned anyway. 'Tell you something: His whole life flashed before him. Always thought that was a myth.'

'Bloody hell. I hope the replay's entertaining when my turn comes. Was his?'

'It was interesting, for sure.' Jed smiled thinly. 'I swear I recognised quite a lot of it.'

'Don't start that again. You're not like him. You're *nothing* like him.' Iolaire hesitated, and bit a nail. 'Not if you're careful.'

'And you think I'm not being careful enough.'

'You're good at what you do, Jed. That's not wrong. Just don't love it too much. Not for its own sake, anyway.'

'I don't.' He had had enough of the discussion already. He did not want to take it further, and he sensed Iolaire didn't either. 'It's not what you are, it's what you do with it.'

'Good.' Iolaire did look relieved. 'Because I have a suggestion about that.'

'Have we talked ourselves in a circle here?' Jed grinned at him.

'Oh yeah.' Iolaire grinned back.

'That's more my kind of conversation.'

'Mine too.'

'Shut up.'

'Oh yeah.'

'Yeah . . .'

Rory

The rhododendrons were so overgrown their clawing branches met overhead, and they dripped spring rain on Rory as he walked up the drive. Turning the corner he paused, shaking rain off his neck and pushing wet hair out of his eyes. Grian was crunching across the gravel, whistling to his yellow-eyed mongrel hound as he aimed his keys at his four-by-four and bleeped the locks. Catching sight of Rory, he nodded.

Rory hoped the healer wasn't going to launch into another rant about his father's abdication of responsibility. It wasn't as if it was his fault. Some days he felt like biffing Grian for insubordination, since Seth never would.

All Rory got from Grian, though, was a smug grin and a wink, and he almost fell over his own feet. He couldn't quiz the man on his change of mood, but it had to be for the better, because Grian was whistling *Boots of Spanish Leather* as he shut the boot on his dog and climbed into the driver's seat. No accounting for that man's temper swings. Rory stared, shrugged, and went on into the house.

Rory was fond of the old place. After the clean rainy air outside it smelt of old wood and books and very slightly of damp. He liked that. He was homesick, sure, but if he couldn't have the dun this must be the next best thing. He never got round to telling Finn how much he liked it, how it felt right, and smelt right. He should. Finn was in the TV room now, he could feel her. Whistling in echo of Grian, he pushed open the door.

Perched on the edge of the sofa, Finn gave him a rueful look, and Rory kissed her cheek. Behind her, on his stomach, lay Seth, his face buried in the cushions while Finn gently rubbed his back with one hand.

She let Rory read her mind. ~ *Your father quit his job.*

'Again?' he mouthed silently. He crouched at Seth's head. 'Hi, Dad.'

'Hey, Rory,' came a muffled voice. With a great sigh, Seth turned his head and offered him a bleak smile. 'Did Finn tell you? I couldn't bear it any more. I'm sorry.'

Rory made his eyes huge. 'Are we poor, Daddy?'

'Aye. I hope you're happy about going up chimneys.'

'Sure. I'll get to be a water-baby.'

Seth grunted. 'And now I would like to ruffle your hair affectionately, but you'll have to imagine it. I'm too comfy in my misery.'

Finn rubbed his shoulder muscle, making him sigh with contentment. 'We're fine for now, Rory,' she said. 'We still have Leonie's money.'

'And when that's gone,' mumbled Seth, 'we can sell that dump Tornashee.' For that, he earned a pummelled spine, and he yelped. 'Okay! Okay! Joke! Ow, Finn, give me a break. No, Rory, we're fine. It's not the money.'

'Your father's bored,' said Finn with a long-suffering sigh.

'So are you,' Seth grunted. 'I mean, bookkeeping?'

'Okay, so that was a disaster,' she admitted. 'I was only trying to be respectable.'

'I've never seen such elaborate paper aeroplanes,' said Seth. 'And so many of them.'

'Oh, and we all thought your job was a great idea, didn't we?

Driving ruddy great lorries up and down the M6. Your blood pressure was in orbit. As for your arteries . . .'

'My arteries,' said Seth primly, 'are fine.' His look darkened. 'It wasn't the work, it was the view. That bloody road.'

Rory flopped down, sprawling half on top of his father. 'Sulaire's not happy either,' he told them. 'Did you hear? He kind of forgot himself and took it out on a deer carcass. Nobody at the hotel will come near him now. They think he's channelling Hannibal Lecter.'

'Oh, not him too,' said Finn. 'Some guy at Orach's office tried to stick his hand up her skirt. They had to rush him to A&E with a crushed testicle.'

Seth stuck his face back in the cushions to muffle his snigger, but Finn slapped his back anyway.

'Well, at least Grian's speaking to me again,' he said. 'Back on the rigs for me, I reckon.'

'Over my dead body,' said Finn. 'And Grian's. And then yours, probably. Rory, do *not* turn on that TV.'

'I'm going to watch a movie with Hannah.' He ran a finger along the DVD rack.

'You've got exams this year,' mumbled Seth, 'and you're never off that bloody Xbox. Haven't you got homework?'

'Nope.'

Finn gave Rory a dark look, but a smooth facility for lying to his father, and his father's equally smooth new facility for accepting it, was Rory's only compensation for the loss of their mind link. She sighed and gave in. 'Fine. But I'm not staying. You and Hannah don't know where the volume control is.'

'Look who's talking,' muttered Rory.

'Why, you little—'

Seth hauled himself off the sofa, grabbed his jacket, and took

Finn's hand. 'Come on, then, lover. I'll buy you dinner. Well. I will if you give me a sub. Be good,' he told Rory airily.

'You too,' Rory sang as he selected a film. As the front door clunked shut, he added, 'As if.'

~ *I heard that, young man.*

~ *Well, pass it along to my dad.* He grinned. ~ *Have fun, love-birds.*

~ *Don't you have too much, young man, just because we're* . . .

'Have they gone out?' Hannah's voice drowned out the rest of Finn's warning. She shut the door, flopped her arms lazily across the back of the sofa and watched Rory load the DVD. 'Does that mean we can have a horror movie?'

'It means we don't have to watch *It's A Wonderful Life* or anything by Richard Curtis.' Rory rolled his eyes. 'Bloody stepmothers. It didn't tell me this bit in the fairy tales.'

'Don't start it yet.' Hannah came round to the front of the sofa and flung herself down on the cushions. 'I want to talk to you.'

'Not you as well.' Rory rubbed his face.

'Hey, don't be like that. It's not like I'm going to nag you about your homework.' She grinned, then grew serious. 'Look, I'm sick of waiting for you to tell me. What happened that day? Y'know, back in October. With the Veil?'

Rory turned back to the screen, prodding the remote. 'Nothing.'

'Seriously, pause that. How come you had so much trouble opening it? And why was it—'

'I said, it was *nothing,*' he snapped, more curtly than he meant to. 'I found a tough bit for once. That's all.'

'That was so not all.' Hannah scowled. 'Why won't you tell me?'

'Because there's nothing to tell.'

'Why are you being like this?' She raised her voice over the thumping drumbeat on the main menu. 'Turn that thing down!'

'You sound like Finn.' He could hear the savage note in his own voice, but he didn't care to repress it.

'Maybe Finn has a point sometimes. What did you find in the Veil?'

'Leave it.' He gave her a venomous look over his shoulder. 'Leave me alone, for fecksake.'

'Fine.' Hannah stood up. 'I will, then.'

It took him till she was outside in the hall to realise she wasn't bluffing. Pausing the movie, he scrambled to his feet and followed her. 'No. Where are you going?'

'Out.' She shot him a glare.

'You can't.' He was alarmed now. 'You heard what Sionnach said. I'm not to let you go out alone.'

Hannah sighed, softening. 'Oh, for crying out loud. I'm only going round to Lauren's.'

'Not without Sionnach.' Alarmed, Rory grabbed the front door and tried to shut it. 'You know what he said. You can't go without—'

~ *She doesn't have to.* Behind them, Sionnach was already pulling on his leather jacket. ~ *Do you, Currac?*

Hannah gave Rory a smirk of victory. Partly, no doubt, because she'd finally persuaded Sionnach to shorten her name from Currac-sagairt. She could talk him into anything. She was the only person Rory knew who could talk Sionnach into anything he didn't want to do; and it worked the other way round, too.

Rory looked from one to the other, vaguely resentful of their tight relationship and not a little anxious. Even he found Sionnach unnerving these days, and sometimes Rory thought uneasily of his mad, dead twin, Eili. He didn't think there was madness in Sionnach, though: only a huge silence where there had once been the other half of him, and a grief that despite its dark immensity couldn't begin to fill the gap. The man's voice, never overused, had almost fallen out of use altogether.

Rory still loved him all the same. And Hannah, who had once loathed Sionnach on sight, now treated him with a fierce protectiveness that seemed to amuse him. In turn she had become his replacement reason for living.

~ *Come on then, Currac,* Sionnach told her now for Rory to hear. ~ *It's not as if Rory has anything he wants to talk to us about. Do you, Laochan?*

Rory grunted. 'No,' he said. 'Because there's nothing to explain.'

With a slight smile, Sionnach spread his hands. ~ *That's that then.*

When the door closed behind them, Rory stared at it for an age.

There's nothing to talk about. Nothing.

It was an accident.

I didn't mean it anyway and it won't happen again. Rory gritted his teeth in irritation as an involuntary shudder went through him.

He flopped onto the sofa and crossed his arms over his eyes, his interest in the movie dead. He wished he hadn't been so bad-tempered, and he wished he hadn't driven Hannah away, and he wished, for a pointless moment, that they could go away somewhere and be alone together for a day. Not that that was an option. And after what happened last time—the whole being-on-the-run thing, and the deaths of everyone who tried to help him, and the should-have-been-mortal wounding of Finn, and the loss of his father's dun, and the exile of their whole clann—well, he wasn't even going to ask permission.

Besides, he knew fine he'd fallen out with Hannah deliberately. She was bound to be curious about what had happened last October, when she was attacked by Darach, and he was attacked by whatever lay sleeping in the Veil.

But just because Hannah wanted to know, didn't mean he had to tell her. *Nothing to tell.* And why suffer a bloody interrogation when he didn't know the answer?

Lolling an arm to the side, he let his fingers twitch for the Veil. It caught willingly in his fingers, rippled against his skin.

~ *What did you do to me? Why did you do it?*

Awkward questions, indeed. And as well as he knew and loved the Veil, it wasn't as if it was ever going to answer.

Lauren

Shania and Darryl were home for a visit. If she'd known that, she needn't have stayed out so late. Lauren swore under her breath at the extra car in the driveway. If her sister would keep her up to date with her plans, she could plot and ration her escapes a little better.

Maybe I should just go and live with Shania. Yeah, her sister would love that.

Lauren turned the key very quietly, laying her hand flat against the lock plate in a futile effort to muffle any click. An ersatz iron lantern burned in the porch, a large moth rattling wearily inside the glass. To Lauren the racket seemed unreasonably loud, but she couldn't reach high enough to kill the thing. She shut her eyes tight and pushed open the inner door of the house.

No sound. The hall and the stairway were in darkness, but when she reached the top of the stairs she saw a thin strip of soft light beneath the door to her parents' bedroom. At least one of them was awake, then. She swallowed, treading softly down the beige carpet of the passageway. If she went straight to her own room, her father would have an excuse to come there and ask her where she'd been all night. Better to go in to their room voluntarily, let her mother know she was in the house, than to have Marty hunt her down alone.

Her hand trembled as she placed it against the door. It barely creaked as she pushed, and it swung wide even as she hoped irrationally that it wouldn't. For an instant the warm yellow glow of the bedside lamp seemed to pulse brighter, then the light settled. The tangle of bodies on the bed stirred, and one of them rose up on a slender arm, sweeping aside a tumble of red-gold hair to peer at her.

Lauren couldn't move, couldn't even close her gaping mouth. The woman who was not her mother smiled affectionately, unconcerned. Beneath her, Marty grunted and struggled up to lean back on his elbows. He stared at Lauren, seeming for a moment not to recognise her. His eyes held a dull glow; oddly blank, thought Lauren irrelevantly, for a father in a passionate illicit clinch.

'What?' Marty mumbled, blinking.

The woman kissed a finger and laid it against his lips, then turned back, cocking her head to watch Lauren.

'We didn't expect company,' she told her with a smile.

'Yeah,' was all Lauren could say, and even that came out on a husky stutter.

Marty kicked away the remaining sheets and leaned forward, swinging his feet to the floor. He blinked faster, shaking his head, as Lauren tried to back off. 'Listen, love, don't you breathe a word to your mother—'

The red-haired woman rested her hand on his flexing bicep. 'Sh,' she said softly, 'the girl won't tell a soul.' And then, gently, 'Go ahead, now. Kill.'

Lauren's blood flow plummeted into her feet and her limbs turned rubbery. She couldn't even summon the strength to run as the bright light of fury finally sparked Marty's eyes into life. Lunging up from the bed, he sprang for her. In sheer shock, she turned then to run, but too late. From behind, hands seized her throat and crushed it with fingers like cold iron.

The soft yellow glow dulled to red. Dying didn't even hurt, not at her throat, though Lauren was aware of a distant agony in her lungs. She didn't think those hands could tighten any more, but they did, and when Marty let her go, she knew her neck must have snapped.

She fell forward, cracking her forehead on the edge of the door, and her vision went black. There were guttering pinpricks of light in the darkness, and even as she wondered how she'd managed to feel that pain in her head, the tiny flashing stars coalesced into a yellow glow. It was way too bright. *Tunnel of light*, she thought. *Nice.*

Not fair that it still hurts. Not fair.

Lauren sucked in a sudden breath and her eyes jolted wide. Her heart was pumping again, overtime, like a huge piston. Her head was twisted to the side but she could hardly see for her own tangled hair, and there was something in her eyes anyway. And there was a stone weight across her legs, and she couldn't move them, and she was soaking.

I'm paralysed, oh God, he's paralysed me, and I've gone and wet myself.

No. No. She could feel them, she could feel her legs, but there was a weight on them, and she couldn't move even if she dared to try. All she could do was blink, and that was when she realised that Marty was sprawled across her, and the surge of revulsion made her want to draw a breath to scream, except that she couldn't, he was crushing her lungs, and what she'd wet herself with was *eight pints of blood oh my God oh my God and don't move don't move don't move.*

'He'd better be alive, Cuthag,' said the woman.

'Sorry. Didn't mean to be quite that efficient.'

That was a man's voice. *Oh God oh God there are more of them.*

'You're so clumsy sometimes.' Another woman was speaking; a

different one. *Oh God how many?* 'Kate, I think the full-mortal's still breathing.'

Through a film of blood and tears and the web of her hair, Lauren made out a figure, walking close, dusting her hands together before dropping to her knees beside them.

The redheaded woman gripped Marty's floppy head in both hands. Lauren felt the weight of it tugged off her but she wouldn't move, wouldn't breathe, wouldn't stir, wouldn't *die*.

A faint gurgle came from Marty's bloody mouth as the redhead pulled back on his skull; then she was arching in ecstasy, her eyes blazing with joy and life. Marty's face went from grey to blue-white, the veins nearly breaching his skin. He made a high-pitched sound like nothing Lauren had ever heard, or ever wanted to hear again. It rose in pitch till Lauren thought with gratitude that it had stopped; but then she heard the dog in the neighbours' garden begin to yap and howl and bark in demented terror.

'Just in time,' said the redhead happily. '*Now* he's dead.'

She let go abruptly of Marty's head. It snapped against Lauren's with a hideous crack. Lights exploded behind her eyelids once more, and the last sensation she felt was sheer relief that the dog next door had finally shut up.

Finn

He whimpered, and I was awake. For seconds I lay in the darkness, letting my eyes adjust. An owl cried, somewhere out towards the line of pines between the house and the road. As my dream faded I could hear the sea again, a languid rhythmic thump at the foot of the cliffs, muffled by distance and the dense green laurels.

Seth made that sound again, a strangled sound of fear mixed with something I couldn't identify. His fist on top of the covers was tightly clenched, the sinews of his arms and shoulders taut and prominent. I reached out a hand to cover his, but at the last moment I drew it back.

His sleep was very deep. I frowned. I wished his dreams would wake him faster.

Hesitantly I slid my fingers to his temple, then down to the sensitive skin in front of his ear. I stroked it there, lightly. If anything he coiled even tighter.

~ *Well,* I thought. ~ *If you won't come to me . . .*

No response; I hadn't expected one. I put my forehead gently to the back of his head, inhaling the scent of his hair, then slipped inside his mind.

It was dark there. It took me long moments to find the dream, and when I did I couldn't tell much more, not for a while. It was still dark, but I couldn't smell the distant sea any more, only damp earth, bitter grass, night air, the blood of an animal. A crossbow lay beside my hand but it didn't belong to me, it was Sionnach's. The blue roan moved in the foliage. I could hear its teeth ripping first at grass, then at a small corpse, but it had eaten and the movements were languid now. A black wolf lay still, head on his paws, watching.

The scents were familiar: I'd been here before, or somewhere like it. I lay motionless, slowly registering my surroundings. Beneath me was cool ground, cropped turf. A leaf drifted unseen to tickle my face, and I raised a hand to brush it away. That gave me away.

Gave me away? Oh, yes, I was being watched. I'd lain here waiting and I'd drifted into sleep and now I was watched, and my guard was down. I swore obscenely to myself, even as lust warmed and stirred my body.

I thought: No no no. I thought: Not this time. I thought: This time I'll tell her to go.

This time I'll kill her.

Yes.

Except that I can't.

Blood thudded in my pelvis, and I was hardening, and—oh. Right.

The Finn in me grinned. At least it was familiar, if not from this angle.

Outwardly I wasn't grinning. My teeth were gritted. *Not this time no.*

'As if you can tell me no.' Long light fingers stroked my hip, and I twisted swiftly to face her. Her amber gaze followed my hand, and only then did I become aware of the hunting knife in my grip.

Kate smiled. Her hand left my hip, stroked up my arm and my wrist, curled round my fingers and eased the knife's hilt from them.

'Don't tell me no,' she said. 'I won't have it.'

Gently she laid the knife on the ground between us, and kissed me.

Gods, the desire that surged through my body. Her hands were busy, unfastening my belt, tugging my clothes from me. Under her short dress she was naked, the wanton bitch; I had far less trouble getting access. And she sure as hell wanted me. Sure as hell.

Hell. Sure as that.

'No,' I tried again, but I could hardly get the word out. All I could utter was a pitiful whimper. It was lust, and fear, and pain, and most of all hate.

'Conal,' I choked, with the last of my self-control.

'He's safe from me.' Her breath caught in her throat. 'I won't harm him. I can't harm him. For your sake, Murlainn. Why would I? How could I?'

'I don't know,' I said, but then I was lost. She howled with delight, and I gave a scream of ecstasy and despair, and then she began to laugh.

The laugh didn't come from this Kate, the one beneath me. It came from somewhere beyond. It came from another place and another time.

I won't HURT him! I won't hurt HIM!

'No,' I said.

Not me, no. I won't hurt him. I won't hurt you.

'No,' I moaned. 'The gods damn you. No.'

That was different.

That was not Seth's voice any more. In the sudden confusion I felt our minds wobble apart and I was slammed back by a terrific force.

When I skidded into reality, I was back in my own head, dizzy, clutching the linen sheets for dear life. Seth had rolled over to face me and he caught my head in both his hands, his eyes dazed and afraid. I closed my fingers over his, holding them against my head.

'Finn,' he said. 'Finn.'

'Sh,' I told him shakily. 'Sh. What was that?'

'Finn.' He kissed me on the lips, with a desperation that was close to violence. 'I'm sorry, Finn.'

My heart was racing out of control in my chest. Gently I nipped his lower lip. 'It was a long time ago. A long time ago. *A long time ago.*'

'Yes,' he said. 'Yes.'

'She's gone.'

'Yes.'

'She can't touch you.'

'No.' His fingers twined in my hair, and he raised himself over me, staring down. His eyes were startlingly brilliant. It was almost frightening.

'Mine,' I said.

'Yours.'

I ran my hands down his scarred back, pulled him against me. He still had his dream hard-on.

Hearing me think that, he grinned.

I grinned back. 'Mine,' I said again.

He laughed. 'I love you.'

'Prove it.'

He did.

Hannah

Twelve Dunnockvale was not much of an improvement on The Paddocks, decor- or atmosphere-wise, but at least it had a better name. Nobody could ever have mistaken The Paddocks for actual fields full of horses. AFS Properties had added the fancy suffix to their development in the plain little suburb of Dunnock, but at least the place looked something like a vale, a little cluster of executive homes snuggled among mature trees in a dip of south-facing land. And since AFS Properties offered very advantageous mortgages, Sheena and Marty had decided to take a step up in the world.

I was glad. I'd hated The Paddocks, for many reasons, and though the worst of them had accompanied his wife in the house move, at least 12 Dunnockvale didn't hold any of my memories. Sheena was cordial enough nowadays—moving out from under her roof had taken the sting right out of our mutual loathing—and I kind of felt sorry for her anyway, being married to Groper Marty. She knew where my mother lived and she was always offering to put me in touch with her. Of course I always refused; if the woman wanted to contact me, she could do it herself. But I thought it was sweet of Sheena to suggest it.

That wasn't why I went round, though. Lauren was never going to be my favourite person, but I knew fine she needed someone dropping in on the family, unexpectedly and frequently. She'd never said so. But I knew. Boy, did I know.

'Try to act normal,' I told Sionnach, who was mistrustfully eyeing a garden full of gnomes in dinky business suits. 'Sheena was absolutely mortified last time, when you scared away the neighbours.'

~ Anybody would have decked that Doberman. It had no manners.

'Sionnach, not many people would punch a Doberman on the nose, and very few of them could knock it out. Just smile and look, uh . . .'

~ Normal, yeah, he said pleasantly. *~ Would you like me to wear a hockey mask?*

'Oh, shut up. Sorry. Just don't scare anybody.' I swung open the gate and walked up the path, between azaleas popping into spring flower. The Rooney garden was all easycare shrubs and paving slabs, but at least Sheena didn't do gnomes.

How did they ever expect to hear the doorbell? Sheena and Marty must be half-deaf. The television echoed through the house, but then it always did, so I wasn't surprised when I had to walk in uninvited. From the lounge I could hear tinny voices and a burst of studio-audience laughter. Groper Marty would be snoring in his armchair as usual, an empty can of Miller Lite beside him. Or with any luck he'd be out. Sheena was nicer when he wasn't around.

'DEBBIE SAYS "UKRAINE." UKRAINE! LET'S SEE IF THAT'S CORRECT, AND IF SO, HOW MANY OF OUR HUNDRED PEOPLE SAID IT!'

~ Too quiet in here, said Sionnach behind me.

~ Ha, ha. I rolled my eyes.

Then I realised he wasn't joking. He had unfastened his jacket and loosened that compact sword in its sheath.

I frowned. The TV was blaring, but I trusted Sionnach absolutely, so I didn't say anything out loud. ~ *Probably asleep.*

He didn't answer that, but pushed in front of me and laid his fingers lightly on the handle of the sitting room door. His brow furrowed slightly.

~ *Wait here a minute.*

Right. As if. I followed him into the room.

The door didn't creak at all; it was polished and oiled like everything else in the house, including Sheena.

'See?' I whispered.

Sionnach scowled, annoyed with me for disobeying him, but then he shouldn't be so bossy and he shouldn't be so paranoid. Sheena was out of it, her head slumped forward on her chest. She was wearing a red t-shirt that clashed with her chestnut hair, but Sheena would not appreciate me telling her so. I'd opened my mind to share the joke with Sionnach when he turned on me.

'Get out,' he barked. 'Out of here.'

I took a sharp step back, confused and shocked. My first coherent thought was that he was going to wake her up, and she'd get the fright of her life.

The notion barely had time to form, because it registered straight away that she wouldn't be waking up. Ever. As for the fright of her life, she looked like she'd already had it.

And then it finally registered that Sheena's t-shirt wasn't red at all. Not when she put it on this morning.

I clapped my hand over my mouth to stop myself screaming, but I couldn't shut my eyes. Sionnach, giving up on ever making me move, was stooped over Sheena's body, gripping a handful of hair to raise her head very slightly. The gaping wound in her throat yawned wide, and I finally shut my eyes, but no blood spurted out. It was all congealed in the cut, what hadn't spilt on her t-shirt and her sequinned jeans. Very delicately, Sionnach let her head sag forward again.

'We need to get out of here,' I told him, my voice cracking. 'You shouldn't have touched her!'

He nodded. Then he hesitated, and glanced at the ceiling. It was darkening with a spreading stain. Perhaps I only imagined its pinkish tinge.

'No,' I said. *'No.'*

'Hannah!' barked Sionnach, but I was already taking the beige-carpeted stairs two at a time. The bathroom door wasn't locked. Sionnach was at my back as I staggered into the room, slipping and slithering on the wet tiles, and he grabbed my arm to stop me falling.

A woman's hand drifted at the edge of the brimming bath. Her hair had caught in the overflow, blocking it, but her hard pretty face was under the water, which wasn't as red as it might have been.

The taps were still running. As I moved to turn them off, Sionnach grabbed my wrist to stop me. He pulled me out of the bathroom, then stuck his head round the door of the bedroom.

~ *Another one. Youngish man.*

I swallowed, but couldn't make myself speak. ~ *Darryl,* I guessed. ~ *Shania's husband.*

He had to physically take hold of my arms and move me out of the way before he strode towards the master bedroom. This time he wasn't so quick. He seemed to stare into it for a terribly long time, and there was pity on his face.

~ *It's your uncle.*

I moved sharply towards the room, but Sionnach only shook his head. That stopped me where all his rough warnings hadn't. I swallowed hard and began to back away.

~ *Sionnach. Sionnach, what about—*

Sionnach lifted a finger to silence me. He tilted his head, frowning, and slid his sword from its scabbard. Shaking my head, I backed towards the last bedroom. The carpet was dense, and it silenced any sound we made.

We hadn't imagined the sound we weren't making. A high muffled whimpering, as if a hand was clasped tightly over a mouth but couldn't stop the sobs. I stared at the cream door of the fitted wardrobe.

~ *Put that thing away,* I told Sionnach.

He sheathed the sword, but left it loose in the scabbard, and his jacket unfastened.

I tried to reach out with my mind, tentatively, but that was silly and pointless. She wouldn't know what was going on, and I'd only frighten her more, and there was something in the way anyway: static or interference. It felt a bit like a crude block, but of course it couldn't be.

I closed my fingers round the gilt handle of the wardrobe and eased it open.

A strangled shriek, and the door banged into my face as a figure exploded from behind it and flung me to the ground. I was too shocked to fight it off, but the creature was yanked away before it could hurt me. I scrambled to a crouch, only to see a struggling demented demon locked in Sionnach's grip, streaky caramel hair flailing across a ravaged face. Tears had made streaky blotches in the endless blood.

'Lauren,' I panted. 'Lauren, it's okay. It's me. Hannah. It's okay.'

It didn't have much effect; it was just that the fight suddenly went out of her and she hung limply in Sionnach's arms, staring at me wild-eyed. I grabbed her hands, and at last her eyes focused and recognition sparked.

'Hannah?' Her voice hardly made a sound. 'It's you. It's you.'

'Yes. Lauren, listen. Is there anyone else here?'

She stared at me for a moment, then gave an awful hysterical laugh.

'I don't know. Are they gone? Please.'

~ *Something terrible happened here. And it's to do with us.* Sionnach's eyes fastened on mine, bright and pitiless. ~ *I should kill her, Hannah. I'll be quick.*

~ *No!* I lunged forward, grabbing Lauren's arms to try to pull her away. She shrieked with fear.

~ *She'll tell. She'll bring down the full-mortals. Too many mistakes, Currac, I've made too many mistakes in my life already. I lost Finn to Kate and I lost control of Eili and—*

'I said *no!*' I shouted aloud, panic making my heart crunch in my chest.

'No?' Lauren's teeth were chattering hard. 'They're not gone? Please, please, they're gone, tell me. It's just dead people now. Dead people! Oh, my God! Mum!'

'Shush. Lauren, shush. Listen, we have to get out of here! You have to calm down. *Please.*'

'But Mum! Dad! Shania! The police, call the police. The police!' Wriggling out of Sionnach's arms, she stumbled to her bedside table and grabbed her phone. It was charging, and it took a second for her to tug it free of the socket, and that was long enough for Sionnach. I didn't have the presence of mind to stop him, but he only grabbed her, thank God. His fingers closed round her temples. She swayed in his grip, then slumped, and he hooked his arm under her armpits to support her.

~ *Get Rory. Call Rory NOW.*

'How many bloody corpses are we planning to hide?' I yelled.

Rory looked shamefaced. I don't think he'd wanted to do it at all; it was just that Sionnach was still angry with me at that point and he wouldn't take *but there's been a hideous crime and we need to tell the police* for an answer. Rory had ripped the Veil, and between the two of them they'd calmly and efficiently disposed of the bodies of almost all that was left of my former family.

'Sionnach did the right thing,' snapped Grian. 'He was in their house with a bloody sword and apparently he'd already beaten up the neighbour's Doberman.'

'Look at his face,' Sorcha pointed out, and Sionnach nodded. 'There walks a man who looks like he's been in many a knife fight. They'd arrest him on the spot.'

'I have been in many a knife fight,' said Sionnach reasonably. ~ *And by the way, don't anybody complain that we brought Lauren back here.*

'Of course not,' said Grian gruffly. 'You had no choice.'

Sionnach glanced at me, and his words were for me alone. ~ *I did have a choice, but I didn't get to make it.*

'How is the girl?' asked Seth, rubbing his head.

'Asleep again,' said Finn. 'That's about all you can say.'

Finn stood in the doorway hugging herself, not meeting my eyes. She didn't look at anyone but Seth. Braon and Grian were there, and Savage Sorcha because she'd taken a lustful liking to Grian; but Orach had dragged Sulaire out to the pub, to keep him out of the way. Iolaire and Jed had reappeared, after a brief trip to the off-license. Sionnach had never left, of course. He hadn't gone far from me at all. Nice of him. Thoughtful.

'What's the situation at the house?' asked Grian. 'How long have we got before somebody asks questions?'

Practical man. Pig.

~ *We cleaned up the blood as best we could.* Sionnach nodded at me. ~ *Moved some rugs. Shifted the furniture. Turned off the sockets. They're on holiday.* And both Marty's car and Shania's were now parked behind our own house, next to my father's ancient Audi, under the laurels. Just as well Sionnach and Rory could think fast and straight.

'Keep the girl asleep,' said Grian. 'I fixed the cut on her head as well as I could. Caorann, you need to work on the inside of it.'

'It's not like Finn can make her forget *that*,' snapped Seth.

'Convince her it's a secret. She's in hiding from the killers. I don't bloody know, do I? If she goes to the police, Sionnach's had it. We all have.' Grian gave Jed a meaningful look, but Jed's expression stayed cool.

Finn didn't say anything. She probably looked more shocked than I did, because I couldn't feel a thing. I was watching it all from space. Rory and I sat curled together on the sofa, feet hitched up, my back against his chest and his arms around me, but I didn't feel like I needed the comfort. I almost couldn't see what the fuss was about. Not from out here in space.

Finn lingered in the doorway as if she didn't know what to do or where to go next. 'I nearly killed Shania once,' she mumbled.

'Well, you didn't.' Seth leaned forward on the edge of a chair, watching her. 'Somebody else did.'

'I can't believe it.' Finn raked her fingers into her hair. 'Hannah, I saw your aunt yesterday morning. In the High Street. Just *yesterday.*'

Nobody said a word. We all tried not to meet her eyes. Then Seth got to his feet and put an arm round her shoulders.

'Oh,' she whispered. 'Oh, God.' She put her hands over her face. Seth put his other arm round her, but she pushed him back, clutching her skull.

'You weren't to know,' he said. 'How were you meant to know?'

'Sheena looked right through me. Right through me, didn't say a word. I thought she was just being snotty. Oh, *hell.*'

'What were you supposed to do? You couldn't know it was just a fetch.'

'I could have warned Sheena,' she moaned. 'I could have gone to her house and warned her.'

Sionnach, propped against the wall with his arms folded, shook his head.

Seth said, 'You know it doesn't work like that. It wouldn't have made any difference.'

'There was nothing you could do,' said Rory. His voice was low and comforting in my ear, as if he was talking as much to me as to his stepmother. 'Nothing, Finn. It's a lousy talent. I'm glad I haven't got it.'

'Why didn't they kill her too?' said Jed. 'The girl?'

He sounded like Sionnach; as if he thought it would be better that way. I shivered a little and Rory's arms tightened round me.

'They thought they had,' said Finn. 'Far as we can tell, she played dead.'

'Smart kid,' said Seth.

'Almost incredibly smart,' said Iolaire. 'How could they possibly make that mistake?'

'Yeah,' said Seth. 'I'm getting a bad feeling about this.'

'Seth,' sighed Finn, with a sarcasm that sounded almost normal, 'four people have had their throats cut. I'd hope you'd have a bad feeling about it.'

'That's not what I meant.' He gave her a wry grin. 'I mean, why didn't they notice her mind was still active?'

'She was blocking,' I said suddenly.

Everybody's attention turned to me. I reddened.

'I felt something,' I mumbled. 'Like a block.'

'No way,' said Iolaire in astonishment. 'No *way*.'

Finn looked doubtful. 'Conal said there might be Sithe blood in that family. He reckoned that's why Shania took notice of me.'

'Come on,' protested Seth. 'A little blood? She can't be Sithe enough to raise a spontaneous block. Without even *knowing* she was doing it.'

'Trauma,' remarked Grian knowledgeably. 'Perfectly possible.'

'Then why wouldn't they sense the block? It doesn't make sense, Gri.'

'Aren't you all missing the point?' I said it quietly, but I was suddenly furious with the lot of them, I don't know why. 'I don't care why they didn't kill Lauren! The point is, why *did* they kill the rest of them?'

They were paying attention now, shamed, but it didn't make me any less angry. By now I was blazing with rage.

'They killed them to get at me!' I shouted. 'They killed them because I went to see them! Because I was related to them!'

Finn crouched beside me and tentatively touched my hand. I snatched it away.

'Hannah,' she whispered, 'it isn't your fault.'

Which is when I started, embarrassingly, to cry.

Kate

'Caorann's onto me,' hissed Kate.

'Or she thinks she is,' said Langfank. 'Which isn't quite the same thing, now, is it?'

Kate had nothing against Lammyr, generally speaking, but nobody could ever say they were sweet when they smiled. She gave it a tight-lipped smirk in return. 'No. And it's not as if there's anything she can do about it.' She drew the falcon charm from the pouch at her hip and turned it in her fingers, thoughtful. She loved the feel of it, the smoothness of the glassy stone, the tingle of the sorcery against her skin. 'And even if she does . . .'

'She doesn't have the strength,' agreed the Lammyr. 'Your Grace.'

Kate's smile became more genuine. 'I like you, Langfank.'

It inclined its head with a little grin, and shot a smug glance at Cluaran, who kept his mouth sensibly shut.

The day was perfect. Thin mist ribboned the valley below, but it glowed bright and pearly, and up here on the higher slopes, the sun dazzled from a sky streaked by a single downy feather of cirrus. The lines of an old fort remained, clear on the lumpy grassland. Some of its singed walls still stood, but at this hour they cast barely a shadow.

'Who are they?' Alainn MacAleister nudged her horse forward

to Kate's side, and jerked a thumb at the cadavers piled in the corner of a ruined hall.

And why was that captain still on her horse when Kate herself had dismounted? Pursing her lips at Alainn, Kate turned to give Cluaran a tiny nod. It amused her that his weather-tanned face could drain so quickly of colour.

'No-one important,' Kate told Alainn at last. 'Not in them-selves, at least.' With one booted foot she nudged the sprawled arm of the gore-drenched man. 'Gracious, Cuthag hasn't any room for sentiment, has he?'

'No,' grunted Cluaran, 'but he's got enthusiasm.'

Kate shuddered delicately. She'd had a sentimental side once herself, but that was long gone, so she could hardly condemn the faithful Cuthag.

'Well. It's rather a mess, but the crows will take them soon enough.' Kate stooped to stroke the younger woman's hair. Hanks of it still shone caramel-gold through the clotted blood. A pity, really. She'd been a pretty thing, even more so than her mother, and she'd probably had better taste in fashion, though now she was wrapped only in a soaking, pink-blotched towel. Kate glanced with distaste at the older woman's sequinned jeans.

She stood up straight. 'The boy's ready,' she told them. She smiled at all four captains, but saved the warmth of her expression for the Lammyr. 'I'd say he's at the peak of his powers. It's time.'

Cluaran muttered his agreement; Alainn and the other two captains nodded; but the Lammyr was the only one who went on holding her gaze, its face thoughtful. As she walked to the edge of the hill to look back at the ruined fortress, it ambled after her.

'It was a long way to ride for a few corpses,' it said. It scraped with a bare foot at the red earth.

'I wanted you all to see that we are ready,' said Kate. 'East, west: they're all one to me.'

'Your ambition becomes you, Your Loveliness.'

All right, the Lammyr was going a bit far now. If she'd had a suspicious mind, she'd have thought the thing was mocking her.

All the same, their impertinent disrespect was part of why she loved the brutes. Any irreverence her own people showed her was a lot more dull. And it wouldn't go on for much longer. And at least you could always rely on a Lammyr for cold-hearted constancy. If nothing else, they took themselves a lot more seriously than they pretended.

'How will your clann react,' it said, 'when you explain what you're really going to become?'

'Will it matter?' She shrugged elegant shoulders. 'We're close now, Langfank. You'll like my world, and the Darkfall can no more break an oath than you Lammyr can.'

'I know. We're quite excited. We've never had a god of our own. What about the young witch you want?'

'That's in hand.' Kate smiled. 'If you want to separate a sheep from the flock, all you need is a well-controlled dog.'

Hooded crows were circling now, and one of them landed close to her. It cocked its head and rasped a petulant cry. *It wants us to get a move on,* she thought. *And so do I.* The birds must have been here before Kate and her fighters; the younger man was eyeless. She kicked casually at his corpse. 'That was a strong one. I'd have liked that soul. The older one was stringy.'

'At least you got it. Tsk. Try to kill his own daughter: how could he?'

She gave it a gimlet glance, suspecting mockery again. 'We know very well how he could.'

'Indeed, and he certainly gave it up to you with enthusiasm. Lustily, indeed. Well, well; you'll have your pick of souls soon.' Langfank blinked its yellow eyes. 'I take it you're ready to proceed, Your Regalness?'

'Now that Murlainn's son is. Yes.' Kate breathed in the scent of whin and broom and April chill. Her nerves and muscles thrilled to it all as she walked back to her captains. She could even stand the blue, blue sky.

Cluaran cupped his hands once again to help her mount. She heard his soft voice as she settled on the mare's back.

~ *These people were true innocents, Kate, but never forget it doesn't matter in the long run. Innocents always die in war, and you'll kill fewer than most.*

Fool, she thought. *Fool.*

His words had riled her more than she'd thought possible. Glancing back at the bodies as she spurred her mare, she thought she felt the faintest resounding, an echo of a residual twinge in her heart. Was Cluaran right? Could that possibly be *regret*? Not that she'd have heeded it, but would the Darkfall be disappointed in her all the same?

~ *I can't be disappointed. So no.* Remembering the beast's retort in the cavern, Kate smiled to herself.

Perhaps there's a shadow of a conscience left in here, she told her-self.

No matter. It's not for much longer.

Hannah

What can I say about those weeks after the murders? I'd hated Lauren and her family for most of my life. What are you supposed to do when they die? Bad enough when it's people you love.

And what could I say to her? Nothing. I hadn't wanted the Rooneys to die, but before they did, I hadn't much cared if they lived. I was genuinely upset about Sheena, but I'd have felt a right fraud playing the grief-stricken niece in front of Lauren. In their hideous deaths they'd leap-frogged over my head to the moral high ground. They'd left me wallowing in the muck, and that's where I deserved to be. For the moment, at least. For Lauren's sake.

Guilt. It's a terrible thing. Makes you take terrible decisions, do terrible things in your turn.

I don't know what trick my friends used to convince Lauren; she seemed to accept it. She remembered almost nothing of the events that night, but at least they hadn't done that to her, or they said they hadn't; that seemed to be genuine trauma. She left school abruptly and completely; Finn made it official with a fraudulent phone call and a twist of some brainwaves. Lauren knew we'd taken her in to protect her; she knew that Something was being Done. As the long weeks passed, I suppose it became more convincing, not less. She spent a lot of time sleeping.

For the first week, she was all out of silliness and bitchiness.

Maybe that was shock; maybe it was just that her mind was being twisted and warped and there was no room in it for thinking. She was blank and rigid, completely withdrawn, but she didn't reject me and Rory, she didn't shove us away. It was like moving a playing piece around a board game: we told her when to sleep and when to eat and she did. She didn't even cry much: only sometimes, silently.

~ *She worries me,* said Sionnach.

Seth said nothing, but to my undying gratitude he didn't tell Sionnach to take her down to the cliffs and slit her throat and throw her over. Seth just watched her, constantly, and he ordered Finn and Sorcha and Orach to keep an eye on her all the time. Jed, as far as I was concerned, kept far too much of an eye on her. I knew he thought the same as Sionnach: that we should have killed Lauren. Now he sat by and watched while they did that thing he always said he hated: messing with a young mind.

And I just watched them, guilty and angry and completely paralysed by doubt. It wasn't right, what they did, but it was more right than Sionnach and Jed and who-knew-who-else being rounded up and jailed for bloody murder. It was more right than the lot of us being exposed to the daylight and the police and the press, and being vulnerable to enemies, and maybe getting killed ourselves.

That's what they said, anyway.

'It's child abduction,' I snarled at Finn one day as we loaded the dishwasher for the third cycle of the night. 'In all but name it is. You're all screwing up her mind.'

'We don't have a choice,' she said for the fiftieth time. 'Hannah, we don't.'

'How can Jed sit there and watch this? Seth did the same to him once.'

'Jed knows that was necessary. In Seth's eyes, there and then. He's not angry any more.'

'He's never forgotten.'

Finn paused to study my face, a little sadly. She turned a dirty cup in her hands, over and over, and didn't notice when drips of cold coffee spattered the tiles. 'No.'

'It's wrong, Finn. Not just Lauren's head. Four people died and nobody's even paying.'

'They will, I *promise*.'

I just sniffed, and slammed a plate into the rack so hard it cracked.

Finn didn't even scold me. She bit her lip as she rinsed another plate. 'Lauren's got us, Hannah. I know you don't like it but at least we can keep her safe.'

'She doesn't have us. Not in real life.' I was torn between anger and guilt. The very idea of trying to talk to Lauren about any of it filled me with horror. 'You lot just spy on her.'

Finn rubbed her damp forehead with an arm. 'We have to.'

'The only reason you have to is because you're terrified she'll realise what's going on.'

'Look, it's not that big a struggle. She's shut it away all by herself. That night, everything that happened, it's inside a locked room in her mind, because she doesn't want to look at it.'

Honestly, I wanted to throttle the woman. 'I thought you were brought up in the real world? Finn, she's *got* to look at it. Some time.'

'True, but not right now. I can't see inside that locked room for now, but neither can she. The rest of it's easy.'

'Easy.'

'Yes, easy.' She shrugged. 'Would you rather we kept her locked up for real? We can only give her freedom to wander because we keep tabs on her head. She likes to walk and I'm glad. How do you think she'd manage if she was stuck in the house?'

'You don't get it, do you? I'm not that girl's biggest fan, but you're hurting her. One of these days she'll realise what's happening and she'll go mad. You can't keep it up forever. That's when it's going to go tits-up, Finn, that's when *everybody's* going to get hurt.'

Finn slammed the dishwasher shut and hit the start button with a clenched fist. 'It's a stopgap, Hannah! We have to think of something, yes, but *now is not the time.*'

'When is it going to be the time? You're all in denial! You're doing nothing!'

Finn leaned back against the gurgling dishwasher and folded her arms. 'I have done something.'

That look in her crystal cold eyes. So aggressive, and Lauren or no Lauren, I knew I wasn't going to like what she'd done.

'What?' I said. 'Tell me.'

A slight shrug. 'Somebody,' began Finn, and licked her lips. 'Somebody called me last night. I invited her over.'

I stared at her. 'We can't have anybody else here!

'You said it yourself, Hannah, you don't even like Lauren. She needs help, and you got that right: we're not giving it to her. She needs family, whatever there is left of it.'

'No,' I said pointlessly, because the frisson between my shoulder blades was horrible. 'Finn. Why did you want me in here helping you? It's not my turn.'

'Because I wanted to tell you. Tell you myself. She's coming round—' she glanced at her watch '—around now.'

She was blocking me, the devious cow. I scowled. Block or no block, I could still make her skin prickle just by giving her a certain look. So I did, and she shivered; and I swear that was the exact moment I heard a car door slam, and hesitant footsteps crunch on the drive.

And, 'You bitch,' I said. 'You bitch.'

. . .

Either the woman had been crying or her eyes were smokily made up. Maybe both. Her hair was red and short, flicked out at the ends. She'd always worn it short. She hadn't always dressed like that, though: all respectable and modest, a navy summer coat belted round her small waist. She blinked, trying to smile.

I was taller than her, I realised as I stood at the open door, blocking her path. It had been so long since I'd seen her, and now she looked so small, and I'd outgrown her.

In more ways than one.

~ *Hello, Mother.*

She didn't hear that, of course. She just forced a hideous smile and said, 'Hannah?' With a question mark and everything.

Finn was keeping her distance, hanging back at the kitchen door and twisting a dishcloth in her fingers, but I was piercingly aware of her. This time four years ago, she'd been a stranger to me. Her and Seth, total strangers, and ones I didn't even like when I met them. Now, though for the moment I wanted to kill Finn— and Seth must have known about this, so my hatred extended to him—they both meant more to me than *she* did.

It wasn't just that they'd been mother and father to me when my real father couldn't, and my real mother couldn't be bothered. It was going through so much together. My mother had never let me go through anything with her.

'Hello, Hannah,' said my biological parent, and nibbled at her lipstick.

It was a mannerism I remembered well, and it infuriated me. I tried not to think about crying, curled up on the sofa, as she tried to hug me and keep hold of her suitcase and check her watch, all at the same time.

'Mother,' I said, and then, 'How are you?'

And *where have you been?* And *did you miss me even a little?* And *was he worth it?* And *do I mean anything to you?*

But I couldn't ask any of that. All I could get out was *How are you?*

So formal. As if I cared anyway.

Trying to be casual, my mother lifted her eyebrows and glanced behind me. Oh, now I had a decent reaction. Her eyes widened, the blood drained out of her face so fast it was cartoonish, and I thought she might trip over her own feet.

I looked over my shoulder. Finn wasn't alone: Seth had come downstairs and he was standing at her side, silent and thoughtful.

Smiling, I turned back to my mother. 'Did you think he was someone else?'

'I—yes.' At last she focused on me, drawing a deep breath, opening her mouth to explain herself. 'Hannah, I've got to tell you—'

'He's not so tall.' I was amazed and pleased at how cool I sounded. 'His hair's much darker. Different look about him, don't you think? Something about his eyes.'

Any blood left in Mum's face was gone.

'Brothers,' I said. 'See?'

'Brothers? Is this Conal's *brother*?' Mum wore a helpless smile, and I wanted to wipe it right off her face. She didn't even ask me how I knew. She didn't even ask who had told me who'd fathered me. 'Is he—how is Conal?' She focused on Seth again, eyes dancing.

Was I really loving this moment? Did I hate her so much that I wanted to revel in it? Maybe. That's what the Sithe are like. But maybe I was only so angry, and so terribly hurt, that I wanted to share it with her.

'How is Conal?' I said. 'He's dead.'

Her smile went rigid. 'He can't be.'

'Why can't he? He is. He's dead.'

'Hannah . . .' Seth had come to my side, and his hand rested in the small of my back. From her perspective it must have looked like nothing but a small comforting gesture, but I felt strength like flexible steel running up my spine.

'Perhaps Aileen would like to come in,' said Seth.

I heard the warning in his voice but I said. 'No.'

Tears filled my mother's eyelids, and she lifted her fingers to push them back.

Damn her, why wouldn't she cry? 'He died this really violent death. He was in so much pain his lover had to cut his throat.' I paused for effect. 'His proper lover.'

She made a little keening noise, put her hands over her mouth.

'If you'd come home,' I said, 'we'd never have had to know that. Neither of us. If you'd come home.'

Tears clung trembling to her lashes but didn't fall. I wanted them to fall.

'But I'm glad you didn't come back. These are my friends. I met them after you left. I was a bit too late to meet my dad, because he's *dead*, but I've seen . . . I've seen . . .' I pressed my teeth together and spoke through them '. . . pictures.'

'That's enough, Hannah,' said Seth.

'No, it's not,' I said venomously. 'It'll never be enough.'

I shook off Seth's hand and walked away, and I didn't look back. I was too afraid he'd come after me. I didn't want any stupid sympathy: I was too ashamed.

I was ashamed I wasn't crying, nothing like. I couldn't cry because there was nothing worth crying over. I hated her, hated her, and I was hers, and so I hated myself as well.

Pictures. Pictures.

I'd seen pictures.

The last time I saw my father he was tied to a stake, whipped and shorn and ready for burning along with the weeping and terrified girl at his side. The last time I saw my father I was on the point of killing him, a crossbow in my capable hands and his heart in my sights. The last time I saw my father, I was Seth.

I'd made him show me that memory. He'd been very reluctant. Not only because he wasn't sure I should See it, but because he dreaded reliving it. It must have returned to him many times in his dreams. It froze his heart, remembering how close he'd come to killing his brother. Foreshadowed the real guilt, too: the guilt he'd live with for the rest of his life.

'What happened to the girl?' I'd asked him, that late and darkening afternoon last November.

It had seemed the safest thing to ask, when he'd only just broken contact, rubbing his face and shivering. I felt cold and scared and shaken too, and it wasn't just the shredded remnants of Seth's old emotions, though those shadowed his face like ghosts. We sat on opposite sides of the kitchen table: just me and Seth. Finn had warned everyone else to stay out, and nobody crossed Finn in that kind of mood. If anyone was hungry, they'd wait.

'What happened to her?' I prompted.

He sounded shocked. 'The girl?'

'The girl. The girl with Conal. What happened to her?'

'She came with us.' Seth looked straight through me. 'She came over with us and she stayed.'

'Her whole life?'

Seth licked his lips. 'Almost.'

'So she did go home in the end.'

'Came back here? Oh, yes. We all did.' He ground his knuckles into his temples. 'She was old by then.'

It was like pulling teeth. 'So she lived for a long time over there.'

'I didn't say that.'

I hesitated, thrown by the coldness of his voice.

'I'm sorry.' He picked at a hangnail. 'She was happy, that was the main thing. Kind of quiet. Brave though. Brave, she was.'

'What was her name?' I asked.

'Does it matter?' Seth shrugged. 'Catriona.'

I let it go. 'What about the guy who saved you? The MacLeod?'

'Died with his men, but not before he'd been outlawed for the killing of the priest. I don't think that bothered him, but I was sorry to hear he'd been betrayed and murdered. He knew about the Sithe. You Saw. One of his men was one of us, and there was a rumour he was the chief's illegitimate son. The MacLeod wouldn't be the first full-mortal to get mixed up with the Sithe.' He laughed. 'Well, I couldn't do anything for him, but I paid back my debt to his grandson. He was a good man too. Misguided twat, though. I only fought for him because I owed his ancestor.'

'Yeah? Which fight?'

He fidgeted. 'Drumossie Moor.'

Had to think that one over for a moment. 'Culloden? Seth, you were at *Culloden*?'

'Yes.' He gave me a beseeching look. 'Don't make me show you that. I'm all for living history but don't *ever* make me show you that.'

'All right.' I shut one eye. 'But tell me how you got away?'

'I crawled off the field while they butchered the wounded around me. Inconspicuous, wasn't I?' There was a catch in his voice. 'There was this boy. Twelve or thirteen, maybe? He wasn't badly hurt but he was scared shitless. I tried to take him with me. I dragged the Veil round both of us, but he panicked. Jumped up and ran. They chased him down and they . . .' His voice faded.

'Oh, God, Seth.'

He rubbed his fist across his face. 'You know what, Hannah? When life's this long, you see an awful lot of people die. And when you're Sithe? You don't see many born to take their places.'

Too many memories, I thought. Standing up, I hugged him, my hard, scarred, cynical, warlord uncle.

'Ach, Hannah.' There was an obstruction in his throat. 'I think I've had enough talking for now. Will you forgive me?'

'Yeah, course.'

'I'll show you more another day, I promise.'

"S'okay, Seth. I've kind of had enough too.' The thought of my father tied to that stake, beaten and brutalised and waiting for a horrible death, was more than I could bear. Yet he'd got out of it, he'd cheated death; that time he had. I didn't want to think about all the others who hadn't. I swear I could hear their pathetic screams, echoing somewhere deep in my ancestral memory.

'Can you hear them too?'

I started. 'What?'

'Can you hear them, Hannah? Can you feel them? I feel them all the time. More and more. The older I get, the louder I hear them.'

Now that was unusual. Seth didn't usually talk about getting older. He was a hundred percent Sithe and he had centuries of life left, so I didn't understand the tired sadness on his face. I was on the verge of tears myself, which was annoying. I ached to See memories of my father, every single one the other Sithe could summon up, but every time it was like a knife to my heart. Because every time I loved him better, but I was never, never going to be able to tell him so.

Do you know me, Dad? I wondered. *I wish I'd known you, and at least I'm getting to know you secondhand, but do you ever See me like I See you? Or is Seth right and you're just not there any more, not anywhere, gone altogether?*

Finn—truculent bloody-minded Finn—insisted he was somewhere. I'd heard her and Seth arguing about it, though they always made it up at embarrassing length.

So if Finn thought my father was still somehow around, I saw even less reason why, all these months later, she'd needed to involve my other parent.

'I didn't involve her,' she told me the evening of Aileen's arrival. As soon as the door had closed on my mother, Finn had gone to the kitchen and poured herself a large neat whisky. She stood there now turning the tumbler in her hand, obsessively, almost forgetting to drink from it. But when she did remember, she took a massive gulp.

She and Seth had talked to my mother for hours, and Aileen had gone back to her hotel shattered. And I don't mean tired-shattered. She was grief-shattered from the news of her sister, and more to the point, her mind had been picked apart. I knew it from the fact that the police didn't show up five minutes after she left; and I knew it from the guilty look on Finn's face.

'You're mad,' I told her. 'I thought you didn't want people to know about the Rooneys? I thought it was our little secret that four people were brutally murdered in their own house?'

'How could I tell her no? Your mother was coming to town and she called, she wanted to see you. I thought I could put her off but she was determined.'

'She picked a fine time to get her maternal instinct back.'

'Listen, it's just like Lauren. I can control her. I can keep her—'

'Grian's right,' I hissed.

Finn knocked back the dregs of her whisky. I'd swear it was only to avoid my eyes.

'Did you hear me?' I wasn't letting her get away with it. 'If it's true that you can control two minds about *this*, you're pushing it way too far.'

She ignored me anyway. 'Aileen knows they're dead. She had to know that.'

'And what does she think about the fact the police aren't involved?'

Finn shrugged. 'She thinks exactly what Lauren thinks. That other people are dealing with it. That Lauren's in danger if it gets out.' She licked her lips. 'That you are, too.'

'Use me, why don't you.' I thought I'd go demented with the lot of them. 'Finn, *somebody has to deal with this.*'

'I know, *I know.* But I can keep a lid on her mind. For now.'

'For now. Your operative words, right there.'

'I don't know what else to do, Hannah. I don't know.'

And for the first time, I realised she was terrified.

Lauren

'Why did you come back?' asked Lauren.

She sat perched on the edge of the cliff with her legs hanging over, the breeze whipping her hair and stinging water from her eyes. Behind her, she heard Aileen clear her throat awkwardly and swallow.

'I've been trying to call your mum. I left messages and voicemails, loads of them. I never called Sheena much but she always got back to me when I did. So I was worried. It wasn't like her not to answer.' Aileen wrapped her arms round herself. 'Now I know why.'

The sky was mottled with cloud and the air had a bite that was less than summery; Lauren thought it was probably going to rain soon. But she didn't want to go inside. She hated that house, the house that didn't even have a name. A house with no name and no number couldn't be home to anyone. She tilted back her head to gaze at the ragged black crow that dived and soared between the low clouds.

'Look at that bloody bird,' she said. 'I swear it's spying on me.'

Aileen laughed awkwardly. 'There's loads of crows around here.'

'No. Look at the size of that one. It's Fionnuala's pet.'

'Well. Maybe that's why it stays around the house.'

Lauren shook her head, burying her face in her folded arms.

Aileen cleared her throat again. 'You can talk to me if you like.'

'What is there to talk about? My mum? My sister?' Bleakly Lauren rested her chin on her arms and stared out over the restless steely sea. She didn't want to look at Aileen for a moment. 'I don't remember much anyway.'

'But maybe if you talked about it a bit—'

Lauren laughed, though she didn't know why. It wasn't funny. 'I'm not supposed to talk to anyone. Least of all the police.'

'I know.' Aileen bit her lip, shifting uneasily. 'Hannah says—'

'Oh yeah. Hannah. I know what she says. She just doesn't say it to me.'

'She probably doesn't know what to say,' said Aileen.

'Seth says it's a gangland thing,' Lauren said. 'Seth says it's something they have to sort out. Seth says, the less the cops know, the better. Seth says they'll deal with these people in their own way. I'm getting fucking sick of Seth.'

At least it all made sense now: the weird living arrangements of all those people, and the weapons she'd seen lying about, and the scars on Sionnach, and Jed Cameron's charming hitman personality. It made a lot more sense than she liked.

'You should be getting counselling. When all this is sorted out—'

'Why would I need counselling? I am in the bosom of my extended family and they are keeping me safe.' Lauren's eyes burned, but she swallowed hard and shrugged.

Aileen stuck her hands awkwardly in her pockets. 'Do you want me to leave you alone?'

'No!' Lauren cleared her throat and looked away. 'No.'

'Because if you like, I can give you a bit of—'

'Don't say that. Don't give me *space*.' Her voice trembled slightly. 'I like it that you're not leaving me alone.'

'Okay.'

'But I don't need counselling, right? I'm okay.' A spatter of cold rain hit her cheek. 'You know what I need? I need to go into town.'

Aileen swallowed. 'Are you sure that's a good idea?'

'I need stuff. And I hate it here. Can you lend me some money?'

'Well.' Aileen nibbled a thumbnail. 'I suppose so. My bank card's at the hotel, but that's right in town. There's a cafe next door if you're hungry. I eat there all the time.'

The huge crow landed with a hop and a skip on the cliff edge, not five metres away. It cocked its head, took a couple of prancing steps towards Lauren. Its eye was black and ferocious, and it opened its massive bill as if it was about to yell at her.

'Fine,' said Lauren. She stood up and brushed bits of grass and whin off her jeans. 'Let's get out of here.'

The cafe was even sleazier, and further down at heel, than her aunt's mangy hotel, and she'd been glad enough to walk away from that. Lauren hung back as the bell tinkled over the cafe door and Aileen went in ahead of her.

It couldn't be quite as bad as it looked or smelled; most of the tables were occupied, largely by what she reckoned were students. There was an old guy with a dog, a fat woman surrounded by plastic bags of shopping, another woman who looked too elegant and well-heeled to be in here. A smell of dampness clung to the yellow walls, even through the reek of stale fat. The rickety tables were draped in oilcloths that smelt of disinfectant—which made Lauren suspect it was camouflaging something—and when she finally pulled out a chair to sit down, there was a scrap of wilted bacon on its seat. She pulled her sleeve down over her hand and brushed it to the floor, shuddering.

'I don't think I'm hungry.'

'The fried egg sandwiches aren't bad.'

She didn't want to imagine an egg fried in that rancid fat. 'I'll just have a beer.'

Aileen's mouth fell open a little. 'I don't think . . . I mean, I'm not sure it's got a licence.'

'Yes it has.' Lauren nodded at the chic-looking customer at the corner table. 'She's got wine.'

'That's Miss Snow. She's a regular. Brings her own.' Aileen wrinkled her nose. 'I don't know how that works. I suppose the police never come in here.'

'I'm beginning to think I dreamed the whole fucking police force.'

Aileen wriggled uncomfortably in her chair. Partly to avoid the conversation, Lauren decided, her aunt stared at Miss Snow again.

The woman wore an elaborate silk turban. On her, it didn't look daft; it looked like a very effective fashion statement, and the statement, decided Lauren, was that she was too hot for fashion. She sat with her legs demurely crossed, one fake Louboutin—or probably not-fake, on reflection—tapping out a light rhythm. There was a newspaper folded neatly at her elbow, and the stem of her wineglass was caught deftly between her thumb and third finger.

The woman lifted her head and smiled. Nerve endings rose under Lauren's skin.

'Hello, Miss Snow,' said Aileen, and wiggled her fingers amiably.

Miss Snow pushed back her chair and rose to her feet, then sidled between the tables to rest a hand on the back of Aileen's chair. It was Lauren who got the brunt of her friendly smile. 'Hello.'

'This is Miss Snow.' Aileen made a slight face, as if mocking the woman's eccentric formality. 'Miss Snow, this is my niece, Lauren.'

'Lauren?' A shadow of horror flitted across Miss Snow's face. 'Oh, my dear.' She dragged out a chair next to Aileen's, flicking crumbs off it before she sat down. 'Your aunt told me. You lost your mother, didn't you?'

Lauren glanced at Aileen, then back at Miss Snow.

Her silence didn't make Miss Snow the least bit awkward. The woman took Lauren's hand, and gazed at her with warm concern.

'I'm so sorry,' she said gravely.

Lauren didn't reply. She was never sure what to say to *I'm sorry*. Why would someone apologise if it wasn't their fault? She shrugged.

'You're very kind,' smiled Aileen into the silence. 'Why don't you join us, Miss Snow? I'm going to get a sandwich. Do you fancy a traybake?'

'Oh, please.' Miss Snow eyed the counter avidly as Aileen stood up. 'That would be lovely.'

Lauren wriggled in her chair. She stared at her hand in Miss Snow's. The woman's long nails glittered with polish. 'Are you a teacher or something?'

A surprised laugh. 'No. Would that bother you?'

'I thought, because of your name and that. I'm not supposed to talk to . . .'

'Teachers?' The woman arched a bemused eyebrow. 'Really?'

Oh God. Why did the bloody woman have to come over? Lauren's head felt fuzzy and chaotic. *I'm not supposed to talk. I'm not supposed to talk.*

'But my dear, you *must*.'

Lauren froze, but the woman's amber eyes were as steady and compassionate as her voice was low.

'Haven't you talked about your loss? That's *extraordinary*. Who on earth is taking care of you, my dear? Because they just *aren't*.' Miss Snow pursed her red lips. 'Would it help if I said my first name's Emmeline?

Not much, thought Lauren.

Miss Emmeline Snow leaned in close. 'I'll tell you who I am, my dear. I'm a friendly stranger. Aren't those the best people to confide in?'

'I don't know . . .'

'You need to talk,' Miss Snow told her again, gently. She ducked her head so that she could meet Lauren's lowered eyes. 'And I promise to listen. Don't your guardians talk to you about your poor mother?'

'They don't really want to,' said Lauren. She looked desperately at the counter, where Aileen was still fumbling with coins and caramel shortbread.

Miss Snow sucked her teeth in disapproval. 'Well, I told you, I'm not a teacher. As a matter of fact, I'm a sort of therapist. Does that make it easier to talk to me?'

'I suppose,' said Lauren after a moment. 'Maybe.'

'Good.' Miss Emmeline Snow squeezed her fingers. 'There's so much hurt inside you, isn't there? Let's see what I can do to help that traumatised mind of yours.'

Finn

'Lauren's gone again.' Sorcha stuck her head round the door.

Seth was sitting on the sofa, his laptop on the coffee table in front of him. Putting his head in his hands, he swore. Sionnach got to his feet and clicked off the radio.

~ *Want me to go after her?*

'Would you? I'm kind of busy.'

'Maybe we should leave her,' I suggested when Sionnach had gone. 'Just for a bit.'

Seth rubbed his temples, biting the corner of his lip. Then he shook his head. 'No.'

'She's a mess. Of course she is. She's been around this house too long and she needs some space, Murlainn.'

'She can't have it.' Leaning his arms on his knees, he gazed up at me. I thought he looked very tired. 'They could come back for her. I don't know why she didn't die, but Kate doesn't make mistakes like that. She just doesn't.'

It was true; it was just that I didn't like dogging Lauren's footsteps, barging in on her shock and grief. The girl needed space. She had a right to take some time to herself, and she had a right not to confide in me, of all people. She knew I'd had a history with her sister Shania. I was sorry Shania was dead and desperately sorry she'd died the way she had, but Lauren had every right not to believe that.

I kept thinking how much I'd changed since I was sixteen: I was barely the same person any more. Maybe I wasn't that Finn at all now. And maybe Shania wasn't the Shania I knew, by the time she died. People change. The most important things in the world—you thought—don't matter any more. People you hate become people you love.

People who hate you love you back.

I laid my newspaper down and pushed the coffee table back so I could hug Seth's head against me. He buried his face in my shirt and locked his arms round my waist. I could feel his mind inside mine but he didn't say anything. He was holding me so tightly he was hurting me again.

'Sorry,' he mumbled. But he didn't break his grip.

I stroked his hair. Then I eased his arms from around me and as he drew back, I knelt down so I could see his eyes better. 'What's wrong?'

'She's inside me,' he said. 'I feel her. Not just that dream. All the time. In my head.'

'I know,' I said softly. I'd known since the dream, I'd known since I'd heard that laugh. I wonder if Kate ever imagined I'd leave it at that? I ran a fingertip down the long scar on his face. 'Seth, I can do something about it.'

He didn't jump at the offer. He only looked apprehensive.

'Can you?'

'I think I can. If you want me to.'

'Of course I want you to. I can't block her. She taunts me, Finn. I can't See Rory but I See her. I *know* her. I wish I didn't; what the hell possessed me?'

'Kate did,' I said. 'She still does.'

'Not that way!'

'No, not that way.' I kissed his nose fondly.

'How is she doing it? She knows me better than my own son does.'

'No,' I said. 'No, she doesn't. That's what she wants you to think. I know exactly what she's doing, and I know where she is, and I think I can find her.'

He sat back, watching me. For a very long time he said nothing. I could feel him searching my mind. Do you know how hard it is to keep a secret from your bound lover, and never to let him even know you're keeping it?

Next to impossible. But not for me.

'How?' he said at last. 'How do you know all that?'

I gave a light shrug. 'I asked around.'

He knew I was lying, if only by omission. He knew that much. His face darkened.

'Finn. Be careful.'

'Always.' I couldn't suppress a nervous laugh. 'You've no idea how careful.'

'You're Aonghas's child. You're Reultan's. You're no child of anything else.'

I felt my lips draw tight. 'A girl can't choose her DNA.'

'She can make other choices. Finn, where do you go when I'm away?'

'I go walking. It helps me think.'

'All right.' There was pain in his eyes now, and it cut me to the bone. 'I won't ask you again, then.'

I nodded. What could I add? He didn't need to know where I walked. He wouldn't want to know. 'So. Do you want me to do this?'

'Finn, I'm scared.'

'I know.'

I hadn't seen him like this for so long. Not since Kate first drew him in and seduced him and convinced him to betray his own brother, and destroyed them both. No-one escaped Kate's thrall without a fight; I knew that as well as he did. But he *had* got away, and so had I. She didn't have us spell-bound any more. She had no right to him. Anger drove out my fear so fast I felt as if a cold river had run right through my body.

'Kate can't have you,' I said. 'Not again.'

'She doesn't want me. Not like before. She only wants my soul.'

'She can't have it. She can't have you,' I said again. I placed the palms of my hands against his temples. 'You're mine.'

'It's not like it was. I mean, she can't control me. She isn't trying to. It's not that. You know that, Caorann, don't you?'

'Of course I do.'

The glow in his pupils was pewter-dull. 'Help me then, Caorann. Please.'

'You don't even have to ask me that,' I told him. I pressed my hands harder against his skull. 'I'm not going to leave you alone again. I'm not going to let you out of my Sight. Not till she's dead.' Gritting my teeth, I let my mind sink into his, winding and twisting. 'I told you that. Didn't I? Didn't I promise you?'

I didn't let him go, though I felt him seize my wrists. I don't know if he was trying to push me away or trying to keep me close, but moments later he slid off the sofa so that he was kneeling too. I was concentrating entirely on his mind, though it seemed effortless. It was more than a connection, different to a binding. I immersed myself in his mind and his soul, found and mapped the familiar pathways; he was like a dark forest I'd known since birth. I felt him give way, felt a forehead press against mine, or was that my forehead pressing against another skull? I wasn't sure; it didn't matter anyway. Beneath the physical contact there was my mind, twining with his like dark tentacles of thought and feeling. I'd felt something like it before. No, I'd done something like it before. I couldn't remember.

I felt him shiver and I shivered. I felt him want me suddenly, and the jolt of desire went through my body too. He kissed me, or maybe I kissed him. There was desperation in it. His fingers tightened on my wrists and he broke the kiss and took a shocked breath. I delved further in his mind. I'd never get out of it, I'd never find my way. Or maybe it was him who was lost in mine. I wrapped my mind round his, let it reach into the labyrinth of his soul. It seemed so easy. So easy. Our minds were made to be together. Locked. Bound.

And there she was. Right in that gash in his self, right where she'd severed him from Rory. Lurking in the wound like gangrene, seeping into him, spreading through him like a virus. I took a breath, stunned by hatred. Intruder. Thief. Witch.

It wasn't funny. So I don't know why I laughed.

She snarled.

~ *You can't have him.*

~ *I already do.*

~ *Not any more.*

She lashed hate at me. I flung it back at her.

~ *You can't have him!*

~ *I already do!*

~ *NOT ANY MORE.*

Dark wings of malevolence buffeted my mind. I spread my own, though I never knew I had them. For instants that lasted forever we were tangled, clawing, raking. Pain seared my mind and I seared hers right back. There was only one way to do this and I couldn't hold back, not now. My soul was open to her. I embraced his at the point of our link, and I held him inside me, and I threw at her everything we were.

YOU. CAN'T. HAVE. HIM.

. . . and she was gone with a scream like a harpy.

I held my breath. Or he did.

Too easy. Too easy.

I laughed again, made myself laugh. And suddenly I was kneeling on the worn carpet, outside him, facing him. He breathed fast, staring at me.

'Don't you dare be afraid of me,' I said. I laughed again—meaning it this time—and kissed him.

'Don't you dare think I am, woman,' he growled, his hands in my hair.

'She can't have you,' I said. 'I won't let her.'

'Don't ever go. Please.'

'I won't.'

'Promise?'

'Nothing she can do will ever make me,' I said. 'Nothing.'

He touched his fingertips to my temple. 'That's a dangerous promise.'

'Of course it is. But she still can't have you.'

'When you did what you did to Eili . . .' He hesitated.

Oh, yes. That was when I'd felt something similar. When I'd thrown the vengeful Eili out of his mind, just before she died; when I'd put a stop to her tormenting of him, I'd done the same thing: put myself right inside his mind, raised barriers he couldn't raise himself. But this had been easier. Like I'd grown up a bit, like I'd learned to do it properly. Like it had developed. Like I was stronger now. Much, much stronger.

I still didn't like how easy it had been.

'You nearly lost yourself back then.' He pressed his palm to his forehead. 'But not this time?'

'Not even close.' I smiled. 'Not that I'd mind getting lost inside you.'

He grinned, wickedly. 'Same here.'

GILLIAN PHILIP

'I promise I didn't look at your Maggie Thatcher fantasy.'

'Ha ha.' He looked like he couldn't tear his eyes off me. 'You're amazing.'

'Of course I am.'

'No,' he said. 'I mean you're really amazing. Do you know what you're capable of?'

I shrugged. 'No.'

'I find that a bit unnerving.'

'Me too.'

He flopped back to lean against the sofa, and I squirmed round to huddle against him. His arm came round my shoulder.

'Want another cheap thrill?' I murmured.

'Try me.' He squeezed my shoulder.

I eyed the newspaper I'd dropped on the coffee table. The corner of page one flickered up. Once, twice. It unfolded with a snap. And then the pages fanned wildly, as if they were caught in a high wind. The rattle of the paper was crazily loud in the silent room: the only other sound was Seth's rapid breathing. This time, when his hand came forward to slap it into submission, I was ready. I caught his wrist.

There was a carved stone otter on the table, curled in on itself, smooth and small and heavy and round. As the flapping pages stilled, the little otter rolled noisily on top and anchored the paper to the table.

Seth swore. Then blew out a breath. Then kissed the top of my head.

'My beautiful witch,' he murmured.

'Who you calling a witch?' I smiled contentedly at the otter. 'Come on, admit it. You're proud of me. I could come in handy.'

'I'm always proud of you. Even when you scare the pants off me. So come on, clever one. Be *really* useful. What's going on in that dark space in Lauren's head?'

'Ah.' I made a face.

'Can't get past that block, can you?'

'No.'

He bit his lip. 'Could be natural. 'S possible, I suppose. But I'm amazed even you can't break it.'

'She's hiding from something, that's all. She's scared.'

'Or she's hiding *something*. Blocking us. Except I don't see how she could. How could she block you? I mean, *you*?'

I shrugged. 'That's exactly why I think she isn't. Not consciously.'

'Hell, maybe it's literally nothing. Maybe the little horror doesn't have a mind to block.'

'Oh, behave. She's traumatised, like Grian said.'

He rubbed his forehead. 'Oh, maybe.'

'You're tired.' I kissed his nose. 'Go get some sleep.'

'And you're still scary. Come with me, scary woman?'

'It's the middle of the afternoon, Murlainn.'

'So?'

I grinned. 'I want to wait till Sionnach brings Lauren home. Get thee behind me.'

'Any time, lover. Don't be long.'

In the end, I took too long. He was asleep when I finally crept upstairs to check on him, but I was glad. He needed sleep. That sneaking dream of Kate's hadn't been the first, but most of his nightmares came from his own subconscious. Every night I'd hear his shallow breathing, feel the tension in his muscles, and slide into his mind to find it full of murder and blood and betrayal. Feeling me there, he'd roll over into my arms, hunting desperately for comfort, and I'd give it to him gladly, and I'd hold him till dawn with our minds bound up in one another.

But this time I was delayed because an hour after Seth left me,

Sionnach came home with Lauren. Hannah was coming downstairs as Sionnach closed the door, and she hesitated on the
bottom step. Lauren ignored her, pushing past to go upstairs in
silence. But she turned, just briefly, and I saw her eyes. And I was
shocked.

Fear: that was fear. I still couldn't read her mind, which perplexed me as much as ever, but I knew fear when it stared me in
the face.

All right. Even that was understandable. Lauren had to be with
us, there was nowhere else for her to go, but what must she have
thought of us? Seth and Sionnach were both frightening to look
at. Even I had wicked scars on my hand: hacked into my palm
where I'd broken Kate's thrall with spikes of silver, slashed across
the base of my finger where I'd ripped it with my own teeth to
escape a kelpie.

Let's face it: we weren't very normal.

'Lauren,' I said. 'Are you okay?'

I bit my tongue, too late. Stupid, stupid question.

She studied my face, then nodded abruptly. 'Yeah.'

'We were worried.'

'Yeah. I was fine.'

Hannah fidgeted. Sionnach gave a small shrug.

'If we can help,' I began.

'I don't think so. Do you?'

Hannah opened her mouth, but I silenced her with a warning
glance.

Sighing, Lauren averted her eyes. 'Look, it's nice of you to let
me stay here. But I want to be left alone. Okay?'

'Okay,' I said. 'I just . . . we'd just like to help. If we can. Ever.'

Her gaze met mine, and I was stunned yet again by the dark
forbidding blankness of that compartment in her head. If I'd
thought Aileen would get her to open up, I'd been a fool. If any-

thing, she'd withdrawn even further since her aunt's arrival. Aileen had taken Lauren shopping, she'd taken her to lunch and coffee and even to a tactfully-selected movie, but maybe that was the trouble. Maybe she never talked to the girl at all. Maybe, to be fair, she was no better around grief and horror and confusion than the rest of us were.

'What are you thinking?' I said softly, and half to myself.

'I bet you'd like to know.'

Lauren turned and ran upstairs, awkwardly, her arms wrapped around her stomach as if she were holding herself together.

I licked my lips, uneasy. 'Sionnach, where was Lauren this time?'

He chucked his keys onto the table, shrugged off his jacket, unbelted his sword. 'That old hotel. You know it? The Caledonian.'

I wrinkled my nose. 'Dump with a fancy name? It's derelict.'

'That's it.'

'What on earth was she doing there?'

'Having a fag or ten,' he growled. 'And a couple of Breezers.'

I was more than taken aback. The Caledonian was due for demolition, for heaven's sake. It was a soulless, deserted shell, and it hadn't been a lot better when it was open for business. There was nothing in it even worth stealing.

'I suppose she's alone there,' I said doubtfully. 'Nobody to bother her.'

'I don't like the place,' said Sionnach. 'I don't like her being there.'

'The last week,' said Hannah, 'she's acting the arse. I'm sorry.'

'They killed her mother,' said Sionnach. 'How would you feel?'

'I'd quite like somebody to kill mine. Lauren's been like this since the pointless cow got here.'

I tried not to smile. Hannah had been through a lot, she'd changed a lot, but deep down she was still Hannah: scathing, cynical, tactless. Hard as nails, and I was glad. She was holding onto her soul, that was the main thing. In other ways she was as soft as butter left out in the sun.

'You've got every right to be hard on your mother, but go easy on Lauren,' I said. 'Remember when you found out your dad was dead? How you felt?'

Sionnach raised an eyebrow. Hannah folded her arms.

'Yeah,' she said. 'I wasn't all that rational. Pretty angry, actually. Remember that? Remember how I nearly destroyed everyone in a five-mile radius?'

I opened my mouth, but couldn't think of a retort. Sionnach examined his boots.

'We didn't do anything to Lauren,' I said at last. 'We didn't kill her family.'

'Seth didn't kill my dad either,' pointed out Hannah. 'But I wanted to think he did.'

'Yes, but . . .'

'I hated him. I hated you all and I wanted you hurt.' She twisted a shining strand of coppery red hair round her finger. 'Bear it in mind, that's all I'm saying.' Turning, she stalked upstairs after Lauren. 'Oh, Finn?'

'Uh-huh.'

'It's not red and it's not copper. It's strawberry blonde.'

Rory

His father was in a fantastic mood. Which was nice, thought Rory, given that that grew less and less common with every passing day, but maybe it was down to Seth quitting the job he'd hated. The *latest* job he'd hated. He'd fairly bounced into Rory's room that morning, brandishing his phone in one hand and his car keys in the other.

'Laochan, you have got to listen to this voicemail! It's hilarious.'

Scrambling up and shoving aside the duvet, Rory had taken the phone and listened. Given that he was still rubbing sleep from his eyes, he didn't find the message quite as funny as Seth had, but he grew a slow grin all the same.

'Gocaman. On a mobile!' Seth scratched his temple. 'I know he's too far away to tell me direct, but honestly, have you ever—'

'Shut up, I'm listening.' Rory jammed a finger in his other ear, concentrating. The Watcher's message certainly wasn't easy to follow.

'*—and I know it will—ach, bugger this machine with a two-by-four to the seventh dimension—it will be of interest to you, Murlainn, and—are you still functioning, the gods damn you? Why are you dead?*' A series of cheerful peeping keyboard tones. '*—is faulty. My message may not reach you, Murlainn. But the creature is here. I do not wish to kill it. Oh, what is the point of you?*' The recording grew echoey as Gocaman hit the speaker button by mistake. *'Be at my watergate within a day and my own horse may be able keep it here. Otherwise—You are as much use as a chocolate sword in hell.'*

The line went dead. Rory made a face, staring at the phone.

Seth choked on a laugh. 'I don't think the last bit's aimed at me. I mean, I don't *think* it is.'

'Would you shut up, Dad? I missed the first bit.'

'To listen to this message again, press 1—'

Rory pressed 1, but it was hopeless; Seth was still talking over it. 'A kelpie came through the watergate! At the Fairy Loch. He thinks it's your filly! You want it?'

Rory killed the phone and stared at him. 'You mean it?'

'Of course I mean it. We've got twenty four hours. Get in the car!'

The pines had always been massive, densely planted and impossibly high, so it was hard to tell if they'd grown at all. The Fairy Loch looked just as it always had: dank and still, as if the sun never reached the water, and the feeble patches of white sky seemed very distant. Branch-filtered light gleamed on tiny ripples as a fish surfaced, then sank back. A remnant of breeze stirred the scraggy reeds.

Seth closed the gate and let the catch click gently into place. His buoyant mood had subsided a little since they'd parked the car on the verge by the wood. 'Don't go near the water,' he said softly.

'I wasn't born yesterday,' Rory pointed out.

'Sorry. Always seems like it to me.' Seth clasped his hand round his son's forearm. 'Can you hear anything?'

'No . . .'

'No. Me either. Bit worrying.' Seth frowned into the trees.

'He's probably sitting in his hut trying to work out the phone.'

'Or hitting it over and over again with a rock. No, I don't think so.' Seth pushed aside a stray pine bough and made his way on down the slope. 'Goc's been edgy lately. I thought I'd have a sword at my throat by now.'

Rory followed. 'Also, I thought he was trying to restrain a kelpie for twenty-four hours.'

'Yeah. You'd think we'd hear that.' Seth shrugged off his leather jacket and slung it over a stump, freeing his way to the blade strapped snugly on his back.

The hut's tin roof glimmered dully through the foliage. Without a word Seth put an arm out to halt Rory. 'He isn't here,' he murmured.

'Where would he go?'

'You try. I don't even feel a block.'

Something tickled the base of Rory's skull, and it wasn't a communication. He shook off the crawling sensation of fear. ~ *Gocaman?*

The call sounded forlorn in his own head, and it got no reply. Rory waited as long as he dared, and a few seconds longer. Then he blocked, swiftly and totally.

'You're right,' he whispered. 'But there's something.'

'Yes. It's the horse.'

Rory shot his father a look that was half-admiring, half-resentful. 'Will I ever get the hang of that?'

'Yes, once she's yours.' Seth moved towards the hut, unsheathing the blade from his back. 'Remember. Get on it, stay on it, don't let it go into the water.'

' *"If it goes into the water, you're dead."* Uh-huh.'

'Oh. Am I repeating myself in my old age?'

'A lot.' Rory grinned.

'Anyway, you're not going to drown in a watergate, but you'd go straight through from here to the other side. That would not be good. You'd still be dead pretty quickly.'

'I know. How are kelpies getting through anyway?'

Seth frowned. 'I was wondering not so much the how. I was wondering why.'

'If Gocaman isn't here,' said Rory, 'the kelpie won't have stayed. It'll either have gone to town to eat people, or it'll have gone back home.'

'If Gocaman's not here,' said Seth, 'it's because he's dead.'

A chill swept down Rory's backbone as Seth softly pushed open the door of the hut. For all the rust, it didn't creak at all.

'Nobody,' murmured Seth, backing out. 'I'm going to check the trees.'

Just as he said it, Rory heard the lowest of growls. His eyes met his father's, and he jerked his head towards a thicket of thorny scrub and bracken halfway up the slope. Where the ground levelled off briefly, a pale shadow moved and something glinted. Seth slowly turned his head as the white horse paced forward.

The mare's eyes glowed deep green as it snuffed Seth's hair. Seth stayed quite still as Rory eased past him and extended a hand.

'Rory . . .' he began.

''S'all right. I think she remembers me.'

'From when you were a *baby*? Like bloody elephants they are,' muttered Seth as the horse let Rory slip his fingers into her silvery mane. 'Where's Gocaman?'

'Dad,' said Rory. 'Dad, look.'

The mare had craned her neck round. She whickered, nibbling the mane of a second horse as it emerged from the scrub. The newcomer, her coat a soft dove-grey, scratched at the white mare's neck with her teeth.

Rory stared at it, half in disbelief. He'd seen it as a foal, not long after he'd failed to tame the kelpie his father had chosen for him: the rogue that was its dam. He'd lived every night with the dream of seeing this one again, but he'd never actually considered what he'd do if he did. He couldn't help wishing he'd done more forward planning.

'Get on it,' muttered Seth out of the side of his mouth. 'Get on, stay on, find its mind—'

'Dad.' Rory gave him a look. 'Leave it out.'

He approached the younger horse from the side, feet soft in the ragged grass, keeping his eyes locked on its blank ones so that he was reflected in the greenish-black sheen of them. Reaching his fingers to its crest, he rubbed it gently. One ear flicked forward; the kelpie bared its teeth and curled back its top lip and sucked in his scent. When it blew, Rory shut his eyes tight and let the hot breath blast his face.

He blinked his eyes open again, pushed his ruffled hair back from his forehead.

'Hello, you,' he growled.

'What are you—' began Seth, but his voice dried as Rory carefully hoisted himself onto the animal's back. It shied once, twisted to watch him, and tossed its mane, striking at the damp earth with a hoof. Rory lurched forward, unbalanced, then righted himself.

A shudder went down the filly's backbone, and she shook herself violently. With a snort of curiosity, she bounded forward into a flying trot, flinging Rory backwards. Once again he leaned forward into her movement.

'Bloody hell,' breathed Seth, and then his voice was lost to Rory as the filly bounded into a smooth canter. Arching her neck, she circled the loch, sending gouts of mud flying from among the reeds. Rory moved with her, accustomed to her stride already, and pressed his cheek to her warm neck. She smelt of loch water and weed; there were fronds of it tangled in her mane. Rory grinned, shut his eyes and sank his mind into hers.

Cool dimness, dark water, loneliness; the weight of water around him, but abruptly it was no weight at all. The sea lifted him up, enfolding him. His hair drifted, tugged by the current of her speed, and he smelt tendrils of blood from a wounded thing in the water. Hunger nipped at his stomach.

When he opened his eyes, Rory was briefly astonished that he was still on dry land. Hooves thudded into soft ground, a flying mane tickled his face, and then the filly was bouncing to a stop, whinnying softly, her brow almost right against Seth's. The kelpie and his father stared into one another's eyes from no distance at all. She tilted her head, gave Seth's shoulder a swift nip, then swung hard, shunting him with her haunches to make him stumble.

'Okay,' said Seth at last, his balance and dignity recovered. He eyed Rory and the horse together. 'That was different.'

Grinning, Rory slid from the filly's back, keeping a hand on her wither. 'I dunno. Why you'd spend years putting the fear of the gods into me about this, I just don't—'

'Shut up, Laochan,' sighed Seth. 'Just shut up.'

''Kay.' He smothered another huge smile.

'Nicely done,' added his father gruffly. 'Nicely and boringly done.'

'Jealous much?'

'Yep.' Seth raised his eyebrows as he walked back to Goca-man's mare and slapped her muscled neck. 'But I still maintain I had more fun.'

'I'm fine without that kind of fun.' Rory's smile died and his gut went cold. 'Dad.'

'What?'

'Dad, just to your left. There's something in that thicket. There.'

Seth shoved the white mare's shoulders and she sidestepped cooperatively. As he moved forward, he drew in a breath. Beneath her powerful legs, half smothered in overgrown whin, lay Gocaman, glasses smashed and askew across his face. A curved blade jutted from between his ribs, close to his sternum.

Seth crouched to work it loose, then turned it in his fingers. A trickle of blood oozed from the half-clotted wound.

'Shit,' he said, and sprang to his feet, raising his sword.

'And here was me,' murmured a drybone voice from the shadows, 'only trying to be helpful.'

'Get out here,' said Seth.

'Oh, I don't think so.'

'Look, you've lost your element of surprise, so—'

'Who said I wanted to surprise you? That horse was on your boy's wishlist!'

Seth narrowed his eyes. 'Stop mucking about.'

'A poor motherless foal! Lonely! All I had to do was bait the mare. The mare baited the other one. It was your son's idea!'

Rory swallowed, remembering his crude plan four years ago for catching the kelpie. 'How would you know?'

'Oh, give me a *break*. You're not the only telepath in the world, sweetie.'

'Gocaman's kelpie wouldn't follow you,' said Rory. 'She wouldn't.'

It popped its head briefly through the bushes, wrinkling a glabrous eyebrow before withdrawing again. 'Well, quite. Have you any idea what it took to make him call it?'

Rory looked down at Gocaman's corpse, his stomach churning.

'Why don't you just get out here in the open,' gritted Seth, 'so that I can put this blade where it belongs?'

'Look,' said the Lammyr, 'much as I'd like to chat, it isn't the moment. It's Laochan's eighteenth birthday soon, isn't it? I'll give you a while to appreciate your pressie.'

'Don't even think about—'

The thing's movement was so swift it was a blur. Off to the left something pale flashed between the pine trunks. Seth was after it but he was already too late; a sleek shape leaped for the watergate and plunged headfirst, leaving barely a ripple. The last Rory saw of it was its webbed toes, stuck back above the surface to wiggle a goodbye.

'God*dammit.*' Seth skidded to a staggering halt in the mud before his feet could touch the water's surface.

Rory couldn't even care about the Lammyr's escape. He looked down again at the shape of the dead Watcher in the weeds. 'What about Gocaman? What are we going to do?'

Trudging back from the water, Seth sighed and crouched at Gocaman's side. Hesitantly he nudged the broken spectacles with a fingertip; then, when they slipped even further the other way, removed them altogether. One arm hitched over his filly's neck, Rory watched as his father pressed his fingers against Gocaman's eyelids, holding them tight till they stayed shut. One eye was missing, but he did his best to close it anyway.

'He was older than anyone I ever knew,' said Seth bleakly. 'I think he was older than Kate.'

Rory said nothing. Seth turned the glasses in his hands, squished the crinkled sellotape till it held the two lenses together more firmly, then fitted them back over Gocaman's broken nose.

'His horse,' began Rory, paling. 'Will his horse eat—'

'No. But something will.' Seth got to his feet, dusting his hands mechanically. 'And I'm damn sure he wouldn't want us to call the funeral directors. You'll have to leave that filly anyway, sunshine; she'll be there when you need her.'

Rory had known that, of course, but he couldn't repress the stab of disappointment. And maybe he was just full-mortal enough to feel a little queasy. 'I hope she doesn't—'

'Why?' Seth turned abruptly to him, and Rory started at the coldness in his face.

Shivering, he blinked. 'Because . . .'

His father looked from him to Gocaman, and back again. Rory narrowed his eyes, searching Seth's for a trace of that grief he'd seen a moment ago. Nothing, there was nothing, and Rory was suddenly afraid to protest any more.

Seth shrugged, sheathing his sword. 'Your filly's had a busy night; she must be hungry. And she seems to have a rapport with that animal of Gocaman's, so it won't stop her. It's quiet enough here. No-one comes.' He turned and climbed back up the slope, and he didn't look back once. 'Let's leave them to it, shall we?'

Hannah

'I mean, the mood swing on him.' Rory sat fiddling with the Xbox controller, but he wasn't focusing at all. He'd died twice in the last ninety seconds, which wasn't like him. 'One minute he's as high as the stratosphere, and then we find Gocaman; and fair enough, he's shocked, he's upset, I could understand *that*. But then it was like somebody threw a switch. Like he couldn't give a rat's arse about Gocaman or anything else. Seriously, Hannah, you should have seen him. Dead behind the eyes.'

As soon as the words were out of his mouth he clamped it shut. He must have realised what he'd said. He didn't move, and his fingers were motionless on the controller, and his avatar exploded in a cloud of virtual blood.

Tearing my eyes away from poor, long-suffering, virtual Rory, I studied the real one. I didn't know what to say, so I just said, 'You imagined it. Seth's fine this morning. Dead behind the eyes he is not. Not when he gave me an earful about finishing the Frosties, anyway.'

'I didn't imagine it.'

Outside, clearly audible beyond the open window, we could hear the hoots and yells of a bunch of faeries messing about with cars and soapsuds. I stood up and leaned out, shaking my head.

'He's out there now, Laochan, and he's fine. Just stuck Jed's head in a bucket.'

Rory came to my side. 'Yeah . . .'

I nudged him cheerfully. 'We should go down and help. I love carwash day.'

'Not you,' said a voice behind me. 'But Rory should go.'

I turned to face Finn, my heart sinking. She wore a sympathetic but deadly serious expression, and I didn't like it. Nor did I much like the woman hanging back behind her, but there wasn't much I could do about her.

'Hi Finn,' I said, and then, 'Mother.'

Aileen wriggled uncomfortably under my stare, so I made one useless dash for the door. A dignified stride, anyway; if I'd dashed I might have made it. As it was, Finn stepped to the side and blocked my way.

'Rory,' she said, not taking her eyes or her solemn tight smile off me, 'Your father needs some help with the cars.'

'My father is arsing about with his mates,' said Rory, 'but I can take a hint.' He glanced at me. 'Hannah? Are you okay?'

'Fine,' I muttered. 'Go ahead. I'll catch up with you in a minute.'

'Bit more than a minute,' said Finn. 'Get out of here, Rory.'

From the window I watched Seth and Jed and Rory and Iolaire sort-of washing the cars. They were swearing now and laughing, flinging water and turning hoses on one another. Grian, Sorcha, and Sulaire came round the corner, shouted with glee, and joined in. Nice to see Seth fooling around. Rory had to be imagining the other stuff.

Jed was already soaked to the skin and the others were getting there; as I watched he grabbed Rory and manhandled his face into the bucket of sudsy water. Rory flung his head back with a gasp and a silver shower of spray, and then he was half-choking with laughter as he chased his brother down with a sodden sponge.

The window was shut and the racket was muted, and I felt horribly detached. They were on the other side of another Veil. I wanted to be out there in a water fight with my best friends, my cousin, my uncle, and my surrogate uncles. Instead I was stuck in the shabby upstairs sitting room, my heart in some sort of cryogenic suspension. Cold as hell.

Finn perched on the sofa, tense and on edge, but that was her default setting these days. Opposite her, hands on her knees, sat my mother. The silence was leaden.

I let her stifle in it.

'Your mother's leaving,' said Finn.

I tilted my head. 'And?'

'I've been here two weeks,' Aileen interjected, as if I needed her to give me an excuse or something.

'And . . .' I said again.

'There's something she should be telling you before she goes,' said Finn. She fixed her silver-blue stare on my mother. 'So go on. Do it.'

'I don't know if I . . .' Aileen shifted uneasily.

'Finn's right. I want to know about my father,' I said. 'Cause get this straight, I don't care what you got up to with old Slimeball. I don't even care if you're still with him.'

'I'm not . . .'

'Yeah, but I told you, I don't care.'

'If you give me a chance?' she said.

'Yes, Hannah,' said Finn. 'Give her a chance.'

I glowered. Mum cleared her throat. Twice.

'Okay. I'm not still with him for the same reason I'm not still with any of them. It doesn't work because . . . it doesn't ever work . . . oh, I'm making a mess of this. I'm still looking for your father, that's all.' Her look was full of resentment. 'I'm looking for your father and I always will be.'

I laughed. Not very appropriate, but I couldn't help it. I thought about my dad, everything I knew about him, everything I'd found out. I thought about the slimeball Rock God with the beer belly who'd been her last shot at finding him. And I laughed again.

'You were looking for my father *there?*'

'I was always looking for your father.' She wasn't provoked, which I suppose was admirable. 'And now I know I'll never find him again, not as long as I live, and if it makes you feel better I'll tell you that dumping him was the biggest mistake of my life and it's made me unhappier than I ever believed I could be and I will never be happy again knowing he's dead.' She took a breath. 'And I'm not lying when I say I hope that makes you happier.'

Finn watched her, thoughtful.

'You can't make me happy,' I said. 'Nothing you can do will ever do that.' I wrapped my arms round my body. My lungs felt painfully tight and I didn't want to do anything stupid, like cry. 'I'm happy in spite of you. I'm happy with Rory, and Finn, and Sionnach. And my Uncle Seth. Dad's brother, I'm happy with him. He's like a father to me, because you wouldn't let me have the real one and then you wouldn't even let me have *you.*'

Silence. A very awkward one.

'I can't change.' She picked at a cuticle. 'I'm sorry for everything but it's the way I'm built. I wish I hadn't done it, I wish I hadn't treated you that way, but you know what? If I got another chance I'd do it all again. 'Cause it's what I am. I'm just *me.*' Her voice faded. 'It's how I'm built.'

Self-indulgent bitch I wanted to scream, but I'd lost my voice. There was a sound behind me. Seth had come into the room. I don't know how long he'd been there but there was an expression of fearful bewilderment on his face as he watched my mother. I frowned.

~ *Seth, what—*

He slammed down a block.

Distantly I could hear the yells and shrieks and splashes continuing without him, but they seemed fainter now, and further away. When Finn reached out a hand, Seth took it.

'Time we left, you and me,' she said. 'Aileen?'

'What?' Her eyes slid from Finn to Seth, and her throat jerked. She couldn't take her yearning gaze off him. Good. I hoped it hurt.

'You need to tell Hannah everything. About her father.'

'Listen, I don't know what you expect from me. I don't have a photographic bloody memory.' Seth's presence had made Mum aggressive and haughty. 'I'll try, but . . .'

'No,' said Finn. She kicked a stool across to my mother's chair. 'Just remember what happened. You don't even need to talk.'

'I don't know what you . . .'

'Trust me.' Finn smiled.

My mother looked like that was the last thing on her mind.

Letting go of Seth's hand, Finn put her hand against Aileen's face. Taken completely aback, my mother forgot even to flinch. Finn's eyes lit, and she froze.

My mother looked dizzy, and sick, but she couldn't move. After long seconds, she gave a shocked cry and jerked away, slapping at Finn's hand.

Finn grinned, not in a friendly way. 'That was him teaching me to swim. Damn, that river was cold. Remember those scars on his chest? I bet you do.'

'How did you—' My mother was pale and furious and frightened.

'Easy. I mean, that was *ages* ago and I remember it all. See how clear it is when you concentrate? Now it's your turn.'

Aileen's eyes widened. 'But I can't . . .'

'It'll flow from the first memory, once you connect. Aren't you always bringing him to mind? Well, do it again for your daughter.'

There were tears in my mother's eyes, but she nodded.

Seth took Finn's hand again. 'Let's go,' he said. 'She'll do it.'

The door closed on them, and I was more alone than ever. I felt shy, and that made me furious with myself. What a coward, to come over all timid as soon as my bodyguards left the room.

Then I realised it wasn't my mother who frightened me. It was *him*.

All her aggression had leached out, too. 'Do you really want me to do this?'

'I really, really want you to do this.' Perching on the stool, I took her face in my hands. I did it gently, much more gently than I'd meant to. She closed her eyes, then jerked them open again.

'Relax,' I said. 'Please. Relax. Think. Think about him.'

So she did.

It was one of those bars with no soul at all. That was what I liked about them. I didn't want some local pub where everybody knows your name. Couldn't think of anything worse. I liked impersonal, I liked mass-market, I liked anonymous.

I liked *him*.

Blinking, I focused on the man at the bar. He was sitting a body-length away from me, but he hadn't looked at me once. He looked out of place, uncomfortable and tense, but as I watched he took a gulp of his drink. Something golden; probably whisky. As he ran his hand across his head, I followed the motion, the eye movement making me a bit dizzy. I took another drink to steady my brain, and watched him again.

He was lovely-looking. Grey-eyed, a wide mouth with smile creases at the corners. His features were a little hawkish, but I liked that. Blade-sharp cheekbones, a strong angular face. I bet the rest of him was strong too. I could tell from his hands and his wrists. There were scars on them, white and long-healed. I was amazed at myself, being able to make that out in the dimness and my befuddled state. I liked the way his dark blond hair spiked out over his forehead. When he rubbed his forehead with the heel of his hand, his fingers tousled the hair a little more. I rested my jaw on my hand, my elbow on the bar—it helped to steady my swaying body, too—and stared at him shamelessly.

The barmaid was ignoring both of us, way too wrapped up in her chatter with the young barman. I wasn't surprised she was ignoring me, but I did wonder why she wasn't taking more notice of the cute guy. Nobody was. It should be wasps round honey, but he sat on alone.

'It's enough to make you believe in the little people,' trilled the barmaid.

'So where'd you find it?' The barman didn't sound that interested. But it was a quiet night.

She lifted her left hand and waggled it so the emerald on her wedding finger sparkled in the bar lights. 'On the shelf down here, can you believe it? I must have looked there already, a hundred times. I was sure somebody had nicked it.'

The silent customer at the bar shifted uncomfortably, and stared into his drink.

'Away,' said the barman. 'You're just getting dottled in your old age.'

'Cheeky wee sod,' she said, and slapped his bum.

I looked back at the cute guy, swirling his whisky in his glass.
He looked tired, and a bit sad. There's an opening, I thought. With
any luck his girlfriend's just dumped him. Rebound on me, baby.
I'm soft as a mattress, me . . .

'Hi,' I said.

He didn't turn. He blinked at his reflection in the mirror behind the bar. I shuffled my stool closer to his.

'Hi,' I said again, and this time he glanced round, as if surprised
to be spoken to.

'Hi yourself,' he said, and turned back to his drink.

'You on your own?' I asked.

He looked to his left, then to his right. Then he shrugged and
smiled. The most gorgeous smile I ever saw in my life. Even though
he was managing to make me feel really stupid.

'Want some company?'

'To be honest, love? Not really.'

'Drinking alone, that's really bad for you.'

Pointedly he eyed my own glass. 'Uh-huh.'

'Ah, but I'm just bad,' I said. 'You don't look like such a bad
guy.'

He laughed hoarsely. 'Anybody ever tell you your lines are
rubbish?'

'No,' I said. 'I never used them on anybody before.'

He gazed at me, so intently I actually shivered.

'Liar,' he said.

Nobody, nobody in my life had ever called me a liar right out
like that. Not after two minutes' acquaintance. He happened to be
right, but that didn't mean he had any right to say it.

'Piss off then,' I said angrily. On an afterthought, I told him to
go and do something physically improbable.

I was so angry I swung off the barstool without really taking time to think about it. That's why my legs tangled, that's why I toppled forward and fell flat on my face. Some guys at a nearby table laughed and stared, and laughed again. I'd chatted to them earlier and I knew they liked a good laugh but I hadn't intended being the cause of it.

Cute-guy-with-cheekbones grabbed me by the arm and hoisted me to my feet.

'You made me do that,' I snapped, swaying. The room wasn't the right way up yet.

'You're drunk,' he said matter-of-factly. 'You've been vaguely and pleasantly tipsy but see that last drink? It's tipped you over the edge of no fun. Go on home and sober up before you do something you regret.' His eyes glittered as he held my eyes again for long moments, and his grin was sudden. 'Like last week.'

I shook him off, trying simultaneously to glare at him and stop the room whirling. 'Have we met?'

'No.' He smiled. 'Believe me, I'd remember.'

'So what do you know about . . . oh, never mind. Piss off,' I told him again, and grabbed my bag. I stalked haughtily from the bar, though it didn't help that I bumped into the doorframe. Still, I carried it off as well as I could in the circumstances.

I was ragingly angry and humiliated—okay, I was drunk, but was I ugly too?—and it never even occurred to me to look back. I certainly didn't think he'd follow me, not after that performance.

So it was embarrassing how enthusiastically I turned when I heard a male voice behind me, felt a hand on my arm. Yes, I was going to give him a piece of my mind, but after that? Who knew where a piece of my mind might lead? Maybe to other, better bits of me.

'See that tosser back there? Nae taste, hen.'

It wasn't him: I worked that out fast. Actually it was three of them: the guys I'd been chatting up. The sniggerers.

'Yeah, but he's my type,' I said. 'Unlike you.'

'Hen, you're the type who doesn't care what type I am.'

The other two giggled.

'Says who?' I yanked my arm away, but he gripped it again.

I was starting to be sorry now: sorry I'd flirted with these chancers, sorry that I'd stormed out in a huff at just the wrong moment. No point in breast-beating, though. I had to get my head together and do something about this.

I didn't know what, that was all.

'Here, c'm'ere.' He pulled me against him and his mouth went over mine. Dis-gusting. Sucking like a hoover. His fat wet tongue seeking mine. Dis-gust-ing. I bit it. Hard.

'Ayya wee—!' Shrieking, he thrust me away but kept his grip on my arms as I struggled and swore. He wiped his mouth with the back of one hand, and glanced down at it, smeared with blood.

'Bitch,' he said, stunned. And backhanded me across the face.

It didn't hurt so much as sober me up. Now I was scared. I was more aware now that the cobbled side street was deserted, that even the main road twenty yards away was devoid of pedestrians.

'Hold her,' said the first guy, and hit me again. That one hurt. While my head reeled, I felt his hand tugging at my waistband. His mate reached to rip my flimsy top. I was sober enough to panic now, so I kicked out, but a leg hooked round mine, and then Number One kicked me back. I yelped. He kneed me between the legs, a pain that took my breath away.

'You asked for this,' he said.

'Indeed,' said one of his mates, and a fist slammed into the side of Number One's face. It sent him sprawling onto the cobbles, his erection sticking ridiculously out of his undone fly.

Oh. Not one of his mates after all.

The third one was just gaping at the vacant spot where his friend had been. He got his composure back in time to turn on the intruder, but the edge of a hand chopped into his throat. He jerked back like a marionette, catspraddled on the cobbles.

The guy gripping my arms was obviously in two minds: let me go and run, or keep hold of me and use me as a human shield. I made up his mind for him, reaching back to grab a fistful of his greasy hair.

'Yuck,' I heard myself say. Then there was a big shape in front of me, saying 'Scuse me' and reaching over my shoulder to grab the man's hair himself. I let go just in time, just as the greasy head snapped back and cracked against the wall.

'Don't even think about it,' said my rescuer mildly.

He must have been psychic. The first guy was on all fours behind him, still conscious and ready to attack again. My hero turned and lashed a foot into his belly, and he crumpled, moaning.

'Are you okay?' Hero-with-cheekbones shut one eye and looked at me, then touched his thumb to the corner of my mouth, delicately wiping blood. 'You're going to have some shiner.'

'Fine,' I said. It didn't occur to me to knee him in the balls, not even when he carefully tugged my top back over my breasts. I fastened my jeans myself.

'You're a halfwit,' he said.

'Yeah,' I said. I was in no mood to argue, but I kicked Number One between the legs as I stepped past him, just to salvage my pride.

'Where do you stay? I'll walk you home.'

'Will you hell.' As I picked up my bag, I saw my fingers judder, and suddenly the rest of me was shaking too.

'Yes. I will.'

'Look, pal, I'm not in the mood any more.'

'I never was in the mood, smart arse.' His fingers closed round my arm to stop me falling on my face, but he didn't get any closer. 'I said I'll walk you home.'

'I'm sober, y'know.'

'About time. I'll walk you home.'

'Okay.'

We walked in silence. After a while my feet hurt so much in my high heels I stopped and yanked them off, and walked on barefoot, my shoes hooked into my fingers and swinging at my side. I had the nasty feeling my companion was amused, but it was my only nasty feeling. Funny, that, after what just nearly happened. Here I was walking home with a strange man, and I didn't feel the least bit nervous. It was like I trusted him, instinctively. Like I'd always known him and I knew his mind and I'd be okay with him.

By the time we got to the communal door of my flat, I wanted him again.

'My name's Aileen,' I offered.

'It would be. I'm Conal.'

'Come on up for coffee, Conal,' I said.

'I'll see you in,' he said. 'But I'll pass on the coffee.'

'Right.' I winked knowingly.

He rolled his eyes. 'I'll pass on the coffee because I'm *leaving*.'

And the bastard did. I couldn't believe it. I was suddenly so exhausted I could have fallen asleep on my feet, and he had to half-carry me upstairs. He had to find my key in my bag and open the door for me. He had to pick me up and lay me down on the bed— fully-clothed—and tuck the duvet round me, and click on the heating an extra hour while the place warmed up. And then he stepped back and said he was going.

'Don't go,' I said, very drowsily.

'You're tired.' He reached out a hand to touch the side of my head but I caught his wrist and stopped him. I don't know why. I wanted him to touch me, after all. Maybe it was my instincts kicking in again, but I did *not* want him to touch the side of my head.

He frowned slightly, as if he couldn't quite make me out.

That made two of us.

'I'm really tired,' I said. 'You can take advantage of me if you like.'

'Uh-huh.'

He leaned down. Kissed my forehead. Then at last his fingers touched my temple, very lightly. I only had a fraction of a moment to enjoy the sensation before I was more tired than I've ever been in my life. I couldn't even move and for a horrible second I thought he'd spiked my drink, but I stayed awake long enough to see him go out the front door and hear the latch click behind him. And then I was asleep.

I laughed. I couldn't help it. I shook off my mother's frustration like a dog shaking off water, and I laughed some more.

'That was so him,' I said.

My mother couldn't quite focus. She blinked as if she was drunk again. 'I thought you hadn't met him.'

'Only in dreams,' I said, 'like now.'

'You're strange,' she said. 'You would be. You're his.'

'I'm not really like him though.'

She shrugged. 'No-one is.'

'Mister Chivalrous,' I said, and smiled.

Mum smiled back at me. 'Yes. But everybody has their tipping point.'

'Obviously. Or I wouldn't be here.'

We both laughed, and I felt closer to her than I had for years.

'What happened?'

Same bar. There was a distinct danger here that they were going to get to know me. A place where everybody knows your name, God forbid. But he drank here. So I went back.

Again. And again.

I flirted for my country. I made so many passes I could have played prop forward in the Six Nations. Every night I went home and looked in the mirror and wondered what the hell was his problem and did I have permanent spinach between my teeth? Every night I only grew more determined. Every night I made sure I was first with the witty conversation.

Except for that one time.

That time, when I pulled up a barstool next to him, I didn't even get a chance to open my mouth. He put his elbows on the bar and his head in his hands. And I knew I had him, because behind his hands he was laughing.

'You're wearing me down, Aileen.'

'That's the idea.' Thrilled, I kissed his cheek and ordered drinks for the both of us. I snuck my arm round his waist and gave him an affectionate hug. A sister-ish, friendly hug. But I felt his muscles tighten, felt his breath sigh out, and I smiled.

'I like you, Aileen,' he said, and drew his hands down his face. 'But I'm not going to lie to you.'

'Oh, go ahead and lie,' I said lightly. 'I'm used to it.'

He didn't smile. He rested his jaw on his hand. 'There's someone else. Someone I'm . . . with. See?'

I took a moment to think about that. It hurt, but then again, it figured. Of course he had someone. Look at him, for God's sake. Of course he wasn't drifting around unattached. If he wasn't with a woman already he was gay. Fact of life. So what?

'It's a *woman*,' he said wryly.

Mind-reader. 'Yeah? Where is she, then?'

'Oh, she's far away. So far away.' He looked quickly at the bar, focused on the inverted bottles, pretended to read the labels. 'She's in another country.'

'Well,' I said, 'I'm here.'

'Yes. You are. There's no future in it. That's all.'

'Yes, there is. Tonight's the future. Just now it is.'

'And tomorrow it'll be the past. That's the thing about time.'

'And tomorrow night,' I insisted, 'will be the future again. Even tomorrow morning it will.'

'Gods, you're even making me feel pissed.' He stood up, and wound his fingers into mine. 'For now, then,' he said.

'For now.'

I don't think my mother remembered much about the walk home. I was very aware of his hand, the warmth of it and the surging happiness, but the actual journey was a blur, jerky and disjointed. I did know

. . . I was barefoot again: I could feel the straps of my shoes in my other hand, the gritty coldness of paving stones and the painful roughness of tarmac as I walked. We talked. He laughed. I was on form. I was trying to impress him and I knew I was managing. I don't know what I said. I didn't remember. I was too happy.

The next time the memory was clear, he was standing there in my flat. He pulled his shirt off over his head, looking a little shy. I put the palms of my hands against his chest. Hard muscle, but badly scarred. Unbelievably badly scarred.

'What happened to you?' I asked, shocked.

He shrugged. 'Wear and tear.'

He was so tall. I came up to his collarbone, which was just right. I kissed his skin, touching my tongue to one of the white scars. He held my wrists, hesitated. 'Aileen.'

'My pals call me Ailie,' I said. 'You can too.'

'I probably would, love. I probably would.' He laughed, a high and oddly tormented sound. 'I'll call you Aileen. Okay?'

'Okay,' I said. 'Whatever.'

He touched his fingers to my lips, then leaned into me and

kissed me, and desire went through my body like flame on dry paper and

and my mother shoved me back just at the moment I jerked away. She gave a small gasp.

'Stop,' she said. 'That's enough. That's enough.'

'Yes,' I said, taken aback. 'Yes.'

'Some things are private.' She looked quite severe. 'And *very* inappropriate.'

'Very.' Watching my mother, suddenly so prim, I laughed again, and took her hands. 'Thanks.'

'I did love him,' she said wistfully. 'It wasn't just a fling.'

'I know.'

'And I think—I'm pretty sure he loved me.'

'I know he did,' I said. I was sure of it. Not like he loved Eili. But he did love my mother and he would have loved me. Seth told me that. And he said if Conal had known about me, he'd have stayed.

'What happened?' I blurted.

My mother's hands went limp in mine, and I let her go. 'You happened, Hannah.'

'He wouldn't have left,' I said desperately. 'He wouldn't have left.'

'Maybe not.' She shrugged, a touch of bitterness returning. 'That isn't what I thought at the time. I had some experience, y'know.'

'You never told Conal about me, did you?' She wasn't the only one who was bitter.

She sighed. 'I knew he wasn't mine and he never would be. I wanted to keep you and I knew I wouldn't have him forever. I didn't want him to know I was leaving because I was pregnant, but even more, I didn't want to give him the chance to leave me. I couldn't have stood it.'

'You wouldn't have had to!'

'What do you know? I had my pride, Hannah, and I still do. It's worth keeping. I wanted Conal to think I was just dumping him. And that's what he thought. He was kind of relieved, you know. That means I made the right decision.'

'He loved you . . .'

'But he was still relieved. Because he loved that other woman more. You're young, Hannah. You'll learn.'

'I hope not,' I muttered.

'My pride was the only weapon I had.'

Weapon? I shook my head in disbelief. All the same, I felt a flash of pity. Maybe I'd never met him but I knew him better than she ever had. I knew him through Seth, and Sionnach, and Finn. I knew him through his goddamn *horse.* And for the first time I was angry with him. Angry? I was livid.

Why didn't you look in her head, Dad? You broke her heart and you broke mine too. You and your precious scruples. You could have known, you should have known, but you wouldn't violate her precious privacy. Was that it?

Misery crept up on my anger. Maybe there was something else. Maybe he couldn't read her. Maybe she was so damn bolshie he couldn't See past it.

No. Not my dad. My dad was strong.

Finn was strong, and she couldn't See past Lauren's shuttered mind . . .

I shook my head violently. I couldn't bear the contradictions any more. At the moment I thought it, the door creaked open and Finn was there.

'Perhaps that's enough moving pictures for today,' she said.

'Yes,' said Aileen, staring at me. 'Yes. I'm sorry, Hannah. Honest I am.'

'I know,' I said, setting my jaw. 'Thanks, Mum. I mean that too.'

It was funny, watching my mother try to sidle past Finn with-out touching her. It wasn't like she was repelled or anything; just as if she was afraid Finn might suck her in if she touched her, absorb her and obliterate her. She knew I'd been sucked in, that she'd never have me back. Tears burned behind my eyelids and suddenly I needed Rory, desperately.

Still, Mum hesitated in the hallway by Finn. She took a breath, changed her mind, then changed it again and took another breath.

'Seth,' she said. 'Him and Conal. They must have been close. About the same age?'

Finn didn't seem sure how to tackle that one. There was hardly time to explain to my mother about the age thing.

'Well,' she said. 'Close, yes. But Seth was a lot younger.'

'Really? He seems . . .'

'*Much* younger. If you think about it. Conal died sixteen years ago.'

'Well, yes, I see that.' Mum blushed. 'Sorry. My mistake. I just thought . . . well. Seth's quite a bit older than you.'

Finn gave a half-laugh that died on her lips. She frowned. 'What?'

'Well, Seth's—I just thought—he looks the same age Conal would have . . .' Mum fell silent under Finn's febrile stare.

Finn forced another laugh, high and scratchy.

'He's been under a lot of strain.' Her voice was cold, like a gla-cier. You wouldn't want to get in its way. 'He's older than me, but actually? He's famous for looking younger.'

'Course.' Mum's cheekbones were dark with embarrassment. 'I'm sorry. Sorry. None of my business. No offence.'

'None taken.' Finn's tone was clipped. She opened the door. 'Come back any time. Hannah?'

'Yes,' I said, shaking myself. 'Yes, Mum. Please do.'

I ought to step forward and kiss her cheek. Hug her or something. But we weren't quite there yet, and Finn standing guard like a malevolent gorgon didn't help. I smiled at Mum, turned away, and went up to my room for a private cry.

Rory

He was trapped under a dead horse and he was damned if he could get out before the Russian shot him from behind. He wasn't even sure he cared enough to try. When his avatar spattered the screen yet again with a cloud of virtual blood, Rory chucked his controller to the floor with a grunt of frustration.

If Lauren were here, she could kill the Russian and give him time to get out from under the horse. She knew this game better than he did and she could get him all the way through this bloody level, if she hadn't wandered off yet again.

The girl was way too good at giving her minders the slip. Finn and Orach and Sorcha were too used to monitoring people with nothing but their minds, and Finn for one was too inclined to give Lauren *space*. In Rory's opinion, they were giving her so much space she'd drift into another solar system.

Rolling onto his back on the bed, he reached idly for the Veil. It caught between his fingers, soft and delicate, and he ran the invisible fabric across the back of his hand. One moment it was like silk, the next like smoke. One moment he could take gentle hold of it; the next it slid from him and curled round his skin as if it was playing with *him*. It was alive, he knew that. An old thing, fragile and desiccated and frayed, but still alive. He ran his palm across its frail softness. It was an old friend; almost part of him. He wanted to mend it. He was pretty sure it wanted to be mended.

He just didn't know how.

~ *I'm sorry,* he told it.

A shrill ringing startled him, almost making him rip the Veil by mistake. For a horrible instant Rory couldn't think what it was—a smoke alarm?—before remembering they had a doorbell. It was just that nobody ever used it.

He rolled off the bed, curious, and was halfway downstairs before Seth intercepted him.

'Don't answer it! It's a god-botherer.'

'A what?'

Finn had come to the foot of the staircase. 'Your father's paranoid. Thinks it's the Inquisition when it's some harmless local minister.'

Hairs stood erect on Rory's neck. 'Why would the god squad want to see you, Dad?'

'They'll take what they can get?' The bell shrilled again. 'Don't, Rory! You'll only encourage him.'

'Dad,' scowled Rory. 'He isn't going away, you know. I'll get rid of him.'

'Rory . . .'

'Dad, grow up.' Ignoring his father's growl, Rory jogged downstairs and pulled open the door.

'Jehovah's Witnesses?' said the minister.

The grin in the shadow of the hat brim was a wide one, empty and horrible. As the head tilted slowly up to face him, Rory felt a bolt of nausea in his stomach, and cold fear in the nape of his neck. He made a sound of disgust, and made to slam the door on the skeletal thing. A foot jammed the door wide faster than he could react. Behind him he heard Seth draw a blade, and his father reached for his shoulder and yanked him aside.

'Ah-ah-ah!' The minister wagged a thin finger. 'My business is the saving of souls. I thought you'd like to talk about that.'

The voice was as thin as its owner, husky like dead leaves. As Seth's blade touched the raised throat warningly, the minister smiled and proffered a business card.

'Murlainn,' rasped the Lammyr, sweeping its hat from its cadaverous head. 'We need to talk.'

Hannah

I was the last to hear about the unexpected guest. By the time I'd washed my face and stuck a cold flannel on my red eyes and made myself presentable enough to go downstairs, everybody else had had the newsflash. Served me right for sulking behind a block for an hour, and it wasn't as if anyone could tell me calmly and intelligibly what had happened. Far as I could make out, there was internecine warfare breaking out in the kitchen.

Jed was the only one who wasn't yelling. He sat silent on the arm of Iolaire's chair, filing his nails, but he watched them all intently. I couldn't quite make out the expression on his face—angry, grief-stricken, indifferent?—but there was no mystery to the others' opinions.

Sorcha was deeply engaged in a verbal scrap with Braon. Orach had an arm round the cook Sulaire, but she was trying to intervene in the other girls' catfight, and she kept having to raise her voice higher. Sulaire looked as if he was going to burst into tears, but that was Sulaire for you. In his worst moments all he wanted was a bacon sandwich, but he couldn't get near the stove for Grian and Finn, who seemed on the verge of blows.

'Cuilean,' Grian barked at Jed, 'talk some sense into your blood brother!'

Jed pushed back a cuticle. 'I have no opinion. Leave me out of it.'

'That's shit and you know it!'

And then Iolaire was on his feet too of course, yelling at Grian.

All I could make out was that Seth had been locked in his study with a Lammyr for forty-eight and a half minutes; and fifteen seconds later Braon was looking at her watch again. Grian wanted to break the study door down and kill it; of course Finn wouldn't let him.

'The hell is it doing here? And why the double hell did Seth let it in?'

'He's talking to it,' said Finn curtly. 'And blocking. They both are.'

'We're aware of that,' said Grian, pacing the floor. 'What's going on in your lover's incomprehensible *head*?'

'I don't know,' snapped Finn, and when he gave her a sceptical glower, she added, 'I *do not know*. I'm not going to pry. He can tell me later.'

'What's the point of having a bound lover, then?' snarled Grian.

Which is when the atmosphere between them erupted like a blaze in a fireworks factory. I couldn't stand it, so I marched out of the kitchen, their company, and earshot. I took the stairs two at a time and gatecrashed Rory's room.

Stretching back on the bed, he put his hands behind his head and cocked his ear towards the floor. 'I take it Grian hasn't calmed down about the Lammyr.'

'It's World War Sithe,' I said, and giggled a little desperately. 'Hey! World War Sithe!'

'I got it.' His mouth quirked. 'Are you okay?'

'Fine,' I lied. 'Why?'

'I haven't heard. How'd it go with your mother?'

I sighed. I sat down beside him, and he rested a hand on my thigh.

'It was okay. Good, actually. It's just a bit . . . much. To take in.'

'Course it is.'

A door slammed downstairs, and the shouting match grew muffled.

'I wish I'd known him,' I said. For maybe the thousandth time. 'My father . . .'

'Come here,' said Rory.

Sighing, I lay down beside him and he put his arms round me. Awkwardly I shifted till his left arm was under my waist and we were both more comfortable. I brushed his dark blond hair away from his glinting eyes, then kissed him, because I couldn't help it.

'I love you,' he murmured. 'I still do.'

'Likewise.' I sighed, and drew reluctantly away. 'We'll get in trouble.'

'I don't care. I love you.' He put his hands over his face and rubbed it viciously hard. 'And I want to tell you what happened. With Darach. With the Veil.'

Months, I'd waited. Months, he hadn't told me. I'd convinced myself it was nothing after all, nothing to worry about at all, because why wouldn't he tell me? Something dark and unpleasant crawled beneath my skin.

'Why now?'

'I've just thought and thought. And thought. And I can't make it out and I need to tell you.' He rolled his head round. 'Swear you'll keep this to yourself?'

I curled up, then propped myself over him and cupped his face in my hands. 'I swear.' I hesitated. 'Rory, what was it? What happened?'

'I don't know, but . . .'

My gut lurched with fear. 'There was something wrong with the Veil.'

'No.'

'No?'

'No. The Veil was the same as ever.' He looked past me, at the ceiling. 'But that wasn't it.'

I opened my mouth, shut it again. I took a breath, trying to think. I couldn't. 'So what was it?'

'I don't know. That's what scares me.' He rubbed his forehead. 'There was something on the other side.'

'I know. I felt it.'

'The darkness, yeah?' He gave a long sigh. 'But there was something else. Something human.'

'Something—'

'Well,' he said. 'Maybe human's the wrong word.'

That cold thing was creeping under my skin again, spreading over my body. 'You saw it?'

He shook his head. 'No. Heard it. It called me.'

'Ah.' I tightened my grip on his hand, waiting till my voice was steady. 'Don't you ever go answering it.'

'Don't worry. Now I know it's there, that won't happen again.' He licked his dry lips. 'I won't open *that* Veil. Not ever again.'

'It's another *Veil?*'

'Uh-huh. I opened the wrong one.'

My brain had seized up. None of it made any sense, and if it did, I didn't want to know how.

The cold thing had got out from under my skin; it was breathing on the back of my neck. I shuddered violently. 'Can we change the subject?'

'Be my guest.' He shivered too. 'In fact, can we just not talk?'

'Be *my* guest,' I said.

I don't think I'd ever needed warmth so much. I wriggled tight against him, and pulled the duvet snugly over us both.

Finn

'This is silly,' I said. 'It's not like you don't know who your ancestors are.'

Seth took my hand as we climbed the stone steps and flashed me his best grin, the one that was close to irresistible and he knew it. 'Indulge me.'

'When do I ever not?'

'Okay. Just the once more.'

'Sure. As if.' I squinted at the building, still annoyed. Sun blazed on pale stone: the day was city-hot and oppressive, and I wanted nothing more than to retreat to Princes Street Gardens with a cold bottle of Pinot Grigio and a good book, and my head on Seth's lap. The traffic had been terrible on the motorway, and the Edinburgh parking worse, and this was why he'd put me through it?

'Register House, Seth. You know they have this thing now? The Internet?'

'I checked that already. I can't get modern records online, and that includes the last hundred-odd years. Anyway, I wanted an excuse to get away from the house. I don't want *her* to know I'm looking.'

The air had developed a sudden, unnatural chill. I scowled. 'Her?'

His gaze slewed away. 'Hannah.'

'Oh, now we're getting there. It's not your own family at all.'

'See? I thought you wouldn't approve.'

'You thought right. This is prying, Seth. Hannah's family's none of our business.'

'I'm always right.' His fingers tightened on mine. 'And I hope you are too. Seriously, Finn. Her mother bugs me.'

'Her mother bugs everybody.'

'Yeah, but she bugs *me* enough to keep me awake nights. Why did she turn up, Finn?'

'She was worried about Sheena. She told you so. You don't seriously think she'd be spying for Kate?'

'Course not. She genuinely didn't know what had happened; we both checked her thoroughly enough. Why would Kate bother using Aileen? She's got plenty Sithe over here to do her dirty work.'

'Exactly. Like whoever killed Carraig.'

His face darkened. 'I wish I knew which bastard that was.'

'Does it matter?' I asked gently. 'He'll be safely back over the Veil. It's not like you can hunt him down, Seth.' I brought his hand to my lips and kissed it. 'At least now we know why.'

'There was no *why*.' He clenched his jaw. 'It was bad, shitty, pointless luck, was all. They must be watching the damned place, all the time. Somebody knew Carraig had been contracted to do that job at Merrydale. He never got within twenty miles of the hellhole.'

Just thinking about Merrydale jangled my nerves beneath my skin. Seth felt it, because he gave me a sidelong glance and squeezed my fingers.

~ *Can totally see the point of the Selkyr now, can't you?*

I was riled. ~ *That place wasn't natural. You can't blame the full-mortals for Merrydale.*

We'd started driving in the early hours so we could make it to the nursing home in time for morning visiting; and part of me wished we hadn't made the effort. But it was the place Carraig was meant to visit on the morning he died, and Seth's curiosity and anger had become unbearable, and he wanted to go south anyway because he was insanely curious about Aileen.

One overnight, Finn. We won't be gone long. I need to know. I need to see for myself.

See what, exactly?

He'd shrugged. *That's what I'll know when I see it.*

It had been easy enough to convince Merrydale's manager that we were someone's relatives. Actually, that part had been way too easy. Mrs Pettingall was a gaunt officious woman who seemed to run on nothing but adrenaline and coffee; talking to her felt like placating a woman balanced on a high ledge above a busy road.

Seth had smiled like a caring nephew and charmed Mrs Pettingall as much as she was willing to be charmed, and he'd talked Liverpool Care Pathways with her while his mind told me: ~ *She's not here, she's hiding behind more than Donna Karan glasses and she doesn't really know it. The woman's not just traumatised, she's broken. Somebody's minced her head.*

Which was nothing compared to what someone had done to the inmates.

Not all of them. Some of them were just sad or lonely, or demented, or old, or ill, or simply dying. A few of them were all of those. One or two seemed perfectly bright and content, peering at quiz shows from plastic-sheathed armchairs. A very few had flowers and slightly strained-looking visitors. But the others . . .

Seth had knelt in front of a withered woman with an electrified frizz of white hair. He'd taken her misshapen hands in his and smiled up into her glazed eyes and talked very softly, while I just stood there, awkward and useless in a situation I'd never had to face. He'd murmured cosily, if one-sidedly, for quite a long time, and then he'd stood up, still sunny and amiable, and found another to talk to. And another. I remembered thinking he was surprisingly good at this.

When he'd finished his monologue-chat with the last one, a skeletal sparrow of a human being, he leaned down and gently kissed her patchy almost-bald skull. I saw him press his cheek against the fragile skin of it, and close his eyes.

Then he'd walked briskly out of the place and I'd followed him. He'd walked out into the dappled gardens with their wheelchair-friendly paths, and he'd found a small plantation of Douglas firs, and he'd taken hold of one broad trunk and pressed his forehead against it, and then he'd screamed, long and softly, with fury.

Just fury, at that point. In a couple of hours I saw the helpless terror start to seep in too.

~ *Nothing left*, he'd raged in my head. ~ *Nothing left of them. The ones without family. Nothing there.*

~ *Is it her?*

~ *Of course it is. I wonder which came first? The soul-stripping or the family-stripping? I should go back in there and kill Mrs Pettingall.*

I'd slipped my arms round his trembling body. ~ *She can't have known, Seth.*

He'd turned in my arms and studied my eyes. ~ *You think? I don't.*

I swallowed. ~ *Better to let her live, then. Because . . .*

'Yup,' he said aloud, finally able to speak. 'Because she's getting the same.'

Hard work at Register House was infinitely preferable to tea and scones at Merrydale. It was cool and vast and calm, and we needed that. A cupola soared above the central archive, and the circular shelves of ancient books stretched almost all the way to the blue hot sky beyond a glass dome.

I liked the place, but I had my limits. Five hours after we arrived in the search room, I stretched and yawned.

'C'mon, that's enough.' I clicked a window shut. 'You've traced poor Aileen's family back to 1832.'

'*You* have. You've got old parish records. I'm stuck in 1870.'

'In more ways than one.' I grinned.

'Ha ha. Look, here's Thomas Andrews. Father to Robert and Sarah and David. Gods, this is addictive.' He was fascinated. 'And here. Thomas's second wife, Catherine.' He drew a finger down the screen. 'Maiden name Munro. Married 1875. I haven't traced her birth certificate yet.'

'There might not be one if she was born before 1855.'

'I know. And they're closing in five minutes. We'll come back tomorrow.'

'Seth, stop,' I said. 'This is the point where you go web surfing at home. With coffee and a whisky.' I fluttered my lashes. 'Hmm? Whatcha say?'

'I wish I could see the originals. I'd get more of a feel for them.' He frowned at a sheaf of printouts. The printer hummed gently in its cubicle. Fresh ink, modern ink, sharp and unmellowed by paper and age. 'Aileen,' he grumbled. 'She's such a crap mother.'

'*Lots* of full-mortals are crap mothers. I thought you were Mister Sensitive about this? Sithe aren't the only bad parents, and all that.'

'Yeah, but it's the way she said it. *I'd do it all again, I can't change, it's the way I'm built.* It gave me a chill.'

'Oh, saints preserve us from your chills.' I squeezed his waist. 'Come on. I'll take you to dinner.'

He hesitated, long enough for me to know he was lost. 'Somewhere good?'

'You choose.'

He grinned, and shut the webpage. 'I'm not letting this go.'

'Yeah, I bet. It's what the Internet's for, Murlainn.'

'Nah. I've got a better idea.'

I groaned, and banged the desk lightly with my forehead. 'Why do I not like the sound of that? Okay, what is it?'

'Aileen,' he told me, beaming like a kid. 'Aileen.'

'I don't know what you think I can tell you.' Aileen looked mighty defensive the next morning. Her arms were folded tightly across her chest, her eyes were hostile and resentful, but she was withdrawing backwards into her hallway and leaving the door wide.

'We tried to phone. I'm really sorry.' Seth was doing his humble supplicant shtick, and if she was looking at him I'm sure he'd have batted his eyelashes. But she wasn't looking. She seemed to be doing her damnedest not to see him at all.

'Can't find my phone. Suppose I should look for it.'

Seth nudged me forward, and reluctantly I trailed Aileen. I was too tired for this. Seth hadn't slept well—because of excitement this time, not nightmares—so, in the usual way of things, I hadn't either. At least the morning was grey, and much cooler, but I didn't want to do this. I wanted to go back to the hotel and get our stuff and go home. *Our* home. Not Aileen's.

Aileen lived in a cramped modern estate of starter houses, so far from the city centre it was practically Glasgow. *Starter homes.* I felt a pang of grief for this woman of Conal's, this woman he'd left frozen in time, this woman who'd never got beyond him. It angered me. And that in turn saddened me, because he was my idol, my angel, my surrogate father, and he slipped further from me every day.

'Sheena's photos, I brought them all here. I haven't looked at them.' Her voice trembled.

'I'm not surprised,' murmured Seth sympathetically. I wanted to kick him.

'I can show you the boxes. They're still in the lounge. There's some documents and stuff too. Sheena was the one who—she was the one who was interested in the family history. I wasn't, really. I mean, what does it matter? They're all dead, aren't they?'

The living room was small, furnished in a bare and careless style. A couple of blue sofas huddled by a gas fire and a television; an IKEA desk and a rusty swivel chair were crammed into a corner, a laptop perched open on the desk. By way of a screensaver the laptop was scrolling through a slideshow of recent family pictures. The room might have been stuffy, but the window was wide open, and the stripy curtains moved in the breeze. I thought it was odd, after what had happened to her sister. I thought she might have locked and bolted and barred herself into her house, but Aileen didn't seem too connected to her home planet. That last remark, for instance. *They're all dead, aren't they?*

Yes, and not just the distant ancestors. Aileen looked more ravaged by grief than she had when she was up north with us. Maybe the shock had only just worn off, or maybe she'd been floored by another unexpected bereavement. There weren't many pictures on display in the room, so I couldn't help noticing the one on the plain pine mantelpiece. I still got a little jolt every time I saw his face. It still hurt, after all these years. Conal grinned at me, his hair tangled and wild in the wind on some hillside.

She had all Sheena's family pictures, I thought, but that was the one she'd chosen to put up there.

'I just found that,' she said. 'I looked it out. I don't know why. I think maybe I'll put it away again.'

Seth raised his eyebrows at me.

~ *Bunny boiler.*

~ *Stop that.*

However sorry I felt for Aileen, she wouldn't thank me for it. 'Are those Sheena's albums?'

I needn't have asked: it was self-evident. My heart plummeted. There was a pile of very fancy silk-bound albums, but there were also two sizeable and chaotic boxes, and it wasn't rocket science to guess where the older photos would be.

Aileen shrugged. 'It's like I say. She had all the family photos.' She nodded at the desk. 'That's her laptop. It's got a lot of picture files too. I still don't really see why you . . .' As if her eyes were drawn against her will, she glanced reluctantly at Seth.

He gave her his best puppydog face. Gently biting his lower lip, not quite smiling. He *was* batting those bloody lashes.

~ *Stop it*, I told him again.

He didn't. 'It's, ah . . . we're kind of doing it for Hannah. You know? A surprise. Unless you'd rather . . . ?' The bottom lip caught between white teeth again. 'I mean, maybe it's a bit presumptuous, seeing as you . . .'

'No! I mean, I'd never get around to doing something like that. I'm no good at it anyway. I'm not interested enough.'

'So you really don't mind if we . . .'

Aileen shrugged again. 'I don't see the harm in it. Help yourselves. Want a coffee?'

'That'd be nice. He kept his mesmerising eyes riveted on her till she'd left the room. As soon as she was gone he was all business.

'Okay. You take the boxes, Finn; I'll start with the laptop.'

'Not,' I said. 'The boxes are all yours. Call it a penance, you flirt.'

Hannah

'You should swim,' I told Sionnach as I dumped my tray and sat at his side, tucking my damp hair behind my ears. 'It's fun.'

I didn't know how he could just sit there mainlining espresso. The air was stickily humid, and smelt of sweat and chlorine. Nothing but a railing separated the big cafeteria from the pool area, so the whole vast hall echoed with whistles and shouts. Sionnach disliked the chaos, but only because he was such a control freak about his environment. To me it was familiar and friendly. I'd come to the Aquadome a lot when I was younger, when I wanted to get away from Sheena and Marty. The thought gave me a jolt of the usual guilt. Well, I was getting used to it.

'I don't want to swim,' said Sionnach. He swiped a handful of our shared basket of chips, and picked at them.

'What's up?'

'The guy with the goggles.' Nibbling another chip, he nodded at the pool. 'I don't like him.'

I turned to look. Goggles was tall, spare, muscled: I'd noticed him already when I was in the pool. His dark hair was pulled back into a slick ponytail. He stopped staring at us—because he definitely had been—and, snapping his goggles onto his eyes, executed a beautiful dive into the deep end, right next to the *No*

Diving sign. A lifeguard scowled, then pretended she hadn't noticed.

'He's Sithe?'

'I dunno. Can't tell.'

'Which means he probably is.'

'Yes. In which case he's blocking. Unusually well. Let's go home.'

'Bugger, Sionnach! I just ordered.'

'So eat fast.' He added, 'Please.'

Please always did it for me, with Sionnach. Obediently I wolfed half my cheeseburger and wrapped the rest in a paper napkin, then grabbed a last handful of chips to eat on the run.

I risked another glance over my shoulder. Goggles had hauled himself dripping from the pool, though he'd only just got into it. Funny, that. He'd struck me as the type who was in there for fifty lengths before his next business meeting.

He stood on the pool edge, ignoring the kids who shoved and shrieked. Draping a towel round his shoulders, he paced towards the changing rooms, passing within feet of our table. Sionnach never took his eyes off him. And frankly I thought Goggles' blue stare lingered a little too long on the both of us. I was getting as paranoid as Sionnach.

I stood up. 'Let's go.'

Sionnach didn't move. 'Phone.'

'Oh. Yeah.' Registering the faint familiar text alert, I fumbled in my swim bag and extricated my phone from a jumble of towel and wet swimsuit. Just as well his hearing was better than mine.

I peered at the display. 'S'my mother. I'll get it later.'

'Your mother's texting you? And she saw you a week ago? Check it.'

I took his point.

I flipped open my phone and read the message. It wasn't long, but it took me a while.

Sionnach didn't rush me. He was watching the swing doors of the changing rooms where Goggles had disappeared, but after maybe a minute he turned back to me.

~ *What?*

I passed him the phone. His face froze a muscle at a time. 'This doesn't make sense.'

I shook my head, my hands clasped over my mouth. I managed to say, 'Yes. It does.'

I just got this from your cousin, said my mother. I don't understand it. Think it's for you.

I didn't. I scrolled down.

hi H, pls have you got stuff, promise promise promise I have £ now, also what I owe u, pls pls meet me at Caley 4pm. will wait

'It can't mean that,' said Sionnach. His scars stood out very white against his face.

'Oh come on.' I wanted to be sick. 'What else could it mean? I don't know who H is but Lauren doesn't owe me a bloody penny.'

'This didn't happen before. It's not what she was doing.' Sionnach stared at the screen again.

'Course not.'

'Drink and fags. That was all. I swear.'

'I know, I know. I also know she nicked Fearna's cigarettes and she bought the Breezers at the corner shop in Fishertown. She didn't have to text anybody and beg for them.' I snatched back the phone and peered into it as if I could put some different construction on the message.

Caley 4pm. will wait

I checked my watch. 'We need to go,' I said. 'Now.'

Sionnach took my arm and half-pushed me towards the exit. 'Let me call Seth.'

'Seth's in Edinburgh,' I said. 'Finn too. And I don't want them to know.'

'Hannah . . .'

I shook my head, cold and certain. 'No time.'

'Then Iolaire and Jed.'

'No *way!* You know what Jed's like! Remember his mother? He'd go straight over and kill H, whoever he is.'

Sionnach tilted his head. ~ *Would that be so bad?*

'Yes, if Jed ends up in jail! Listen to me. I don't want anyone else involved. Jed would kill the guy. I don't want Lauren in trouble. She just needs . . . she needs . . . oh, I *dunno.* She needs family, she needs *me.* You guys don't know about this. It's not Sithe stuff. I'll handle it.' I took a deep sobbing breath. 'Oh, God, I'll *kill the little cow.*'

He furrowed his brow. 'So leave her to it.'

I shook my head violently. 'I need to go get her before I kill her.' I tried to laugh, wiped my nose with a sleeve. 'It's my job, Lauren's *my* responsibility. She's screwed up. It's my fault, kind of. It's my fault.'

~ *Don't be stupid,* he said calmly.

'Can we fight later? We need to go and get her.'

He didn't argue any more. 'Come on.' ~ *And calm down. Don't run.*

Finn

My fingers ached and so did my eyes. If I smelt another coffee I was going to throw up. I pushed the chair away from the desk and stretched as I glanced over my shoulder at Seth. He'd been sitting cross-legged on the floor, until he got cramp; now his preferred position was flat on his back on the sofa, one hand idly delving into the box of papers on the floor, even as he held the last one above his face to study it. He rubbed his eyes.

'Feeling the strain?' I asked sarcastically. I was unreasonably cross that he'd picked the better job by default, or rather by having it thrust upon him. I could see the attraction of it for him over a computer: frail documents, the smell of old ink and paper, words and photographs faded to sepia.

He gave me a sidelong grin. 'You wanted to do the computer files, babe. Want another coffee?'

'Urrgh. I *want* a humonguous Scotch.'

I could tell Seth was enjoying himself. He stroked ancient signatures with a fingertip, touched inscrutable faces. He must have known, as he gazed at the stiff-necked Victorians, how that fabric had felt against his skin, what the women's soap had smelt of, how to make hair tumble loose from elaborate knots, what sounds and sights and stinks had surrounded these people in the clattering streets beyond their parlours. I couldn't share that.

Well, I could have, if I'd asked him to remember. But I didn't want to. I was jealous. I felt it like a nagging heart-burn. Not of the women: of the time. The long, long time without me.

His hand went back into the dusty box, disturbing a little spider. He shook it off, and it scuttled under the sofa. 'Sorry. I've wasted our time.'

'Nah. It was worth a shot. But if I see one more picture of Marty in his Speedos my brain'll explode.' I wrinkled my nose. 'Or my stomach.'

Actually my most disturbing moment had been clicking on a picture of Shania, polished and cocky in her school uniform. A knowing lipsticked smile. Shining caramel hair. Chills in the nape of my neck. I'd been scared of her, so scared. And now all I was seeing was a teenager, full of herself, not seeing the world and the life and the death ahead of her. I'd thought she was the devil incarnate; there on the screen there was only an innocent. A bitchy, hyper-confident innocent who probably grew out of it, and promptly got killed for being at home on the wrong day. It was knowing me that had led her to her horrible death.

~ *Aye. Knowing you and persecuting you,* said Seth.

Which didn't actually make me feel any better.

Standing, I shook myself and stretched my shoulders. The picture on the laptop screen faded, switching back to its family slide-show. I watched it, sleepily interested, but I didn't know these people. Just to stretch my legs, I wandered over to the mantelpiece and gazed into Conal's grinning frozen face. With my forefinger I stroked it lightly, trying to see only his laughing eyes, trying not to see the skull beneath. What was wrong with me?

'Finn, c'm'ere!' Seth was on his feet, jabbing frantically at the laptop touchpad.

'What?' I was beside him in an instant, taking over.

'That photo that just came up. Bring it back!'

I leaned over, clicking on menus. 'Which one? I can't. They're random, Seth. They only come up for a few seconds.' I clicked hopelessly through the picture folders. 'You're not helping . . .'

'Holidays.' He rubbed his forehead. 'Abroad.'

Sheena wasn't bad at labelling but boy, she took a lot of photos. 'Tenerife? Spain? Help me out here.'

'Damn. Oh damn. *There!* Go back. Like that but—that's it! Antigua! That's Antigua, Finn, I recognise it.'

Me too. It was spooky seeing Sheena and Marty propped grinning against the parapet at English Harbour, the Caribbean shining like a bolt of silk below. We'd taken a photo of ourselves in the exact same spot, two summers ago. I clicked the keys, going through the pictures individually so that they filled the screen. Sheena and Marty on a beach. Sheena, Marty, and Shania. Shania and Darryl. Darryl and Marty, bonding over beers at the cricket. Must have been a family holiday. Though I didn't know that couple with them in the seventh picture . . .

'I do,' said Seth. 'Shit.'

I don't know why I had such a doomy feeling. 'Sure? It's not very good . . .'

'It's good enough. They're both Sithe. He's one of Kilrevin's lieutenants from way back. And there's—*damn*, there's Cuthag. They must have latched onto the poor old Rooneys ages ago. Got pally with them, won their trust and—' He made a guttural sound and drew his finger across his throat.

A feather of unease fluttered in my gut. 'I don't like how planned that sounds. I thought they were afterthoughts. I thought Hannah had it right, that they killed them to get at her.'

'Doesn't look that way. Why would they be so interested in the Rooneys?' He shrugged, exasperated. 'C'mon, we'll give it another fifteen minutes.'

'No more,' I warned. 'Or I'll be so hungry I'll be eating *you*.'

'Any time.' He threw me a wicked wink before flopping back onto the sofa.

Bored, I got back to the photos. At least in the Antigua folder there was something of interest. Here they were on a beach again, and here in an open-sided restaurant. That couple was still around. The Rooneys had spent a lot of time with them. Hannah always said Sheena was gregarious.

A thought brushed my brain, and vanished. I frowned. No getting it back. It would come to me later.

Seth tossed aside a photo and rummaged for another. Frowning, he picked strands of cobweb off his fingers and shook the yellowing picture, then picked at its edges. Two stuck together, obviously.

'Don't go tearing them,' I said.

'Like Aileen would notice.' But he eased them apart quite carefully.

'Finn,' he said.

'Huh?'

He didn't answer. Glad of another distraction, I stood up again, then leaned on the end of the sofa to look over his shoulder. His head was right there, so I kissed the top of it. 'Mm? Want to get a late lunch?'

'Finn,' he said again.

I was alert now. I squinted at the stiff photograph in his fingers, which shook a little.

He'd torn it a little bit, just a tiny spot where the surface had come off, but the rest of it was clear and unfaded. Maybe it had helped that it was stuck to the back of the other one for years.

'It's dated. Edinburgh 1876. This is her, the woman I couldn't find at Register House. Catherine Andrews.'

He lifted the photo so I could see it better. Thomas stood a little behind his wife, hand proprietorial on her shoulder, pride blazing out of his handsome face. He looked strong, intelligent, slightly startled, and irredeemably in love. There was something far more self-contained about Catherine, more secretive, but no wonder Thomas looked proud. She was beautiful, exceptionally so. Her glossy hair was coiled in an elaborate bun; her tilted face held a look of sweet mischief and solemn promise. Her eyes were large and luminous, demanding the camera's full attention so that the rest of the picture seemed almost out of focus; but that was an illusion. It was only that the eyes were so bright. They were lovely, and seductive, and oddly empty.

I stared at the smiling bride and her besotted husband. Couldn't take my eyes off them. But Seth stroked the pad of his thumb across the lovely monochrome face, gently at first, then again and again, harder, as if he could obliterate it.

'What now?' I licked my dry lips.

'Oh, Finn, I dunno,' he said miserably. 'Let's go home.'

Hannah

I tried not to run, like Sionnach said. The Caledonian wasn't far from the beach and the leisure centre, but it was on the town side of the bypass. It wouldn't take us more than ten minutes to get there, if I didn't run under a lorry.

What was this, her first time? No, she owed him money. Second or third, then? What were the signs?

Trouble was, I didn't know. Drugs had never done anything for me, so I'd never bothered to find out.

'Don't kill him,' I said suddenly, grabbing Sionnach's arm.

Sionnach smiled sideways. He'd already unfastened his jacket.

'I'll scare him,' he said.

'Only scare.'

'Promise.'

Despite myself, I slowed as we approached the old ruin. I didn't know why the hotel was still standing. There was wire fencing round it, plastered with *Keep Out* and *No Entry* and *Danger* signs. And a board, chipped at the edges, that read *Acquired for Development by AFS Properties*. It must be at the bottom of AFS's priority list.

The wire fencing was so saggy and ripped as to be pointless, and Sionnach, familiar with the place already, stepped through a gap into a tarmac car park, cracked and pitted with weeds. The

Caledonian itself was a doleful rickle of concrete, crawling with vines, every window broken. Prowling shadows froze to stare: scrawny cats, half of them bulging with kittens.

There was a faint stink of urine that became overpowering the closer we got to the deserted building. The entrance doors were long gone, ripped from their hinges, so we walked straight into reception, where the floor tiles were crazily tilted. A fire had been built in the middle, still smelling of smoke and charred plywood that might have been the remains of the doors. Beer bottles and cigarette ends and scrunched-up fag packets were piled in the ashes, and shattered glass lay everywhere.

Sionnach gave a shrug, as if to say *We should have known.*

So we should. Why else would she come here? Guilt stole over me again, for not looking after Lauren better, for not giving enough of a damn. She didn't need space, I thought suddenly. She needed us. And she didn't get us. So she took this place instead, and her new pal H. I shuddered.

The place seemed very quiet. Sionnach drew his blade, stepped across a gap in the floor, and pushed at a swing door.

Must have been a conference room at some point; it was that kind of size. One forlorn metal chair was propped against a wall that was scrawled with obscene drawings in marker pen. Incredibly, a couple of broken frames still hung on one long wall, the glass gone, the prints washed out and corrugated by damp. They were common pictures you saw in just about every pub and hotel on the coast, as well as the foyer of our school: the mercat cross of the town; the ruins of a mediaeval cathedral; a Highland cow standing picturesquely in front of a loch. Wires straggled where appliances had been yanked from the walls and ceiling, and greasy water dripped steadily through the roof into a yawning hole in the floor.

Chilled, I approached it. Sionnach stayed very still, his blade held ready at his side.

I halted on the edge of the hole, then stepped instinctively back from it. Tiles and concrete had been wrenched up, leaving support beams exposed: rotten and broken, some of them charred by fire-raisers. The smell was even worse here. I could see a faint dark gleam, deep in the hole, and when the light moved I realised the hole was flooded. That was the source of the smell: a dank stagnant pool in the guts of the building.

No wonder AFS Properties couldn't bring themselves to get started. I rubbed my arms and stepped further back, not liking that pool.

'Sionnach?'

No answer.

'Sionnach?'

I turned, reluctantly because I hated that hole in the floor, hated to turn my back on it.

'All right, Hannah.'

He spoke calmly, despite the two men with the naked swords. I hadn't heard their steps and I didn't recognise either of them, though I was plenty familiar with the glint in their eyes. I took one step forward.

'Stay back,' said Sionnach. 'Go if you can.'

A quick look to left and right confirmed what I suspected: I couldn't go. The only way out of this room was past the guys with the swords—or perhaps through the hole in the floor, and frankly I'd rather take my chances with the Chuckle Brothers.

'Then stay,' said Sionnach, a smile in his voice. 'I'll be a minute.'

They went for him. So fast I hardly saw them move, but he was no slouch himself. He'd half-turned in a wicked little feint—I'd watched him practise it—and ducked and sprung back before the first of them could double back for him.

It was the only way he could have done it and he did it beautifully. He should have had the blond one's head off, but the man jerked aside at the last instant and Sionnach's blade went only halfway through. Reflexively I shut my eyes as blood arced in a great spray and the man stumbled forward, juddering, twitching, flailing, but not in any danger of getting up again. His kicking legs jerked him to a halt by the pool, head hanging into the hole, blood spilling over the edge. The drip of it echoed in the new silence.

Down to one opponent, Sionnach eyed him, breathing hard, and before I could catch my breath they were at one another again. This one was shorter, and bearded: he was good, but strong rather than fast. Sionnach somersaulted low to avoid a slash, rolled easily to his feet and lashed his blade across the man's hamstrings. Beardie howled, fell forward then stumbled back, and Sionnach drove his blade between his ribs.

I didn't have time for revulsion, or nausea, or relief, or anything else. Sionnach raised his blade yet again, manic fear and aggression in his eyes, and my own blood ran like iced water. For seconds that seemed like minutes, we couldn't move or make a sound.

I made my throat work.

'You,' I said.

I was too shocked even to be very afraid. At that moment I was. The fear came later. Just a little later.

I'd never forget that face. It wasn't forgettable, even though the left eye was missing, the lids stitched roughly shut. His left hand was hideously scarred too: lumpy and ridged and misshapen, the forefinger missing from the second knuckle. It looked like it had been savaged by a wolf. Still fit for purpose, though, because it was tight round the throat of Lauren, while his good hand pressed a sword lightly against her throat.

What a delicate touch he had. The blade creased her skin but didn't break it. She looked stunned by terror.

The Wolf of Kilrevin gave a world-weary sigh. 'Do I have to do everything myself?'

As he rolled his eye, it was caught by the damp print of the cathedral ruins. He shook his mutilated head in admiration. 'That was a job well done, that was. How that Bishop squealed.'

'You're alive,' I croaked.

'Of course I am. Alive, and not very happy with your uncle.' He examined the wrecked hand round Lauren's throat. 'You think I'm going to die of falling down a hill? I've been keeping my head down since MacRothe's healer fused its bloody bones, but you can't blame me.' He grinned. 'And after that I was in Kazakhstan. Bit of a busman's holiday. What a place. Even more fun than Chile in seventy-four.'

'Hannah.' Lauren gave a barely audible squeak. Impatiently the Wolf shook her.

'Speak up, speak up,' he told her.

'Hannah. I'm sorry.'

I swallowed. My throat hurt. 'You didn't send my mother that text?'

'I did.' She nodded her head, with difficulty. I could hear her breathing catch and rasp. 'They told me to. But they've got your mum's phone.' She dragged in another breath. 'More convincing. Than sending it straight to you.'

I was so numb I could barely feel my fingers any more. 'Why? What did they tell you?'

'I met a woman. Friend of your mum's.' Tears spilled from her eyes, though it might have just been pain and breathlessness. 'She talked a lot. Said you were lying. Said Sionnach and Seth killed my family.'

Sionnach wasn't speaking or moving, but as if he'd elbowed me in the ribs I remembered suddenly what Finn used to say. *She can make anyone believe anything.*

'Was she pretty?' I said bleakly. 'Redhead?'

'Miss Snow,' rasped Lauren. 'I don't know. She wore this turban. It was a redhead killed my—'

'That's quite enough,' said the Wolf, and tightened his grip. Lauren's voice dried, and her tears dribbled onto the broken tiles. 'There now,' he went on, 'if that's all cleared up, perhaps we can get on with business?' He smiled at me. 'Could you move? I want you breathing.'

'Yeah, Hannah,' said Sionnach. 'Stay clear.'

'Sionnach!'

'All right, Hannah. S'okay.' He didn't look at me; all his attention was fixed on the Wolf, even when someone walked in through the broken door from reception.

'You're late,' said the Wolf irritably. 'Hold this.' He shoved Lauren hard.

She tripped and stumbled but she didn't have time to fall. The newcomer caught her, seized her by the hair and hauled her against him. Goggles. He gave me a cool smile.

The Wolf examined his sword blade, tilting it to catch the light. 'I'm not sure I can bring myself to do this. It's a *twin*, for gods' sake. Killing his sister was like shooting a myxied rabbit.'

Sionnach growled.

Sighing, the Wolf stepped forward, and Sionnach flew for him.

I knew Sionnach was fast. I knew he was good. He could give Seth a run for his money, in the big empty basement at home where they kept their skills honed. I used to sit at the side, out of the way, and hoot and cheer, never sure who I was egging on because I never was sure who would win, who I wanted to win.

Here, now, I was silent. I wanted to howl for Sionnach, and I was afraid to. He was tired, and he'd fought two already, and he'd used up much of his speed. He barely held off each hacking stroke, and I was terrified of distracting him fatally. I could only breathe in and out, when I remembered to, and beg Sionnach's gods to give him a break, an advantage of sorts, a lucky strike, a bit of *mercy*.

Two more Sithe fighters waited at the edge of the conference room, but no-one tried to hold me: there was nothing I could do. The blades glittered, snapping and flashing in the dreary light, but the Wolf was easy and slick and fast where Sionnach was only furious and desperate. He backed away in one of the few lulls, panting for breath, eyeing his cool opponent.

'Go, Hannah. Run.'

'No,' I said.

I wasn't being foolhardy and I certainly wasn't being brave: I hadn't a choice. I knew fine they'd bring me down before I got halfway to the only door. And anyway, I knew Sionnach would need me. He'd need me, or he'd be dead, and if he was dead I no longer cared anyway.

Not right then.

Just as I thought it, Sionnach staggered and slipped on the blood of the man he'd half-decapitated. His feet faltered, he lost his balance, and the Wolf stepped forward almost casually and lanced his sword into his guts.

He whipped it out, and as Sionnach glared hatred at him, he plunged it in again. My best friend fell to his knees, clutching his belly.

I didn't scream and I didn't panic and I didn't run. Later, when I had more than enough time to think, I was pleased about that.

I walked to the nearest corpse and tugged the blood-slippery sword from its limp grip, ignoring the laughter of the Wolf's fighters. I raised the sword and shut my eyes just once, briefly, and pressed it hard against my own throat. I knew exactly where my jugular was. The things I'd learned.

The Wolf's smirk had faded to a perplexed frown.

'Don't be silly,' he said.

'I'm not. They're going to want proof of life, yeah?'

'My. You're not as stupid as you look.'

I swallowed, but I was more angry than scared. If the shithead thought I wouldn't do it, I'd show him how wrong he was.

And he didn't think I'd do it. So I pressed my lips together and pushed the sword till I felt my skin break.

Someone took a step forward but I don't know who, because I didn't look. I kept my focus on the Wolf, who raised a hand to stop his fighter in her tracks.

'I'm not quite with you,' he said.

'They're going to want proof of life,' I said again, because that had worked, and anyway, I needed to remind myself what the hell I was doing. 'And if Sionnach dies, they're not going to get it. Cause if he dies, so do I.'

There was silence, and in my head the broken static of Sionnach's dying voice.

~ *f he dsn't kll you. I bloody wll.*

Tears stung my eyes. A warm trickle of blood meandered down the hollow of my throat, pooling at my collarbone.

'Oh for gods' sake,' snapped the Wolf. 'Have it your way. He'll be company for you.'

I didn't move the sword. I was scared to: the hilt was slippery in my shaking fingers and it was close, so close to the vein. I flicked my gaze at the woman fighter, hoping she was superstitious.

'On Kate NicNiven's life,' I said. 'I get to heal him.' Though I didn't even know if I could.

The woman exchanged a glance with the Wolf, who looked furious, but she nodded.

'Her life. My word.'

I didn't look at them again. I knew how superstitious these tossers were, Finn had told me often enough. I didn't even hesitate to turn my back.

I let the sword fall with a clatter, and fell to my knees at Sionnach's side.

Finn

I woke with a cry, thinking for an instant I was dying. I thought the car was exploding into burning shards like Carraig's; I thought I was already dead and done for. And then I was blinking at the windscreen, and back in myself, and Seth was driving. Which was just as well.

'What?' he said, glancing at me, taking his foot off the accelerator and veering into the left-hand lane. 'What?'

I rubbed my shoulder. I was going to have a bruise where I'd lurched violently forward into the seatbelt. 'Trouble. Don't stop. There's trouble.'

'Who?' He swerved just as abruptly into the outside lane, earning a furious hoot from a lorry driver, and put his foot down.

'Is Hannah in range?' I asked.

'Of course she is, she's my—'

'Yes, yes. Can you See her?'

He had to ease off the gas again to focus, infuriating the lorry driver, who overtook on the inside and gave us another volley of horn.

'Shit,' he said. 'No.'

'We have to get home,' I said.

'Rory?' His voice caught.

'I dunno. I don't think it's him.'

'Sionnach?'

I found I couldn't speak for a second. I'd just remembered what woke me. Blood and pain and an ebbing life.

'Sionnach's in trouble,' I managed.

Seth said nothing, but he put his foot down.

Sorcha and Grian met us on the drive. Seth didn't even bother to park the car, just slewed it to a rough halt against the laurels, bringing down a shower of rain from the leathery leaves. He got out and slammed the car door. I followed, my heart leaden with foreboding, and I caught Grian's eye.

~ *Don't say it,* I snapped.

He shrugged.

'Where's Rory?' said Seth curtly.

'With the girl,' said Sorcha. 'Jed and Iolaire are there. And Orach. They're not going anywhere.'

'Why the hell did you waste a bodyguard on Lauren?' said Seth bitterly. 'They don't want her.'

'The guard is for Rory, Murlainn,' murmured Grian. 'To stop him following.'

'Right. Yeah. Okay.'

'You can't go after Hannah either, Murlainn.'

'Sorcha. Shut up. I can't not go after her. If she's dead I can't not kill them. You bloody know it.'

Sorcha shrugged. I gave her an apologetic look, but there wasn't really any need. She was used to it.

We were inside the house by now, and Seth slammed into the sitting room ahead of the rest of us, then stood stock still and stared at Lauren. Right behind him, I put my hand on his back. A tremor rippled down his spine, but he didn't fling me off.

Rory sat in a daze on the edge of an armchair. Jed had a hand on his shoulder and he left it there as he rose to his feet. His face was wild. Rory's though, was dull and haggard, and he stared at his father with empty desperation.

All Seth's attention was on Lauren. 'What happened?'

She'd only opened her mouth when she began to cry. She'd been doing a lot of that; I could tell from her red swollen eyes.

'She's dead,' she gasped. 'Hannah's dead.'

'Dead how?' Seth's voice was expressionless.

'They drowned her.'

Nobody spoke.

'I didn't know. I didn't know what they—'

'Shut up. How did it happen?'

I took a breath, startled. 'Seth, don't. This isn't her fault.'

'If it isn't hers,' he yelled, 'whose is it?'

'Ours.' ~ *Murlainn. It's ours.*

'I don't give a damn. The little bitch'll tell me every detail or I'll throw her off the cliff. And I might do that anyway.'

Lauren looked wildly at me but I couldn't help her. I could barely think under the buffeting of his rage. And I couldn't bear to look at Rory's face.

'Sionnach got stabbed,' she said, breathing hard. 'I mean, there was a fight. Hannah was trying to help him. I don't think she could but she was trying. The guys who were there, they took them both and shoved them down a pit, this flooded pit. They threw bodies on top of them.' She hesitated. 'They didn't come up.'

'Bodies?' said Seth.

Lauren swallowed. 'Sionnach killed two of them.'

'Well. Good for Sionnach.' Seth's jaw was tight.

'There was a woman,' said Lauren, her voice hoarse. 'Miss Snow. Hannah knew who she was, soon as I told her.'

'Daughter of the Snows,' I said bleakly. 'Nic Nevin.'

Lauren rubbed her nose fiercely. 'I'm sorry, I'm sorry, I'm sorry. Miss Snow said you killed my mother. You.' She had the guts to look Seth right in the eyes, and maybe it calmed him down a bit. 'And it wasn't just that she told me, I *knew it*. I knew it like I know you're standing there right now wanting to kill me. I could see it, I remembered it, I *saw you do it*.'

'We didn't.'

She gave Seth a glare that was almost contemptuous. 'I know that now. *I know*.'

I took her hand. 'Listen to me. I've said it already. This was not your fault. It was ours, all along.'

This time Seth didn't contradict me. He just stared at both of us. But I couldn't read his eyes.

Shock made me giddy. I had to tell it to myself again, as I stood there with Lauren's hand in mine and stared at my bound lover. *I couldn't read his eyes.*

He turned to Lauren. 'And how did you get away?'

'He told me to run or he'd kill me.'

'Who?'

'I don't know, do I? A one-eyed guy. He had a bad hand, all scars and missing fingers and stuff.'

Seth was very still. 'You noticed a lot.'

'It was round my fecking throat,' she spat. 'Of course I noticed. And he said I was to run *to you*. Or he'd find me. And kill me.' Lauren said it with an air of self-loathing. 'So I did all that.'

Seth struggled to say it, but to do him justice, he managed. 'It's okay. Nothing else you could do.'

'He probably thought you'd kill her anyway, Murlainn.' Jed's eyes were cold. 'After she'd given you the news.'

'What was Hannah doing there?' Seth asked it so quietly Lauren went absolutely rigid.

'I had to get her to come to the Caley,' she mumbled. 'And as soon as they knew she was coming'—she rubbed her nose so fiercely it began to trickle blood—'they changed. I thought they were going to kill me. And then they told me what was really happening.' She wiped at the tendril of dark blood under her nostril.

'I see,' said Seth. 'Rory?'

Rory looked up at his father. I'd never seen his face so ravaged with misery, and it hurt my heart. 'I can't See her, Dad. I can't See Hannah.'

'The girl's dead, then,' said Sorcha.

Seth said nothing. He glanced back at me.

I shook my head. ~ *I don't think so.*

'But you don't know.'

I shook my head again.

His eyes were dark and he wouldn't look at anyone but Lauren, sodden with grief and rage and loathing.

'Well,' he said more gently. 'But I have to know. Don't I?'

'It's deep,' said Jed. 'But not that deep.'

He was up to his waist in the dank pool; Seth crouched on the edge, watching him. Iolaire and Orach guarded the broken-down entrance to the shattered conference room, but that was a formality. I think we all knew the danger was gone from the Caledonian, that it had never intended waiting for us.

'You think it was him?' I asked.

'I know it was him,' said Seth. 'I took his eye out. I ate his fecking hand. Jed. Any gap at the bottom?'

Jed shook his head, prodding at the unseen bottom of the black pool with a length of broken pipe. 'No. Wait . . . there.'

Submerging himself to his shoulders, he dropped the pipe,

and it vanished with a dull clanging echo. We didn't hear it hit bottom.

'Oh, it's deep.' Jed straightened. 'Take my hand.' He reached upwards, and Seth gripped the edge and leaned forward.

'Careful,' I said.

'Two seconds max. All right, Jed?'

He reached down and clasped Jed's hand. It was only just over a second when Jed cried out, and Seth grunted, and tore their hands apart with a sharp cry of pain.

'Close one,' said Jed, a little shakily. Reaching up, he jumped for a charred length of support beam, caught it and hauled himself dripping from the pool. Making a face of disgust he swiped at his body. 'Jesus, that stinks. Evil. You were right, Seth. It's a watergate.'

'So she's alive,' said Seth, half to himself.

'Maybe Sionnach too,' said Iolaire, half-turning. 'Sounds like she was healing him.'

'Why would they let her?' Seth's tone was dead flat. I tried not to think how long he'd known Sionnach. 'Where do you suppose this comes out?'

'I suppose the same as you,' I told him. 'Kate's caverns, or too close to make a difference. We can't use it.'

His look made me want to weep. 'What else can I do, Caorann?'

I looked up at Orach, and then at Iolaire. They were so expectant. They fully trusted me to get Seth out of this. And all I wanted to do was keep him safe with me, and all I wanted to do was bring Hannah back, and Sionnach, if there was anything left of him to bring.

The two things I wanted most in the world, and they were mutually exclusive. Meanwhile, back in the house I'd found, the protected bolthole I'd struggled to provide, Seth's son sat guarded by the hardest hearts of all Seth's clann, to stop him going after the love of his life and bringing destruction and death on us all.

Time to make my last choice, then. Time to go to our likely death, before it could find us first.

'Murlainn,' I said, linking my fingers with his. 'I'll show you what else we can do.'

Finn

Seth stood on the edge and watched the grey sea foam and break on black rock. The higher air was a chaos of wind and gulls, and below us stiff-winged kittiwakes hugged the cliff. A high late-summer sun struck sparks off water and made wings dazzling-white against the low cloudbank.

Branndair, summoned from his happy hunting ground on Ben Vreckan, whined doubtfully as he stared down the rockface. Dancing on an updraft, Faramach mocked the nervous Beast, but Seth wound his fingers into the wolf's black fur and scratched his neck reassuringly.

'You say there's a way down, Finn?'

'There's always a way down.' Five of his favourite words.

'But an actual path that Branndair and Gelert can manage?' He smiled at his wolf and Grian's hound, then, ruefully, at me. 'Ah, Finn, the things you keep from me.'

I averted my eyes. 'There's no point trying to get down there till low tide. You've time to prepare.'

His smile died. 'And talk to my son.'

We walked slowly back to the house, just us two and our familiars, the wolf at Seth's side and the raven strutting beside me. When the going got too tough, Faramach flapped clumsily up onto Branndair's back. Ignoring the wolf's offended growl, he stayed for the ride.

Seth's hand found mine, and he lifted it to kiss the back of my fingers. 'It's the end, whichever way it turns out.'

'I know.'

'She won't let us live. I can't stretch this existence any more, Finn. She has to die or we do.'

'I know all that.' I gave him a sidelong grin. 'Am I allowed to be scared?'

'I hope so. I am.'

'Please don't be hard on Lauren. She couldn't have fought Kate. You know that as well as anyone.'

'I don't blame her,' he said. 'I was angry. I wasn't myself and there's a reason for that. Lauren's done me a favour, Finn.'

'What?' I shoved hair out of my face.

'She's kicked me off the fence. What she's done, it forces me to go back. Because I *have to*. Not just for Hannah. I have to cross the Veil, Finn, and if Hannah and Sionnach were at home waiting for us now, I'd still have to go.' He stopped, his fingers tightening on my hand.

A cold fist clenched on my heart. Somehow I knew what was coming—what kind of a bound lover would I be if I hadn't known something was badly wrong?—but I didn't want to hear. Even now, I didn't.

'My soul, Finn.' He pulled me close on the windswept grass and whispered it to me, his voice breaking. 'My soul's dying. Almost gone.'

I tried to say *No* and I couldn't get the word out.

'You thought Kate was gangrene.' His lips curved in a melancholy smile against my ear. 'She was . . . more like a blood clot.'

His face was wet but he wasn't crying. And then I realised the tears were mine.

'It's not your fault.' He pushed me gently away and his finger stroked my cheek.

'Yes,' I whispered, 'it is.' *Oh, my arrogance. Oh, the arrogance of a witch. Child of the Darkfall.*

'I don't know why,' he whispered, his hand stroking the back of my head relentlessly. 'She was inside me, playing with me, stopping it. Without her, I bleed. Faster every day. It comes and it goes, have you noticed? But there's less of it every time.'

The wail of remorse started low in my belly, and I thought it would split the sky. Instead it came out of my mouth as a pathetic, helpless whimper. He pulled my head into his shoulder.

'Can't lose it, Finn. Can't lose it before I die.' He kissed my wet face, again and again. 'Have to die first. Christ, I'm sorry, I'm sorry, I'm sorry.'

'Kill it,' I screamed at the top of my voice, yet only a hoarse croak came out of my throat. 'I'll kill it, destroy it, wipe it off the earth—'

'It?' he said softly, and tilted my chin so I had to meet his eyes. I swallowed, or tried to.

'Her,' I whispered brokenly.

'Her,' he repeated, and shook me gently. 'Kill *her*. Feel very free to do that.' He laced his fingers through my hair, and held my head rigidly still. 'It's this watergate, isn't it? That's where you used to go. On your long, long walks.'

I managed to nod, muted by despair and fury.

'But I still don't know where you went on the other side, and I still don't want to.' He released my head, and hugged me again. 'There are things you can't kill, Finn, and you mustn't ever try. Please.'

'But.' I pushed him away, gripped his shirt, tightened my fingers till my knuckles were white. His soul: was that the one that was bleeding? I thought my own was going to die, right there. 'But you can keep your soul and live, Murlainn. If you kill her instead. If we can stop her—'

'But,' he said. 'Too many buts. Let's just go home.'

The drive was busy with cars, and when we opened the door we could hear the buzz of talk, an occasional shout of glee. Friends had appeared who I hadn't seen in months. I wished I could be happier to greet them.

'See?' Seth squeezed my hand. 'No worries. Everybody wants it over. Nobody likes being picked off one by one.'

I still couldn't speak. I cleared my throat and tried to smile at Orach. Her brow furrowed, and she looked from me to Seth.

'Finn,' he murmured in my ear. 'Act like we're going to live to see winter, will you?'

I gave a hoarse, difficult laugh. And smiled, properly, at Orach.

'I hope,' said Seth, and paused in the hallway. 'Finn, we don't know how long she's had Hannah and Sionnach. Do we? The time might have warped.'

I wrinkled my nose, cleared my throat. 'I don't think so. She's aware of the warps, isn't she? This seems so terribly well-planned. And Seth? I don't think she'll hurt Hannah.'

'Please be right.' His mouth twisted with doubt. 'And Sionnach . . .'

'Yes,' I said. 'Let's be quick, shall we?'

'Finn?' He scratched at his temple.

'Uh-huh?'

'Speaking of quickness, there's no point having Rory take us through the Veil. It's too far from here to there. We need the watergate to close the distance.'

'Yes. I know.'

'But Rory has to come. I'm not going to stop him.'

'I know that too.' I put my hands against his face.

'Yeah. Course you do.' He closed his eyes and leaned his head into my hold. 'Am I wrong?'

I hesitated. 'He won't stay behind. You know he shouldn't. You'd be wasting your time. And talking him out of being your son.'

He smiled. 'That's kind of what I thought.'

'We live or die together. Or we die apart.'

'I know,' he said. 'But it's what makes me scared.'

'You think you're scared now?' I kissed him. 'You haven't broken the news to Jed yet.'

Just as I expected, Jed lost the plot. He fumed, and spat, and yelled at Rory, and swore violently at Seth, and made a hideous scene in front of forty-odd fighters. Even Branndair whimpered unhappily.

Still, it didn't last as long as it might have. He fell at last into silence, breathing hard, his every objection turned aside or just ignored. He ran out of fight because he was wrong. He knew what we knew: that he couldn't talk Rory out of coming, and what was more, he shouldn't. And the hunger on his own face betrayed him. He couldn't deny Rory what he wanted so much for himself.

Anyway, the tide below the cliffs was withdrawing.

No-one wanted to wait for the next one, and we all lived ready to move at a moment's notice, so only three hours later I was leading them to the hidden cliff path. Seth stopped on the brink, and watched the first of his clann climb down. He laughed hoarsely.

'What?' Jed walked back towards him, hitching his pack higher.

Seth didn't look at him; he looked at me, and grinned mirthlessly.

'I'm afraid of the height,' he said. 'The bitch. The bitch. She sucked it from me.'

'Look at me,' said Jed. 'Look at me when you talk at me, Murlainn.'

His voice was hard, but when Seth did turn to him, Jed's mouth quirked. 'I know how far it's drained, Murlainn. I know what she's taken from you. How did you think I wouldn't?'

Seth licked his lips. Made a rueful face. 'Right.'

Jed brandished the palm that was marked by his blood-brother scar. 'You really don't think ahead, do you? But you're not going to lose your soul.' He gave Seth a sudden genuine grin. 'Because we're going to kill her.'

Seth laughed. I squeezed his hand.

So he was afraid of the height, now, but he climbed anyway.

Some twenty feet down, I paused to glance back. On the lip of the precipice, Lauren stood watching us. Her fists clenched and unclenched at her sides, her fingers twitching. She didn't shout to stop us, she didn't call a goodbye. She didn't look disbelieving: just stunned, and lost, her face smudged into emptiness by experience. I wondered what would become of her, and yet I couldn't afford to wonder too much or too long.

Out in the free air Faramach swooped lower, taunting Branndair, who clearly hated the descent even more than Seth did. Light backpacks held all we needed of our otherworld lives, and the only other things we carried were our weapons, retrieved and polished and honed for war.

Seth overtook me at the foot of the cliff, then turned to lift me down beside him. I almost laughed at the uncharacteristic chivalry, but when he set me down he wrapped his arms round me. My hair blew in the breeze, tangling with his.

'This gate,' he murmured in my ear. 'It comes out . . . ?'

'Sea to sea. East to west.'

Behind him his fighters jumped one by one to the shingled beach. Some of them had already started a sand-fight. Bunch of big kids.

'East to west,' he echoed softly. 'And the sea. And the basalt caverns.'

'Not inside them. A mile or more away. And you know,' I whispered, 'why I never told you.'

He gave a small shrug, and stepped back. He stroked my wind-blown hair behind my ear. 'So now,' he said, 'just show me.'

The withdrawing waves smashed foam against the rocks, but the way through at low tide was easy. The fighters fell silent, so-bering, spitting out sand, brushing it off their clothes as they fol-lowed me. I led them the way I'd gone before, the way I'd picked out when I found the gate, the only way there was through sea and rock and cliff. I'd known from the day the estate agent brought me here that this house was calling to me, that it had a drag on my soul. I'd known that if I looked long enough, I'd find the source of that drag. I'd sensed the watergate then and I could sense it now, tugging on my spine and my blood.

Well. Not so much the watergate, I suppose. The force that had pulled me then, that pulled me now, was no innocuous portal, but for the moment the call of home was the only call I wanted to hear.

A low scramble into the exposed cave and I blinked, adjusting my eyes to green dimness, and wet salty air, and the pool the tide had left behind.

Carefully I skirted it as Seth and the others ducked into the cave behind me. A murmur went round the assembled fighters, forty or more of them, a yellow-eyed hound and one grinning wolf. It was the sound of happiness, of a long wait almost over. I smiled. I couldn't help it.

'Well, Lost Boys and Girls,' I said, and stepped to the deep pool's glassy rim. 'Shall I be Mother?'

And I stepped into the water, and went home.

PART TWO

Finn

.

It was the same, the same as always, but it felt so inevitably different. True, the landscape was as I remembered and loved it. Rock and hill, scree and loch: they don't change. We went as far as we could from the watergate exit, heading north, and as we passed the cove of the basalt rocks, I didn't even pause to smell the air.

I did not let myself think about my lover's suppurating soul. Not even once. And as far as I could, I didn't let him think about it either.

Coming home had helped, there was no doubt about that. Returning had in itself bought him time. I lay at his side that night in the open air, *our* air, and as he fixed his stare on the Milky Way, I stroked his scarred face and smiled. He was no lorry driver any more, he was no roustabout working the rigs, he was no unemployed forestry worker or occasional mercenary. He was a Sithe warlord and the Captain of his clann. Not to mention of me.

He lolled his head to face me. He was outlined in low firelight and I couldn't quite read his expression. 'Didn't really suit me, did it?'

I gave him as much shrug as I could manage while lying on my side, then leaned in to lick his chin with the tip of my tongue. 'It suited you at the time.'

'Not.'

He gazed back at the stars, so I could enjoy a further close study of his slightly dented profile. 'Honey, you looked great in hi-vis gear. It was so your colour.'

'I look great in *anything*.'

'You look great in *nothing*.'

He spluttered a laugh. 'Quit it. You're not seducing me in the open air in front of my entire clann. I said you're *not*.' Firmly he removed my hand.

'There's a beach,' I told him, wickedly.

'Jed and Iolaire are on the beach. I'm not hunting for a free sun lounger like some tourist.'

'One, Toto, we're not in Antigua any more. Two, Jed and Iolaire are on guard,' I whispered as I tickled his ear. 'On the headland. And three, if you want an excuse for the clann, we need to call the horses. Best place to do it.'

'True.' He shut one eye thoughtfully and trickled my hair through his fingers. 'Sand gets everywhere.'

'Not if you go in the sea afterwards.'

He cocked an eyebrow at me. 'Why am I even arguing?'

'I wondered that.'

'It's your woman's wisdom that makes me love you.' His teeth flashed. 'So, d'you fancy a swim?'

He was dead right about the sand. It chafed and gritted absolutely everywhere as I ran naked towards the waves with Seth at my heels. I was giggling, because I was faster than he was and I knew it annoyed him; and he wasn't helped by the fact that he was out of breath with laughter too. I hit the Atlantic's edge three strides ahead of him and as a massive swell rolled towards me I dived headfirst and swam under.

Shit, it was cold. If my body hadn't been alive before, every nerve in it would have jolted into action now.

But hey, it had been perfectly alive anyway.

I surfaced, swept my hair off my face, gasped for breath. If anything the air felt colder than the water, but I was growing numb to the temperature already. I swam a couple of strokes, then twisted and trod water.

Seth wasn't on the shore; he was nowhere in sight. Not that kind of sight, anyway, but I wasn't born yesterday. I was ready for him and I knew where he was, and I'd taken a lungful of air before arms went round my legs and yanked me under.

I blinked and blew bubbles, smiling. There was enough underwater moonlight for me to make him out, drifting there in front of me. Shards of it striped and rippled his skin. I reached a hand for him, right where he wasn't expecting it, and his eyes widened with his grin. He spluttered to the surface, and I let go and wound my arms round his neck.

His arms slipped round my waist. I pushed back his hair and kissed him. Our legs, still treading water, bumped and tangled.

'Can we get back into our depth?' he mumbled into my mouth. 'Need a bit of leverage.'

'Already?' I drew back and licked the salty skin on his throat.

'No sand here.' His tongue found mine.

'Horses,' I managed to gasp.

'Spoilsport.' He wound his fingers into mine and we both struck out one-armed towards the shoreline.

My toes found shifting sand and weed, and I stood up, my breasts clear of the water. Seth was eyeing those, but I turned a slow circle, searching the water's surface. 'Back to business, sweetie.'

He growled, took a mouthful of sea and fired it with annoying precision at my left nipple. 'Fine.'

'Bugger.' I swept a fan of water into his face.

'Didn't you call him already?' He raked his hair back. 'I called the roan five minutes ago.'

'Yeah.' I frowned. 'Give them time.'

He ducked his head underwater, then resurfaced. 'Well. Mine's coming.'

I felt my heart quicken. However long I'd known the blue roan, it never seemed altogether trustworthy. I peered down into the black waters below me, trying not to visualise any iconic movie posters.

I shouldn't have worried. When its savage head breached the surface it was thirty metres out from shore. White water cascaded from its crest and forelock, streaming down its black face, and then it was cutting through the waves towards Seth, hooves rising out of the sea in its excitement, plunging back in an explosion of foam to power it forward. Seth smiled through his wet hair as it reached him, and then he was embracing its neck, dragging himself over its withers and onto its back. He reached down an arm for me and cocked an eyebrow.

I shook my head. 'I'll wait.'

He bit the corner of his lip, slightly apologetic. 'How long, Caorann?'

'Maybe he's on dry land,' I sulked. 'Maybe he's hunting.'

Seth leaned forward to rub the roan's flicking ears. 'Not according to this one.'

I gritted my teeth. Called the black again. Trod water for long minutes at the roan's side. I was so close to it, my hair tangled with its mane. I felt Seth's hand touch my head.

'Maybe you'll have to go back for his bridle.'

'It's in my pack. I can't be arsed.' I sank under the water, let myself drift for long seconds, then resurfaced. Still no sign. Seth had ridden the roan closer to shore; it stood up to its shoulders, mane blowing free in the salt breeze, tail hanging heavy in the water like tendrils of weed. I swam back to them, floated beside the roan's flank.

'It's not like he can refuse you,' said Seth into the wave-lapped silence.

'Apparently he bloody can.'

'Come back to the camp for your bridle,' said Seth again. I resented the note of sympathy in his voice.

All the same: 'Looks like I'll have to,' I said.

'I'm not even sure—'

I don't know what he was about to say, but his words were drowned out by the shattering explosion of water. I laughed with glee and pure relief as the massive black head and shoulders erupted from below, barely ten feet further out. The black was so close I ducked, reflexively, shielding my face with an arm. The blue roan plunged and screamed, and Seth had to grab its mane to stay on.

Brutal white teeth grazed my cheekbone as the black lunged forward. Its silky sodden mane slapped my face, but I seized it as it swam, hauling myself onto its back as it pitched through the swell and suddenly dived underwater.

I had time to take a breath. Luckily. My fingers tangled in its mane, and I saw a sudden flash of memory in my mind's eye. It felt real and frightening, as if I'd never been master of this horse at all, as if I was sixteen years old and trapped in time on a blue roan kelpie that was planning to eat me. My free hand pressed against the black's neck, feeling the power of its muscles, and as I blinked through dark water I saw its head turn, saw its empty eye swivel towards me. Then it breached the surface again, spray showering around us.

Its legs plunged strongly. Seth and the blue roan were fifty metres back—had we really swum so far?—but we reached them while the shock was still etched on Seth's face. The black splashed to a halt alongside him, seawater cascading off it and me, nipping affectionately at the blue roan's rump.

'Well,' said Seth, and blew a wet lock of hair off his face. 'I've never seen it that reluctant.'

'Funny, isn't it?' Avoiding Seth's stare, I scratched gently at the black's shoulder, exactly where it liked to be scratched. There had been something in that glare it gave me in the gloom beneath the water, but it was here now, wasn't it? It had come to me, it had answered my call. Why shouldn't a wild thing take its own sweet time? The kelpie arched its neck and lifted a hoof high to strike a swelling wave. I rubbed its ears and it nickered with nothing more than calm fondness.

'Or indeed,' Seth added, 'quite that keen to drown you.'

'Nah,' I said. 'He was only playing.'

Seth nodded at the landward horizon, paling now behind the black hills.

'Dawn,' he said grimly. 'Hannah and Sionnach have been gone more than a day.'

'End of play.' My lips twisted ruefully. 'I suppose we'd better go back. Get dressed. Before anybody else wakes up.'

'Yeah,' he said, and turned the roan's head. 'And try to imagine what the hell we're going to do next.'

Rory

'Isn't it obvious?' said Grian, poking at the ashes of the fire with his dirk. 'We take the dun back first. Get ourselves a secure base. Evict the Lammyr. I've been aching to do that.'

'I'm with Grian,' said Braon brightly, glancing from his face to Seth's.

It was Seth's favourite time of day, Rory thought, when the world was grey in a thousand tones, but he didn't look as if he was enthralled with it right now. A rain blew against their faces, a rain so faint that Rory couldn't feel the drops, only the wetness on his skin when it had passed.

'No,' said Jed, who was sitting on a rock, lovingly examining the edge of his blade.

'"No?"' Grian twisted round to stare at him. 'Who died and made you Captain?'

Jed shrugged. 'That's not Seth's plan. Ask him.'

'I thought I did.'

Jed shrugged again. Seth looked exasperated, but he said, 'Jed's right. There isn't time to besiege a bloody dun, Grian. You know what the defences are like.'

Grian rested back on his elbows, letting his yellow-eyed hound lick his face. 'You haven't got a plan, have you, Murlainn?'

Seth hissed though his teeth. 'I didn't exactly get time to make one. But taking back the dun certainly isn't part of it. Yet.'

Something tickled Rory's ear, and he reached up a hand to scratch the grey filly's nose. She'd come instantly when called, so he reckoned she must simply have been waiting for his return. He felt guiltily smug about that, given that Finn had apparently had so much trouble with her black.

The filly's lips explored his scalp, then nipped a hank of hair and tugged it. If he'd known she was going to be so obsessive about Polo mints, Rory thought, he could have brought a few packets, and she wouldn't have been limited to the few lint-fuzzy ones he'd found rattling around in the crannies of his backpack.

Finn and Seth's kelpies were being a little more stand-offish, grazing on a knoll some fifty metres away. Branndair, jealous of the filly's closeness, was flopped across Rory's lap, his eyes half-closed, his tail thumping lazily. Rory threaded his fingers into the wolf's neck fur, not wanting to look at his father in case Seth managed to read his face even without a mind link. He was desperately impatient to get to Hannah—and Sionnach, of course—but he couldn't help thinking of the time Seth had made him learn the whole of *Art of War* cover to cover. All that stuff about forward planning and superior forces, and decisiveness without impulsiveness, and winning the battle before you fought it. According to Sun bloody Tzu, as far as Rory could make out, they were all going to die.

Orach nudged him mischievously. 'Know when to walk away and know when to run.'

'That's not Sun Tzu,' said Braon beside her, 'that's Kenny Rogers.'

The two of them giggled like schoolgirls.

'Oh great,' muttered Fearna. 'We really are gonnae die.'

'We're not going to die,' Seth growled. 'But we need horses, weapons, more fighters. I'd suggest Dunster . . .'

Grian shook his head. 'Dunster has never been fond of you, Murlainn. You killed their Captain—'

'For good reason,' Rory butted in. Hell's teeth, his father and Braon and the rest had scalpeled a nest of Lammyr out of that village, for no thanks, and their wretched Captain had promptly sucked up to Kate by betraying rebels in a neighbouring settlement.

'For no better reason,' agreed Grian, 'but did he expect their undying adoration?'

'No,' grunted Seth. 'Which is why I was going to say we'd have a better chance at Faragaig. Apart from anything else, it'll help me gauge what support there is out there.'

'I don't understand.' Braon had stopped laughing with Orach. Rory realised she'd stopped some time ago, and her expression was cold and challenging, and Orach looked nervously supportive of her. He wondered what had passed between the two women's minds. 'There are ways into our dun. You've got in twice.'

'And saved your scrawny arse both times.' Seth stopped honing his blade. 'And ever since the second time, the Lammyr have known about the tunnel.'

Braon snorted contemptuously. 'There has to be another way. Lammyr are cowards and they won't hold out for a long siege.'

'Lammyr aren't cowards, they're pragmatists,' said Iolaire. 'They'll hold out as long as it suits them, and they don't mind dying. Positively enjoy it.'

'Still, the fewer of them are at our backs, the better chance we'll have. And Grian's right, we need a base. Your father never met a Lammyr without cutting its head off, Murlainn. He certainly wouldn't have let a mob of them keep his dun.'

Orach stiffened, reddening, and detached herself very slightly
from Braon's side as if to distance herself from that remark. Seth
looked as if Braon had stuck a dagger in his gut. He paled with
fury, and Rory couldn't imagine what he might have said to her
if Jed hadn't flicked his dagger into the centre of the group. It
smacked blade-first into the peat.

Jed cracked his fingers casually as they turned.

'I've got a personal interest in Skinshanks's lot,' he said. 'And if
Seth says leave them alone for now, that's fine with me.'

Grian looked as if he wanted to punch him. 'So they'll be free
to come at us from behind as soon as we head for Kate's caverns.
Good plan,' he ground out through his teeth. 'I want to know
what Langfank talked to you about, Murlainn.'

'That's my business,' said Seth. 'You trust me, or you don't.'

'I don't know how you can even say that to me,' said Braon.

'The watergate's that way.' Seth got to his feet and pointed
back the way they'd come. 'I'm going to get Sionnach and Hannah, and whoever wants to come with me can take my word that
I know what I'm doing. The rest of you—' he glanced at his
otherworld watch '—I think the pub's open for another two
hours.'

Grian stood up too, his face close to Seth's. 'I don't know
what's got into you, Murlainn. Unless it's something that's finally
drained out of you.'

'That is *enough*.' Finn walked up to Grian and placed her hand
against his ribcage. She left it there for a second, maybe two, long
enough to feel his heart beat. Then she shoved him away from
Seth. 'Grian and Braon, you make good points and it's your job.
But Murlainn's your Captain and it's his decision. He's right about
that, at least. You don't like it, you leave.'

'I'm not leaving.' Braon scowled. 'And he knows it.'

'Yes, I think he does.' Finn smiled at her.

'And nor am I,' said Grian, 'though Murlainn might trip over his own complacent arse one day.'

'I'm not the only leader who's complacent,' said Seth softly, 'which is why I want you to trust me. Grian, do not ever imagine I take you for granted. But I will not attack the dun, not now.'

Grian shrugged. Branndair whimpered, and licked his hound's muzzle. Iolaire looked relieved that the squabble was over. Jed kept his cool eyes fixed on Seth.

And if that uneasy silence hadn't fallen at just that moment, they wouldn't have heard the horses.

Seth turned on his heel. Jed was on his feet, and a fraction of a second behind him, so was everyone else. Rory couldn't help noticing that Orach backed close to his father as she drew her sword. She wasn't just guilty about Braon's brutal comment; she'd been anxious and protective around her old lover since they'd got here. Rory had noticed that. He was totally sure Finn had too. He was fair-to-middling sure that Finn didn't mind.

'Where the hell are they?' Grian sounded perplexed.

'This way.' Iolaire took a step towards a crevice in the granite rocks.

'No, said Braon. 'Beyond the treeline.'

'Here!' a fighter yelled from the edge of the machair. He stood on a fringe of scrubby sandbank, his dirk indicating the beach below.

'This is absurd,' muttered Seth. He pushed aside Orach's defensive blade and walked towards the kelpies. Rory's filly had the same idea; she galloped past Seth, heading for the reassuring company of her kin. As she halted beside the roan it gave her a sharp bossy bite on the neck, then shouldered her into its shadow and raised its head, and screamed at the invisible threat. Then it swung its head and screamed another challenge, in the opposite direction.

The black did not scream. Its head was high, its nostrils flared, its lip peeled back, but it was very still.

'Are we surrounded or what?' said Iolaire. 'Where the hell are they?'

Seth was up on the roan by now, turning its head towards the treeline, but it backed a few paces, resisting. It shied to the right, its flanks bumping against the grey filly.

'It doesn't know either,' shouted Seth. The roan had stopped its aggressive squealing now, and the only sound was the rustle of stiff grasses in the light breeze.

They waited a breathless age, till hilts began to tremble in tense fists, but the sound of hoofbeats had died away. Seth shook his head impatiently.

'Let's call that a mass hallucination, shall we?'

'If you like,' growled Grian, still eyeing the pines. 'But I suggest we move.'

'Fine.' Seth sheathed his sword on his back. 'If anyone fancies joining me, I'm off to Faragaig.'

Rory knew Faragaig. He'd always liked it and his father had visited it often when he was a boy: negotiating trade deals, adjudicating arguments (or trying to), keeping its temperamental Captain onside. It nestled very comfortably in the crescent of a white-sand bay, protected by two long headlands; to its landward side rose low green hills thick with bramble and wild raspberry and rhododendron. They approached the place on foot, through cultivated fields of barley and oats, potatoes and kale. A blowing, stamping herd of fat bullocks thundered close to a fence to watch them pass, puffing inquisitive steamy breaths, earning an evilly hungry glare from all three kelpies. In a smaller paddock the sun shone on the glossy flanks of pregnant mares; others had foals at foot already. Rory noticed his father having a good look at those.

'Faragaig always bred good horses,' Seth remarked to Jed.

'I wonder why there's any still here.' Iolaire had already climbed to the crest of a grassy slope, and he turned back with a warning look. ~ *Seeing as they've been raided lately.*

'Raiders?' said Seth, his brow furrowing. 'They didn't steal much.'

He hoisted himself onto the blue roan and rode it to Iolaire's side. The roan shied violently as soon as it crested the ridge, and Seth put his hand to his nose and mouth and swore. He was silent while the rest of the clann caught up. When Rory reached the hill's crest and the sea breeze caught him, the stench came with it like something solid, and he recoiled and gagged.

'They may not have taken anything.' Grian cleared his throat and spat. 'But they left a lot of dule trees.'

A track of gritty sand wound from the ridge down into the outskirts of the village. The first houses weren't far away, but the zigzag of the path down into its streets must have been three-quarters of a mile long. In dips and hollows it meandered out of sight, but it was very clearly marked now: they could see the line of it all the way, punctuated at fifty-metre intervals with gibbets.

Not particularly sophisticated ones. The dule trees themselves weren't much more than wooden spikes hammered into the ground, no more than fifteen feet tall, and sharpened at the tip. An upright body was impaled on every one, arms pinned against its sides with an iron band. The closest corpses were definitely the newest; further down the track towards the village, some of them were barely recognisable as human. Those ones were staked much closer together; the executioners must have been busier in the first days of whatever had happened in Faragaig. Crows flapped up as they passed, but lazily; it wasn't as if there was a shortage of meat. The flies were more industrious.

'God, Faramach, don't,' whispered Finn at Rory's side as her raven took off from her arm. He rose on the wind and swooped between the gibbets, provoking the crows to defensive cawing, but he didn't settle on any of the bodies. Rory could make out his distinctive ragged shadow on the track as he flew far ahead towards Faragaig. Finn shut her eyes and exhaled with relief.

Seth had remained on horseback, letting the roan find its own feet down the windblown grit of the track. He stared at every corpse as he passed it; the last one had fallen from its spike and collapsed into a pathetic pile of bones and flesh-rags. He halted by that one, gazing with his head tilted, as the roan snorted and snarled and struck up sand-flurries with a hoof. Seth had the look of a man who was passing the time, waiting for something, and in no more than a minute they heard hoofbeats again.

It was easy enough this time to tell where they came from. Six riders came out of Faragaig at a canter, the late sun glowing on polished flanks and glinting off tack buckles. When the first animal was almost within biting distance of the roan, its rider yanked on its reins. He and Seth stared at one another for long seconds.

'I'm a little surprised to see your face, Glanadair,' said Seth at last. He nodded at the nearest gibbeted corpse. 'Especially looking as good as you do.'

The man didn't answer at once. His lips tightened; there were red patches high on his cheekbones.

'And where were you, Murlainn? I haven't seen you and your principles around here for, ooh . . . four years, at least.'

'You know fine why.'

'Of course I do. You scuttled off to the otherworld with your son and your lover and your well-honed sense of self-preservation, and good luck to you.' The corner of Glanadair's lip lifted. 'But some of us stayed.'

'I'm not surprised. You've done very well for yourself. Nice horse.' Seth studied first the animal, then his fingernails. 'I thought for a minute there you'd been attacked.'

Rory had to admire Glanadair, though he'd never let on to his father. He could feel the anger radiating off the man in waves, but Glanadair stayed perfectly calm.

'In a sense we were, Murlainn. From within. Seems I'd been breeding a right nest of rebels. They must have thought I'd be suicidal enough to support them.'

'Instead of which you sold them off to Kate, I take it?'

'Kate asked for them. You didn't.' Glanadair cocked his head to examine the rickle of bones left on one of the gibbets. The way the skull was, all twisted and gaping, suggested the man—or woman, maybe—hadn't died very well; but maybe that was just the ravages of time and weather. 'I mean, you weren't here to do any asking, but that wasn't my problem, was it?'

'Not at that point,' said Seth.

'Are you threatening me, Murlainn?'

'Gods, no. I don't do idle threats.'

Glanadair shrugged. 'We're a small community. Kate treats us remarkably well, considering what was simmering here for a whole year. She gives us advantageous trade, she gives us protection; she accepts counsel and she gives a hearing to any request we care to make.'

The fair-haired, sharp-faced man behind Glanadair nudged his horse forward; must be his lieutenant, Rory realised. Jed mirrored the man's movement, walking forward to stand at the roan's shoulder. He hadn't drawn a blade yet but his fingers were twitchy.

'We hear a lot of bad things about Kate,' said the lieutenant.

'She wipes out resistance if they won't negotiate. She makes free with her Lammyr and she likes to keep them well content; she'll let them destroy entire communities if they're selfish enough to disrupt the Queen's Peace.' He lifted a shoulder. 'She's never done that to us. We've never given her reason.'

'No, Leoghar.' said Jed. 'She let you do it to yourselves.'

'Hello, Cuilean.' Leoghar gave him a thin smile. 'I would've thought you of all people would sympathise. I thought you and the Lammyr had a special relationship going.'

Rory's breath stuck in his throat, but Jed didn't rise to it, and he was dizzy with gratitude. His brother just smiled at Leoghar.

'Well. It's like you say. Some communities are just asking for it.'

'I've heard enough from you and your warmongers, Murlainn.' Glanadair turned his horse, then twisted on its back to face Seth again. 'You came here for support. You came for horses and weapons, maybe even fighters. It should be obvious that isn't going to happen.'

'Oh, believe me, it's obvious,' said Seth; but Glanadair was already riding away.

Leoghar hesitated. He looked up at the line of stinking corpses, then back at Rory's father, with a faint smirk. 'Sorry we can't help, Murlainn. Try Howedale: I'm sure they'd be more your type. Or who knows? They might do you an even bigger favour. They might convince you that you're wasting your time.'

'Nobody's going to do that,' gritted Seth. 'The bitch-queen has my brother's daughter and she has my lieutenant.'

'Then kiss them both goodbye.' Leoghar's expression was suddenly full of hatred. 'You lose two? That's nothing. Call them casualties of exile. And then go back into it, and drink yourself to death while you still have a soul. I see you, and I See what's nearly gone. You're out of time, Murlainn, in *so many* ways.'

Nobody spoke as Leoghar turned and rode casually back down the trail. All they heard was his voice, drifting on the suddenly still air.

'Abandon a world long enough, Murlainn, and it'll abandon you.'

Finn

Howedale must have waited a long time to teach us its lesson. The salt breezes had blown through its ruins for months, if not years. There were no people here, no horses, no cattle, except for their charred and crumbling bone-houses. What hadn't been taken by the crows and the insects had been desiccated by dry winds and time. Even the smell of death had deserted the place.

Seth separated the clann into small detachments and sent them out through houses, store-rooms, stables and bakeries, hunting for life; but it was a formality. I was assigned with Grian, but I had to drift away from him because I couldn't bear the buffeting of his tormented mind. He didn't mean to do it; he didn't know he was doing it. I certainly wasn't going to confess to him how much of it I could feel. I just reached out and squeezed his healer's fingers, and left him in the middle of a burnt out kitchen, staring into shrivelled humanoid cinders, lost in his helpless impotency.

As I picked my way through a shattered doorway into the yard beyond, my boots crunched on what might have been burnt wood or broken shells or much worse; I didn't want to look down. A twig gusted past me, caught by the breeze, bouncing across the rough overgrown beds till it was brought to a stop by a crumbling dyke. I picked it up, then flung it in the air to let it blow away across the fields towards the machair. Irrational, sentimental, but if anything wanted out of this place, it should go.

There was a compact two-storey barn on the right of the field; maybe it had been a stable or a byre. I didn't expect to find anything in it, not really, but I wanted to do something, or look as if I was. Anything to avoid the awful churning horror that was Grian's mind, anything to kill the time till we could leave here.

I pushed through waist-high weeds, feeling with my feet for the hidden raised rigs—God, if I tripped and fell I might land on something terrible—and tugged at the broken door of the outbuilding. It resisted for seconds, then collapsed outwards in a clatter of rotten wood, and I stepped quickly back.

The wind moaned around me, rattled a loose plank, but no life stirred. I shivered. Inside the barn the quietness was complete, and the air was dim and cool. A shaft of sunlight caught swirling dust-motes like a tiny galaxy. My steps echoed on the bare floor, hideously loud.

The stairs to the hayloft were intact. Above them a hatch lay open, the blackness beyond it forming a square of absolute night in the dusty indoor twilight. I couldn't not go. I *wanted* not to go, but I didn't seem to have a choice.

So I climbed. At the top of the stairs I felt inside the loft with my fingertips, heart crashing with dread. I didn't want to touch a body, if there was one. I didn't want to touch a fat spider, gorged on fat contented flies. I didn't know which would be worse.

I blinked. There was light after all, just enough of it: cracks in the roof beams let in the tiniest shards of sun. Hoisting myself up, I fell onto all fours on the rotting plank floor and stared at the children.

Dead, of course. The bigger one was curled round the little one, its arms tight; partly protectiveness, I guessed, partly the contractions of death and rigor. I couldn't tell the sex of either one. I couldn't tell its sex even when it raised its blackened cratered head and spoke to me.

~ Where were you? it said.

I stayed where I was, crouched on the floor. It wasn't as if I could move. My eyes were wide and the light in them crackled with terror. It hurt. Flakes of charred skin fell from the little corpse's lips.

~ We waited and we waited and you didn't come, it said.

I opened my mouth but the excuses wouldn't form. Even if they had, my throat muscles had contracted. Speak? I could barely breathe.

~ We were sure you were coming, it said. ~ You never did.

And the little one, the one in its arms that had maybe not lived long enough to learn how to speak, raised its head as well, and there were fresh live tears streaking its charred skin.

That was when I screamed. I crossed my filthy arms across my eyes and screamed, and it wasn't just terror; I knew that if I shrieked loud enough, and the child spoke again, I at least wouldn't be able to hear it. Running out of breath was one of the worst prospects of my life, and I thought that when the scream stopped, and I heard the child's voice, I would die.

But I had to stop. I forced out a last, choked, scratch of a whimper, and I crouched there, frozen. I had to inhale, that was the thing. I took my arms down from my eyes, and filled my lungs, and waited to die of fright.

There were two little corpses in the corner, nothing more. Two long dead children, and not a twitch of motion or a whisper of sound from either of them. Why would there be? They were dead.

I started to shake, then. My whole body juddered so violently I was afraid the rotten planks would give way beneath me and I'd fall through and break my wretched neck, and oh God, then I would have to see the children again and hear them accuse me.

Because only the dead could hear the dead; not the living. *Not the living.*

What have I done? I screamed in my own head. *What have I woken? What have I done? You stupid, stupid bitch. You stupid witch. What have you done?*

I crawled to the rickety wooden steps and stumbled down them, and I ran out of the barn. I tripped and fell at least twice; might have been more. I was bruised and bleeding and gasping for breath by the time I raced into the village square.

'Finn!' Seth turned and stared at me. He was standing with the rest of the clann, and they were all holding naked weapons. They looked confused and angry, and not on my account. Seth left them, striding across to seize my arm. 'Where were you? What is it?'

I clutched my side, trying to kill the agonising stitch, and for the first time since the horror in the barn, my brain clicked into some kind of working order. 'Nothing,' I panted. 'Nothing. Panicked. Nothing.'

He chewed his lip, narrowed his eyes. 'Nothing?'

'Sorry. Nothing.' I creased my mouth into a smile. 'Biggest. Spider. Ever.'

He laughed, a sort of strained gasp. 'Fine. You're creeped out. No wonder. I think we all are. Could you tell where they were coming from this time?'

I raked my fingers through my tangled hair. 'Who?'

'The horses. The hoofbeats. Didn't you hear them?'

I shook my head.

He creased his brow. 'They were loud. Thought they were attacking us, that they'd pinned us in the village. You didn't *hear* them?'

I didn't hear them, Seth. I wanted to say that, but I was afraid to. If I hadn't heard a pack of fighters riding down on us, it was because I'd been sealed in a bubble of witchcraft, or worse, and listening to the dead talk. I didn't want to say it and I didn't want him to hear it. I didn't want to know.

'Well. They disappeared again.' Seth scratched at his neck. 'I don't know why they're playing with us. But they've gone.'

The clann were indeed sheathing their weapons. Their faces were grim, their hands filthy with soot; they must have ransacked the whole place. The unseen riders were clearly not top of their list of concerns right now.

Jed flung down a charred bow and a rusty sword with a badly nicked blade. 'There's the contents of the weapons store,' he said bitterly. 'I'm guessing Howedale said no to a decent trade agreement and a plantation of dule trees.'

I glanced at Grian. His face was pallid and sickly. 'Are you okay?' I whispered.

'Bastards,' he whispered back, not particularly to me and not to anyone else. 'Bastards.'

I reached out to squeeze his stiff fingers again. He had a crap job. But not having a need to do it must have been a lot worse.

'Well, well.' Jed's voice was suddenly loud in the silence. 'One of them's decided to come out of the burnt woodwork. Bags I kill her.'

Everybody turned and stared. A rider approached down Howedale's main drag, such as it was: a woman on a bay gelding. Her choppy-short brown hair was flicked out by the sea breeze, she wore a leather jacket and a longsword, and her eyes sparked with something like aggression. She didn't seem in a hurry, though; she didn't even seem afraid. A green rag fluttered from her horse's mane.

'If that's a flag of truce,' called Jed, running a finger down the flat of his blade, 'you can stick it right up your—'

Seth seized his arm to shut him up. 'Alainn.'

'Murlainn.' She reined in the bay gelding.

I had to rack my bruised brain. *Alainn?* I knew he'd had a captain once, when he was Kate's henchman and he killed for her. There had been an Alainn then. It might be the same one: the captain who wasn't so bad, the one who wasn't his direct commander. I'd heard all his stories from those days . . . *Orach*, I remembered suddenly: Alainn had been Orach's Captain. I glanced over my shoulder at the blonde fighter. She'd come forward three or four paces and a look of torment crossed her face. She was probably hoping her old commander wasn't going to get impaled on her old lover's sword. Gods, I thought, did the Sithe have to be so few? Did we all have to know the people we killed; the people who killed our friends? It was all so hideously intimate.

Seth folded his arms. 'Where are the others, Alainn?'

She looked genuinely taken aback. 'What others? I'm alone.'

'You're lying.'

'Try me.'

'Fine. Get off the horse.'

She hesitated, but she must have known she didn't have a choice. She was encircled by forty cold-eyed Sithe who were just looking for an excuse for a brawl, especially with someone who might well have been in Howedale on its last day of existence.

Her feet had no sooner touched the ground than the point of Jed's sword was in the small of her back. She froze, then twisted her head to flash a tight smile at Seth.

'I realise you're all nervous,' she began.

'I don't have a sentimental attachment to you,' said Jed in her ear. He slid her dagger from its sheath and tossed it to me. 'Give us the sword.'

Very slowly she drew the blade from its scabbard and held it at arm's length. Iolaire took it delicately and turned it, examining it.

'Haven't you seen a sword before?' she said testily.

'Just checking for scorch marks.' Iolaire gave her a dazzling smile of promise.

'That,' said Alainn, with a brief glance towards the village houses, 'was a long time ago.'

'We know,' sighed Jed with a roll of his eyes. 'He's just kind of joking. And he kind of isn't.' Alainn winced as his sword tip dug in.

'I've got something else to give you, if you're not too homicidally snotty to take it.' She glared at him over her shoulder as her hand slipped inside her leather jacket.

Forty hands went to their blades this time.

'Oh, grow up,' she muttered. 'Like I've got a death wish.' She pulled something small and rectangular from her inside pocket and tossed it to Seth.

He caught the phone, turned it in his hands, rubbed his thumb across the touchscreen. Nothing happened, of course, since the battery was dead. 'Hannah's,' he told me, and placed it in my hand.

'She's alive,' said Alainn. 'Sionnach too, for now.'

'So you say.' He took back the phone from me and thrust it in her face. 'This proves what?'

She shrugged. 'Nothing. Token of good faith, you can call it.'

'Oh, I need more than that.' Seth crooked a finger at me, but he didn't take his eyes off Alainn.

Alainn eyed me warily. 'Just how malevolent a witch is she?'

'Want to find out?' I gave her a Iolaire-style smile.

She huffed a strained laugh. 'Fine. I don't suppose Murlainn will trust me without a scan anyway.'

'Trust you how? You're not seriously saying you're on my side.'

She sighed and jerked a thumb at the ghost village. 'Somebody has to be. You'll get a choice of two results wherever you ask. This, or Faragaig-style.'

A few of the fighters behind us shifted uneasily, shared glances.

I wanted to give them a death-glare but I had a feeling that would be tactically bad.

'Kate's left you no constituency, Murlainn. You might pick up a few fighters here and there, but nothing like an army. This land's devastated by Lammyr and militia and politics, and I don't know which has done most damage.'

Seth looked genuinely mystified. 'And the point of telling me this?'

She shrugged. 'Just a warning. I thought you might like to go home, and then I can go back to Kate and live out my shrunken life.' Her tone was acid. 'Otherwise I'm with you, Murlainn. May the gods have mercy on my soul.'

There were a few more murmurs behind me. I thought, this time, they sounded a little more optimistic.

'Alainn. If my lover can read your motives,' said Seth silkily, 'so can your queen.'

'That's a chance I'll take.' Alainn nodded curtly at me. 'Kate's afraid of Caorann. That's no small thing. It means that at the very least, Caorann can tell my motives without me dropping my block.'

'I can take a good guess,' I said flatly. 'So can Kate.'

'Kate has more to think about than me. And she's complacent. Always has been. Can't help herself.'

'She has reason to be.' Seth smirked. 'Go on.'

'I may be a fool. My lieutenants too. But I wish you well, Murlainn. And you really have to trust me.' Alainn lifted a shoulder. 'You don't have much of a choice.'

'I have the choice of killing you,' Seth pointed out. 'Finn?'

I stepped close to Alainn and put my hand against her forehead, studying her eyes. Faramach hopped to the ground and stalked round the woman, cocking his head to give her an insolent stare.

'That's a good block you have,' I murmured.

'You bet it bloody is.' Alainn gave a derisive laugh. 'So would yours be, if you were me and you lived where I live.'

'No.' I smiled thinly. 'Mine would be so much better.'

Alainn's smile died, and she swallowed reflexively.

I pushed her away. 'You're not a captain any more, are you?'

'No.'

'What happened? Express an opinion?'

'Not one she liked.' Alainn glowered.

'Your lieutenants?'

'Demoted along with me. They'll turn with me, once you're in and if things go well for you.'

'Not entirely altruistic, are you?'

'So? I was her captain for five centuries. I balk at a hanging, on the grounds of the offender's youth, and wham-bam, I'm a bottom-rank fighter again and Raib MacRothe captains *my* fighters.' She spat, as if the name had caused her physical pain. 'Bitter? You bet I am, Caorann. I probably have sounder motives than half these airy-fairy idealists of yours.'

Folding my arms, I turned and walked back to Seth.

'She's for real.'

'Sure?'

I shrugged. 'Far as I can make out. Can you pass up the chance?'

He shook his head. 'Alainn. Tell me Kate's thoughts.'

'She wants you in the tunnels. She won't meet you outside, where you'd have room to manoeuvre. Well, she'd be mad to meet you in the open, with the advantage she's got. On the other hand she knows you can't afford a long siege, because she has more supplies than you do.' She added snarkily, 'Or should I say, any supplies at all.'

'So she wants us in the caverns.'

'Of course. She won't come out. She wants her fighters in

front defending her, and Langfank coming at you from behind. Like stoats in a rabbit warren, and you bunnies will have nowhere to go.'

I was watching the back of Seth's neck. He must have felt it, because he scratched at it with a fingertip, but he didn't turn to me. And still he wouldn't tell me.

~ *Seth?*

~ *Later. I'll explain later.*

~ *You'd better.*

He shivered, shaking me off. 'If all this is true, Alainn, you're backing the wrong horse. Late in the race and all.'

'I'm backing the horse I want to win, the only time it'll ever have a chance. How long have you been gone, Murlainn? And then your brother died and screwed everything? Come on. I'd have been pissing my life away. But *now* I think you have a chance.'

'Murlainn,' hissed Iolaire. 'She's been Kate's captain for five centuries. Kill her.'

'Aye, right. Like I killed you when you came to me?'

Glowering, Iolaire turned away.

Alainn reached a hand to her horse's wither, rubbing it absently. 'Go find what fighters you can, Murlainn. You don't have all the time in the world. I'll be in touch again.' She glowered at Jed. 'Assuming your attack dog isn't going to stick me in the ribs.'

Seth gave Jed a brusque nod. Jed, somewhat reluctantly, stepped a pace back and let Alainn mount her horse. But before she could turn its head back towards Kate's lands, Seth reached forward and seized the cheekpiece of its bridle. It shied, its eyes rolling to show the whites, but at a word from Seth it quietened. Alainn gave it a filthy look.

'And the others?' asked Seth. 'The troops we keep hearing?'

'What others? There are no troops, unless Cuthag's grown an extra stupid.' Anger ignited in her eyes. 'I told you, I came alone, or I'd be dead already.'

Seth shot me a questioning look. I twisted my mouth. ~ *She's not lying.*

'You find them out there?' he told her, releasing her horse and slapping its neck. 'Make sure you tell them I will too.'

'I'll be keeping my mouth shut,' she said. 'And you can go rootle up weapons and horses. And some more supporters. Good luck with that, Murlainn.' She nudged her horse around. 'I'd say you're going to need it, but that'd be too much stating the bleeding obvious.'

Seth was walking towards the cluster of blown pines that had protected Howedale's northern border, albeit not very efficiently. I felt him go, or I might have missed him; the rest of the clann were busying themselves to leave the dead settlement, and only Branndair loped after Seth, claw-scrabbling across a stone dyke after him. I saw Seth glance down, smile, and ruffle his neck fur, but he strode on swiftly into the woods as if he wanted no company but his wolf.

So anyway, Branndair went after him, and so did I.

When I found him in a small glade he was standing in dappled shadow with his back against a pine trunk, his arms folded. 'Hello, lover.'

'Hello yourself.' I returned his rueful smile.

He reached out a hand and took mine, pulled me in and kissed me. I raked his hair back from his face and drew reluctantly away. His eyes were very silver in the green dimness.

'You know the worst of it, Finn? I don't care.'

I stroked the scar on his face. 'You mean, about what you're going to do.'

He nodded gently, which brought his forehead against mine. 'I'm going to kill them.'

'I know,' I whispered.

'Yeah.' He kissed my nose. 'Yeah, of course you do. Here's the thing, Finn.' He swallowed and shut his eyes. 'I've been trying so damn hard to be Conal. And I can't be. I shouldn't be.

'Thank God you've got that straight at last,' I murmured. 'But I'm worried about you.'

'That's the problem.' He sighed. 'I'm not.'

'We deserted those people,' I said.

'I don't even care about that. I don't give a tuppenny shit, Finn. They deserved to be abandoned, every mother's child of them.'

'I'm not sure that's . . .'

'In my head it's true. And that's where it matters, isn't it? Because I'm the one who's going to take what we need, and strip them of everything they have, and cut their worthless throats. It doesn't matter to me. I don't regret the thought of it and I don't regret that it doesn't matter, and I'll feel no shame when I've done it.'

'Right,' I whispered, my head still pressed against his. Dread twisted and tightened in my gut.

He kissed me again, and his mouth smiled against mine.

'Will you still love me tomorrow?' he asked.

'Yes,' I said.

'Good,' he said. 'Because it's the only thing that I still give a damn about.'

I had to make my limbs move, I had to focus on every step that I took after him as he walked back out of the wood. Maybe I wouldn't have managed it if his fingers hadn't been tangled round mine. I was more afraid of what was happening to him than I was of death, I realised, but I couldn't take a side against him: not Kate's, obviously, but not the clann's either. *Bound,* I thought as my soul chilled inside me. *So this is what it means.*

And then I thought: *What's the point of it, if there's nothing I can do to help him?*

Which was when I began to want to kill them all, too.

Hannah

'Sionnach,' I whispered. 'Sionnach, are you okay?'

The room was dark, so dark. I was scared of the dark but I kept trying to forget that, and by now I almost had. Or I'd almost convinced myself I had. I kept shutting my eyes. Pretending there was light, and that I just couldn't see it.

I'd paced round the walls, over and over, feeling the length of them. The cell was maybe three metres by three, and there weren't any windows. It might have been stiflingly hot, if we weren't so far underground, but it only felt airless and threatening. I felt like I was already in the belly of some beast, a wooden beast. The walls and the floor were lined in smooth timber: I knew that only because they were warmer to the touch than stone, and I'd run my fingertips down narrow panels and grooves.

I'd tried to reach out my mind—to anyone, even one of the cold-faced guards who'd put us in here—but my mind could go nowhere. There was nowhere for it to go. It was a horrible sensation, as if the world had shrunk down to this cell and no more. Like we were all that was left of everything.

I felt so scared and lonely I huddled down against Sionnach's inert body, fingering his throat desperately. Yes. A pulse. Blood in his veins and a heart beating. A little pathetically, I lay down and put my arms around him, willing him to wake. Like I was a small animal and he was my mother. Well. That was pretty close.

'Rowanwood.'

I thought I was hearing things. His voice was very hoarse and dull, but it was for real. I whispered, 'Sionnach?'

No response. Unconscious again, but he was alive. I cuddled against his back, slipped my hand under his shirt and touched his belly very tentatively. I was afraid of feeling my hand sink in his guts again, the hot slippery blood leaking where it shouldn't.

The instinct had taken over again, or he'd be dead. I still barely knew what I'd done, but I must have done it right. The scars were thickly raised and they'd be ugly, but to my fingertips they felt clean. No swelling, no heat. Well, of course not. That wasn't a problem. Everything else was, maybe, but not infection. He'd die of something soon, but not that. Me too. But not of infection. I rubbed my eyes with the heel of my hand.

Sionnach stirred again, a few times, but it felt like hours before he woke properly. I was so glad I could have cried, but I hugged him tighter instead.

'Easy,' he gasped.

'Sorry. Oh, Sionnach. Sorry.'

I let him go and sat up, then knelt over him. His hand grasped mine, and I pulled him upright as gently as I could.

~ *What are you apologizing for? Thanks.*

~ *It's okay. Oh, I'm so glad you're okay.*

~ *I'm fine. I'm still going to bloody kill you.*

I laughed unsteadily. His arm went round me and we leaned together against the wall.

'You said something earlier.' I licked my lips. '*Rowanwood.*'

'Oh, that. The cell. Lined with rowanwood. It blocks you.' ~ *Can't get your mind past rowan.*

'Oh.'

We sat in silence for what might have been an hour. Or five minutes.

'How long have we been here?' he asked.

'Four days? Maybe five? I think, anyway. Going by the meals. There's no light except when they put the food in.'

'Four days? I was a mess, eh?'

'Yeah. You were.' My voice shook. 'You hungry?'

He laughed quietly. 'Yeah. We recover . . .'

'Fast. I know. You guys still make my head spin, honest. There's bread left. Dried meat. Some water. Here.' I crawled across the floor and fumbled for it, desperate not to knock over the jug, not when I'd rationed it so carefully. Sionnach's hands found mine in the dark and he took the jug from me. I heard him gulp it, desperately.

'Take it easy,' I whispered. 'There isn't that much.'

He stopped, put it down. 'You're thirsty, Hannah.'

'I'm okay,' I lied, and put some bread into his hand. 'The food's crap, by the way. I'm kind of glad I can't see it.'

He gave a dry laugh. 'It'll do.'

They must have been watching and waiting. Sionnach had only just swallowed his last bite of bread when I heard a plank of wood slide sideways, and a single strip of light appeared at the top of the cell. Even that hurt my eyes. When I'd blinked away the dazzle, I could see that the ceiling was panelled with rowan, too.

I smiled at Sionnach, and he squeezed my hand.

The door swung open, and two guards came in, flanking Kate.

I didn't remember her being so beautiful. She was astonishing, I've got to admit. She wore amber silk that turned her eyes to gold, and spike-heeled boots I'd have killed for, if the sight of them on her hadn't put me off. How did her skin get that glow underground? She was like a patch of sunlight. I looked at the boots again. They had a distinctive red-lacquered sole, and I thought, *I know that look, it's a trademark.* There stands a woman, I realised, who goes over the Veil a lot more than any of us suspected. In my mind's eye I saw Lauren, all alone and all vulnerable to her, and my heart turned over with remorse, and with a sudden recognition of my own stupidity.

Sionnach had moved slightly in front of me, but Kate simply gestured to one of the guards, who shoved him aside. He winced with pain, and suddenly Kate didn't look so warm and beautiful after all.

Tilting her head, she stood right in front of me.

'You have such pretty hair,' she murmured.

'Thanks,' said Sionnach, earning a blow from the guard.

Ignoring him, Kate trickled my hair through her fingers. I tried not to shudder, not to jerk away. But she knew I wanted to. Her lovely mouth curved in a broad smile.

'Pretty hair,' she said again, 'though that's to be expected. A little faded, of course. That happens with the dilution. Bad blood, bad full-mortal genes. But yes, for a fifth generation mongrel you're not unattractive.'

What the hell? Second generation, I was second generation. I hunted for Sionnach, caught his bewildered eyes.

'I dunno what you're on about,' I snapped. But an icy trickle of fear was creeping down my spine.

'Dear me. I'd have expected more intelligence, but perhaps that suffers from the dilution too.'

I wanted to say something really cheeky. I wanted to be cool and hard. I wanted to say *You don't scare me.* Fat chance. I was so very scared, and I didn't want to ask why. And I didn't want to test what the guard might do to Sionnach.

I also wanted her to leave before she said anything else. Because I could feel it coming. Whatever it was.

'You don't block so well as your cousin. Shame on you, child!

Not enough practice, I think. Your mother was a natural too—never knew it, of course—but that child Lauren has real talent. She didn't need a lot of help from me. All I had to do was create a space in her mind, then come back later and inhabit it. And then, when I asked her to block, you'd think she'd been doing it for centuries.' Kate tutted. 'You should have learned the same tricks.'

I wanted to say *I don't do tricks*. But I was too afraid.

'Sit down, dear.'

'No, I—'

'Sit *down*.' Kate didn't even gesture to the guard, she put her delicate hand on my shoulder and shoved, and my knees buckled underneath me. I grunted with shock. Kate sat down and put a slender arm round me.

'You are easily as talented as your cousin, and you're stronger. Gods, a turban fooled that girl; She saw me suck out her dying father's soul and she still didn't recognise her new therapist. Well. I assure you you're better than that, and I can help you develop. What do you say?'

I could only gape at her.

'Join me. You owe it to me. You have no idea of your potential!' She beamed with something like pride. 'Your uncle's cause is lost and your father is dead. Choose the winning side, Hannah! Now, here's a sign of my good faith: I'm not going to tinker with your mind, the way I did with Lauren's. Partly because you're strong and it would be such a terrible shame to break you—' she laid a finger against my lips to still my protest '—but mostly because I want you to come to me willingly. *Lovingly*. I want you to come to me out of love and loyalty, Hannah, and I *think* I have a right to expect that.'

I could barely get the words out, but this time it wasn't just fear, it was goggle-eyed disbelief. 'I don't owe you either of those things! I *hate you*.'

'You *do*. You have a duty of love to me, and I to you.' Kate tapped her cheek coquettishly. 'I want to be able to spoil you. It's my privilege! And I'd so like to spoil you in a *good* way.'

Sionnach was staring at me, then at her. I didn't want to see the look in his eyes.

'Stop,' I said. 'Stop.' I had no idea if I was talking to him or to Kate. And then, because I simply couldn't stop myself, I said, 'What privilege?'

'A great-great-grandmother's privilege, dear.'

In the leaden silence Kate leaned over me, cupping my face in her hands and tilting it to her. She studied me for long, adoring moments, and then she kissed me. She tasted like the sweetest poison.

'There, dear,' she said. Her fingers caressed my face, spreading their gentle coolness across my skin. 'I knew the Bloodstone would be a human child. I *always* knew that. Gods, I was so far ahead of Leonora she wasn't even tasting my dust. So I went to all that trouble. To the otherworld, and a suitable mate! Your great-great-grandfather Thomas was adorable. Stupid, but adorable.'

I couldn't swallow, couldn't speak. I could still taste her.

'You've the bloodline of witches, the strongest ones of all the Sithe world. Accept it!'

'No,' I whispered.

There was no shutting her up. 'Oh, it should have been you! *My* descendant with *my* blood! And a father like Cù Chaorach! You should have been the Bloodstone, Hannah. *You.*'

'No,' I said, pointlessly. Honestly, could I not come up with another word? Something obscene enough to melt her on the spot, like rain in Oz?

'There.' She clasped her hands in her lap, smiling. 'I know you'll have to let it sink in.'

That wasn't all that was sinking in. 'Aunt Sheena. Shania. They were—'

'Mine too. Yes, yes. And I *do* regret that, from the bottom of my heart, Hannah. But you were the one I truly wanted.' Her beautiful face was alive with eagerness. 'You should be proud of that! I had to sacrifice those two, my own bastard full-mortal children, so that I might finally have *you*. Do you see?'

'Not me,' I croaked. 'Rory.'

She wiggled her fingers. 'Yes, yes. Him, of course. That goes without saying. But you—you are my bonus prize, and what a prize you are!'

'I'm not your bloody bonus,' I said.

'Well. There's something else you might like to consider, Hannah.' She folded her hands in her lap again; her eyes were bright and happy. 'I'm not a sentimental person, but what sentiment there is in me, you appeal to it. You weren't kind to my friend Alasdair last time you met, were you?'

'Who, the psycho?'

'Hannah, let me tell you something. Fond as I am of Alasdair—and that's very fond, since he's so loyal—I can admit that he's not a very nice man. I'd like to protect you from his *extremely* high dudgeon regarding the loss of his eye.'

'He was about to cut Seth's tongue out,' I cried.

'Yes, because I told you, he's loyal. And I was upset when I thought him dead, my dear. I'd go so far as to call it grief. If it hadn't been for Raib MacRothe nursing him back to health, keeping him hidden and protected for a whole year, I might never have seen him again. Hannah, he has many fine qualities. I'd like you two to be friends. And I'd very much like for him not to kill you.'

My jaw felt loose. I mumbled something and I'm not even sure what it was. I thought: he's going to kill them anyway. They're all going to die, all my friends, and I love them but I don't want to die with them. I especially don't want to die of Alasdair Kilrevin. I didn't even want to imagine what it would be like to die of his pique and his *dudgeon*, and I had a choice now that I'd never expected to have.

And I was a coward.

And I wanted to live.

And I wanted, really wanted, to live to know what I was capable of doing.

And she was looking at me with actual warmth and affection.

Sionnach wasn't. But there was something in his expression that wasn't just regret: something kind, something that understood me. As I stared into his grey eyes, I saw the skin around them crinkle with an almost-smile, and he gave me a barely-perceptible nod. He glanced sidelong at Kate, then back at me.

~ *It's all right, Hannah. She's right.*

'Sionnach,' I said through tears.

~ *Do it, Currac. Live.*

Kate had heard him. Her face lightened, and suddenly she giggled, like a favourite conspiratorial aunt. 'I'm your mother in all but full-mortal generation. Join me, Currac-sagairt! Find your destiny!'

'You tried to kill me,' I whispered.

'Oh. Darach?' Kate sniffed. 'Poor girl. She wanted approval and a captaincy, and she rather . . . shall we say . . . exceeded her remit. If Sionnach hadn't stuck her like a pig, I'd have had someone else do it. It's why I absolutely insisted that Alasdair left Lauren alive; I wasn't having anyone else make that mistake. If anyone's to decide my family members will die, it'll be me, not some *employee*.'

I shook my head. I wasn't denying anything, I was just trying to get my head straight.

'There. I want you with me, Hannah! Come back to your true family!' She held out her arms for my embrace.

I managed to stagger upright. I stared down at her. And this time, I picked the right word. This time, I truly meant it.

'No.'

Kate's face fell. When I say *fell,* I really mean it froze, turned to a death-mask carved out of ice. She cocked her head, and watched me. For a long moment of nothingness, I felt her, probing my brain, twisting my soul this way and that to examine it.

'Oh,' she said, and rose elegantly to her feet. She spread her hands in a gesture of acceptance. 'Whatever. Pity.'

All I could do was stare. My mind, my past, my self, they were all crumbling and I didn't know what to do about it. If I moved I would die.

'No you won't, dear.' Kate caressed my cheek with the back of her hand; soft and fragile and scented with hazelnuts. She kissed me again, and smiled a loving grandmotherly smile.

'Not yet.'

Jed

Glanadair was right about one thing, Jed thought: Faragaig was a small community. Prosperous, but small. Smug, but snug. The assault was tantamount to a massacre, but Jed cared no more than Seth did. He only had to rattle his blade softly on the bones of a rebel as he passed a dule tree in the darkness, and what was left of his conscience could be soothed.

Glanadair had posted guards, of course; he wasn't stupid, just undermanned. *And he didn't have to be,* mused Jed viciously, as he wrapped an arm round the throat of a sentry and jerked him back onto his blade. *He had twice the fighters, but they're all spiked on gibbets now.*

Even forty fighters would have been enough to take Faragaig without casualties, though Seth had drawn fourteen more to his cause in the last twenty-four hours. And the very destruction of Faragaig, with a tasteless irony, should bring them more supporters. Jed knew that Iolaire knew it, and he knew that was why Iolaire pressed on, silent but for an occasional grunt of murderous effort. Jed saw his lover's blade flash, latticed with blood-streaks, in the shadows on the other side of the street; then Iolaire nodded at him and they moved forward together on parallel paths towards Faragaig's centre.

Faragaig had to be taken, and taken without mercy, and it was the inhabitants' bad luck that they had, in this particular instance, backed the lamer horse. And, of course, that they'd had another horse inhumanely destroyed. The memory of Howedale stirred the anger in his belly again, and Jed was glad of it.

A shape moved at a tight corner as he edged towards it, but when he brought his sword round ready to strike, he recognised the glint of a half-moon on bright blonde hair. 'Orach,' he murmured.

'Where's Seth?' she said softly. 'Have you seen him?'

Iolaire, guarding Jed's back, half-turned and winked at Jed. 'He'll be cutting his bloody way to the hall steps, Orach. You know? Like we agreed?'

Jed grinned at Orach. 'You need to stop worrying. Apart from anything else, Finn's starting to look at you sideways.'

'Oh, shut it.' She gave him a rueful grin, then jerked her head round. 'Listen!'

The place had erupted. Perhaps two streets away, there was the echo and ring of metal, newly raised voices, a scream or two and a hideous vocal gurgling. Lights blinked on across the settlement, and Jed gave a hoot of satisfaction. No more silent, skulking deaths, then. He raced for the central hall, Iolaire and Orach close behind.

A man skidded in front of him as he ran into the square, sliding low and slashing for his belly, and Jed was forced to jump high. He twisted as he fell, and as he swung his blade he felt it bite into flesh. No time to check the man was dead, but Jed was sure enough. He yanked out his blade with effort and turned for the next one.

The melee was close-quarters and rapid and intense. Faragaig had not expected an attack, and their certainty of protection had done them no favours when one came. Morale was almost visibly collapsing every time Jed could take a breath to glance beyond his immediate sword-reach. One by one, blades clattered to the steps outside the hall; and once the surrenders had begun, the chain reaction was swift. Seth ended the fight sweating and bleeding from a cut to his arm, but his wound was one of three, and his clann had suffered no fatalities. The dead of Faragaig obscured the village square.

When Jed's last opponent flung his sword to the ground and he stepped back, Grian was already wiping his blade and sheathing it, and striding swiftly towards Seth.

'Where's Glanadair?' he asked grimly as Grian pushed aside his t-shirt sleeve and set to work. 'Gods, Grian, leave it, it's a scratch.'

Grian sighed, but he didn't release Seth's arm. 'Give me strength,' he muttered.

Braon shoved the village Captain forward; he stumbled, but recovered before he could actually fall at Seth's feet. The man gritted his teeth and spat on the ground.

'Leoghar,' he snarled. 'You call that a defence?'

His lieutenant stepped from among the clustered captives, his mouth tight with fury. 'You were adamant we didn't need one. What with Kate watching over us so benevolently.'

'I didn't tell you to as good as open the frigging gates to Murlainn.'

'Carry on,' murmured Seth. 'Talk amongst yourselves.'

Sorcha and Fearna were flinging together a pile of captured blades in the square; Leoghar barged forward, snatching his own sword from the pile. Lifting an eyebrow, Sorcha kicked a stray dagger onto the heap and reached up to her own scabbard, but Leoghar ignored her. Formally he marched up to Seth, went down stiffly on one knee and offered him the hilt. The blade, Jed noticed, was cutting Leoghar's palm, but then the man was clearly seething.

'Yours, Murlainn,' he gritted. 'I've had enough of this shit.'

'You fucking turncoat,' shouted Glanadair. 'This is a peaceful community and Murlainn's a murdering bandit!'

A few of Leoghar's men shot Glanadair looks of distaste, and some of them were already gathering supportively behind their immediate commander. *Bloody hell,* thought Jed. *So much for loyalty. But it's not as if we can't use the fighters.*

Seth took hold of Leoghar's sword hilt and presented it back to him. 'Ask my healer to fix your hand,' he muttered. 'And watch your sodding temper.' He turned to Glanadair. 'Want to change your mind?'

'And follow a man who'd loot and murder a village the size of Faragaig?' Glanadair spat again.

'Oh, you're small.' Seth tilted his head to examine the Captain's face. 'You could've been bigger. You could've had a useful ally down the road. Pity you let Howedale burn.'

'Howedale made their choice,' growled Glanadair. 'Kate never threatened us. They asked for war and they got it. And I have responsibilities. So long as the Lammyr were at Howedale, they weren't here.'

'But I'm here now,' said Seth. 'And you don't have responsibilities any more.'

Glanadair's face went shades of red and white. 'You have no right,' he yelled.

'Conqueror's rights,' said Seth, shrugging. He glanced up at the subdued ranks of non-fighters gathered at the edge of the square. Nobody seemed especially keen to support Glanadair.

'Murdering bandit's rights,' snarled Glanadair. And spat again, this time hitting Seth's foot.

'Did your mother never tell you that was unhygienic?' Seth wiped the toe of his boot on the back of his calf. 'Gods' sake, somebody gag this bugger.'

Wiping his sword blade, Jed watched from the corner of his

eye as Seth turned and walked away. Jed didn't like the speed of his stride. Seth, he thought, was angrier than he ought to be in the wake of a fast successful raid and the recruitment of another fifteen-odd fighters; not to mention the acquisition of enough horses and weapons. *Finally.* Yet with all that, and a cathartic bloodletting to avenge Howedale, still an aura of frustrated savagery seeped off the man. Seth yelled to two of his fighters to summon them, and Diorras and Oscarach leaped to their feet as if newly afraid of him.

'And bring whoever's in charge of the armoury,' he barked.

After a moment's heavy silence, while the villagers looked uncertainly at one another, a shaven-headed man pushed truculently out of the crowd. Jed got to his feet, and followed. Jed knew where the Faragaig armoury was located, in a barred stronghold behind the village hall, and Seth was heading straight for its ironbound door. He tested the strength of it, then stood back and watched while the armourer wrangled the three locks.

Seth watched him the whole time, but the man didn't resist and he didn't demur. When he'd freed the locks he stepped back and made an elaborate gesture of invitation. 'Help yourself, Murlainn,' he grunted.

Diorras and Oscarach stepped forward, but Seth put out a hand to hold them back, and edged into the armoury himself. Jed sidestepped between the two men, who shot him a questioning glance, but he shook his head and went to Seth's side.

The air within was steel-cold and speckled with dust, and slanted moonlight hatched the tiled floor through a high barred window. Darkness pooled in the corners and behind racks of swords and longbows. Jed's palm prickled.

'Seth.'

His warning was too low and too late. A human figure flew

from the space between two racks, a shard of metal glinting lethally in its fist. The short blade made an arc of light as it swung for Seth's neck, and if he hadn't doubled himself backwards his head would have been clunking on the floor. Crashing forward with the impetus of the attack and the unexpected evasion, the attacker stumbled and twisted on the tiles, swiftly leaping back to his feet.

Jed shoved Seth back as the blade swung for him again; Seth rolled with the shove but crouched and sprang upright, his own sword in his hand. Catching another movement in his peripheral vision, Jed took a wild guess and slammed back his fist. A grunt of pain, and the attacker slammed back hard to the tiles. An agonised wheeze betrayed that he was winded.

Jed felt Seth grab his arm and drag him out of the way; then Seth was on top of the oddly small figure, slamming his fist twice into its face before rising to give it a breath-stealing kick in the ribs. He grabbed the figure's collar and drew back his blade.

'Seth!' yelled Jed, grabbing both his shoulders. 'Seth, it's a kid.'

The small figure sucked in air at last, wriggled desperately loose and cat-crawled sideways. Seth seized it by the hair, hauled it upright, slammed his boot into the small of its back. It smashed forward into one of the sword racks, and this time it lay stunned, fingers twitching hopelessly for safety. With a snarl of fury Seth flipped his sword in his fist and raised it to stab downwards.

Jed flung himself forward, knocking him off balance. 'Did you hear me? It's a child!'

'It's a bloody assassin.' Seth's words hissed through clenched teeth. His blade lunged forward again. Jed intercepted Seth's arm with a jab of his elbow, just enough to deflect it through the sleeve of the boy's shirt.

'*It's* defending its own frigging armoury! Are you mad?' Jed seized a handful of Seth's hair and dragged his head back, forcing the man to look into his eyes. 'Kill it and I'll pulp your face, *Captain.*'

Rasping breaths were the only sound in the echoing space, until the boy gave a trembling sob that he choked off mid-gasp. Seth jerked out of Jed's grip and turned to look at the cowering child, confusion etched on his face.

He dropped his sword with a clatter and swore.

Panting, Jed straightened.

The armourer was drawing back into the moonlit rectangle of the doorway, his mouth tight with frustration; but he'd forgotten Seth's other two fighters. Diorras and Oscarach seized an arm each and held him while Jed stepped over the shivering boy on the floor. Snapping his sword back into its scabbard, he drew his dagger.

'This,' he said pleasantly, 'is for getting an infant to fight your battles.' He jammed his blade between two of the man's ribs. The armourer sagged at the knees, his mouth gaping. When dark blood spilled from his mouth and his weight went dead, the fighters let him collapse.

'Jed,' said Seth quietly. 'Cuilean. Come with me. Now.'

'You are pathetic,' murmured Seth. 'How many times are you willing to do this?'

There was a distinct bite to the wind that moaned across the moorland in the greying dawn. A lemon-gold aura glowed behind the mountain to the east, outlining an ominous silhouette like a hunched ogre hoisting itself above the horizon. You could see where the fairytales came from, thought Jed. He half expected red eyes to blink and open, for the mountain to rise to its feet and crush them with a gigantic arm.

'I thought you were some kind of vicious predator,' Seth added. 'And look at you.'

The black wolf cocked his head, grinned, and dropped the stick at Seth's feet. Panting, he gazed up at him with limitless optimism.

Sighing, Seth crouched to pick up the birch twig and launched it into the breeze. It flew far downhill and Branndair bounded after it, elated.

Seth stuck his hands in his pockets and stared bleakly seawards. 'Sorry about that business back there.'

'Nah,' said Jed. 'Makes a nice change. Me having to rein you in.'

'I nearly killed him.' Seth looked sick.

'He nearly killed you.' Jed nudged him cheerfully.

'I'd have been on a level with Glanadair. I'd have had to give up and crawl home and drink myself to death like Leoghar suggested.' Seth licked his dry lips.

'Give over. Not without Sionnach and Hannah, you wouldn't.'

'Maybe I should just get them and go home. Maybe I'm not fit to fight Kate.'

'Like how can you do one and not the other?' Jed lifted a shoulder. 'She's the one who asked for this. We don't have a choice, Murlainn. She's the one who forced us back here.'

'Yeah. Finally. Some of them hate us, you know. They hate us for staying away so long and I think they hate us even more for coming back.'

'So what?' said Jed lightly. 'I'm not that keen on a lot of them myself.'

'Thing is,' said Seth, 'I understand Glanadair's choice. I understand why he did what he did. Maybe I'd have done the same.'

'Take it from me: not in a million years.'

'I said I understood him.' Seth gave him a rueful smile. 'I didn't say I forgave him. Branndair, for gods' sake, can't you just kill that twig and be done with it?'

The wolf's tail thumped. Seth took the stick from his jaws and threw it again.

'It's a clever trick that woman's got,' he said, as they watched Branndair wrestle the twig down and disembowel it. 'She can't take your soul without consent. But if she can drain it to next to nothing, you don't care. You'll give the dregs of it up like you were chucking an old wrapper.'

'Seth, my soul's intact, for what it's worth. And I'm a *complete* bastard.'

Seth laughed. 'Yeah, fair point. But I've known bigger ones.'

'Like Glanadair. Give yourself a break, is what I'm saying.'

Seth rubbed his hand across his face. 'I would, but they're watching me. The whole clann, all the time. They know how close I am to the edge and they're worried, and you know what? They don't even trust me any more. You can bet it's got back to them that I nearly gutted an eight-year-old. You can bet Glanadair's grinning right now. If I pull any more stunts like that one tonight, half my clann might leave me.'

'They trust you. I trust you, for heaven's sake.'

'Do you?' Seth lifted a sceptical eyebrow. 'Really?'

Jed's anger came out in a choked scream. 'Listen to me, you pigheaded fool. If Conal had been our Captain, we'd all have been *dead by last week*. And your precious clann *know it*.'

A muscle jerked in Seth's throat. Words caught in his throat and he swallowed.

Jed threw up his hands. 'Listen. I'll prove I trust you.'

'Yeah? Are we going to do that knife-between-the-fingers thing, like we all do when we're drunk?'

Jed clicked his tongue in exasperation. 'No, we're going to do that thing I don't even do when I'm six feet shy of a straight line and I'm falling-down pissed. That thing where I tell you what I've never told another living soul.'

'Ha. Given that your tongue's as loose as a bishop's morals when you're—oh.' Seth actually paled. 'Wait a minute—'

'Yup. I'm going to tell you what happened between me and Laszlo the day I killed him.'

Seth's double take nearly made Jed laugh aloud. Nearly. 'I didn't actually think—'

'Yeah, you thought I was such a drama queen afterwards and I wouldn't tell anyone, and I made this big deal about it, and you thought I really *was* being overdramatic and I'd forgotten by now.'

Seth chewed his lip guiltily. 'All that. Uh-huh.'

'So you want to know? Because I haven't forgotten, and I still don't want you to know, but I want you to understand that I *know* you'll never use this against me. I'm going to trust you with this, Murlainn, and the only reason I'm doing that is because I *know you won't lose your soul.*'

He realised he was shaking, and his voice had grown furious. He swallowed.

'Murlainn, I know what it's like for you. I feel it, don't I? I'm your blood-brother.'

Branndair was at Seth's heels again, the birch twig jammed absurdly in his jaws, but this time Seth just placed a hand on his head to quieten him. 'Does Iolaire know?'

'He knows what Laszlo said to me. Most of it.' Jed swallowed. 'And he knows I mind-linked with Laszlo.'

Seth stared. 'You did *what?*'

'Right as he died.' Jed shrugged. 'I fell into him and he fell right back.'

Seth had gone ashen. 'How did Iolaire react to that?'

'Not well.' Jed forced half a smile. 'You can imagine. You don't look shocked. Well, you do. But you don't look surprised.'

'Of course I'm not surprised. It happened to me.' Seth laid his palm against Jed's face. 'I told you. I couldn't avoid your bloody mind, not even the first day we met. Iolaire'll understand.'

'Iolaire did. Eventually. But Iolaire doesn't know the half of it.'

Branndair reared up and planted his forepaws on Seth's chest. Seth rubbed the wolf's head, scratched his jaw.

'In that case,' he said slowly, 'are you sure you want to tell me?'

'I'm not going to tell you. I'm going to show you.'

Narrowing his eyes, Seth slanted them disbelievingly at Jed. 'You are?'

Jed tapped his temple. 'You've been in here before. What's one more time?'

Seth's breathing was harsh now. He pushed Branndair down. 'You mean that? No, of course you do. It's not like you'd joke.'

Jed clenched his teeth. *I won't back away, I won't. This is for him.*

All the same, when Seth took a pace forward and seized the back of his skull, he couldn't help his instinctive flinch. It didn't deter Seth. The force of his mind hitting Jed's made him reel backwards and he almost lost his footing. He felt Seth grab him to stop him falling, but suddenly he didn't know which of them was holding the other.

Bayside pines. The smell of salt and sea. A fire.

Jed's brain swung. Seth gasped.

Small houses, roofed in turf. Not old, though: modern. Trailer-park caravans.

Jed clutched Seth's upper arms, gritting his teeth. Felt strong hands grip his own arms.

Wind turbines and a playpark. John MacLeod's belligerent ruddy face. Mila laughing and waving to him. Eyes lingering.

Guitars. Hippy chicks. Beer and the scent of marijuana. A fat moon playing hide-and-seek behind the summer clouds.

Jed winced as Seth lurched deeper into his mind.

Feet pounding over soft pine needles. Laughing, running for the darkness under the climbing frame. A woman's hand in his, tightening. Her pale hair trickling through his fingers. His reflection in her eyes.

Naked limbs. Sweat and quickening breath.

'Holy *shit*.' Seth flung himself free, staggering back from Jed. '*SHIT*.'

Jed clutched the back of his neck, panting, trying to keep his balance.

Seth was rubbing his forehead wildly. Branndair crouched low, ears flat, whimpering as he gazed up at his master.

'Not your memories,' said Seth, breathing hard.

'No. But I kept them.' Jed let his head hang down, wishing the blood would come back to it. 'I'm not sure I had a choice. I don't think I could ever get rid of them.'

'Nils fecking Laszlo.' Seth's eyes were still wide and stunned.

And suddenly Jed was blindsided by regret. *What did I think I was doing? I should never have shown him this. NEVER.* Shame racked him down to the bones. He bit his lip hard, straightened, looked Seth grimly in the eye.

'You see? You see why Skinshanks liked me? See why it thought I had so much promise?'

There was horror etched on Seth's face, and Jed didn't want to see that. 'It knew. The bastard.'

'It knew.' Jed lifted his shoulders, tired beyond imagining. 'So did Laszlo. And I found out.' He gave a desperate laugh. 'But not till the day I killed him. Know what Laszlo's exact words were, the ones I didn't quite tell to Iolaire? *Welcome to my world, son.*'

'He was nothing to you,' said Seth, his voice hard. 'It was Conal who was everything. I can tell you that from experience.'

'There's a lot to biology,' Jed said. 'There's method in genes. And if you don't want me around, I'll understand. I'll get it.

Totally. I'll leave if you want. But I wanted someone to know.' He hesitated, and his voice cracked. 'I wanted *you* to know.'

Seth came so close to him, their faces were almost touching. He put his palm on the back of Jed's skull, watched each eye carefully in turn. 'Don't go. Don't you dare go. I need you more than I ever did.'

'All right.' Jed's heart clenched. 'Since you asked. I won't go, then. And on your own damn-fool faery head be it.'

'Good.' Seth kissed his lips gently. 'The gods know we can't choose our fathers.'

Finn

'Can you sense *anything* off those riders? A mind, a block?'

Seth sounded curious, but not frantic, not overly alarmed. Since that dawn after the raid on Faragaig, when he'd gone off and talked with his blood-brother for hours, there was something calmer about him. It might have been Jed's counsel; it might have been that we were properly armed and equipped at last: we had weapons, more than enough horses, more than thirty new fighters. The odds were shrinking in our favour, but I didn't think that was all it was. It couldn't be, since Kate's troops in her underground fortress were still more than treble our number.

Anyway, I was glad. Seth's mind was not a constant turmoil any more, grating harshly against mine; and even the clann had sensed the change in his mood. They seemed more confident altogether, more relaxed about the prospect of following him, even if it was to bloody defeat. I reckoned they'd begun to trust him again.

'I can't sense anything,' I told him as I cantered the black up alongside the blue roan. 'Not a mind, not a block, nothing. And have you ever heard a voice? They say nothing. They don't call out, not ever. You know what I think? It's witchcraft. Some trick of Kate's to throw us off balance.'

And no Lammyr stalked us. That confused me, but I wasn't

going to object. I felt them sometimes, watching, keeping their distance, but they never came in sight.

We'd raided a couple more settlements, but bloodlessly. We took food and yet more weapons at swordpoint, but we never actually had to use the swords, because the villagers put up token fights or none at all. A couple of times, groups of fighters rode out of the settlements in our wake and quietly joined us. The village Captains would have liked to give us supplies and fighters voluntarily, that's what Fearna thought, but they wouldn't dare. Our threat of violence was as much for the villagers' good as for our convenience. Even then, I doubted it would do them much good if we came back defeated.

By 'came back defeated,' of course, I mean 'never came back at all.'

But that likely prospect didn't haunt me today, with my lover at my side and the sun overhead and my black powerhouse of a water-demon beneath me, its muscles warm and bunched, its eyes sparking green from its long years running wild and unmastered. The blue roan was happy too. It tossed its head, not resisting the bridle so much as proving a point. The two of them were high as predatory birds from bullying the new horses, and having their wicked way with some of the mares.

We rode the pair through the steep green oakwood above our latest camp, Branndair close at the roan's heels, Faramach playing slalom-flight with the oak trunks. When we reached open high ground, we galloped the kelpies till they'd grown marginally less hyperactive and savage.

'Brute,' said Seth fondly, caressing the roan's shoulder, bending his face to its neck. 'I thought you'd eat that poor bloody mare of Grian's.'

'Hah. I didn't like how he was looking at Grian.' I trickled the black's silky mane through my fingers, and aimed a dark look at

Seth. 'And speaking of merciless predators, I'll tell you something that's worrying me. There haven't been any Lammyr.'

'Yet.' He avoided my eye, caught Branndair's yellow one instead, and smiled.

'You've made a deal. With that . . . minister.'

'You knew I had. You knew, Finn. What else could I do?'

'All right. But a deal with Lammyr's never simple. I don't know what you agreed.'

He just shrugged.

'The things you think it's fine to keep from me. So is it a good deal?'

'I don't know.' He sighed, and I took it no further. I didn't want to break his mood.

Silly me.

The horses were calm enough by now to descend the steep hillside at an easy walk, and spare us a couple of broken necks. Beyond the trees the slope was drenched in bluebells. I'm not sure it registered, till I saw the drifts and shoals of them, that the summer was younger on this side. You'd think the sky had too much blue in it, that raw pigment of sky had leaked into dark puddles on the earth. We stayed silent as we rode down through them, leaving the oakwood to the south and east.

'What are we looking for?' I asked after a while.

He gave me a sidelong smile. 'A good place.'

'And what makes a good place?'

He turned away to stare westwards, and the impatient roan scraped the ground with a hoof. Laying a hand on its neck, he took a breath.

'Wild running water,' he said.

.   .   .

It turned out that he knew the place he wanted, and we rode around the perimeter of it. It was a broad stretch of flowering machair, hemmed in, but not too tightly, by cracked grey rocks that lurched out of the turf and ridged the skyline. And yes, there was water. A stream from the craggy northern hillside broadened to a tumbling river, broke into a meandering delta beyond the dunes, and met the sea. Wild water, running water.

Plenty of space for a fight.

'The ground's good,' he said.

'So I see.' I was too angry to say more.

'Finn, give me a break.'

'Yeah,' I said. 'Yeah, I know.'

I reached for his hand, brought it to my lips and kissed it. Then thrust it away quite sharply, and lifted my arm for Faramach. I was still angry, after all.

He grinned. Nodded at the roan, who had angled his black head to give me a supercilious look.

'He wants a run.'

'He's a spoilt brat.' My black nipped fondly at the roan's muzzle.

'But he's lovely really.'

I rolled my eyes.

'Oh, what the heck. I think I want a run too.'

The black and the blue roan plunged down the dunes, furrowing the soft sand. They were already straining at their bits, flinging their heads up, dancing their hindquarters sideways, and when we reached firm sand we let them rip. There was a mile and a half at least of open beach, and the tide was out. All I knew for a while was the salt wind in my ears and nostrils, and the sharp air filling my lungs to bursting, and the limitless strength of the black horse, the deafening reverberation of its hooves.

I was laughing as I reined it in—just—beneath a black sheer rockface. Its massive hooves plunged in dry sand, sending tiny sandstorms flying. My laughter had a hysterical edge of ecstasy, and I leaned forward to embrace that familiar neck. How long had it been since we'd last done this? I didn't care to remember. I didn't care to remember how long he'd run wild without me. It had made him rebellious, and he'd played sillybuggers with me that night when I called him. Well, of course he would. But I'd never been afraid that he wouldn't come to me.

I twisted to jeer at Seth. 'Beat youse! You pair of old ladies.'

The blue roan canted sideways as he dragged it to a halt beside me. Seth's eyes were dark and almost as sinister as the horse's. Faramach was ahead of us all, Branndair several lengths behind and sulking.

'You'll be sorry you said that, Caorann.'

'Hah!' ~ *Make me sorry, Murlainn!*

'You asked for it!' Grinning, he leaned out of the saddle to snatch the black's reins.

I shrieked as his arm went round my waist, dragging me towards the roan. I shouldn't be so happy in the face of war, and the endgame. But just for those moments, I was. I was high on adrenalin, on speed, on love, and on the world where I belonged.

'Finn! FINN!'

My head was spinning. It didn't occur to me that my horse was trying to spin too, thrashing wildly, until Seth finally stopped yelling at me and spoke straight into my mind.

~ *Finn!*

There was desperate shock in his yell as he lost his grip on my waist. The blue roan was bucking and plunging and it was all he could do to stay astride it as he reached hopelessly out for me. Branndair yelped with fear.

~ *FINN!*

'Seth!' I was too shocked to be frightened as the black went back on its hind legs and screamed like a ban-sithe. Reflexively I leaned low on its neck, tightening my grip. It shook its neck and roared, then shot forward across the hard sand like a bolt from a crossbow.

It was going back to the sea.

I knew it like a bolt of electricity to my brain. It was going into the waves, because it had as good as forgotten I was there. It had as good as forgotten *me*. It was going into the sea whatever I did, and it did not know or remember or care that it would kill me.

What? It was wearing its bridle, but I knew that the bridle was going with it, and that if I didn't remove its bridle, so would I. The horse wouldn't break its contract: it would simply take me too.

So why was I suddenly so ambivalent about ripping the damn thing off?

No point trying to get off the horse. I let go of the reins and flung my arms around it, pressing my cheek to its sweat-soaked neck. *'What is it, eachuisge? What's wrong?'*

The shouted words were almost inaudible, flung back into my throat by the speed of the wind, but its black eyes rolled back in its fearsome head, and I saw a spark of recognition there. It scrabbled to a halt, still tossing its head wildly.

'STAY!' I screamed. Suddenly I'd rather go into the waves than lose it.

It froze, its entire body shuddering and jerking.

'No!' The grip of my legs began to fail, and I felt myself slide sideways even as the blue roan galloped foaming to my side. An arm went round me, and I smelt horseflesh and sweat, and leather, and Seth. It was all so real and primeval that my fuddled brain

swayed in my skull, locking it down to sand and rock and the solid earth.

Seth pulled with all his strength and I was in his arms, astride the blue roan in front of him. By that time the black horse was ten metres away, hooves slamming through the shallow waves. It swung its head, fixing me with those black emotionless eyes, but its breath came in fiery snorts, and its scream was a tormented one.

'DON'T GO!' I howled.

It tilted its head so far back on the black muscular neck it looked double-jointed, its jaws open in a scream at the sky.

'Finn!' shouted Seth in my ear. 'The bridle!'

'*What?*'

His voice quietened. 'It can't go if you don't take the bridle off.' He hesitated. 'Not without you.'

Instantly the blue roan stilled, its entire body trembling as it stood foursquare before the black. The black calmed too, almost unnaturally quickly. It did not come towards us but watched me, head lowered, foam dripping from its bit.

'Aw, no,' I moaned.

Seth's arms tightened around me, but I pushed them away. Swinging my leg over the roan's neck I slid to the ground, Seth's fingers around my arm. I hardly knew if he was trying to help me down or trying to hold onto me, and I had the feeling he didn't know either. But as my feet touched the ground, he let me go. Tentatively I took a few steps towards the black.

I reached out a hand, and it put its warm muzzle in my palm. Hot breath jetted out of its nostrils. Shaking, I unbuckled its throatlash and pulled the headstrap over its ears.

The horse lifted its head, black eyes fixed on mine as it opened its jaws and let the silver bit fall into my hand. The bridle fell across my arm, a tangle of leather straps, the bit cold and heavy against my palm. I found I was crying.

'But you're all I've got,' I whispered in its ear. 'You're all I have of him.'

The black horse nuzzled my hair, nibbling with its blunt teeth and giving it a rather sharp tug. Then it lifted its head and whinnied towards the west and the islands. The glare it gave me, as it glanced back, was devoid of all affection.

Behind me I heard a soft thud as Seth dismounted, then his footsteps on the firm sand. In an instant he was beside me, but he was looking at the black horse.

From across the years I remembered something Iolaire once told me: *You know these beasts, Finn. We call ourselves their masters, but they're nobody's servants.* Not since that day, the day Iolaire had said that, had I seen Seth look at a kelpie with that strange minatory kinship, that funny mixture of aggression and humility.

And look how that had ended: with Seth nearly eaten by a rogue. A chill rippled down my spine.

Without looking at me, Seth held out his hand but stayed motionless. Reluctantly, so reluctantly, I passed the bridle into his hand.

He didn't hesitate, but turned on his heel and flung the bridle as he'd flung it before, far into the roiling sea. Then he stepped back.

'Go if you must,' he whispered.

The black horse reared and starfished, screaming with unearthly excitement. My own heart was brimming with that excitement, and the dread of separation. The horse wasn't gone yet. It was turning on its hind legs, yearning back at me. I was half-aware of Faramach dancing in the air above us, watching the scene, uninvolved, transfixed.

I could still go. If I ran to the horse now, threw myself onto its back, I'd go with it and I'd never be parted from it. It was going somewhere I wanted to be, somewhere I'd *always* wanted to be, and there I'd have a happiness I'd only ever dreamed of.

Churchill County

Library

Date: 7/26/2016

Time: 3:58:07 PM

Fines/Fees Owed: $0.00

Total Checked Out: 3

Checked Out

Title: Hades
Barcode: 31427800675768
Due Date: 08/16/2016 23:59:59

Title: The heir
Barcode: 31427800683253
Due Date: 08/16/2016 23:59:59

Title: Icefall
Barcode: 31427800683002
Due Date: 08/16/2016 23:59:59

An ecstatic, heartless happiness that no-one could take from me. *No-one.*

Seth had not moved, and I realised he had barely even breathed. But his mind brushed against mine, tangled achingly inside it, and I knew he wasn't speaking to the horse. He never had been.

~ *It isn't time, but go if you must. I'll follow. But not now.*

I didn't turn. I didn't even glance over my shoulder. But I took a step back, then two. I stretched back my hand, very hesitantly, and felt his fingers lace into mine. I was touching blood and bone and skin and sinew once more, and I closed my eyes and breathed, sliding my fingertips up his wrist to feel the throb of his pulse. I didn't open my eyes again.

I heard the guttural scolding cry of a raven. Through the soles of my feet I felt the hoofbeats of the black horse as they thudded across hard sand, the vibration altering with the distance, then deepening and echoing dully as the kelpie went into the water. I didn't even see it disappear.

~ *Love of my heart,* said Seth into the terrible silence.

I twisted into his arms, my tears damp against the skin of his neck. His pulse jerked unevenly.

'He's gone,' I said bleakly. 'Forever this time.'

~ *You let him go.* Seth stroked my hair, relief and gratitude spilling out of him. ~ *Love of my heart. You let him go.*

I think I might have stared into the ocean, addled with confusion and grief, for hours if I'd had the chance. Seth was calming the roan, or at least pretending to; he rubbed its nose and spoke to it softly, letting me walk to the water's edge and try to understand why the black had left me. Left me *now,* of all times. I hated it for that, and I loved it, and I missed it already like a chunk of my heart.

'Why hate it?' crooned a thin mocking voice. 'It would have taken you, after all. It's hardly the animal's fault if your heart's onshore. Locked down in dullsville.'

I lifted my head and stared. Only a few feet away from me the lanky thing stood, skeletal hands in its coat pockets, a flat tweed cap tilted rakishly over one hairless brow. It stirred the sand coyly with bare webbed toes. The coat hung open to show ribs and cratered skin, and a belt of elaborately curved blades.

I gave a cry of disgust and drew one of my own daggers. The Lammyr didn't move, and I'd have let the blade fly into its heart if a hand hadn't closed round my arm, stopping me.

'No, Finn.'

I swung round in disbelief. 'Seth!'

'No,' he said, and looked from me to the Lammyr, and back to me. He nodded at the thing, and watched its yellow teeth grin wider.

'Leave it, Finn,' he said. 'It's time.'

I don't like to describe Grian's face when we rode back into the camp, two of us on the roan and a Lammyr walking nonchalantly at its side. Branndair hung back fifty yards; he seemed incapable of lowering his hackles. Faramach rode on his back again, pecking at them, but Branndair couldn't even spare enough aggression to shake him off.

One by one the clann were rising to their feet, reaching for weapons, some of them simply gaping. The newer recruits didn't seem so fazed. They raised a few eyebrows, exchanged glances, but maybe under Kate's reign they were too used to Sithe and Lammyr acting as one.

Seth didn't dismount till he was right in the centre of the crowd. That meant the Lammyr could walk protected at his flank, bestowing its eerie grin on fighters whose fingers visibly itched on their sword hilts. When the blue roan stopped before Grian, Seth slid from its back and faced the seething healer. I jumped down behind him. The silence was ghastly.

'I can't fight on two fronts,' said Seth.

Fearna stood sharpening his longsword, watching him. Braon and Sorcha exchanged an unreadable glance. Iolaire and Jed leaned against one another, shoulder to shoulder. Jed wore a slight smile. 'You don't want a war on two fronts,' said Grian through his teeth, 'though you've always known you'd have to have one.'

'Obviously.'

'And this means you'll do a deal with *Lammyr?*'

I moved a little closer to Seth, keeping my eyes on Grian. Seth lifted a shoulder, very slightly. 'I don't expect any of you to like it. But hear me out.'

Sorcha snorted.

'I don't like *this.*' Grian pointed at the Lammyr as if he wanted to shove a finger right through its pallid eye.

'Grian,' said Seth wearily. 'It's not like I have a choice.'

'Oh. Dear me. May I say something?' The Lammyr removed its cap and patted down its strands of lank hair. 'Because I think this conversation is going to go in ever-decreasing circles.'

It smiled amiably at Seth and Grian. Neither of them said anything. Too busy glaring at each other.

'Well, then. Here's the thing. None of you have the faintest clue what you're dealing with.' It wagged a bony finger. 'And I never read that one in the rules of war. Y'know: *Make sure you have no idea what your enemy's up to.*'

That drew Grian's attention as well as Seth's. 'So,' said Grian coldly, 'explain it. Not that I have to believe a word that comes out of your foul mouth.'

'Do you mind if I sit down?'

'Yes,' said Grian and Seth together.

'Have it your way.' It gave them a sulky look. 'I'll tell you what I told Murlainn, back in the otherworld. We've had a small re-think. About this whole war thing.'

Grian wore a sour grimace; he was visibly struggling not to cut its head off. 'Give me a break. Lammyr won't pass up a war. *Ever.*'

'It's complicated,' said the Lammyr brightly. 'I mean, it's not as if there *won't* be war. There's going to be fighting whatever we do. It's not as if you lot need the provocation.'

Behind me, Rory gave a grunt that might have been agree-ment. I glanced back at him, gave him a rueful wink.

'I thought you liked to join in,' growled Fearna. 'Especially when Kate's your Mistress of Ceremonies.'

'Frankly, there are times we just like to watch.' The Lammyr sighed and dusted down its cap, then twisted it again in its fin-gers. 'Let me tell you about Her Loveliness. She doesn't appreci-ate us.'

'My heart just bleeds,' remarked Sorcha.

'I'm sure it will, dear,' it said tartly. Then its face fell mournfully, and it shook its head. 'That woman takes us for granted. Never bothered to renew that ten-year oath she asked for four hundred-odd years ago. That's just *rude.*'

The silence had grown a sudden edge, an expectant one. I could almost feel it physically, the way the atmosphere shifted. Nobody wanted a Lammyr alliance, but if Kate couldn't have one either, it did change the sallow complexion of the thing.

'I mean, *we're* not important. I mean, she's never asked *us* if we want a lovely peaceful otherworld. I mean, *we're* not worth a spe-cial effort, like the Darkfall is.'

The mass inhalation was audible. 'What?' said Seth and Grian as one.

I kept my mouth shut.

'What does she want with the Darkfall?' Sulaire's voice was very small. Because he was often too timid to open his mouth—unless he was channelling Hannibal Lecter in some hotel kitchen, obviously—everybody turned to look at him.

'Good question,' shouted Oscarach from the back.

The Lammyr put its hand to its hollow cheek in astonishment. 'You see, it *amazes* me that you'd go to a war when you don't even know *that*.'

Seth gave a growl of frustration. 'That's what you're doing here, Bonehouse. And I'm getting really tired of the dramatic pauses, by the way.'

'Langfank, if you don't mind,' it told him snippily. 'And she's positively besotted with the Darkfall. It's been an awfully long time since she was besotted with *us*.' It looked downright hurt. 'Oh, she throws us scraps, of course. A village here, a village there. It's the sheer presumption of the woman that gets my goat. If she ruled the otherworld, we'd be under her thumb as much as anyone else, and we'd play only at her pleasure. That's not what Lammyr *do*.' It sounded offended. 'And did she ever ask if we wanted peace in the otherworld? *She* might want love and affection, but it's the last thing we want. What on earth would we do with ourselves?'

Grian spat. 'She doesn't want love. She hasn't got a soul!'

'Don't be silly. You don't need a soul to want the love of millions.' Langfank pouted. 'I don't know what your obsession with these things is. What do you people *want* with a soul? I mean, what's it *for*?'

Grian opened his mouth, then shut it again.

'Kate wants rainbows and unicorns.' The Lammyr spread its hands at the ripple of scoffing laughter. 'She wants unity, she wants world peace, she wants souls that are perfectly happy to be eaten. I'll tell you what she wants.' Its skin tightened over its cheekbones, and two spots darkened to ochre, almost as if it was angry. 'She wants *everything her own way.*'

We all stared at it. It shrugged lightly.

'Gosh, she makes me testy,' it said, and crossed its arms.

'She's got immortality,' I said suddenly. 'But no power.'

The Lammyr clapped its hands in delight. It even did a little dance. 'Yes! Aren't you the clever witch.' It turned on the others. 'Don't you numbskulls get it? She doesn't want to be *queen* of the otherworld. She wants to be a *god.*'

Well, that shut everyone up.

'And if the Lammyr have no use for peace,' added Langfank, pleased with the reaction, 'we have even less for gods.' It gave a little shiver.

'Her clann.' Seth cleared his throat and tried again. 'Do her clann know about this?'

'Not yet they don't. Some of them are starting to have their suspicions, but really, who believes what they don't want to know? They wouldn't want some jumped-up new god any more than the Lammyr do, but once she's got her way and she has the otherworld, it won't be up to them. The Darkfall will see to that. I mean, it's not as if she'll tolerate free will.' It inspected its fingernails. 'Free will is an awfully big threat to anyone's immortality. That's why most gods don't like it. They might *pretend* they do, but just you try exercising your free will in front of a god. Go on and see where they'll put you.'

The clouds seemed to have thickened overhead, and somehow they looked lower, sketched with charcoal. I shivered.

'So all we have to do is tell her clann,' Sulaire said hopefully.

'You think they'd take our word for it?' said Seth. 'I'm not sure *I* believe it.'

'Oh, suit yourself,' said the Lammyr.

Seth gazed at it glumly.

'I don't care,' said Grian at last. 'Kate can take her bloody god-head. I won't be around to see it. I'm still not fighting alongside any Lammyr.'

'I thought you'd say that.' Seth sighed, and his eyes met the Lammyr's. 'Plan B, then.'

'All right!' Braon jumped forward happily, her sword raised.

'Not that Plan B.' Seth smacked the blade aside, rolling his eyes. 'Plan B, the new oath.'

I cleared my throat nervously. 'Oath?'

'Yup,' said the Lammyr. 'New oath. No problem. To you this time. And we'll sit this one out. How about it?'

Grian seemed dumbfounded, finally. He cracked his fingers. Stretched his arms. Let them fall back to his sides. 'Well, that sounds fine to me. Straightforward. Yes?'

'It can be,' said Langfank. 'But oaths need ceremonies.'

'I assure you they don't,' I muttered, thinking of my mother after brutal widowhood and two whiskies. One rash oath straight out of her mouth and it bound her for life, and me for quite a lot of it.

'They do for us, witchy-girl,' said the Lammyr petulantly. 'We need a ceremony or we won't play.' It grinned suddenly. 'Or rather, we *will* play. And you won't like that.'

'So what is it?' Jed spoke for the first time. His gaze was very steady on the Lammyr. 'What's the ceremony?'

Seth coughed, and everyone turned to him.

'They want a challenge.' He avoided my eye. 'A one-on-one. Single combat. Y'know.'

I felt as if he'd punched me. I had to take a breath and steady my heart. 'I see.'

'Not you, Murlainn,' said Braon. 'That'd be stupid.' She turned to the Lammyr. 'Not Murlainn!'

'Yes Murlainn.' The Lammyr folded its arms. 'Deal or no deal?'

'This is insane,' snapped Grian.

'It's *perfectly* sane. He's your leader.'

'*Quite,*' barked Fearna.

There were a lot of opinions being expressed now, though with the racket, none of them were intelligible.

'I'm not going to get killed by one bloody Lammyr!' Seth snapped them into silence, exasperated.

'Look, it's simple,' said Langfank patiently. 'We fight. To the death, obviously; I mean, where would the fun be otherwise? And then the winner has to kill one of his own kind in cold blood to seal the oath, and boom! Sorted!'

'You little bastard,' said Jed, studying Langfank with interest.

'Oh come *on.*' It raised its eyes heavenward. 'I'm a *Lammyr.*'

'That's enough.' Seth shoved the Lammyr aside. 'That's the deal, that's what it offered me in my own bloody office over my own sodding *coffee.* And when the fighting with Kate's done, we get our own dun back, right? The Lammyr leave peacefully.'

'Which is why we never had to fight for it,' said Grian sourly.

'Damn right. I need your agreement, though. All of you!' At last he managed to look at me again. 'But I *cannot fight on two fronts.*'

Jed stood up. He turned a slow circle, studying the whole clann. 'What kind of a captain do you think Murlainn is?' His soft voice carried amazingly clearly. 'One Lammyr. *One.* I'll say it again. *Lammyr.* How can you trust him so little?'

A few of the clann still looked doubtful, but most fidgeted, embarrassed.

'I like you, Cuilean!' Langfank clapped its hands in delight. 'You think straight, you do.'

'Shut up,' said Jed. 'That really doesn't work any more.'

'But it's *true!* I like you so much I let your little brother go. Four years ago!' It looked brightly at Rory. 'Remember? Beside the watergate? I could have bitten your throat out, *and* your girl-friend's, but I jolly well didn't!"

Rory swallowed so hard I saw his throat jerk. 'That was you?'

'We don't change our minds in twenty-four hours, you know. We've been thinking this over for a *while*. That was a sort of to-ken, you know? A goodwill gesture!'

'I believe that,' said Jed, picking idly at a fingernail. 'And I be-lieve it'll stick to a deal. And I believe it'll die in single combat.'

'But, Cuilean . . .' began Orach.

'To be honest,' said Fearna, darting embarrassed glances to his left and right, 'it makes sense to me.'

The clann were edging into excitement now, and anticipation, and the hope of a new and better war footing. Shrugs, glances, optimistic murmurs were exchanged.

'You won't have to fight two forces, Murlainn.' Jed sheathed his blade, stretched idly. 'And we won't lose our Captain. It'll work out, I can feel it in my bones. And my bones are *extremely* trust-worthy.'

Hell, even I was almost convinced by Jed's confidence. And why not?

It was just as Seth told us: he hadn't a choice. And things could hardly look bleaker than they did.

And so I never did get time to mourn the black kelpie. I couldn't afford to mourn it anyway; I had time only to feel terror for Seth. The Lammyr's timing was good in that respect.

One Lammyr. One Lammyr. I repeated Jed's words to myself all that last evening, like a mantra. It was quite soothing.

Seth seemed to regret the loss of the kelpie more than I did, but that was fair enough, because the black was a terrible loss to a fighting unit. But I wouldn't let myself miss it. I was still angry at its capricious desertion. And I kept thinking that we'd already lost more than a horse, that there was every chance we'd lose more lives and likely our own.

Of course, Seth and I had a fight about it. Only a short one: it wasn't as if we needed the thrill.

'Someone called him, Seth.'

'That's horseshit, Finn, I'm sorry. He just went. They do.'

'No. He was called away. Someone needed him.'

'*You* needed him,' said Seth bitterly. 'Did that make him stay?'

'Someone had a prior claim, Murlainn.'

'Don't start that, Finn. Please. Don't start it.'

So I sighed, and kept my tongue behind my teeth.

None of the fighters spoke about the black, but I knew its loss was a blow to them too. They were even more subdued now, sobered stone-cold by the nearness of a fight. And, I realised, the deal with the Lammyr might shorten the odds in this war, but it had focused everyone's attention that there still were odds, and from our perspective they were hideous.

Orach seemed especially nervous, casting constant anxious glances at Seth, and in the twilight of the clear day I saw them together, his arm round her slender shoulders as they talked. She'd loved him once. He'd loved her back. Conal had wanted them bound to each other but she'd waited in vain and finally lost him to me. It must have been hard for her to contemplate his death without being the lover who'd guard his back or die with him; I felt for her, and was glad the duty was mine. They probably remained in a love of sorts. I knew the clann saw it and I knew they gossiped, but that didn't bother me. It made me smile. She knew and I knew she wasn't a threat.

When Seth released her and walked away, I went across, let my fingers touch hers.

~ *He'll be fine*, I said. ~ *He always is.*

~ *Course he will.*

~ *If I can't watch him, Orach. If I can't protect his back when we get to Kate's—*

~ *Don't even ask.* She nudged me fondly. ~ *Of course I'll watch him for you.*

'Lay*deez!*' Jed was in a particularly hyper mood. He'd actually been whistling. 'You'd better not be fretting your petticoats over our hero. You'll only put him off tomorrow if you start throwing your knickers at the stage.'

We both chucked clods of peat at him, and he laughed, batting them away. I couldn't help smiling. When he grinned back at me, my heart twisted. If Seth was still a little in love with Orach, it was no more than I was with Jed. Since we'd come home, it was as if his whole body had been lit from within, as if there was life in his veins again instead of dark sluggish blood. He moved differently. He was fluid and easy, and he belonged in the landscape like a tree or a rock or a pool of water. His happiness seemed to overflow into Iolaire, who laughed more easily than he had in four years.

Jed's surly standby mode, I knew, made his occasional sunniness all the more disarming. It was easy to be infected, and I think he was all that got the clann through that evening and night. He was what Seth needed at that moment; he was what we all needed.

I just really hoped he was right.

Rory

Rory couldn't sleep. Not that he wasn't used to roots and stones digging into his bones, to snatching sleep where and when he could, but every few minutes an image of the captive Hannah flashed in his brain, tormenting him, jerking his eyes wide open. If he drifted close to sleep, it was worse; half-dreams of her came, feeling more real than anything around him, and they weren't happy ones.

Seth said Kate wouldn't hurt her. Rory wasn't so sure; and there was Sionnach. Rory was fighting not to grieve for him yet, fighting to believe he was alive, but if he was alive, Hannah would be protecting him. He lay watching the clouds drift across the moon, and imagined the terrible risks she might take to do it.

'Hey.'

He turned at Jed's soft voice. His brother crouched above him, smiling. Jed had calmed down a little since his manic clowning earlier, and his eyes were calm and sympathetic.

'Can't sleep?'

Sometimes Rory thought he'd always be his brother's child: eight years old forever in Jed's mind. Sometimes that drove him crazy. Sometimes, like now, the comfort of it brought hot tears to his eyes.

Silently Jed held out a hand. Rory took it and let his brother haul him to his feet.

'C'mon,' murmured Jed, releasing his hand. 'Don't wake the others.'

They'd moved camp, closer to that broad expanse of machair where his father wanted them to be at dawn. Rory followed Jed's shape through the small copse of trees, then over a ridge where Orach stood guard, her eyes brilliant as she twitched a hand in acknowledgement. Beyond the ridge the ground fell away into a small gully that ran almost to the sea. Between Rory's bare toes the salt-cropped grass was damp and cool, and the night air was intense with the sea scent of tangle.

When Jed sat down, Rory didn't think twice, but slumped against him the way he used to. Jed started, but Rory felt him smile as his arm went round his shoulders. Strange feeling, when they were nearly the same height, but it was good. They sat for minutes in silence, and then Jed said, 'I'm sorry. About Hannah.'

'Not your fault.'

'No. But I'm sorry.' Jed hesitated, awkward for the first time. 'About everything.'

Swiftly Rory kissed Jed's cropped scalp. 'Not your fault either.'

'Yes. It was.'

Rory put his arms round Jed and hugged him hard.

'I'll never go back to the otherworld,' said Jed quietly. 'Never.'

'No. But none of us will, I don't think.'

'You're in danger. I wish you'd stayed home.'

'You know fine I couldn't do that.'

Jed gave a low laugh as Rory pulled away. 'Yeah. I know. But I thought I'd better throw some kind of a hissy-fit.'

'Jeez. You're so *maternal*.'

Jed laughed again, shaking his head. 'Somebody had to be, motherless brat.' He sobered. 'I'm sorry about that, too.'

'Stop being sorry about things that weren't your fault.' Rory head-butted his shoulder. 'I'm glad you're happy. What a pain in the arse you've been.'

'*Insolent* brat.' Jed squeezed his shoulders a little too hard.

'Speaking of Mum. Will you be okay seeing the Lammyr?'

'I'll be absolutely peachy seeing the Lammyr,' said Jed grimly.

'Jed . . .'

'Shush, it's okay. Joke.'

For long moments there was only the lonely cry of a night bird, and the whisper of the river, and the distant thump and hiss of the sea.

'Don't let them wind you up,' Rory blurted.

'Nah. Course not.'

'Because they'll try. Look what—'

'Listen, bruv, I know how their minds work. Mine works the same. Me and Skinshanks and Nils Laszlo: sisters under the skin.'

'Oh, quit doing that!' Rory grabbed Jed's head and shook it. 'You know what you've got in common with Laszlo? Self-fulfilling prophecies, that's what.'

Jed slewed his eyes sideways, and Rory thought for a moment that his face had darkened with pain, but when he looked at him again he was grinning. 'Oh, yeah?'

'Yeah. You believe all that bollocks about yourself, just because a Lammyr wound you up once. You see why I'm worried? Skinshanks would be laughing its head off.'

Jed twisted swiftly and wrestled Rory to the ground. 'Aye. If your barbarian father hadn't cut it off already. And by the way, I do *not* have a Lammyr hangup any more.'

Rory giggled, aiming a few useless punches at Jed's solar plexus. Jed slapped his fists away like mosquitoes, caught his wrists and sat on him till he was squashed into submission.

'Bloody hell, bruv. You're going to have to do better than that.'

Jed bounced on his belly, making him grunt. 'Don't let me catch you picking a fight with a Lammyr.'

'Gerroff.'

'No fighting. Don't get involved with them, whatever happens. Swear on your mother's grave.'

Going limp, Rory stared up at Jed's eyes. They were cold and serious now.

'Okay.'

'Grand!' The mockery was back in Jed's eyes, and he let Rory wriggle up.

'Pig,' said Rory.

Jed squeezed him hard again. 'I love you, runt. Know that?'

'Yeah. Me too.'

'Good. Now shut it. And maybe we'd both better get some sleep.'

'Are we ready, Murlainn?' said Langfank, clapping its dry fingers. 'Are we steady? Are we go?'

It stood in front of a phalanx of fifty or more: Rory had given up counting. At least twice that number watched from outcrops of grey rock, from the hillsides, from the edge of the dunes. The Lammyr murmured happily amongst themselves; Rory wouldn't have been surprised if they were taking bets.

Rory stood by the blue roan as he'd been ordered, his hand on its neck, more afraid than he'd wanted to feel, watching his father walk up to Langfank. Seth looked more corporeal somehow. The Lammyr was so thin, it might have been made of paper: paper made of milled steel, maybe. It couldn't wipe the empty, starving smile off its face, and it sounded a lot less obsequious than it had when it was alone in the middle of a small Sithe army.

'We're all sorted,' said Langfank. He gestured grandly at the dense ranks of Lammyr. 'They're forming a block over the playground. Aren't my friends clever?'

'They'd better be,' said Seth. 'They'd better not squawk.'

'What about yours?' It sniffed. 'I hope you've left your newbies behind. You can never be sure.'

'These are my own clann,' said Seth through his teeth. 'Obviously. Sulaire MacTorc's with the rest. If I was in the otherworld I'd be giving Kate three months' notice, but I'd really rather not do that here.'

'We're all of one mind, Murlainn, we really are! The secrecy's part of the deal. We're here to help!' It clapped its hands. 'So. Down to *your* part. Where's the prisoner? Come on, come on. You know the rules.'

Seth jerked his head, and Braon and Fearna between them dragged forward a wildly kicking, bound figure, dumping him next to Seth and the Lammyr. Faragaig's Captain bit down hard on his gag, mumbling unintelligible curses, but his arms were pinned securely behind his back and Fearna held him down with the tip of his sword on his belly.

'Sorry about this, Glanadair,' Seth told him, 'but it's you or my army. And I never met anyone who asked for it louder.'

Langfank inspected the red glowering face. 'He looks very nice. That'll do grand, Murlainn.'

'This oath is binding,' said Seth, shrugging off his jacket and unbuckling his sword belt. Fearna and Braon were already dragging Glanadair backwards to the edge of the arena. 'Ten years.'

'Not a problem.' It bounced on its heels, brimming with eagerness. 'And don't forget, it's to the death. No sneaky cheaty.'

'Fine. And don't even *think* about reneging once Kate's dead. Or I am.'

It giggled like a rockslip. 'Now, I won't pretend we wouldn't be happy to dance on your corpse, Murlainn. But it's like I said. I've no affection for Kate either.'

'Langfank, you've no affection for anybody.'

It loosened the blades in its belt, patting their edges with a fingertip. 'True. But I confess, Murlainn: on a personal level, I'm still a bit miffed about my brother.'

'A Lammyr's never miffed about death,' said Seth darkly.

'Well, no. But Skinshanks was grand company. I miss his quirky sense of humour.'

'I know you don't have principles,' sighed Seth as he half-drew his sword and examined the edge, 'but just tell me. Do you give a toss about the outcome either way?'

It shrugged bony shoulders. 'No, my dear. We really don't give a damn. Enough of the chat, I say.'

'You're on, then. I—'

'No.' Jed shoved forward.

Seth turned on his heel, exasperated. 'What now?'

Lammyr or Sithe, every one of them stared as Jed walked to Seth's side. He raised his voice so there was no chance of anyone mishearing. 'It's mine, Murlainn. I claim it. Its brother killed my mother and it's mine.'

Rory opened his mouth to shout, but no sound came out. His voice had dried to dust, and for a moment he had no breath. The blue roan nuzzled his neck, blew into his hair. Branndair slunk to his side, and Rory thrust numb fingers into his neck fur.

'Oh!' Langfank brightened, grinning. 'You!'

Seth's irritation had faded to shock. He paled. 'No, Jed.'

'I'm not sure this is quite kosher,' remarked Langfank to its lieutenant. 'Is this acceptable in the rules?'

'No!' barked Seth. 'No, it bloody isn't!'

'It's his blood-brother!' said the lieutenant, clasping its hands in excitement. 'If it's not in the rules it *should* be.'

'Absolutely no way. Out of the question.' Seth clenched his teeth and raised a fist as if he wanted to punch Jed out of the arena.

'Is this all right with you guys?' called Langfank to its assembled Lammyr. The polite and delighted applause seemed to tell it it was.

'Lovely!' called one from the rocks. 'Blood-brother! That's adorable.'

'Perfect!' wheezed another, and had a fit of coughing. Its nearest neighbour patted its back.

'No. I don't accept this,' yelled Seth, grabbing Jed's collar. 'The combat's mine.'

'He claimed it.' Langfank pouted. 'That's your rules, not mine. It's a yes from me!'

'It's a bloody enormous *no* from me.'

'Too late, brother.' Jed slapped Seth's fist off his collar. 'Look, I've claimed it. You know how this works, right? It's a done deal. No get-out clause, so shut your trap.'

'You *bloody* little tosser.'

'Thank you. Shall I get on with it?'

Seth breathed hard, and in the ranks of the Sithe there was expectant silence. Iolaire's head was bent, his eyes shut, his mouth a tight line. There was nothing to be done, thought Rory, feeling nauseous. If Seth carried on this quarrel, no-one would benefit but the Lammyr.

At last his father put his hand against Jed's face.

'Cuilean. Be careful.' He kissed his cheek and stepped back.

'I do like being a Lammyr.' Langfank was shrugging off its coat, fully revealing the dagger at its waist and the belt of hanging blades. Unscabbarded, some had cut its flesh at the waist, and colourless blood had dribbled down to darken its trousers. 'Speed! Strength of purpose! Decent metal, not your shit steel! But the best of it, Cuilean? I don't care which of us wins.'

'Bollocks to that,' said Jed.

'Ahhh!' Langfank grinned. 'My brother liked you. I quite see why.'

'And bollocks to that too.' Jed unbuckled his sword belt, drew his weapon and threw the belt aside. Three curved blades flew from Langfank's fingers, and met his swift deflecting sword, and then he and Langfank collided in a tangle of blade and body.

Rory wanted to shut his eyes and couldn't. The blue roan had its head pressed to his, and he could feel its hot breath on his neck. Branndair stood silent against his legs, and it felt as if the wolf was propping him up. They all seemed small in the huge threatening amphitheatre, watched by that idle circle of Lammyr perched like vultures on the rocks, but Jed looked smallest of all, penned in the inner ring of Sithe and Lammyr. Rory did not want to look at Iolaire. He didn't dare.

Langfank twisted in mid-air, its webbed foot lashing into Jed's belly, but Jed was already snaking his body back, lessening the impact. He grunted, but his blade flashed through Langfank's ear, sending a colourless spray spurting onto the water meadow. Grass where it fell crackled to yellow, but red blood spilt on top of it. Jed fell clumsily back, rasping in furious breaths, crouching. His blade raised in defensive warning, he reached to touch his shoulder blades, brought his hand back wet with blood. There was a long gash of red in his t-shirt, right across his back.

Iolaire gave a groan of fear. Langfank made a petulant face.

'*Tiresome!*' it tutted. 'How did that miss your spinal cord?'

'You're pissing me off,' said Jed through gritted teeth.

He sprang at the Lammyr as it reached to its belt for another blade. Catching its arm, he twisted with it as it tried to writhe out of his grip. For hideous moments they were wrestling in mid-air, feet kicking and hooking, torsos wound together like lovers. Then they crashed to the ground.

Jed shoved Langfank's face sideways hard into the earth, twisted its scrawny arm up, pressed his sword to its throat. It strained to watch him with one eye. Thrashed its legs a couple of times. Gave up, and let the last blade fall from its fingers.

Rory heard Iolaire's pent breath sigh out of him, high-pitched with relief. The other Sithe stirred restlessly, but Seth didn't move.

'A death, please, Cuilean.' Langfank spat out earth and grinned. 'Soon as you please, slow as you like. And may I say how glad I am that it's you!'

Jed said nothing but he hesitated, his blade point pressing into its sinewy throat.

'Because I like you. I really do!'

Something crossed Jed's face, a look of half-forgotten torment. He tightened his grip on the sword hilt, twisted the blade so it broke pale skin.

Langfank gave a tremulous sigh of contentment, closed its eyes, licked papery lips.

'Oh, Cuilean, yes. My brother always liked you, and I do too!'

Jed went rigid, and his face emptied. He twisted, the knuckles of one hand digging into the peat, and his eyes met Seth's.

'For my soul,' he said.

He wiped his sword on the stubbly grass, rose and spat on the ground by the Lammyr's face. Then he turned, and walked away.

'Just you get back here!' Langfank rolled up to a crouch. 'A death! Cuilean!'

'Fuck you,' said Jed, and kept walking.

It snarled.

Rory only saw movement, swift and sleek. Langfank's discarded blade was back in its fingers. Livid, it screamed at Seth.

'Murlainn! There are *rules*, you know!'

'JED,' screamed Seth.

The flight of the blade was too fast to see. Rory only saw Jed jolt forward, his body bowing into a backwards curve, before he slumped to his knees, shock in his eyes. Only when he pitched forward with a sickening sound did Rory see the blade, sunk so deep in his brother's back only one glittering point was still visible.

Seth yelled with pain, clutched at his left hand as if the blade had pierced the scar on it. He recovered and ran, but by then Finn's knives were drawn, flying one after the other at Langfank. It didn't try to dodge, or perhaps didn't have the time or the concentration, too busy watching Jed with a joyful fascination. Finn's knives sank almost as one into its chest, and it swayed sideways. Grabbing the scrawny neck, Seth drew his sword, and plunged it into Langfank's throat. As it fell twitching at his feet, a sigh of rueful elation went round the ranks of the Lammyr, and there was a polite ripple of applause.

'That's half,' called Langfank's lieutenant. 'I'm sorry to interrupt but that's half . . .'

Seth hesitated for less than a second. His teeth clenched, he swung his blade at Glanadair, slicing his throat. He spun round before the spray of blood could even hit him, running for the river, and flung the blade into the shallow water.

Rory was stumbling to his brother, reaching him half a second ahead of Iolaire. Jed's eyes were open, but they were glazed as if with ice.

'Grian!' screamed Iolaire, but the healer was already on his knees at Jed's side, his frantic fingers working at the sunken blade. Frothy blood bubbled from the wound as he tugged at it.

Jed's eyes met Rory's, and he moved his head very slightly sideways. More blood choked from his mouth.

'Heart,' he murmured, and almost smiled. 'My heart, bruv.'

'No,' Rory shouted.

'The blade's barbed,' muttered Grian. *Fuck!*

'Yeah.' Jed coughed blood on Rory's hand. 'Fucked.'

'NO.' On his knees, Iolaire slipped his arms gently beneath Jed's head, cradling it. 'Jed. You wait for me! You bloody wait!'

His body was juddering violently, but he gritted his teeth and tried to smile. 'Iolaire. 'S'better. Really. Think about it.'

'No! Don't you dare!'

'Jed.' Rory stroked his face, kissed it, pressed his forehead to his rough cheek.

'Iolaire, hold *still!*' yelled Grian. 'Tip him. Finn, help, gods almighty. To the side. Left lung's flooding. *Tip him.*'

Rory was only vaguely aware of the people around him. His father. Finn. Grian, panicking now, his fingers digging desperately in Jed's back as the others tilted his body as best they could. But he was really aware only of himself, and Iolaire, and Jed. Leaning close as his brother was tugged onto his side, he heard his grunt of agony, felt a spray of blood on his face as Jed coughed. Rory caressed his face, whispered low. 'Jed.'

The glazed eyes crinkled with pain.

~ *Jed. Please. Now.*

Jed smiled. His lips moved, and though Rory couldn't read them, he heard his answer. With that, the world tilted and pain tore into Rory's back, and he gave a cry that would only come out as a cough, and he felt grass and cold earth, and his head cradled tightly on Iolaire's lap, and the world was receding too fast, and

Long time no see, old girl . . .

the bay mare blew gently on his face, ears flickering. She was not locking him down to reality, not this time. There was nothing doing that. And never would again

Hoofbeats. Hoofbeats?

his eyes were blurred, but he knew that rider. Oh, the irony. Finally he was in a place he belonged, but the hold it had on him was loosening. He wanted to grip it tighter but there wasn't any strength in him. There was no longer a life much worth living . . .

'JED!'

He blinked. Iolaire. Oh, no. Hell no, he didn't want to leave him. He didn't want to leave the others. No. But he didn't have a choice any more. He could feel it.

'Jed, wait.' He could feel Iolaire's hot tears on his face. 'If you won't wait for me, wait for Grian. Give him time.'

'Iolaire.' His fingers gripped Iolaire's shirt till his knuckles were white. At least, he knew that was what his fingers were doing, but he couldn't feel them any more. He frowned in perplexity, then almost laughed. It was so silly. He hadn't expected to get old, anyway, so he hadn't put in any practice at doing it gracefully. Damn, but he'd make a lousy old guy. Iolaire young and beautiful, and him a bad-tempered old fart. *Iolaire, I never wanted you to look at me with pity. I wanted to stay beautiful like you. I wanted to stay beautiful for you.*

No, it really was better this way. He could just about convince himself of that, except that it hurt. Oh, but it really hurt. He wondered how long it was going to last. Not long. Oh, please. *Too long already.*

'Don't go! Stay, Jed!'

arms went round him. Smelling the sleeve of a familiar woollen jumper, he managed a grin

~ *Jed! I found her for you! She's waited. So long. Me too*

he shut his eyes and opened them again, and smiled.

'Mila,' he whispered. 'Mila Cameron.'

Iolaire's fingers were stroking his bloody face. 'Jed Cameron,' he whispered. 'You are my Jed. My Jed Cameron. Please stay with me.'

But I can't. I would, and I want to, but I can't.

Feeling crept back into his heart, a spark of stirring happiness. It was belonging. Being wanted, and missed, and loved.

But mostly belonging.

'Jed! DON'T GO.'

'I love you. I love you.' But he didn't think the words were coming out. He couldn't even see any more, let alone speak.

'Seth Rory Finn.' Tried to suck in more air but it wouldn't go. No place for it to go. *Iolaire oh Iolaire I love you*

But at least it had stopped hurting.

'Rory, NO! *Somebody. Get. Rory. Away.*'

His father's distant scream sliced into his mind and Rory felt a hand on the scruff of his neck: Fearna's hand, yanking him back with a frantic shout. Seth stumbled to Fearna's side and hauled with him. The opposing tug was strong, so strong, but Seth and Fearna, if not stronger, were more desperate. A gaping maw that was bigger than distance opened between Rory and his brother. With a single yelping scream, he was himself again.

Grian released Jed, who rolled onto his back, deadweight, staring at the sky.

~ *The sky, Jed, look at the sky.*

Rory heard someone say it. Who? Finn? He was almost angry. A waste of thought: how could Jed see that? A corpse on the cold ground.

Smearing Jed's face with his bloody hands, Grian drew his eyelids shut, and Iolaire pressed his face to his torn body and wept.

Hannah

'You're an idiot,' said Sionnach, cradling me against his chest. 'Honestly, you're an idiot.'

'I know.' I huddled into him for warmth. The cell was freezing. 'Shit, I could have been a fairy princess by now. And I always wanted—oh no, hang on. I didn't.'

He huffed a laugh. 'That figures. But honestly. You could at least have been a *live* fairy princess.'

'I look terrible in pink. Clashes with my hair.'

'So does blood,' said Kate. 'Take my word for that, dear.'

Sionnach lolled his head to the side and eyed her lazily as she walked in. The door had opened silently and only now did a light flare beyond the cell, so that Kate was fetchingly backlit. She'd done that deliberately, the bitch, to give us a fright. Good luck to her if she thought that was possible any more.

'Hello, your Maj.' Sionnach managed to give three words all the amused contempt in the universe, and I admired him for it even as I wished he would shut his trap and stay alive a bit longer.

'Look a little more cheerful, Sionnach. You'll be seeing your twin again soon.'

'Can I just ask you something, Kate?' His fingers tightened a little more on my shoulder, protective. 'You're going to live forever, right? What in the name of the gods is wrong with doing that here?'

'Live forever here?' She trilled a laugh. 'You've answered your own question, silly boy. I would die of boredom, except that I *can't*.'

Her face was frightening, but he didn't turn away. 'And what about after? When you're in the otherworld. What happens when you're bored with it?'

Her mouth tightened. 'Bridges to cross, dear. And that was quite the most pathetic delaying tactic I've ever witnessed.' She made a sharp gesture towards one of the guards. 'Now. Out.'

He leaned down, grabbed my arm, and yanked me out of Sionnach's arms. I stumbled and he dragged me out of the cell, ignoring Sionnach's snarl and my cry of protest. The other guard stepped past him and hauled Sionnach to his feet.

My guard didn't take me far, though. Just outside the cell door he stopped and swung me to face Kate.

Kate walked calmly round me, then grasped a hank of my hair and tugged it hard. I winced, couldn't help it. She pulled me against her, swung me so my back was to her chest, then twisted my head back and drew a dirk.

I was facing Sionnach, so I saw him try to lunge for me, but his guard whacked a rabbit-punch into his wounded stomach. As Sionnach gasped and staggered to his knees, his arm was twisted up behind him and a blade pressed to his throat.

Don't, Sionnach, I thought desperately. *Don't.*

I heard Kate laugh. The blade tickled my throat, teased my earlobe, then she wrenched her handful of my hair so hard I cried out. I felt the slice of the dirk, the bite of it as it severed my hair at the roots and nicked my scalp. I felt the dampness of blood, too, but I didn't put my hand up to my head. I damn well wouldn't. The blood swelled and began to trickle down behind my ear.

Shoving me away, Kate held up the hank she'd cut. Making a

little face of distaste, she shrugged and separated it into two strands. She reached to her own hair, and with one delicate slice, cut a single lock of her own shining hair. Then she began to braid the strands together.

Backing away, caught by the guard, I watched her fingers, quick and lithe and skilful. I could tell which strands of the braid were mine. Paler. Not so coppery. But the two strands were alike: so terribly alike.

'Oh dear.' Kate eyed the patch of scalp she'd cut. It really hurt now, and I hoped she'd leave soon, in case it hurt worse and I started crying. It was only hair, for God's sake.

'Take the twin: I'll see to him later. Leave the girl till her lover comes. My power. My Bloodstone. My Rory.'

Rory

His heart had fossilized inside him. Rory knew there was something beating in his chest but it was hard and heavy and unyielding. A stone. Was that what the mad old prophet had meant when she told Leonora Shiach what to look for? Had she Seen even this?

In which case, why hadn't she warned them?

Old bitch, he thought coldly. *May you rot. You and Leonora and Kate. My brother is dead, and I can't even cry for him.*

'Rory.' His father sat down beside him on the coarse machair grass.

'Dad.' His voice was perfectly calm. That wasn't right: but it was the way things were. A misty dawn was bringing the landscape into three lightly glowing dimensions, and something told Rory it was going to be a beautiful day. 'How's Iolaire?'

Seth nodded towards the encampment. In a glimmer of dying firelight Iolaire sat cross-legged, sharpening his sword, rhythmic and slow. His silhouette looked a little different. Oh yeah, thought Rory. He'd shaved off his tangle of dark hair.

He raked a hand through his own. Needed a cut anyway. It was falling into his eyes, tickling his neck. 'Sorry. I forgot.'

Seth put an arm round his shoulders. 'Don't, if you don't want to. It's not life and death, it's a bloody tradition.' The arm tightened. 'And I'm keeping mine. I haven't got time to mourn. I'm sorry. I can't and I won't. I'll do it when she's dead.'

'I know. Don't be sorry. I'd better go through the motions, though. How's your sword?'

'It's fine. No damage . . .'

'Laszlo was his father. I Saw.'

Seth's muscles went rigid. Rory heard him take a breath to speak, but clearly he couldn't think of the right words.

Rory said, 'I wish he'd told me.'

'I wish it too.' Seth pulled back a little, to look into his eyes. 'He didn't know.'

'He's known for four years.'

'He was ashamed.'

'He didn't have to be.'

'He didn't die ashamed,' said Seth.

Rory managed to twitch the corner of his mouth. 'I know that too.'

'Of course you do.' Seth hesitated. 'Rory. I'm glad he let you in at the end. But he's gone and I know how it hurts. If I could, I'd share it.'

'There's nothing to share. I don't feel it.' Rory looked away, out towards a sea that was calm and silken, burnished by silver dawn, teased by a light wind. 'We can share anything you like when I've killed her.'

He drew his dirk, tested the edge. His hands were shaking, he noticed. Why was that?

'Here.' Seth took the dirk out of his hands and stood up. 'I'll do it.'

Rory clasped his hands around his knees, stared down at the camp and tried not to think. He felt his father behind him. There was a brief silence, a brief hesitation, then Seth grasped a handful of his son's hair and sliced through it, close to the roots. He let out a sigh, as if the worst was over, and cut the next hank, and the next.

Rory closed his eyes. He could feel the gentle tug of Seth's fingers, the give with each swift cut. Cold air on his scalp, the breath of his own world. Funny: he could taste the dawn. He was sure he could. Like ash.

Seth lifted the last lock of blond hair, running his thumb across its silkiness. Holding his breath, he sliced the blade through it.

'*Ah!*' Fiery pain bit into Rory's scalp. Half-rising, he stumbled forward.

Seth dodged his defensive flying fist. 'What the—'

'Bloody *hell,* Dad, what did you—' Rory put his hand against his shorn head, where the knife had cut him, but there was no blood. No *cut.* Bewildered, he stared at his palm.

Seth had spun away. 'Finn?' he shouted.

She was already running up the hill towards them. When Seth met her, she stopped in his arms and rubbed her own head, angry and scared.

'Hannah's alive.'

'She hurt her!' screamed Rory. '*She hurt her!*'

He tried to barge past them, race down the hill. Releasing Finn, Seth caught him and wrestled him to a halt. 'Rory, *calm down.*'

'Rory, listen.' Finn stroked his shorn head, then took his furious face in her hands. 'It isn't serious. That's our proof of life. She took some of Hannah's hair. It isn't bad. I promise.'

'I felt it! *Why can't I feel her now?*'

'Me neither. There's nothing, I've tried.'

'Rowan. They'll keep her behind rowanwood. Must have taken her out of her cell for that . . . for the proof. You were meant to feel that, and Finn too. She's not dead, Rory, she's not dead.' Still gripping his son, Seth stared across the machair to the north.

Split grey rocks formed a distinct defile in the slope, and in the gap something moved.

'What?' Despite his misery, Rory looked too.

'Here we go,' muttered Seth, and unsheathed his sword, and walked back towards the camp.

At the foot of the small hill, Diorras met them. 'Murlainn,' he said. 'A visitor.'

The others all had swords drawn as the rider approached across the grassy plain, unhurried, one hand resting lightly on his thigh. Within a horse's length of one another, Seth and the rider both halted.

'Cuthag,' said Seth.

'Murlainn.' The rider took his time gazing around the encampment, a slow smile curling his lips as he openly counted Seth's fighters. 'Is this it?'

'Get on with it, Cuthag.'

'Given what I see here, I think you'll be glad of the deal.' Cuthag reached into his jacket and drew something out. Seth took it from his hand as if he was taking a snake. Then he laid it flat on his palm and held it out to Finn. She stroked it with a finger.

'It's Hannah's,' she said. 'And Kate's.'

With a high breath Rory pushed forward and snatched it. It was a thin braid of hair, one woven strand of it darker, more coppery. The other two were lighter red. *Strawberry blonde*, thought Rory, a fist of fear constricting his windpipe. He touched the lighter strands. Some were cleanly severed, some had been ripped out by the roots. There was blood on them. He clasped the braid in his fist and looked up at Cuthag with hatred.

Cuthag smiled. 'Kate feels nothing but sorrow that it's come to this. There is no reason why we should take this to the death. All Kate has ever wanted is the Bloodstone.'

Seth's laugh was derisive.

Cuthag gave an eloquent shrug. 'Your attitude has always been a stumbling block, Murlainn. Yours, and your idiot brother's. You have no hope of winning. *None*. But Kate is willing to preserve the lives of your clann, her great-great-grandchild, and even of your son. Even now, your queen offers you reconciliation. It's not too late. Deliver the Bloodstone, accept the death of the Veil, and allow your clann to renew their loyalty.' He looked over Seth's head, scanning the silent fighters. 'Murlainn and Caorann will die, of course, but it needn't be slow. Kate is willing to be merciful. This is our offer. Time to think is not part of it. Kate expects me to take back your acceptance, Murlainn.'

'Piss off, Cuthag.' Seth spat at his horse's hooves.

'I see. Your clann may disagree, since your death is inevitable and theirs isn't. Not *yet*.' He looked round the others again. 'The traitor's interest is somewhat *vested*, you have to agree.'

'You heard our *Captain*,' called Fearna. 'Piss off before we cut it off. The bit that hurts.'

Cuthag's smile was thin as he turned his horse. He aimed a special smirk at Finn.

'See *you*,' he said.

If she shivered, she didn't show it. Her eyes were steady on him.

'Don't be long,' he called over his shoulder as he rode away. 'Keep us waiting, you filthy little traitors, and we'll keep you waiting longer for your deaths.'

Seth shot a look at Finn, but she was rigid with fury and he didn't undermine her pride by putting an arm round her. The others were silent. But they didn't look sorry.

'The man's the very soul of charm,' said Grian.

'Always has been,' said Orach, venting her feelings with a finger at his fading shape. 'But I've no intention of keeping the bastard waiting.'

'Dare I suggest we leave Caorann behind?' said Fearna.

'You dare not,' spat Finn. And he shut up.

'Iolaire, you know where the cells are. Between the two of us we know all the entrances, I think. Seven at the last count?'

'Faramach would know if any more had been opened,' put in Finn, tickling the raven's throat. 'He's overflown the caverns to check. There haven't.'

Seth raised his eyebrows in mild surprise. 'I thought you couldn't see his mind.'

Finn only smiled at Faramach. 'Can now.'

'Fine.' He shook his head. 'Look, it's not so impossible. According to Alainn she wants us to fight in the tunnels. She won't meet us outside. Forcing us in will give us all the disadvantage of a siege situation, with the added factor of the Lammyr coming from behind.'

'We'll have it relatively easy in the early stages,' said Iolaire. His eyes were dull but focused. 'The entranceways were narrow in my day and they haven't been widened much, as far as I know.' He drew in a patch of sand with his dagger. 'For the first thirty feet of any of them, you can only properly fight one person at a time.'

Braon craned her head to study the rough sketch. 'And she won't mind a good few casualties on the perimeter; she'll keep her best around her.'

'Yeah,' said Seth. 'It's their numbers that'll wear us down, but that won't happen for a while.'

'It'll happen eventually,' growled Grian.

'Yeah. So it's simple. I need Hannah, and Sionnach if he's alive. And I need Kate. Quickly.'

They digested it in silence, for an age. Then Fearna barked a laugh. 'She's telekinetic! So that'll be no problem, then.'

Seth smiled. 'I never said it would be easy.'

'Or indeed possible.' Fearna grinned.

'Finn?'

They all waited. Finn was very quiet for a moment, and then she said, 'Yes.'

'You think you can do it?' asked Seth. He glanced at the raven, which tipped its head and gave a sneering caw.

Finn shrugged. 'I think I can try. That's all.'

'*I* think you can do it. So does your bird, by the look of him.'

'See those eyelashes of yours? Quit it.' But she was smiling.

A hiss cut the darkness, and Seth stood up abruptly. Sorcha, who had been on sentry duty, was at his side. She was blocking, they all were, and alerts could no longer be soundless.

'Intruders?'

'One. Just one. She's coming from the caverns.'

Seth spat. 'Are they having a laugh?'

'It's Alainn, I think.' Orach rose to her feet.

A slender shape formed out of the darkness and starlight, weaponless, pale hands spread so they were clearly visible. Orach smiled with relief, walked forward to meet her and kissed her cheek. Alainn looked a little surprised, but gratified.

Seth hung back, warier. 'This isn't a good time to make an appearance, Alainn.'

'It's going to be a quick one, believe me. I could hardly use my mind.' Alainn shrugged. 'I take it you know the girl's your key.'

Seth stiffened. 'She's all right?'

Alainn shrugged. 'She's all right. So's Sionnach, by the way. But Kate will kill them in the end, and it won't be quick. She's full of bile for you and yours. I'm not the only one who has sympathy with your cause, Murlainn, but you won't find many willing to risk sharing your fate. And there's plenty just gagging to inflict it on you. And your lover.'

'Nice.' Seth's eyes were icy.

'Good. You get the idea. If Kate has your friends she'll use them against you and you know it. You have to have them back in your hands before you get to Kate.'

'No shit, Sherlock,' muttered Grian.

Alainn shot him a glare. 'Iolaire knows the way, but I can get you straight to Hannah's exact cell, and you're going to need all the speed you can get. The Lammyr will be coming down on you from behind and you're going to have to be so fast, I honestly don't know how you're going to do it. But I'm sure you've thought about that.'

'Yeah.' Seth exchanged a quick look with Finn. Rory felt a shuddering wave of relief. So Langfank had kept its promise. What his father had said about Lammyr oaths was true.

Unless, of course, Alainn herself was lying.

Seth bit his lip. 'So what do you suggest?'

'Iolaire comes with me now.' Alainn pointed at him. 'Between us we can get your friends back into your hands. Apart from that, it's up to you. And you'll have to guard your back against Langfank.'

'Iolaire?'

The man stood up. 'I'll go with her. And slit her throat if she's lying. Believe it, Alainn, you'll die before I do.'

Alainn looked a little startled, but she gave him a wry smile. 'You seem different, Iolaire.'

'Yes,' he said coldly.

Rory knew Seth didn't want that subject going any further. He pushed forward, and Seth turned. His expression of relief, though, quickly mutated into grim anger.

'Oh, no,' said Seth. 'Forget it, sunshine.'

Rory's gaze didn't waver. 'I'm going in, Dad. Whatever. So you want me in the thick of it? Or you want me to go for Hannah?'

'Go for—' Seth exploded. 'You're not going to ring her bloody doorbell and ask if she's coming out to play!'

Rory folded his arms and glared.

'No. No, no, no.'

'Yes. I'm going to get her. I'm not staying out here while Hannah's in there.'

'Iolaire!'

Iolaire only shrugged, as if to say *Don't expect me to control the wee bugger.*

Seth clutched his own head and gave a roar of exasperation.

'Right,' he said. 'You take my son. On these conditions. He stays back and stays in hiding, till *you* tell him otherwise. At Hannah's bloody *door* he stays back till you allow him forward. And you may wallop his arse, Iolaire, if he disobeys you at any point.'

'Happy to,' said Iolaire. 'Won't be the first time.'

In the salt-scented quietness the roan blew, and pawed the ground. Branndair gave a tiny whimper of impatience.

'Murlainn,' said Fearna, examining his sword blade. 'I'm bored.'

'Me too,' said Sorcha.

A ripple of laughter went round the fighters. An edge of nerves to it, but it was laughter and it tasted of blood-hunger.

'So,' said Seth. 'No point waiting any longer.' He ran a finger along his sword blade and gave them all his best shit-eating grin. 'For our deaths or anything else.'

Finn

There's no word for the colour of the dying sun on the moor. Amber, ruby, bronze: it's all of them, lit from within like stained glass as a lilac-and-cobalt sky dies behind it and takes the light. Night is coming, and night on the moor is not a place or time to be when enemies are close, but for those minutes it's beautiful, and all the more beautiful for being the last moor-twilight you'll ever see. Maybe. If things go badly.

We'll wait for nightfall, Seth had said.

I walked up towards the ridge that overlooked the Atlantic, shining in the last dusk, but once I reached it, I couldn't look at the sea. *We all go back there,* Conal had said once, and I didn't want to go, not now.

So I turned my back and watched the moor-glimmer fade till the sun sank, and the last shadow crept across my land, and the horizon vanished into night and the darkfall.

Hannah

Without Sionnach, the darkness was worse. Emptier. I had nothing to do but go over and over Kate's family bombshell, and it made me sick and cold. She'd used me against my friends once, and now she was doing it again. Had that ever stopped, or had she been pulling my wires all along? Since I was born, even?

After they took Sionnach, it seemed ages before they brought more food. I was edgy with hunger by the time I heard the locks slide loose and the bolts shoot back, and the racket made me start and cringe against the wall. It was a reflex, kind of, and now that Sionnach wasn't with me I couldn't help it, the place being so pitch-black and soundless otherwise, but it made me furious with myself. I think that was part of the point.

The door swung inwards and light filtered in, a guard silhouetted against it. I blinked him into focus: the oily dark-haired one. He dumped a plate on the floor but this time he hesitated, running the key chain through his fingers and grinning.

'Suspense killing you, is it, love?'

'Don't call me love.'

'I'll call you what I like. Witch-spawn.'

There was something about the guy I really didn't like. 'Your boss know how you talk?'

'My *queen* doesn't mind how I talk to you. Don't think you'll get any favours, by the way. Kate isn't sentimental.'

'Fine. I wasn't expecting her to knit me anything.'

He gave me a filthy glower. 'You'll have company soon. We're expecting your pals.'

'Don't worry. Seth won't let you suffer.'

With two swift steps he had me by the throat, and now I regretted my cheek. His fingers tightened.

'You're a mouthy little bitch.' He shoved my head against the wall and slapped me.

That hurt. Oh God. I tore uselessly at his hand, and my feet flailed, but I couldn't connect with his balls. He probably wouldn't have felt it if I had. Balls of steel, I thought, struggling, feeling rage fill me alongside the terror. I managed a stretched grin. ~ *Balls of steel, or none at all.*

He snarled, slapped me again, his other hand tightening like a garrotte. I couldn't breathe.

'Cuthag!'

Never been so glad to hear a hostile voice. Oily gave me a last glare and let me fall. Buckling against the wall I sucked in breath, clutching my throat. Behind him a woman stood in the open doorway, arms folded.

'Gods' sake, Cuthag, control yourself,' she snapped.

'She's an impudent slag,' he growled.

'That's all she is. I'm taking over guard duty here. Go get something to eat.'

'Aye, Alainn. I'll need the energy.' He gave me a grin, then turned on his heel. The woman shut the door behind them both, and I was in darkness again.

Dark or not, I felt my face red and hot where he'd slapped it, and my throat was on fire, and suddenly my eyes were burning

too. I gritted my teeth. I wasn't about to cry. No way. I put my
hands over my face and swore at myself for the umpteenth time
for letting them fool me. By the time I'd gone through my exten-
sive repertoire of obscenities, I was a bit calmer. God. If I'd listened to Sionnach. If I'd never gone to the Caledonian. If . . .

'If you hadn't gone, they'd have cut your cousin's throat. Or
more likely they'd have taken her instead. Would have come to
the same, wouldn't it?'

I blinked through my fingers. The door had swung open again—
silently this time—and the woman guard leaned against the door
frame. She had choppy brown hair and eyes so brilliant she could
have been on drugs.

'Well? Murlainn would have come after that Lauren creature,
wouldn't he?'

I glared at her, best I could. 'Doubt it. I wouldn't.'

She laughed, not very nicely. 'You'd have begged him to. You
mongrels and your consciences. Never mind. This is how it worked
out.' She stood aside. 'Get out.'

'What?' I asked stupidly.

'Get *out.*'

I hesitated, expecting a trick.

'If I have to say it again I'll die of boredom.' She half-turned to
look over her shoulder. 'Come and get her. I'm not standing here
till she develops rudimentary intelligence.'

I staggered to my feet as someone barged past the guard. Barefoot. Dark v-necked t-shirt, very cool jeans. Gold earring.

'Iolaire?'

They had him too? And Jed? For a moment I wanted to howl.

Then I wasn't sure it was Iolaire at all. Hair too short, eyes too
dead. Then he smiled, or something like it, and I knew it was him,
and for some reason I felt both overjoyed, and sick with dread. I
blundered forward and into his arms.

'Hannah. Come on.' He eased me away and gripped my hand. Nervously I eyed the guard, but she stood well aside, and Iolaire's body protected me. No chance of kicking her shins, even.

As soon as I stepped over the cell's threshold, a figure stepped from the shadows and grabbed me into a fierce embrace. I gasped a sob and let myself hug him back, even as Iolaire growled in frustration.

'Did I say you could show yourself, you little shit? Did I say it was safe?'

'Give it a rest, Iolaire.' Rory's voice was muffled in my hair.

And his hair? I reached to stroke its softness and it wasn't there. Ice balled in my stomach.

Before I could say a word, Iolaire pulled me sharply away from Rory. I was shaking so much I was afraid of falling, but Iolaire kept his arm round me as he turned to the woman. 'Alainn.' His voice was menacing. 'Where's Sionnach?'

'They must have moved him,' she muttered. Sour, but she looked nervous.

A new fear gripped my guts. From somewhere, far away in the tunnels, I could hear the distorted echo of familiar sounds. Some things never changed.

Screams didn't change. Yells, crashing bodies, clashing blades.

Too far away to get the detail, but close enough. I knew how several dozen people fighting to the death sounded. I'd heard the same thing four years ago in the dun.

I gave Rory a warning look as he seized my hand. 'I'm not going without Sionnach.'

'We never thought you would.' Iolaire squeezed my shoulders, and let me go. 'Let's find him.'

Finn

Iolaire had been right about the passageways. The narrowness of them gave us a distinct advantage, even if it wasn't quite so simple as one-on-one.

I found it hard to fight: not that I didn't want to. But I wasn't a swordfighter. My weapon was throwing-knives and I hadn't room for manoeuvre. When Seth flung aside a fighter or took a leap, or dived, I was behind him, I could spring on them. I could engage them close-to, fling myself on a snarling fighter as he turned. I could stop them turning on Seth. I could protect his back, the way I was sworn to.

What I mean is, I could kill.

It's in my blood. And I'd seen enough friends die.

Orach was close to me, though, and took many of them. Sorcha and Fearna, too, and Leoghar, the turncoat lieutenant from Faragaig. And Branndair, of course, who was better at finding an exposed throat than any human fighter. Faramach was a terrifying ghost in the dimness, coming at Kate's fighters like a rag of darkness, buffeting faces, clawing eyes, blinding and disorienting. It all left me freer to do what I had to do, and that was lock on Kate's mind.

Damn, but she was strong. I was strong too, but I could feel her malice battering against my brain. My head stung. My eyes watered. A fighter stumbled beneath Seth's feet: he took a leap from her shoulder at the next one. She rolled, got her balance, started to turn on him. I staggered forward, brain burning, but Orach got to her first and finished her. She was protecting Seth, doing my work, and just as well. I wouldn't have got there in time. I could barely think, let alone coordinate my arms and legs.

I knew there was noise, a hideous cacophony, but to my ears it was blurred. I could focus on nothing but the black malevolence that was Kate's mind, and for a fraction of time I couldn't see. Then Leoghar parried a dirk that came at my belly, slammed his foot into my attacker's chest and sent him reeling back. I yelled with rage, turning Kate back in my head.

I was strong too. *I was strong too.*

Slowly, we gained ground down the long tunnel. Orach howled with pain and slammed herself bodily into her opponent, sending him reeling off balance. Blood flew from a gash in her arm as her sword split air and Sithe-flesh two feet from me. Ahead, on the point of Seth's sword, someone screamed long and horribly. I heard the sound of metal in flesh. I smelt blood. Ours. Theirs.

I was tiring.

No.

I couldn't tire. A little behind and to my right, Fearna shouted an obscenity, and his sword rang, and rang again, and thunked in something softer. A bolt of pain went through my head from temple to temple and I clenched my teeth and flung it back at Kate.

I had to contain her. Had to. Could, couldn't, could.

Could. For Seth. I'd already cut her from his mind. She couldn't have him.

~ *You can't have him.*

~ *I already do.*

~ *Not any more.*

I came to a standstill, couldn't move another step. I could only clench my jaw till I thought it would shatter, tighten my fists, hack at her mind as if with an axe.

So difficult. That black mind. It was slippery, shapeless, viscous. Striking it was like striking treacle. Beside me Orach shoved through to protect me.

~ *You can't have him.*

~ *I already do.*

~ *Not any more.*

Her voice. My voice. Screaming together in my head. I didn't know which was which.

~ *You can't have him.*

~ *I already do.*

~ *Not any more.*

Hannah

Part of me—the chickenshit selfish part—had hoped Iolaire and Rory would drag me bodily out of the caverns. At least I could admit it. At least the chickenshit wasn't going to win out. I kept telling myself that, because I was terrified, sidling deeper into the caverns behind Alainn, cold rock beneath my feet for a thousand miles. *So afraid.*

Rory was with me, Iolaire at my back: my shaven-headed body-guards. I didn't want to know why they'd cut their hair. I didn't want to know why they were alone.

I think I knew already, and I didn't want to know.

'Stop,' hissed Alainn.

Rory put his arm across my chest, the gesture of warning turn-ing into a hug. Light glowed faintly round a corner. Alainn looked more nervous than ever but she drew herself up arrogantly and stepped round the corner.

'My prisoner,' I heard her say.

'Not that I heard,' said a surprised male voice.

'Gods, do you not know what's happening up there? The bloody rebels are at our throats.'

'Aye, and I'm to hold this guy at all costs, or slit his throat.'

'Aye,' she mimicked, 'and now it's my turn. They've a familiar, a bloody raven. It's causing mayhem. Kate needs a close-quarters archer. Get your arse up there.'

'Right.' He broke into a run as he rounded the corner, so his shock had only an instant to register before he was dead on the point of Iolaire's blade. I turned my face away.

Bolts clanged back on a wooden door, and Alainn pulled Sionnach out into the dim light. He swore, lashing out at her, but at Iolaire's low voice he froze.

'Sionnach.'

He rubbed his eyes, blinked and grinned. 'Iolaire. *Hannah!*' He hugged my head. 'What's Rory doing here?' He snatched up the sword and bow of the dead guard.

'Nice to see you too.' Rory was grinning happily at Sionnach.

'Her?' Sionnach raised his new sword to point its tip at Alainn.

'She's okay. With us,' said Iolaire. 'But Hannah won't leave without you.'

'Yes she will. Hannah?'

'Too right she will.' Rory's fingers tightened on mine.

'You *have to go*,' snarled Iolaire. 'No time. Everything rests on getting you away. You *have to.*'

I took a breath to argue, then caved in. This time it wasn't cowardice: I'd felt that often enough to recognize it, and anyway I felt safer with Sionnach than anywhere else. It was just that there was no point being self-indulgent. I'd only get them killed. And Iolaire sounded like that so rarely, I believed every word he'd said. 'Okay.'

'I'll take her out.' Alainn kept flicking glances over her shoulder into the tunnels.

'And Rory.'

She shrugged. 'And Rory.'

Iolaire looked suspicious. 'Sionnach, you go with them.'

'As if.' Sionnach snorted. 'I've scores to settle. Iolaire, you go. You know the place better. If she's going the wrong way. Yeah?'

'If she goes the wrong way?' Iolaire gave Alainn a level stare, then drew his finger across his throat.

She laughed. 'Drama queen.'

'Go, then.' Sionnach didn't wait to see us go, but ran into the tunnel's darkness and towards the sounds of battle.

Fínn

In Kate's hall there was more than quietness. There was that strange vacuum of sound where the ring of blades and the flying bodies and the screams and grunts of the dying and their killers had been like a solid, living force.

Every entrance forced. Every passageway taken. Seven narrow battles won, and the war still to come.

Our fighters were exhausted. So were hers. But ours had won the ground.

Kate sat white-faced on her dais, gripping the arms of her silver chair. I'd never seen anything so ornate, so beautifully carved and chased. When had she ordered a throne? The sheer demented vanity of the woman. Seth stepped slowly forward, bloodied sword held in front of him.

'Heretic,' she hissed. 'Traitor. Vermin. Filth.'

He didn't answer, only watched her eyes.

My brain hurt so much I thought it would explode. I could barely stand it. I didn't think I could stand it. I certainly couldn't fight. I couldn't stand alone. I could only prop myself against the wall, Fearna and Sorcha and Orach in a protective circle in front of me.

But Kate's teeth were clenched, and her temple throbbed. The pain wasn't all mine.

Her gaze skittered quickly to me, then back to Seth.

She screamed, *'Langfank!'*

Seth gave a low laugh. 'When did its oath expire, Kate?'

'LANGFANK!' Kate's eyes were wild.

'I have its oath,' said Seth. 'And the oath of a Lammyr is binding.'

Once more, Kate turned to look at me. How many souls had she taken since we'd last met? Oh, she was strong with them, and she oozed with the power of the dead. And when she had the otherworld, how much stronger? Her hatred seared my mind, and the pain of it was so bad I had to bite my mouth till it bled. But at least I didn't scream.

'You distracted me, Caorann. You blocked me. You *deceived me.'* She hissed it through her teeth, and I had a sudden, terrible foreboding. As if our duel had been gameplay to her. As if she'd been passing the time while she waited for her Lammyr to come from behind and slaughter us. As if she'd only just realized the seriousness of her position, and she was only now going to defend it. Only now.

'How dare you.' Her lips formed the words, silently, directly at me, and her pupils ignited with cold flame.

'Stand back,' she ordered her fighters. '*Stand. DOWN.*'

They hesitated, but her eyes were pure silver. Swords lowered; bows lowered; their fists clenched tight on daggers but stayed at their sides.

Kate's mouth stretched in a grin. She stood up, and opened her arms to Seth.

'Come and get me then, Murlainn. Son of the hound Griogair. At last. Come here and get flesh.'

Hannah

Why was I leaving? My friends were dying. My friends were fighting and dying for *me* up there and I was leaving.

'You think I like it?' whispered Rory. 'You and I need to stay away from Kate, because she'll use us. I don't want to go but it's all that'll let my father win.'

'He's right,' said Iolaire behind us.

'Would you three shut up?' hissed Alainn. She seemed more furtive now, more scared, if that was possible. She was on a knife edge, she was. The passageways were narrowing and darkening, but they were definitely rising under our feet. I could almost feel the outside world. Air, daylight, freedom. So close I could taste it.

So close I could *see* it. That light wasn't torchlight any more, and it wasn't the flickering glow of wind-generated electric strips. It was the light of a starlit sky and the open moor. Safety must be round the next corner. Alainn held up a hand to stop us.

She edged into the next tunnel and was gone, her raised warning hand the last thing to slip out of sight.

Silence. She seemed to be gone for a very long time. I watched the place where she'd disappeared, till I began to wonder if she'd abandoned us. Behind me I could feel Iolaire's anxiety growing, and he'd silenced his breath. His muscles tensed.

When Alainn reappeared, I let out a shuddering sigh of relief.

Her left hand rested against the wall, her right still held her sword. She stood stiffly, her expression unreadable.

And then a figure stepped out beside her. Tall, powerful, ugly as sin.

'No!' I shouted.

'Bitch,' said Iolaire, and raised his sword to kill her.

It was struck from his hand, from behind. He lunged for it with his slashed hand, but the ambush was too tight, there were too many of them. An arm went round his neck and a blade pressed against his throat. He rolled over and kicked once, the blade nicking his neck, then looked up into the eyes of his captor.

'Cluaran.' He swore.

'Renegade.' The blade tip pressed harder.

Rory grabbed me, pulling me behind him, snarling. 'You're dead, Alainn!'

She gave a tiny shrug of her shoulders, and a coughing laugh, and opened her mouth to say something. All that came out was blood.

I looked at her belly. The blade impaling it drew back into her, vanished. That awful, soft, sucking *thwick* as it left her flesh.

And then the man behind her thrust it though her neck. It flashed out of her throat, sending a dark spray of blood across Rory. Reflexively he turned to cover my body, but beyond his shoulder I saw our attacker kick Alainn hard in the back, jolting her off the blade. She pitched forward, her face hitting the rock floor, stone dead as Darach so many months ago.

The blade was still held out towards us, glistening prettily with Alainn's blood. Her killer eyed us along it, smiling.

'Drop your pathetic weapon, Laochan, and I won't kill the girlfriend.'

Rory's breath rasped through his teeth. He still held me protectively behind him.

The Wolf rolled his single eye. 'Look, if we do this now, you know I won't kill *you*. Just her. Give yourselves time to say goodbye. Hm?'

Rory's blade clattered to the floor, and I buried my face in his shoulder blades.

Too much silence, and yet I knew in my heart the real fight was on.

Please God please let Seth kill her NOW before we come

We were thrust stumbling along the passageway. I tripped on a corpse—*Diorras, who liked Blackadder and buffalo wings*—and the Wolf grabbed my hair and hauled me to my feet. Rory, stumbling to keep up, his wrists bound behind him, snarled a curse but the Wolf ignored him, shoving me on. The rock floor was slippery with blood, and I slid on smooth steps, but once again he grabbed me and kicked me in the back to get me moving.

He didn't say a word. I hated that. He didn't even snap back at Rory's relentless swearing. I tripped on the slumped body of another fighter, righted myself, and caught sight of more: Kate's troops, and some of ours. And I thought: *Seth's doing.*

Oh, God, Seth, finish it please finish it now

Because I knew if he didn't, he'd pay for it.

The Wolf thumped me in the back, and I staggered forward, and the passageway opened abruptly into space and light. Startled, I flinched back.

Kate's hall wasn't *great*, it was gigantic. Its roof was so high it was barely visible, and the pillars supporting it were snaked with vines, their huge white flowers heavy-scented and sweet. So inappropriate, because the whole hall was piled with bodies and body parts. There was a sound I didn't recognize and didn't like, but after a couple of seconds I twigged. All around, from countless wounds, blood leaked and dripped onto rock.

Two forces, and a soundless stand-off. The fighters stood in two opposing semicircles, nervously eyeing the high dais and the last fight, the one it turned on. No-one moved, no-one attacked, no-one did anything. No-one could. That was clear.

Kate and Seth faced one another, close as lovers. She stood tall, arms flung wide, eyes riveted on his, as if she was defenceless and pleading for mercy. The fingers of Seth's left hand were wound tightly into her hair. In his right hand his sword quivered. You could barely see the tremor but it was there, making the steel sing and the torchlight dance. The tip of the blade was maybe a thumb's width from Kate's throat.

Bewildered, I watched. Why wasn't he plunging it right in? *Seth, do it!* What was this, second thoughts? Conscience? Oh, for God's sake, for our sake, *no*.

It took me a good half a second to register the silent struggle.

Kate's face wasn't quiet and accepting, but taut and trembling and savage. Seth's arm shook as he pushed his sword tip millimetre by millimetre towards the soft hollow of her throat. His teeth were gritted and there were beads of sweat on his temple. One swelled and trickled to his jawline, and he pressed harder. The sword-tip moved closer, closer. A finger's-width from her throat now. *Less.*

That was when I noticed the other half of the deadly struggle: Finn, surrounded by our fighters. Her agonized face was the mirror of Kate's. Fighting back Kate's telekinesis, forcing Seth's blade forward. Slow and inexorable. My heart swelled with pride and fierce hope. I forgot where I was. I forgot what was happening.

I forgot, till the Wolf thrust me to the ground and said 'Murlainn.'

Nothing changed on that high dais. The struggle went on. Kate smiled a little more, but her focus never wavered. Seth blinked, that was all, shook something from his eyes. His lip twisted back in a wolfish snarl.

But the fighters around them turned, one by one, and watched us.

Rory was kicked to his knees beside me. He caught my eye, desperate, but like Iolaire he had a dirk at his throat.

Straddling me, the Wolf stretched out a hand. His lieutenant handed him a length of chain, and the Wolf grabbed my arm and dragged me against the wall.

And all the while Kate and Seth fought, still and silent, in the centre of the hall.

The Wolf hauled me to my feet, and lifted my arm above my head. Snapping it into a manacle, he drew a dirk with a hiss like a snake. He pressed its needle-tip to my wrist, dug it in and slashed.

I didn't even get a scream out. It didn't even hurt, not for a second or two. I just gaped in disbelief, like an idiot, as blood pumped out of my lacerated vein and down to my armpit.

Seth's eyes slewed towards me, then back to Kate. Nobody moved except Grian, who took a step towards me, then halted abruptly when the Wolf's dirk nicked my throat.

'Hey, Murlainn! Want Grian to reach her?'

I hung stupidly against the wall, swaying. Blood pumped. Strange. One instant it didn't hurt at all, the next it was like fire in my flesh. I was trying not to make a sound but it was hard. God, it was hard. I was trying not to cry.

'She could even heal herself, maybe. If I let her.' The Wolf shook my slashed arm in its manacle.

Rory shouted with horror, but I turned my face to the rock wall. I didn't want him to see the terror in my eyes and I knew it must be showing. I'd felt a helpless tear roll down my cheek, and I didn't want any of them to see it. I didn't want to die but I didn't want to be the one who made us fail, the one who blew it all to hell.

The Wolf tightened his savage grip on my free arm. His fingers bit so hard they were cutting off the blood flow, and my unhurt hand felt numb already. I wondered if my blood would race to my slashed wrist instead. I wondered how long I had. I shut my eyes but I could still feel warm wetness pulse out and down.

'Losing your focus, Murlainn?'

Terrified, I looked wildly at Finn. Her eyes were shut, her teeth sunk in her lip, and she was pressing Seth's blade harder, closer to Kate's throat. Seth's grip tightened in Kate's hair, so hard she winced. But his blade trembled even more.

'Not like you, Murlainn. Getting angry.'

'Told you once before,' gritted Seth. 'Do get angry. Don't lose my temper.'

Smiling, the Wolf touched his stitched eye. He tapped his cheek with a finger. He examined my wrist.

'Could take a while in this position, Murlainn. Won't be fast but it'll be sure. I suppose there's a chance it might clot.' He gave a low laugh. 'I'll unclot it.'

'Your soul, Murlainn.' Kate's lips were almost touching Seth's face.

He gritted his teeth.

'Your soul,' she said again, and smiled. 'I can see it gushing out of Currac-sagairt's open vein.'

'No,' he said, but he didn't sound as if he was arguing.

'There it goes.' Blinking her silky lashes, she flicked her serene gaze to a spot above my head, as if watching a small bird fly. 'It'll be gone so soon. And I thought you'd hold onto it harder.'

The tip of his blade glinted on her skin, depressing it very slightly. She swallowed, and the sword tip pricked flesh.

'She's losing so much blood, Murlainn. And you're losing so very, very much more.'

Sweat dripped from his temple. 'My clann,' he said hoarsely.

She smiled fondly. 'They'll live. On my royal word.'

I shut my eyes. They burned like my wrist. God, *don't let Seth see me cry* . . .

I heard the clang of metal on rock.

'No,' I shouted at Seth.

He ignored me. It was too late anyway. They'd moved like oiled lightning. His sword was kicked aside, his arms were seized, some-one punched him hard in the gut and as he doubled over his arms were yanked up behind him. Four of them had Branndair by the scruff of the neck now, and I saw others piling onto his cowering form with ropes and a muzzle. Tears stung and blurred my vision.

Grian raced to me, shoved the Wolf violently aside, and un-snapped my wrist from its manacle. I thought Kilrevin would kill him but he only smiled, stepping back and giving me up with a casual shrug. Desperately Grian shoved his finger into my wrist, hunting for the vein.

God, the healing stung a lot worse than the cut. I clenched my jaw. Seth had straightened, sucking in air, and he was watching me. I couldn't help crying, now.

'I'm sorry,' I whimpered as Grian cursed under his breath. *'Aow.* I'm so sorry. I'm sorry.'

'It's not your fault,' said Seth. A fist caught his cheek, and he snarled and snapped his teeth.

'I didn't want you to do that. I didn't mean to cry. I'm sorry.'

His arms had been twisted behind him and I heard the hid-eous metallic snap of shackles once again. Going on him, this time. His eyes didn't leave mine.

'Right, get this. Didn't make a difference. You crying. Get that into your ginger head.'

Another rabbit-punch silenced him for seconds, and that was time enough for me to cough it into the silence.

'Strawberry.' I gasped. 'Blonde.'

Seth's head jerked up once more, and he was grinning at me, eyes brilliant. 'Ah, Gingernut, but I love you. It's the same as before. Same as it ever was and ever will be. I won't stand by and watch him kill you.'

Now I could hardly see for tears. 'He's going to kill me anyway, you stupid faery! He's going to kill us all!'

There were two swords at his throat, and Kate at his back. Our fighters, one by one, were dropping their weapons, spitting, cursing, falling silent. You could cut the emptiness with a blunt dirk.

'Hannah,' said Seth, and his voice was clear and bitter. 'If Kate and I are no different, does it honestly matter who wins?'

'A MacGregor makes a deal with Lammyr,' said Kate softly, bringing her lips close to his ear. 'It shouldn't have been possible. It *wasn't* possible.'

You could see she was in his mind. He shuddered with it, but his face stayed dark and angry.

Kate bit his ear gently, then raised her head and smiled around her fighters. 'Yet I *made it* possible. I took so much of his soul, he gave up his blood-brother to Lammyr, and sealed an oath with them, and because of that and that alone, Murlainn almost defeated me. The blessed, beautiful *irony*.'

As her protectors surrendered their weapons, Finn flung down her knives. Ignoring the threatening jab of enemy blades, slapping aside spearpoints, she stalked to where the guards had taken hold of the disarmed Seth.

'Finn,' he said urgently, 'Finn. I knew there'd be a price for what I did.' He raised his head, desperately seeking out Rory. 'I just never thought the price would be Jed.'

'Dad,' yelled Rory, 'you didn't kill him. It wasn't you.' The Wolf thunked an idle fist into his cheekbone and he staggered.

'I paid the price and it broke my heart, Finn. I couldn't let the price keep rising.'

'I know.' Slipping her arms around his neck, Finn kissed him, and she went on kissing him even when her arms too were wrenched behind her and manacled. One of her captors seized her by the hair and began to drag her away.

'Now, now. Let them say goodbye.' Kate smirked. 'Don't worry, either of you. You're not going to die. Yet.' She brushed down her coat, making a face of distaste as her fingers touched a splash of blood. 'Be assured, you'll still be able to hear one another later. It's nice that you can exchange a last few intelligible words.'

Seth smiled into Finn's eyes. 'I love you. It's not going to be good, Finn.'

'I know. It's okay.' She smiled back as she was tugged away from him. 'I'll be with you.'

'No, you won't,' said Kate.

Finn turned on her. 'You can't stop us.' But she sounded truly afraid through her rage.

'Watch me. Dear.'

'No.'

'I know where you're linked, Caorann. You showed me that yourself. You showed me your link and you had the *utter insolence* to drive me out of him. I can cut that link like butter.' Seizing Finn's hair, she ripped out a tangled fistful.

'Don't do that to them,' Rory shouted. He'd got maybe three paces from his guards before they grabbed him.

His guards pulled him across to Kate, so she could slap his face. 'Don't *you* tell me what I can and can't do, you infant. Ah, look at you! A sickly stripling the first time I saw you. Small, like your father. You were such a surprise to me, Rory.' She glared at Seth. 'I never thought it right that Cù Chaorach's runt brother could sire the Bloodstone.'

'Aye, Kate.' Seth's eyes glinted. 'Now if you had any balls yourself—'

His guard didn't have to strike him. Kate strode swiftly to him, and did it herself.

He licked his lips, shook his head clear of the blow. Smiled.

'Ah, Kate, all this time. All the time in the world, and you did this with it.' He smirked. 'But you're still looking good, sweetie. Is that surgical?'

Kate breathed deeply, her high colour receding. I could tell she wanted to slap him again. Instead she dusted her hands in contempt.

'It's a soul that ages you. But I can understand how you might have forgotten that.'

'You do talk mince,' said Seth. 'You've got lucky skin genes, is all.'

'And you've *such* unlucky genes yourself.' She gave him a brittle smile. 'One could never accuse a MacGregor of immortality. Which brings me back to business.' Kate stroked his cheek. 'I confess, a soul's a devil of a thing to get rid of. You may not be incorruptible, but in some ways you're incorrigible. You loved being that close, didn't you?'

'Actually,' he said, 'I don't mean to sound rude, but it made me feel a bit dirty. Sorry.'

Snatching her hand back, she struck him again on the side of the face.

'You will be, Murlainn,' she said softly. 'Things were never going to go well for you, but they just got a lot worse. Take him, Alasdair. And his lover. Have fun.'

Finn

He was gone: from my soul, my mind, my heart. I was torn apart. The pain of the wound was astonishing and I realised I'd never really known how it was for him. How could I not have known? How could I not even have tried to know? We'd never known each other, not truly. We'd never been bound. We were strangers and now we were lost to each other.

The guards were relaxed. They sat against one wall of my cell, gossiping, laughing, giving me occasional contemptuous glances. I sat curled on the floor, hugging my legs against me because I was afraid my whole body was going to collapse into pieces. I'd have liked to look fierce or at least impassive, in front of Cuthag in particular, but I didn't care enough to try. I wanted to die already, and she'd only started. I was shrivelled, nothing left of me but fear and despair. Where had my strength gone, all that power I'd grown so stupidly proud of?

Wasted. Vanished. *No no no.*

Yes!

The guards didn't say a word and that was almost the worst part. The waiting. I say *almost*, because when it came down to it, it wasn't the worst part, of course it wasn't.

It was an age, hour upon hour upon hour. When the door swung open at last, Kilrevin walked in, cocksure and grinning. There was blood on his face and hands and clothes: Seth's blood. The knife in his right hand was wet with it: a long curved evil blade, jagged along one edge.

I thought I heard it. One more time.

~ *You can't have him.*

~ *I already do.*

~ *NOT ANY MORE.*

Now I knew whose voice was whose. Pain and terror sawed into me.

I wanted to scream but I didn't. No. Rowanwood or no, I'd know if he was dead. Forget my mind: I'd know it in my soul.

Kilrevin shut the door firmly behind him and bolted it with a flourish. Tenderly he laid the knife down on the bench, right where I could see it best.

'This is how we play the game, Caorann.' He looked into my eyes, and I made myself hold his Cyclops gaze. 'You have a choice to make. The longer I'm with you? The longer I'm not with him.' He laughed. 'And vice versa. You've each got to let me know if you ever want me to go back to the other. Let's see how long you can hang onto your souls.'

'Please don't,' I said. Just once.

He didn't listen. I didn't think he would. I didn't beg again.

'Right now your lover's a bit upset, Caorann. He couldn't take that blade any more, and he passed out. He didn't actually ask me to go to you instead, but it's a start, and I took the hint. Anyway, I brought him round to let him know I was coming to see you.' He stroked his mutilated fingers along my cheekbone. 'Do you know, Caorann, he cried?'

If my hate could have killed him then, it would have.

That's what I had to remember later.

Rory

He didn't know how much time had passed. It could have been hours, it could have been days. Rory's brain swam as the guards marched him down another passageway. His cell had light, constantly, so he had no way of knowing how fast or slowly the hours passed. As for his sense of direction, it was screwed. This was another tunnel he didn't recognize. They weren't rushing him, and he knew why. They wanted him to hear the enraged screams of the chained and hobbled roan in the cavern they passed, and the whinnying of his own heartbroken filly. They wanted him to see Branndair, muzzled, collared, whimpering his grief in his tiny lightless kennel. They wanted him to see the raven's corpse, hung like a tattered black rag on an iron stake, wings stretched.

They particularly wanted him to see Seth's fighters, sullen but obedient, drilling with wooden swords under Gealach's contemptuous command. There were some missing, and he couldn't help but count names in his head: *Braon, Diorras, Oscarach, Meachair, Osran . . . Leoghar of Faragaig.* He stopped. Too many. At least Sulaire was there alive, miserable as he looked. And Orach, and Fearna. Rory tried to smile at them as he was marched along a high walkway, but no-one looked up at him, although they must have heard the footfalls on metal. Not one of them would meet his eye.

They looked despairing and defeated, but at least Kate was keeping her word. At least they were being treated reasonably. He wouldn't let himself think about how they were treating Seth and Finn.

The room they steered him into was no cell. The starkness of the black stone walls was warmed with silk brocade hangings, the chairs and the table were elegantly beautiful, and there were sculptures in alcoves around the walls. Nothing he'd have wanted in his own room. He averted his eyes from the vile carved faces, and concentrated on the far viler flesh-and-blood one smiling pleasantly at the head of the table.

A chair was pulled out, and one of his guards put a hand on his shoulder and shoved him into it. He didn't take his eyes off Kate's.

'I want to see my father.'

'No.'

'I want to know if he's alive. There's no way I'm helping you till I know that.'

Kate chuckled. 'First of all, Laochan, you will help me, sooner or later. Secondly, of course your father is alive. You think I'd kill him now? You think I'd let him off so lightly?'

He twisted his fingers tightly together so he wouldn't launch himself across the table and make a grab for her. His hands ached to be around her throat, and he knew she knew it. She was loving this.

'Now, Rory.' Rising to her feet, Kate walked a languid circle round the table, trailing her fingers across his cropped scalp as she passed behind him. 'I've had your father here for forty-eight hours.'

His guts froze. *Two days?* You've left me doing nothing for two days while—'

'Forty-eight hours, Rory. Put that into perspective: it's been *such* a long war! I dare say by now your father wishes he was dead, but I assure you he isn't. Imagine how much he'd like it to stop, hm? The longer you hold out on me, the longer he'll suffer, it's as simple as that. His lover, too. Alasdair is having the time of his misspent life.' She returned to her chair, sinking gracefully into it and smiling. 'And Alasdair's life has been a long one.'

Rory stood up so fast, his own chair fell with a clatter to the floor.

'You'd love to kill me, wouldn't you, Rory?'

'I will kill you,' he said. Staring into her amber eyes, he saw a brief spark of fear. It was gone quickly. She smiled.

'No, you won't. You see, your uncle Conal told me the same thing, once upon a time. He was mistaken; so are you. Now, Lao-chan. You have only one decision to make, and your father would like you to make it quickly. You *will* cooperate with me. If you do it now, Murlainn and his lover will hang. If you leave it too long? They'll burn. Understand?'

The guard behind him had righted the chair. Rory stared at Kate, breathing hard, but of course there was nothing to say. He sat down and put his head in his hands.

'Now, let's get down to business. Tear a gap in the Veil here, Rory. A foot or so. Let's see if there's anything I can do to . . . enlarge the wound. Keep it open.'

'Bitch,' he whispered.

'Come, come.' She waved at the air between them. 'We'd better work this out quickly. You don't want it to take days, do you? Alasdair doesn't need much sleep.'

He lifted his fingers. Trembling again. Angrily, he clenched his fist, and when it was steady he flicked her the finger. The guard gave him a clout that made his head reel.

'Don't play silly games, Rory.' Kate sighed. 'I have the patience of angels, but please don't provoke me.'

Shaking his head, he raised his hand again, extended his fingers. Beneath them he felt the Veil. Soft, silky, insubstantial. *Oh, gods.* He wanted to weep but instead he lowered his hand, and pushed back his chair from the table.

'I can't. Not here. It's an underground dun. The Veil's too strong here.'

Kate, examining the back of her hands, sounded bored. 'You're lying.'

'No, I—'

'Your hold on it has been strengthening since you were an infant, Rory. Four years ago you tore the Veil close to a dun, remember? Just last May, you tore it inside one.'

'No—'

'Yes. You did. You tore the Veil at Dùn-Cnuic.'

He gaped at her. 'I haven't been in a—'

'Oh, sharpen *up*, child. Dunnock. Dunnockvale, as Alasdair's wretched marketing people insisted on calling it. And may I say, you showed a mature ruthlessness in dealing with those bodies. I'm sure your father was very proud of you.'

'Shit,' he whispered. He wished his bloodstream would find its way back to his brain.

Kate brightened, her face all innocence. 'Yes, your father! Do you think he'll last a week? I'm quite sure he will. Alasdair and his men would love to have more time with him and your stepmother.'

'Stop it. Stop. I'll *try*.'

'You'll do more than try, Laochan. I'll have my personal guard start building the pyres. That'll focus your mind.'

Clenching his teeth, he stroked the Veil, gripped it hard.

~ *I'm sorry,* he told it.

Kate gave a little chuckle.

What was the point in pretending she was wrong? She was right, and she knew that he knew it. He was stronger, and the Veil was weaker. That much he could feel. That, and the fabric of it stretching and giving and ripping. It had the strength of tattered linen, perhaps. No more. His face contorted with grief as he tore it wider, a ragged awful wound.

'It heals itself. Am I right? We don't want that. What we want is to . . . oh, push the self-destruct button, metaphorically speaking. Hm?' Kate tapped her cheek with a long finger, nibbled on her lip and closed one eye. Stretching out an idle hand, she ignited the edge of the tear in smoky black flame.

Rory started, gasped a protest. But before his eyes the flame guttered, and died.

'Dearie me.' Kate pouted.

He took a breath. 'You're not even trying!'

'Do make up your mind, child. Of course I'm trying! But I've waited a long time for this. And Alasdair has scores to settle.'

He sank his face in his hands, swearing. 'If this is it, let me say goodbye to them. Please.'

'Oh, grow up. Of course this isn't it! You think after all these centuries I'm going to destroy the Veil in an underground cave with three witnesses? This is a rehearsal, Rory!'

'You want to grandstand?' he growled.

'You're joking, aren't you? Of course I do. I deserve a little spotlight, and so does your father, for all he's put me through. We're all going to have an audience! They'll be screaming for you, believe me.'

This time, she couldn't keep the vicious hatred out of her stretched smile.

Dad, he thought dully. *Dad, just die.*

Oh, Kate was right about too many things, but she was wrong about one. He'd make sure his father was dead. He'd make sure Finn was too, and Hannah, and everyone else he loved.

After that he had an oath to keep. He had a claim to take, for that matter. It was a matter of honour as well as desire, he thought. You couldn't fight tradition. You couldn't fight the blood and oaths of centuries.

He wouldn't die, not before his time. And his time would only come when he'd killed her.

Finn

There are things you can't kill, Finn, and you mustn't even try.

I reached out for it.

Hannah

There was no pleasing me. So the guard said. I didn't seem to like a torchlit cell any more than I'd liked the dark one. My wrist hurt, with a deep stinging pain, and I rubbed and rubbed at the ugly scar, but I knew it was nothing. Nothing. I had too much time to think about it, that was all. Too much time to think, full stop. About other damage being done, other hurts inflicted, other terrible things happening beyond my cell.

I don't know how I managed to sleep, but I did. When I woke I didn't feel any better, but my senses immediately zinged into overdrive. There was someone in the room with me.

I leaped to my feet, taking a harsh breath, panicking too much even to reach out with my mind. I was still trying hard to block, anyway, though I'm sure it wasn't keeping Kate out. I'm sure even rowanwood couldn't do that. How did we ever imagine we'd beat her?

'Hannah.' The voice was low and calm.

Sionnach. I gasped with relief as I made him out in the flickering shadows, sitting against the wall with his arms resting on his knees. He didn't look too bad. He'd been roughed up a bit but not much more than that. He looked up at me but he didn't move.

'Don't be scared,' he said. 'It's me.'

I don't know what came over me then. I burst into tears, I

couldn't help it. Sionnach reached out a hand. 'Come here,' he said gently.

I sat down against the wall beside him and he put his arm round me and hugged me in silence. My tears dried quickly. I didn't see any point in them. When I rubbed my hands across my face and gulped, he said, 'Are you okay?'

'I'm fine. They haven't laid a finger on me.'

'Since they slit your wrist?' His voice was dry.

'I'm sorry, I've got no right to cry.'

He squeezed my shoulder gently. 'Yes, you have.'

'What about you?'

'Fine. I wanted them to take me instead. It doesn't bother me. I didn't want to live this long anyway. I told them to take me instead of him but—'

It was a long speech for Sionnach and it ended very abruptly as if he'd run out of words. But the silence was so heavy I turned my head and saw something I'd never seen before, something I'd never expected to see: Sionnach weeping, silently, as if his heart would break.

I wriggled round and put both my arms around him, pressing my face into his shoulder. He put his cheek against my hair. After a while he stopped crying, and he didn't start again.

'Are you scared?' he whispered.

'Yes,' I said. It was long past the point for playing games.

'That's okay. Don't feel any shame, that's important.'

'I promise.' I hoped I could keep it.

'I don't have long, Hannah. They've only parked me while they look for a free cell, so listen. They won't let you near Rory but he'll be with you, okay? Even if she blocks you both, his mind will be as close to yours as he can get it. Don't forget.'

'No. I won't.'

'You'll see him again, Hannah. After all this is over.'

'Yes.' I was trying to believe it.

'I'll stay as close to you as I can, okay? If I can be in your mind I'll try. I don't think she'll bother to block us.'

'I'd like that. Thanks. Thanks for everything, Sionnach.'

'Same to you. Be brave, Hannah. If you are, I might be too.' He pulled away a little and winked at me. 'Okay?'

I nodded and hugged him tighter, but he raised his head sharply at the sound of footsteps.

'They're coming for me,' he whispered. 'I'll see you later, okay?'

I kissed his scarred cheek and then held him as tight as I could until they opened the door and bright light flooded in and they dragged us apart and manacled his hands behind him. He gave me a last wink and then they'd taken him.

I felt as bereft as if they'd pulled off a limb, but I didn't have time to cry about it, thank God. I stood up as someone else came into the room, knowing who it was. Not that I could read her mind: I could just feel her. I just knew her. I was *part* of her.

Kate gave me a smile that was the smuggest I'd ever seen. 'We're all done here, Hannah. You'll be glad to hear we won't be needing you.'

I felt cold, and very sick. 'I want to see Rory.'

'Out of the question, I'm afraid.'

'Then let me see Finn and Seth.' I was trying not to sound aggressive but I had to grit my teeth.

'Seth? Absolutely not. But you can go and see your . . . what is she? Stepmother-in-law? Aunt? Cousin thrice removed?'

'She's my friend,' I spat.

'Oh, of course. You care for her. You all care for each other, don't you? Let me tell you something, Hannah. If you'd truly cared for your friends you should have talked them out of their treason.' She laughed. 'And you should never have baited a trap for them.'

I could only struggle to breathe properly, struggle to keep my fists at my sides. 'You took me! *You* made them come!'

'Ah, yes. But only because I had to. I had to put a stop to you somehow.' Her eyes glittered. It wasn't the glint of madness; the old bitch was all too sane. 'I wanted you, Currac-sagairt, and you spat in my face. The rest of them kept my Rory from me. I killed his clann one by one and still Seth wouldn't come, the coward. I had to take Conal's bastard to force that, do you see? But if you'd all given up this nonsense earlier . . . ah, too late now, isn't it?' She stood back by the open door. 'Go to Finn. Get her cleaned up a bit, will you? You'll be on parade within the hour and you'll want to look your best in the circumstances.'

I shoved past her. The guards fell in at my sides but they didn't try to grab me. They all knew fine we were beaten. The fight was out of us. It was over.

They escorted me even deeper into the caverns, down twisting tunnels that stank of misery. I recognized Goggles as soon as we turned the last corner, lounging against another rowanwood door and laughing with a second guard. As we approached he unfolded his arms and stepped lazily aside to let us through, jerking his head.

'There you go. Murlainn's whore.' He smirked.

There were scratches on his face, and real hatred in his eyes. My stomach was heaving, but I think I managed not to let it show. I didn't even give him the satisfaction of my hate, but ignored him and went into the cell. Behind me the door crashed shut and I heard the bolt shoot home.

My heart was slamming. It was gloomy in there, but I saw her quickly enough, crouched tightly in a corner of the cell. Her arms were wrapped round her knees, but the fingers of one hand twisted and wrenched obsessively at a lock of her hair.

Finn looked up at me, her twisting fingers going still, the dull misery and fear on her face turning to something like relief. Her left eye was bruised and swollen, her cheekbone gashed. There was a bad cut on her eyebrow and a thick rivulet of dried blood under her nostril. She tried to smile.

I sat down beside her and put my arms round her. She pressed her face into my chest but she couldn't let go of her knees, as if she was desperately trying to hold herself together. She choked out a single dry sob.

'Are you okay?' I whispered. Stupid question, but what else was I supposed to ask?

'I'm fine. I'm fine.'

'Did they hurt you, Finn?' Another stupid question. I was full of them.

She shook her head, far too quickly. When she lifted it, her eyes were filmed and clouded with grief; the Sithe light that should have been in them was barely detectible. There was something else there instead. Maybe it was my overworked imagination, but I didn't want to look at it too hard.

She whispered, 'Not as much as they hurt him.'

'How do you kn . . .' My voice dried.

'Alasdair showed me.' Her voice was a husk. 'Some. In his head. He let me See.'

I couldn't answer. I was too scared of throwing up.

'Hannah. Have you seen him? Have you seen Seth?'

'No,' I said. 'I'm sorry.' I hugged her harder.

'I want to see him. *I want to see him.*'

'Sh,' I said. 'Listen, Finn, you mustn't cry. Please. Please don't cry. It won't be long. They're taking us out soon.'

She pulled away a little, searching my eyes. 'I see,' she said very quietly. 'You're right.' She let go of her knees at last to rub her eyes with her fists. 'Sorry, Hannah. I'm acting like a child.' She took hold of my arms. 'Listen, you might be all right. She's your great-great-grandmother.'

'That means nothing to her. Nah, Finn. We're in this together, okay? Hold it together. It'll be within the hour.'

'So they broke Rory. Did they hurt him?'

I looked away, but that was cowardly, so I met her eyes properly. 'No. No, I don't think so. They didn't have to.'

'Of course.' She hugged her knees again and laid her cheek on them, closing her eyes in grief and exhaustion. 'I wish it was over.'

'Me too. Soon it will be. Finn?'

'Mm?'

I swallowed, and muttered, 'Is it true, what you saw that time? When you saw Conal. Are you really sure?'

'Oh, God, Hannah, I don't know any more. I used to be sure. Maybe I was seeing things.' She opened her eyes and tried to smile. 'But if it was real, I'll see you over there, okay?'

They'd given me a cold damp rag, that was all, but I turned her face towards me and tried as best as I could to wipe away the blood and filth. I wished I could stop her shaking, but when I'd done what I could we put our arms round each other and sat like that for a while. I don't know how long. Until I heard distant footsteps in the corridor, and I pulled gently away from her.

'Thanks, Hannah. Listen, I'll be fine. I promise I won't lose it.'

'I know you won't.'

We stood up together and held hands until we heard them shoot the bolt back on the door.

The sunlight seemed intolerably bright after the darkness of Kate's caverns. I put my arm over my eyes to shield them, but still they stung. The first shape I could make out was the biggest: the blue roan, hobbled and chained between two terrified horses, its jaws strapped shut, its flanks heaving with fury. Hot jets of breath shot from its scarlet nostrils.

'She's hoping to sacrifice him.'

It was Sionnach's sceptical voice close by me, but glad as I was to hear it, it broke my heart to see him when my vision cleared. He was shackled and guarded, and he was the only one who seemed destined for execution with us. The rest of our surviving clann stood in Kate's ranks, their faces sullen and beaten. She hadn't trusted them enough to arm them yet, and they were scattered and separated among fighters who glanced at them with barely-concealed scorn. Kate's captains stood a little apart, talking quietly.

I knew some of the captains. I recognised Gealach from Finn's description, a woman with scarlet hair. I'd seen Cluaran before, the brute-faced shaven-headed one with the gold torque. Iolaire had always said he was a decent guy. Iolaire maybe didn't think so any more, because he slouched behind them, guarded and mana-cled. He'd taken a good thrashing, but he didn't look as if he minded. His eyes were dull and dead, as if he didn't care what they did to him, but the faster the better.

As we passed, Cluaran glanced up, then frowned and stepped across our path. I glared at him, and pressed protectively closer to Finn, but he spoke a curt word to the guards and they pulled me back. Cluaran grasped Finn's chin and tilted it to look into her eyes. She didn't flinch.

Cluaran did.

I heard an intake of breath. For the first time Iolaire seemed conscious of what was happening around him. He stared first at Finn, then turned savagely brilliant eyes on Cluaran.

Cluaran took a step back, as if he couldn't help it. Then, angry, he snapped, 'Not my doing, Iolaire. But she's a rebel. You're all rebels. You made your choice, Iolaire; all of you did.'

'I don't know you, Cluaran. I never knew you.' Iolaire looked at Finn again, the ghost of a smile on his lips. 'Hey, Finn. Soon.'

'Not soon enough for some of you.'

Kate's voice resounded, as clear and sweet as ever, and the fighters hustled back to allow her through. Behind her stood Rory. He met my eyes, but his were entirely cold. He wasn't manacled or anything. He stood unspeaking behind Kate, flanked by a man and a woman fighter. I tried to catch his eye again, but now he wouldn't look at me.

'Kate.' Cluaran kissed her hand, drew it to his forehead, then withdrew with his fighters and Iolaire. I guessed the gallows in the dun courtyard was for him, and I hoped they'd hang him fast. I hoped Cluaran would have the decency to haul on his legs, or something. Break his neck.

I couldn't really believe these were actual thoughts going through my head. I wanted to scream, but no way was I doing it.

Kate gave a great sigh, and clapped her hands with satisfaction. 'We're all done. We're through with these rebels.'

'So soon?' murmured Goggles, and ran his finger hard down Finn's spine. 'You know, they've neither of them asked for us to go to the other, yet.'

Finn twisted to gaze at him. There it was again in her eyes. That dark un-Sithe light I didn't like. I can't imagine he liked it either.

'I know, Raib, and that's disappointing. But I'm afraid it's time we got down to some proper work. I promise you it won't be an anticlimax.' Kate's golden eyes were sparky with anticipation.

Two fighters were leading out horses, and one of them held out a hand for Kate's foot as she slipped elegantly onto the back of a white mare. She pointed to a bay gelding and said to Rory, 'Mount.'

I was shocked that he didn't argue. He just went to the bay, and hauled himself onto it. He picked up the reins in one hand.

Kate tutted. 'What on earth is keeping your father?'

The sky above us was grey and bleak, with a blustering threat of rain, but I'd swear the breeze died the moment we heard footsteps. Brisk steps. And dragging ones. Gealach's unit divided to let the Wolf stride though, his eye bright with glee.

He stopped in a good central spot, where we could all see him. Loving it, the bastard. I tried not to look at him but I couldn't help it.

'Alasdair,' called Kate affectionately. 'Welcome. To you and your *favourite* prisoner.'

'May I say,' said the Wolf, 'he's good. He's very good. The things he called me! The filthy tongue on him! He even spat, till he ran out of spit.' He grinned at Finn. 'But that was only the first day.'

He took a swaggering step to the side. Seth was hauled forward between guards, one gripping each arm, and he was walking, after a fashion. A murmur went round Kate's troops, and there was something strange about the sound, because it wasn't contempt: it was pity, and horror. The Wolf stared at the ranks and they were silenced.

Seth was stripped to the waist, but I could hardly stand to look at his arms and torso. Every visible bit of him was marked with a slash or a ragged rip or a brutal deep puncture, and the raised hideous ridge of recent healing, and why in God's name wasn't he dead? Bile rose in my throat, tears in my eyes. I could just see his left hand, hanging limp in its manacle. It had been sliced between each finger, almost to the wrist. Then it had been put back together.

The Wolf grabbed his filthy tangled hair and yanked his head back. Seth blinked, slowly and painfully. One of his eyes was gone; there was only a red angry hollow.

'Well,' said the Wolf, shrugging. 'He did it to me.'

'Fair enough, Alasdair.' In the awful silence, Kate turned to gaze at her clann and ours. 'And you'll be doing it to the next person who expresses any sympathy.'

Alasdair grinned.

Someone in the ranks was weeping, very quietly. Orach, I think. The guards released Seth's arms, and he took one step, but his leg wouldn't take the weight and he collapsed to the hard ground.

For an instant I couldn't move, but Finn could. She broke away from her guards and tore across to him, leaving them speechless and prisonerless. Then, since I'd promised to stay by her, I ran too, getting away from my guard by sheer surprise. And of course Sionnach came after me, so I got further than I should have because they had to restrain him first. I was only a few yards from Seth and Finn when they grabbed me and held me. No-one on earth could have caught Finn.

She flung herself to her knees beside him, leaning her body protectively across his. Then she whipped round like an animal, and gave the men who'd come after her a supernaturally vicious snarl.

Cuthag got the brunt of it. I saw his eyes darken with terror, just for an instant. Then he recovered, and both guards seized first Finn and then Seth, dragging them to their feet.

She yanked away and forced herself close to him, her face against his neck, but her eyes stayed open and fixed on the guards. Seth leaned his bloody face against her hair with an expression like bliss.

'Kill us now,' he mumbled. 'Not long, lover. Not long.'

'I know.' She clenched her teeth and whispered, 'Let me in.'

I could see Seth's face. His single eye was open, but the pupil stayed resolutely dull. 'No.'

'Let me in,' she said more fiercely. 'Let me in so you can walk.'

'No . . .'

Kate took an involuntary breath. I watched her. I saw her perplexed frown. But Finn paid her no attention at all.

'Love,' Finn told Seth, softly but clearly. 'You can't stop me. And nor can she.'

I knew he couldn't fight her. I knew it even before I saw a single tear roll from his single grey eye.

He turned reflexively away, so that her face swung towards me. As her pupils lit up her eyes jerked wide, and her mouth opened in a soundless gasp. For an instant I thought her knees would buckle and she'd fall, and I started towards her again, but as the guard jerked me back she recovered. She turned her face to the Wolf. She held his eye directly, and the two of them were immobile for long seconds.

It was the Wolf that blinked.

There was shock on Kate's face, and incomprehension. Then she snapped, 'It doesn't matter. Not any more.' She yanked her horse's reins.

I didn't know how Finn had done it. I didn't even know what she'd done. But *Thwarted!* I thought, and if I hadn't wanted so badly to cry, I'd have laughed.

'Bring them up to the cliffs.' Angrily the Wolf jerked his head, and the guards tugged us forward. 'And take his shackles off. I don't want to have to carry him.'

Without the shackles and with Finn in his head, Seth could manage a stumbling walk. Finn was close against him, her arm supporting him. It wasn't a long walk, thank God, though the wind grew stronger near the top, flattening the salt grass. Seth wavered as it hit him, then ducked his head and lurched grimly on.

I hesitated, afraid, because the hoofbeats were there again.

I could hear the murmurous crash of waves far below, and I could hear the sad whisper of the wind in stunted oaks and piled timber, but none of that could drown out the sound of countless running horses. A bit jangled; breath snorted through flared nostrils; hooves thudded on peat. Still, the horses I could see were calm and quiet. It wasn't them. The blue roan they'd dragged to the clifftop already, and it had taken four of them plus the terrified horses; now it stood with its hooves splayed and its head low, its mouth foaming blood beneath its muzzle, its flanks heaving. It was silent, but for its furious breathing. The noise wasn't coming from the blue roan.

I think Finn could hear what I could hear, but she was taking no notice. She was white and strained with half Seth's pain, but the mercury fire in her eyes wasn't strained. They slanted once towards the Wolf. I saw him tug his collar, rub his neck, and he glanced angrily back at her to meet a look of diabolical hatred. His tiny smile was contemptuous, but he looked away swiftly. She'd beaten him, I realised, however she died. She wasn't afraid of him, not any more.

Despite his quirking little smile, I'm pretty sure he was afraid of her.

Rory turned his head, as if listening to the hoofbeats, but then he stared straight ahead again, expressionless. He held the reins in one hand, ignoring the mounted fighters on either side of him, who were glancing nervously at the moor. I'd seen that frightening look on Rory before, but it seemed to have etched itself permanently onto his hardened features. There was nothing I could say to him, I knew it, even if Kate wasn't blocking us from one another.

Sionnach lurched forward, fast enough to surprise his guards and come briefly abreast of me.

~ *Speak to him. TRY.*

I did. Nothing I could say, but I tried. Gently, I reached out to his mind with mine.

~ *Rory.*

He looked over his shoulder, right at me.

I took a breath of surprise. Maybe Kate hadn't made the effort, after all. She had a piece of my hair, and she had Rory's. She should have been able to separate us and it seemed unlikely that she wouldn't. I frowned, perplexed, because it seemed that Kate couldn't keep our minds apart, any more than she could split Finn from Seth. I don't know why that made me shiver, but it wasn't with fear.

Rory smiled back at me, mirthlessly.

~ *Hear the horses, Hannah?*

Kate glared at him, but he took no notice.

~ *We're all going to die,* he told me. A slight smile touched his mouth. ~ *I'm sorry.*

I just smiled back. What else? Nothing to do. Nothing to say. Nothing to forgive.

Rory

'You'll have to be patient,' he said.

Kate eyed him as he jumped down from the bay gelding.

'Really?' Her tone was rimmed with ice, but she seemed just a little wary. It was clear, he thought cheerfully, that nothing was going quite as she'd expected.

'Really.' Rory gave her a thin smile. He walked onto the jutting headland, faced out to sea, and lifted his hand to touch something unseen. He stroked it, first with his fingertips, then even more gently with the back of his hand. Then he turned on his heel, and walked back to his place by Kate.

'The Veil,' he said crisply. 'It's very strong here.'

Kate's lips were a thin compressed line. She stared pointedly over her shoulder at the heaped brushwood and the stake twenty metres away, prominent on the edge of the bluff. Rory followed her gaze.

'How ironic, Rory dear.' Kate's remorseless smile seemed a little forced. 'That it should be so tough in this very place.'

'Isn't it?' Rory smiled too, but his was much more genuine.

'You'll manage, though, won't you? When the kelpie bleeds out, that'll help.' Her eyes narrowed. 'Kelpie blood is a powerful thing.'

How could someone so beautiful, Rory thought clearly and loudly, look so bloody ugly?

Kate turned to Cluaran, and he dismounted and came forward, shooting Rory a glance that was almost guilty. So he should, thought Rory. He'd spared the man's life, or made Iolaire spare it, and look where it had got him.

'Where's Iolaire?' he asked Cluaran coldly.

'Iolaire is not one of you,' hissed Cluaran. 'He's in my custody and he'll hang when this is over.'

'You're wrong,' said Rory. He didn't specify on what count.

'And you, Laochan,' snapped Kate, 'are too damned arrogant. Cluaran. Burn them.'

Cluaran gaped at her, shocked.

'Don't make me repeat myself. Murlainn and Caorann: put them to the stake.'

'What?' said Cluaran.

'Oh, and put in an extra stake for that misbegotten spawn of mine.' Kate flapped her fingers. 'The girl. Currac-sagairt.'

Rory felt as if he'd been hit hard in the gut. 'You promised me,' he hissed.

'You're not cooperating, Laochan, you're irritating me.'

'Wait a minute, Kate.' Shoving Rory aside, Cluaran took a step forward, tracked by Kilrevin's cold empty eye. 'That was a bluff. They're rebels and I'll happily hang them but I'm not burning anyone.'

It happened so fast. Kilrevin drew the sword off his back and plunged it casually into Cluaran's heart. He drove it in further, up to the hilt. As Cluaran sagged against him and the light went out of his stunned eyes, Kilrevin withdrew it. Then he wiped the blade casually on Cluaran's jumper, and sheathed it.

Dusting his hands, he turned to Kate's front line. Two other captains glanced at each other, swallowing, and dismounted to take hold of Seth and Finn.

Closing her eyes, Kate shook her head sadly. 'I can't bear

uncooperative people. Now, Laochan, there's still a chance I'll have them strangled first. A very slim chance, and entirely at my own whim. So I suggest you start ingratiating yourself with me.'

He knew she wouldn't. He knew she'd burn them alive even if he kissed her feet and begged. There was no choice. Never had been. And the horses were close, so close.

Rory walked back to the cliff top. Teeth gritted, he tightened his fingers into fists, then flexed them.

Oh, gods forgive me.

He drew his hand back in a claw, then lashed out like a big cat disembowelling a deer. Dug in his nails. Growled. Raggedly, violently, his fingernails ripped the air.

Easier than last time. Would it go on getting easier?

He was never going to know, so what the hell. He shut his eyes, grabbed the Veil in two hands, and dragged it apart.

The gap shimmered in the air, bulged, widened. Kate laughed, quick and breathless. Sweeping to Rory's side, she stepped past him and touched the edges lightly. They smouldered like paper, curling back, but nothing ignited, no proper flame would catch. Resisting, thought Rory. It was strong.

Don't mess with me . . .

The gap was widening, though, remorselessly. Kate's excitement was a tangible thing.

She could have done this back in the fortress, thought Rory. She could have had her way then. But she wanted a show, a victory celebration, a public execution. Oh, that vanity of hers. It'd be the death of her.

It'd be the death of them all, but who cared?

The gap was perhaps ten metres wide and three tall when she stopped burning the Veil. It was clearly a struggle. Hesitating, she stepped forward. She frowned at Rory.

'This isn't how it behaved before,' she said.

'No, it isn't.' He studied it with interest. It was a fascinating thing. He wished he could have longer with it.

It wasn't dark this time. It wasn't *black*; it was positively summery. But he felt the breath of it, the menace, raising the roots of his hair. He tilted his head and touched the edges, curious more than afraid.

The sunlight on the other side was just dazzling. Her eyes blazing its reflection, Kate stepped briskly through the gap. The landscape beyond looked much the same, Rory thought. That was comforting despite its empty strangeness.

It was beautiful. He liked it. Funny it should look so welcoming, and so like the world they were about to leave forever. A thrill buzzed at the nape of his neck.

Kate, though, was scowling. Turning a full circle beyond the torn Veil, she stared around as if she was blind to the moor on the other side, and the glittering sea, and the crying gulls. As if there was nothing there.

'There's nothing here!'

'Not for you, bitch!' The yell came from behind.

Rory turned and grinned at Hannah. *Oh, Hannah*, he thought. *Trust you to get the point.*

Told you I'd trust you to the end of the world.

Hannah's captors eyed her warily, and they were gripping her arms now. But she didn't need restraining. She was laughing too hard. 'Not for you, ya soulless witch!'

Rory said, 'She's right, Kate. You haven't got what it takes.'

Kate gave a shocked gasp and looked down at her fingertips. In the clear light beyond the Veil they were greying, shrinking, and a hint of white bone poked through the tips of them. Her face paling too, Kate hurried back through the gaping maw of the hole, and took a shaking breath as she lifted her hand to her eyes. Her fingers pinked and fleshed out once more. She sighed her relief, but there was real fear in her face now, where last night there had only been the ghost of it.

With one nervous scowl at Rory, she turned back to the ripped Veil, but took an involuntary step away from it. The edges flickered again, and combusted. With no help from Kate, the fabric of it was kindling, the black invisible flame spreading, unseen in the brilliant light. She backed further from it and Rory followed her with his eyes, smiling.

'You haven't got what it takes.' He barked a laugh that was half happy, half savage. 'You only went and gave it away.'

'Shut this Veil!' she yelled in panicked fury. 'Shut it! Shut it!'

'I don't think I can, Kate.' Rory gave her a cool smirk.

She spun in a rage. 'Alasdair! *Burn them!*'

'*You're too late!*' Rory screamed back in her face.

'Shut it, damn your soul!'

'*At least I've got one!*' He wanted to howl with laughter, but the joy of victory was so fierce it choked him.

'Congratulations, Kate! We're all going to die! It's open and *I can't close it!*'

And that was when the riders came.

Hannah

Why wasn't I scared? There must be something wrong with me: my teachers were right all along.

Is something amusing you, young lady? Do you find this funny?

Hell, yes.

The landscape beyond the Veil-gash was blurring, but only because the sunlight was so white and fierce. They came out of it, hooves thundering loud and clear now, fighters on horseback. I spun and ducked, then had to fling myself onto the ground as the leader's horse took a flying leap over me. The horse was a black kelpie. I couldn't see much of the man on its back, except that he was blond and scary and there was a white wolf running with him.

I wanted to go and hug Rory for being so damn clever, I'd have liked that to be the last thing I ever did, but there wasn't time. There was nothing more to be done. I hadn't expected dying to be this much fun. I was still laughing as the rest of the horsemen hurtled past me and fell on Kate's ranks.

They were terrifying but some of them seemed familiar. A crop-haired beautiful woman, her horse's throat clotted with blood; right behind her, a skinhead with a thin grim mouth. There was a blond bearded guy with burnt-sugar eyes. A tawny-haired woman, eyes even bluer than Finn's. A goatee-bearded, black-haired barbarian, handsome as all-get-out. Finn dragged Seth to the ground and flung herself across his body, her arms over his head, but the black-bearded man twisted his head to stare down at Seth as he galloped past, and I'd never seen a barbarian look quite so gobsmacked.

I was still watching him, still grinning, when the flesh began to slide from his face.

I squealed in horror, rolled onto my back and kicked away frantically, afraid to look at him, afraid to look away. As if some invisible blade had hit him, a gash opened from his eye to his jaw. His throat split wide, and I waited for the spray of blood, but it never came. And he never even paused. He just swung his own sword at one of the guards, taking her head off in one blow, and rode on.

~ *Hannah! Hannah!* I heard Sionnach's panicked voice, saw him elbow-crawling towards me on his manacled arms, but there was too much carnage between us. He tried to get up and run to me but the crop-haired beauty's dappled horse shouldered him to the ground.

Sionnach couldn't break his fall and he crashed hard, but he seemed stunned by more than the impact. The female rider's chest opened in a bloodless burst but she didn't fall, she didn't even wince. She just galloped on, straight for Gealach's unit, and im-paled the first fighter who came at her.

Kate's ranks were in chaos. Some of them were trying desper-ately to fight back, some of them were running. Incredibly, some of them were rooted to the spot, just gaping, and then I realised: those ones were ours. Our clann, weaponless and defenceless and conquered, but maybe that was why they weren't attracting the attention of the cavalry. The tawny-haired woman rode straight through, scattering them even as she ignored them, and swung a spear in a low elegant arc through a guard's chest. Gobsmacked

Barbarian turned on his horse to give her a gruesomely adoring smile. The woman reined in her horse and hesitated, seeming undecided, but the dead guard was still flopping around on the point of her spear. Impatiently, effortlessly, she flicked him off.

I lay on the ground, holding onto fistfuls of peat for dear life, and goggled up at her, thinking *please don't kill me please don't kill me.* She wasn't that beautiful now, to be honest. Her face had putrefied fast, and her limbs looked bloated, and there was rank seaweed tangled in her hair.

She looked at me with curiosity in her eyes, eyes that were no longer very blue because they'd sunk back in their decaying sockets. Then she calmly turned her horse's head and rode back at the screaming, panicking, human fighters.

There was a low outcrop of granite not far from me, and I stumbled for it, running low. A pale blood-dappled wolf streaked by me, its ribs exposed by its peeling flesh, at the side of a black horse. I thought my heart would stop, I thought I was headed straight for decay and death myself, but the wolf, the horse, and its rider all ignored me. The blond captain rode straight for the captive blue roan, circled it, and his sword slashed its chains like spiderweb. The roan reared, lunged free, and bolted seawards, and the black watched it go, giving a screaming whinny that was too much like laughter.

I was panicking now, frantically and uselessly wriggling down in the shadow of the granite slabs. The skinheaded ghoul nudged his horse round at my movement, blade raised, but he shrugged and turned away from me, and he couldn't seem to find another opponent. He jerked his head at his captain, who was riding back at a trot, his blade bloodied and filthy. He didn't speak. None of the strange riders yelled or spoke. I thought, *Oh yeah. Their tongues have probably rotted already.* And then I thought, *Oh my GOD their TONGUES HAVE ROTTED.*

The blond captain turned his horse on its hindquarters, and peered around the battlefield with fascination. The horse shook its indignant head, and its eye caught me lying there. It peeled back its lips and screamed a whinny.

And that was when I finally recognised its rider, stupidly enough: from Finn's horse.

He was the father of my dreams, the father of other people's broken memories. He was beautiful. He was terrifying. His throat was slit in a single deep bloodless slash. His faded blue shirt was torn, and as his body moved with the horse's gait I glimpsed a jagged rip in his belly. His barely-contained innards sagged out of him with every pace. He was still beautiful, though. Still terrifying. His eyes glowed silver, the irises, the pupils, everything.

I wasn't terrified, not now. But Kate was.

She was standing rigid in the middle of what had become a rout, clenching and unclenching her fists, her lovely mouth open in disbelieving horror. Slowly she turned, and shouted at one of her fighters who was scrambling away on all fours, but her words were inaudible among the screams and he ignored her anyway. A bloodied space was opening around her, and when she spun again, the captain on the black horse was watching her. Her eyes snapped wide.

For a few seconds she seemed frozen, couldn't tear her eyes off him. Then her muscles gave a violent twitch, like she could move again. She took a step back from him. Then another.

He furrowed the dead, flaking skin of his brow, studying her with a detached curiosity. Behind him, Seth had pushed Finn off and was struggling to his feet.

'*Cù Chaorach.*'

His voice was cracked and barely audible, but this time the rider seemed to hear. He twisted on the horse's back, peered down, and his skull split in a grin.

Seth staggered forward, his teeth clenched. '*I claim her.*'

'Seth, no!' I heard Finn's yell, saw her snatch at him, but when the blond rider reached down his rotting skeletal hand, Seth seized it.

'Not without me,' he rasped. And the rider yanked him bodily up onto the horse behind him.

Conal—*my God*, I thought as I named him in my head, *Conal*—craned his head round, smiling a delighted, death's-head smile, shrunken lips peeled back from his teeth. Seth locked an arm round his brother's waist, his maimed hand flopping loose; then the two ruined men, the living and the dead, rode together towards Kate.

She turned, and ran.

Not fast enough. I got the impression she could never go fast enough. Conal nudged the kelpie on, and it picked up effortless speed. Within ten feet of Kate, it broke into an easy gallop. As the two riders drew abreast of her, Seth leaned down, gritting his jaw against pain, and seized her arm.

Kate flailed wildly, screaming, but Conal made not a sound, and neither did Seth: Conal because he clearly had no working voice box, Seth because his last scraps of energy were focused on dragging the queen behind as she kicked and punched and shrieked.

The black horse jolted to a halt, and Conal swung round to grip Kate's other arm. He yanked her easily onto the horse, dumping her backwards across its withers, but it seemed he'd lost interest immediately, because he was smiling at the blue roan. It was galloping back now and drawing alongside his black, grazing its teeth fondly against its neck.

Seth hauled himself painfully from the black to his own horse, and wound his fingers into its mane. He sagged low on its neck for a moment, drawing agonised breaths, but with an effort he straightened. His eye fixed on Kate, slung upside-down and squealing across the withers of his brother's horse.

Conal was surveying the chaos as if it was a social occasion and he didn't quite want to leave yet. I couldn't tear my gaze off him. His eyeballs had sunk in his skull and the flesh was wasting from his face. His torn shirt hung on his bones, and the fingers of his free hand, tapping lightly on his thigh, were decaying with the rest of him: bone showed at his fingertips as the flesh withered and fell away.

I scrambled over to Finn and grabbed her arm as the two brothers rode calmly back to us, Kate flopping helplessly in front of my father. Conal smiled at Finn as if to reassure her, and made a wild try at a wink, but the effect of it, without much eyelid left, was pretty unsettling. Seth's fingers were white where they were knotted through the blue roan's mane. His lips parted but he couldn't seem to get any words out. Finn was frozen, shaking in my hold.

The black kelpie shifted restlessly and sidestepped, yearning towards the gash in the Veil, but Conal nudged it back towards me. He raised what was left of his eyebrow at his brother.

'Currac-sagairt,' croaked Seth. 'Touch her.'

I bit my lip. Kate was still slung backwards over Conal's horse, sobbing and raging, and her amber eyes were locked helplessly upside-down on mine. The last thing I wanted was to touch her.

All the same, it didn't occur to me to disobey Seth. I reached out my palm and pressed it to her forehead.

Kate stopped screaming, just like that. Instantly. Her mouth was still wide in a howl of mortal terror—and it wasn't her best look—but no sound was coming out of it.

Strangest thing I've ever felt, my body sucking the power out of her. Mostly I felt it in my eyes. They sparked and crackled so much they hurt, and I could barely see, but I gritted my teeth and held my fingers against her clammy skin. I didn't take my hand off Kate till she went limp, empty of magic and gibbering with fear.

Conal turned the black horse lightly on the forehand so that it trod a delicate half-circle and my great-great grandmother no longer hung gabbling between us. Smiling that skull-smile, he leaned down and brushed my cheek with his rotting fingers. The air stank of death but I didn't care.

Seth had collapsed forward on the roan's neck now, but his head was twisted towards Finn so that he could see her out of his remaining eye.

'Finn,' he whispered hoarsely. 'I have to go. I'm sorry. So sorry.'

'No,' she moaned, but already Conal was turning his horse, and he beckoned to Seth, and smiled.

'Oh, I'm coming,' said Seth. 'You and me.' And he actually grinned.

Conal nodded happily, then urged the kelpie into a gallop; Seth dug his heels into the roan's flanks and rode after him. The pair of them were twenty metres away and heading hard for the Veil before Finn got her senses back.

She tore away from me and ran, screaming her panicked anger. 'Conal! *Don't you dare! Don't you dare!*' She stumbled to a halt as Seth craned to look back, his ruined face tormented. I knew what struggle was going on. *Claim, Binding. Binding, Claim.* I gulped, wanting to cry.

Binding, please trump Claim.

Finn straightened. Hair whipped around her face and she tightened her jaw. And I heard what she called to him; I think the whole battlefield heard it.

~ *Go if you must!*

The black horse slowed to a canter, then a flying trot. Its cadaver of a rider hesitated. Seth reined back the blue roan.

~ *It isn't time,* Finn cried. ~ *But go if you must!*

The kelpies had both drawn up now, snorting and pawing the peat. The brothers exchanged a look. I never imagined a corpse could look so rueful and amused. Then Conal's arm, all bone and sinew and bloody ragged cloth, reached out for Seth.

'Conal. Don't,' whispered Finn, but she didn't call out again.

Conal seemed to pause, torn in more ways than one. Then he slipped his rotted arm round his brother, and pulled him close in a fierce, fond hug. And then he lowered him awkwardly to the ground.

Seth swayed, found his balance and stepped back. Finn was already running to him, and she threw her arms round his shoulders, holding him determinedly in the world of the living. The blue roan, riderless and confused and blowing, was backing away from the Veil-gash now. Conal simply shrugged, lifted the wild-eyed queen from the black's withers, and tucked her under one arm.

By now his friendly grin was altogether a death's head rictus, but I still wasn't afraid. I wanted to run after him and hug him, torn belly and all, but it was too late to ask. With a last regretful smile, he snuggled his pathetic wriggling burden tighter under his arm, and spurred the black horse back through the ragged split in the Veil.

All of them were riding back now at a canter, all the ghoulish fighters. Some of them had jumped their horses through already, and the rest were galloping hard as if they feared the Veil might close, but I couldn't see that happening. If anything, it looked as if it was ripping wider.

The blond with what had been burnt-sugar eyes flew past me so fast he almost knocked me over, but I dodged and caught myself from falling, and searched desperately for my father again.

~ *Don't be gone, don't be—*

He wasn't gone. He'd halted his horse just on the other side of the Veil, Kate still tucked under his arm. I blinked. He was whole and beautiful again. There wasn't a wound on his body, despite the torn shirt. He looked just as Finn had described him when she was dying of the Wolf's sword-thrust. My father was beautiful, and unharmed, and he was grinning.

Not, I thought, the nicest grin I'd ever seen. Even when his face wasn't melting.

Something small and black fell from Kate's clothing and Conal caught it in his fist. Creasing his brow, he turned the thing in his palm, shrugged, then tossed it back through the Veil. It bounced once on peat and Finn darted forward to catch it. Then she crouched on the heather, and stared wide-eyed through the Veil-gash as it sagged towards her.

Playfully Conal tossed Kate skywards, caught her by her glossy hair and dangled her like a child's toy. She hung limp and shrunken in Conal's grip, eyes glassy with terror, as he jiggled her. As I watched my great-great-grandmother's frantic furious face, she began, quite gently, to dissolve.

It was a slight translucency at first, that was all, as if she was starting to stop existing, starting to be a ghost. Her body shrank as she hung there, brittle and desiccated, her flesh shrivelled and dried on her bones, but she was still *there*. I could see her, as clearly as I'd seen Conal when he rode across the Veil to get her. But Kate must have been on the wrong side too long now, because the decay didn't stop. Her flesh wasted and her face hollowed to a skull, and grey putrefaction crept across her like the light of a gruesome sunset.

There came a point when only Kate's eyes were alive, but the last thing to go was her mind: I knew that, I could see it. The strongest part of her, of course. There was something peculiarly horrible about that, and if it had been anyone else I might have felt sorry for her.

But then her mind went too, like a thrown switch, and the lights went out in the eyes of a would-be-god.

Rory

Kate's awful end was going to be theirs now. Hannah's, Seth's, Finn's, his own. It didn't bother him half as much as he'd expected. Almost happily, Rory watched the gap in the Veil swell. Finn was backing away from it now, reaching desperately for Seth's good hand.

The gash was going to go on growing, inexorable, as the other side swallowed them all, ate their world. Oh, and the otherworld too, Rory guessed, as soon as that other Veil died: the one he'd known and loved all his life. It made perfect sense, now. Thing was, thought Rory, something of them would be left, some remnant of every Sithe and every full-mortal. Maybe it would be a better remnant anyway. At least there would be *something*.

Of Kate there was nothing, nothing at all. She was scattered bone and ash and dried flesh below Conal's upraised hand, and all that was left in his grip was a hank of silken copper hair. He shook that contemptuously onto Kate's remains, then turned a gaze like cold fire on Rory.

Rory shivered. ~ *I can't close it.*

Conal tilted his head and frowned his disapproval.

~ *I've tried and I can't. It doesn't matter.*

For the first time Conal looked angry. The black kelpie took a pace towards the gash, pawed the earth and snorted.

~ *Even if it does matter, I can't—*

Conal's eyes closed, then blinked open again. He leaned forward on the horse's back, stretched a hand back through the yawning Veil, and tilted it palm-upwards as the flesh greyed and shrivelled. Clenching it into a fist, he yanked it back.

~ It must close, Rory MacSeth MacGregor MacLorcan Mac-Luthais. NOW.

God and gods and wannabe gods: what was he thinking? As if he'd snapped from a dream into a waking nightmare, blackness surged through Rory's veins and his brain and heart contracted with terror. Lunging, he grabbed a handful of the dark Veil in both hands. He pulled it, tugged and dragged. *Nothing.* He pressed it to his face. Cajoled it. *Flirted.*

And he forced it, or tried to. But it wouldn't listen.

It wanted to stay open, that was the thing. It wanted to swallow everything. That was how it was. Like a snake was a snake, or a wolf was a wolf, it was the Veil. *The* Veil, the *Sgath Dubh.* Endlessly hungry, that was all, and there was no changing it.

The dead riders watched him in silent anticipation, but he tried not to see their eyes. He tried to think they might live, all of them: him and Hannah, Seth and Finn. Sionnach and Orach and Grian. By some miracle they might even fight their way back to the fortress and save Iolaire and Branndair. Miracles happened. Maybe.

But that Veil still wouldn't seal.

~ *You'll close!* he told it, furiously.

Sweat prickled on Rory's temples. If there was magic he could work he'd do it, witchcraft or not. For a magic word, he thought, he'd go to hell and back right now.

It was strange that as he thought that very thing, he felt Finn behind him. Her hand pressed the back of his skull and the icy torrent from her fingers chilled his blood, his bones, his brain, and he could think again.

Think was the wrong word, perhaps. See and feel and hear everything that had ever happened to him, more like it. His whole life coalesced into the instant. He heard the wail of a baby and the despairing shriek of its mother and every word he'd heard since, and one of them was magic, the gods knew, because even his father, who didn't believe in magic, never shut up about one magic word, and Rory heard it echo in his head as if it was every time Seth had drilled it into him, all in one moment. It was the only one Rory knew.

~ *PLEASE.*

He didn't scream it to the strange Veil in his fists; he screamed it to the one he knew, the one he'd known all his life. He needed it now like it had always needed him, he needed the flesh and the skin and the substance of it, and it yielded, stretching, melding, sealing; and he knew with a hideous certainty what the foremothers had felt when they twisted the damned thing to protect their homes and their fortresses, and remorse went through him like a knife.

The world swung on its axis and the two Veils wrapped him like matching shrouds and his mind was one with them both. His whole consciousness expanded and contracted, he felt death and life and everything in between, and then he was falling back, a handful of Veil in each fist, crushing the gap together as his mind came back together too. The last thing he saw, as the gash shrank and coalesced and vanished, was Conal's satisfied wink.

Rory came back to himself, realising how stupid he must look, on his arse on the ground. Half-sitting up, he stared in stupefaction at the empty air. At a sound he started, but it was Seth, falling to his knees beside him. Rory scrambled round into his embrace, felt Finn's arms around them both.

'It's not over,' said Seth through gritted teeth. 'It's not over, Rory, but you did your job. Listen, I love you.'

'Oh, it's over.' Gealach slid, trembling and blood-spattered, from her limping horse. 'Kate's dead. My unit's dead. Every man and woman of them. I don't want any Veil gone. Let ours survive or rot as it will. It's over.' She grabbed Sionnach by the shoulder and fumbled to unlock his manacles. 'Over. So help me. *Leave us alone.*'

Finn started to get to her feet. Seth, though, stayed on his knees, holding Rory as if he knew for the first time that there was a time limit to his life.

'*I have a last right!*' A cold voice cut the air, bitter and hateful. Kilrevin stood up, chest heaving, his sword in two hands. Maybe he knew he was done for now, but there must be someone he wanted to take with him.

'A last right, and you all know it. I claim it. Now.' Backing towards Cluaran's body, he bent to yank the dead man's sword from the scabbard on his back. He had to kick Cluaran's shoulder to free it, and the corpse jerked and collapsed again as it slid free. Someone in the dead captain's unit gave a cry of protest.

Kilrevin ignored that. He tossed Cluaran's sword to the ground beside Seth. 'Pick it up, Murlainn.'

Rory pulled back from his father, searching his face in disbelief. Seth only shrugged, half-smiled, and shut his eye. As he staggered to his feet, Finn seized his arm, but he eased out of her grip, then turned and kissed her gently on the mouth.

'I love you,' he whispered.

Seth bent to grab the sword. He stumbled, righted himself, and hefted the weapon, its tip dragging on the peat.

He could barely lift it. Laughing hoarsely, he stood and hauled the blade up to a defensive position. His body swayed.

Rory felt the rage and hate coming off Finn like a physical force, but he couldn't get off his knees to stand by her. He couldn't take his eyes off his father. Couldn't believe what he was seeing.

The Wolf threw him a smug look. 'It's my right, Laochan, so no tantrums. One-on-one with the victorious Captain.'

There were murmurs of dissent from Kate's surviving fighters, a few shouts of protest and shocked whispers, but the Wolf took no notice.

'Not a right that's often claimed, understandably,' he mused aloud, 'but under Murlainn's circumstances . . .'

Taking three running steps to Seth's blind side, he casually lifted his blade and slashed down at his shoulder. Seth wavered aside and parried him, just: but only because the Wolf was still playing. Seth's arms were too weak to hold Cluaran's weapon. It bounced from his hands, and clattered to the rocky ground.

Seth reeled, but kept his feet. Finn's jaw was clenched and she gave a tortured cry of—what? Rage, thought Rory? Frustration?

Seth could only turn as well as he could, finding the Wolf with his surviving eye.

'Do it fast,' he said. 'You've had your fun.'

'That was my pleasure,' said the Wolf. 'And so is this.'

Seth raised his head defiantly as the blade swept towards his neck.

And stopped. It didn't shiver or slip, just jolted to a halt in mid-air as if it had met a soft but impenetrable wall. The Wolf goggled at it, tried to move it back or forward, but failed. It was held fast.

Seth was gaping at it too. He turned, dumbstruck, and stared at his lover. 'Finn?'

She'd sunk to her knees, drained. With an effort she shook her head. 'Tried. Couldn't. Didn't.' She fell forward onto her fisted hands on the peat. *I couldn't.*

Swaying, Seth searched the faces in the ranks. His voice, when he spoke, shook. 'Who's the telekinetic?'

Good question. Apart from Finn there had been only one telekinetic, and Rory had felt safe assuming she was dead. Bewildered, chilled to the bone, he looked around him. So did everyone else.

Except one. Wearing an expression of utmost contentment, Hannah stepped forward and slapped her hands lightly together. 'I am.'

'*You!*' The Wolf stared at her. 'You never—you didn't—'

'Only just,' said Hannah, idly admiring the sword as he tugged futilely at its hilt.

Finn shoved herself to her feet, sucked in a breath, and straightened. Her face was cold stone as she strode past Hannah, right up to the Wolf.

'You failed,' she whispered venomously in his face. 'You failed to kill our Captain.'

'Beaten only by witchcraft!' the Wolf snarled.

Seth took a breath. 'Pots and *fecking* kettles—'

'All right,' Finn interrupted. 'I'm next in line to the Captaincy, Alasdair. Try your luck with me.'

Open-mouthed at his good fortune, the Wolf couldn't repress a broad grin as Finn walked back to where Seth crouched, exhausted. She touched his cheek.

'No, Finn,' he moaned. 'No. No.'

'Yes.' She kissed him. 'I love you too.'

Lifting the blade she walked back to the Wolf, her tone turning formal. 'Not only is it my right, Murlainn, I claim him from you anyway. I think we have plenty of witnesses.'

'Finn, don't. Please don't.'

But Seth must know it was already too late, thought Rory, heartsick. They all did.

'Didn't you get enough of me, Caorann?' The Wolf laughed, and winked at Seth.

Hearing the low wolf-snarl in his father's throat, Rory lunged, just in time to seize Seth before he could fling himself at Kilrevin. With a yell of rage and misery, Seth gave up the struggle. Rory's arms tightened round him.

Rory looked anxiously at Finn but she was shaking her head in wonderment as she gazed at the light dancing on Cluaran's blade.

'Oh, that.' She gave Seth a smile. Then she turned back to the Wolf, shrugging. 'Listen, I don't want you to die with the wrong idea in your head.'

He barked a mocking laugh. 'Killed by you, you fumbling amateur? Have four years made you marginally better than useless? I'm not going to die.'

'Yes, you are. But I'm not going to kill you for anything you did to me. I'm going to kill you for hurting my lover.'

He laughed again, but he sounded less certain this time, because Finn had stopped admiring Cluaran's blade. She turned the sword in her hands so that it was pointing at the ground. Both hands on its hilt, she thrust it hard into the peat.

'Now, wait a minute,' began the Wolf.

Finn glanced over her shoulder at Hannah, who nodded. Finn smiled.

'My weapon of choice,' she told him.

'No, that isn't—'

'That's fair, Alasdair.' A voice shouted it from Kate's decimated ranks: Gealach. 'You chose weapons last time.'

'And was beaten by witchcraft!' he yelled again.

Thoughtfully Gealach looked from him to Finn. 'Uh-huh. And you tortured Murlainn half to death before you took him on. I think it stands at a fair draw.'

There was a ripple of agreement from Kate's surviving troops.

'Back to business,' smiled Finn. 'Now. Did Kate mention how talented I am?'

'You can't do this!' He was straining at his sword with both hands but it was immovable.

'*Can't*, Alasdair? Of course I can!' She laughed a little rippling laugh.

'It's the young witch that's got the power. Kate told me. It's her. *Not you.*'

'I know, isn't this funny? Couldn't you just *die*?'

She was scaring the hell out of him, thought Rory, so the gods knew what she was doing for Kilrevin.

'I told my lover the night I was bound to him,' Finn murmured, 'that I'd kill the next person who hurt him. You've been a dead man walking for four years.'

'Get away from me!'

'Like you got away from him?' Her smile was lethal.

'*Get away!*'

'Oh, look, forget the stupid sword,' she said, sounding almost like Finn again. 'You'd better fight me.' Her eyes lit up like nitro-glycerine, like phosphorus. The explosion of light filled her pupils, her irises, even the whites of her eyes. 'It's the only chance you've got left.'

Kilrevin leaped to his feet, clenching his fists, vicious hatred igniting his eye. The bolt of energy was almost visible, rippling the air between them before it slammed Finn right between the eyes.

She brought her fingertips to her forehead, then studied them with mild interest. Shook them lightly, and smiled at the Wolf.

He sucked in an angry breath and snarled. When his second attack came, she lifted a lazy palm towards him, and the skin of it rippled just as the air had. Finn made a fist, loosened it, and shook her fingers again.

'You're almost tragic,' she said. 'Go on, one more.'

His face reddened, and this time his teeth bared like an animal's. Finn opened her arms to him, and the unseen missile crashed into her chest. She gave a small wince, glanced down, and brushed her ribcage.

'Oh, Alasdair,' she said, and took five steps, and placed a tender hand against his face.

The Wolf tried his damnedest, he really did. With something like pity Rory watched him fight, recognised the struggle, witnessed his hopeless panic as he went under. But Finn was wrong, he thought: Kilrevin never did have a neutered tomcat's chance.

The Wolf knew what was happening, Rory could see that. Physically he shrank before Finn as she cupped his face, motionless but for her black hair stirring gently in the sea breeze. His brutish malevolence died into utter horror, and he whimpered.

Finn tilted her head curiously to watch his eye. Her gaze flicked left, flicked right, as if following the flight of tiny invisible birds. She looked back into his eye once more.

'Please don't.' The Wolf's voice was a thin scratchy wail.

Finn furrowed her brow. At least, Rory thought she did. His view was blurred by the insanely intense silver of her eyeballs.

'Faster?' she asked distantly.

She answered her own question. Small white flames flickered around the rim of the Wolf's single eyeball. One of her forefingers twitched, and the Wolf jerked. Once more. And again.

'Oh, gods,' moaned a voice from the ranks. 'Oh, gods.'

Grian, thought Rory.

Finn gave a small sigh; Rory thought solar wind might sound like it, out in the vacuum of millions of miles of darkness. Lazily she flicked her fingers again, stripped another layer of consciousness. Closed her eyes, stripped another. A fighter in the closest rank fell to his knees, retched in terror and threw up. It was Cuthag, but Finn didn't notice. She stood still and silent and contemplative, and tore the Wolf's mind into tiny glittering pieces.

He crumpled, and crumbled, flailing his sword one last pitiful time as Hannah disdainfully released it. A reflex, Rory thought sickly. It could have been nothing more. Finn didn't even flinch as the blade whispered past her ear, and clanged to the ground.

The Wolf was drooling and gibbering now, and he was twitching on the ground, empty-eyed and foetal, when Seth limped to Finn and slipped his arms around her waist. He pressed his forehead to the back of her head and closed his surviving eye, and whispered.

Her inhuman eyes flickered.

Seth placed the palm of his hand on the side of her head, and turned it very gently towards him. He murmured again.

The light in her eyes sparked and guttered like a candle starved of oxygen. She blinked hard, her face turned a tiny degree closer to Seth's, and she swayed. After seconds that felt like forever, the silver light gave a last fierce glaring pulse, and subsided.

Finn blinked again, and her eyes were close to normal. Staring down at what she'd done she began to tremble, but Seth held her and murmured to her till the shaking stopped.

Even the sea wind had died. There was silence on the bluff, except for the ugly racket of Raib MacRothe, vomiting next to Cuthag.

Seth turned to Sionnach. 'Get rid of that,' he said quietly.

Grimly, Sionnach took the lifeless arm of the shell on the ground. He dragged it to the lip of the cliff and half-kicked, half-rolled it over. It seemed an age until the dull thump and splash, far below.

Hannah couldn't take her eyes off the place where the Wolf had lain. Rory approached her quietly, took her hand in his and kissed it. She shivered, blinking at the cliff-edge, and he knew what memory was in her head.

'No,' he told her softly. 'This time he's gone. This time he really is. He was gone before he went over the edge.'

She sighed and turned into his arms. He decided he wouldn't let go of her again.

'Anyone else?' Sionnach turned on the ranks with a snarl.

No-one answered for a moment, but a lot of heads shook violently.

Gealach was first to recover. She gritted her teeth and glared somewhere to the left of Finn's shoulder.

'I think we're all done, aren't we?' she said brittly. 'I'll pledge my allegiance to Murlainn tomorrow.'

Seth straightened, but he held Finn firmly against him.

'You can all have twenty-four hours to get used to the notion.' His voice was flat. 'This time tomorrow I want every one of you back on this spot to pledge me your swords. I know every wretched one of you. Anyone who isn't here, I'll hunt you down and kill you myself.' His lips twisted in something like a smile. 'Or maybe I'll let my lover do it.'

Visible shudders in the ranks. 'Yes, Murlainn.'

'I'm your king, just long enough to tell you this: I abdicate. No more kings. No more queens. Enough of that shit. Now get back to your hellhole.' His lip curled. 'Release Branndair and Iolaire and Rory's filly. Gealach, you bring my bridle here. *You personally.*'

Gealach nodded curtly. Her face was pallid. 'Murlainn.'

They turned one by one and limped away, or sagged on horseback, led by their exhausted unwounded comrades. When they were gone, there was no sound but the breeze, rising again in rock and grass and abandoned pyres.

Reluctantly Rory eased his hand out of Hannah's, but he did

have to let her go. For this he did. He turned to Finn, and she eased herself gently from Seth's embrace.

She opened her fist. A black talisman lay in her palm, an obsidian falcon with threads of faded golden hair wound round its neck. Finn laid it on a flat slab of rock and ground her heel onto it. For a second it resisted, then shattered explosively into glassy splinters.

Connection sparked and flamed in Rory's head. Seth was in his mind, and he was in his father's arms, and a heartbeat later Rory felt pain sear his body, slicing into his limbs and his guts, knocking his breath from his lungs.

It didn't matter. In an instant Seth was gone from his head, and the pain evaporated. Seth was grinding his forehead against Rory's so hard it hurt. That didn't matter either.

It really was over, thought Rory. He'd kept the promise he made the day he claimed Kate, a stupid fourteen-year-old boy who barely knew what he was promising. And Finn had kept whatever promise she'd made his father. *Over,* he thought.

Except that the other Veil, the one Kate had wanted him to open, the one he stroked fondly beneath his fingertips? It felt frailer than ever, a rotten skein of silk that would blow away in the next puff of wind like an abandoned cobweb.

Finn

Did I feel any remorse for what I did to the Wolf? Honestly? No. Regret for what it did to me, that's all. I knew the ability had only come to me with a visceral soul-deep hatred. But there was a saving grace: if it had been only about hate, only about me, I'd have been able to do it before, when I could have saved myself from him. What I did to the Wolf had to do with love, too. And it was saving the life of someone I loved, not just punishing his tormentor. That's what I told myself when I lay awake in the small hours, lost and scared of myself and very, very small beneath the skyful of stars.

Besides, every time I looked at the wounds on Seth's body, the patch that hid his eyeless socket? I wished the Wolf alive again, so I could kill him again the same way, and again.

'How okay are you?' Seth asked me, on the first night we could be alone together, the first Grian would let him out of his sight. We lay on our sides, facing each other. His fingers touched my face, combed through my hair, stroked my neck, like he never wanted to stop touching me, ever. That was fine by me.

We watched each other for a while, letting our minds mingle. 'Don't,' he said abruptly, pulling away when I intruded too deeply in his memories.

'I'm not keeping you out.' I stroked his hair.

'That's different.' His thumb traced my temple, my cheekbone, my lips.

'That game of Kilrevin's,' I said. 'He didn't really understand, did he? I'd have done anything to stop them going back to you.'

He took my face in his hands and pressed his forehead to mine. It felt light and fierce all at once as his mind caressed mine. 'Same here.' His lips curved in a smile.

I tried to touch his mind again, but he blocked me abruptly. 'Don't. No, don't try to See. It hurt, but it'll hurt me more if you feel it.'

'Don't keep me out. Seth, don't. I know what he did to you.'

'Please, Finn. Later. Not now. Wait till it's faded. Because it will fade, it will.'

His harsh breathing quietened again, and we lay very still for a while. Thoughts skittered across my mind: *No. I never did forget. I never did lose him. I always knew him. She was nothing.*

I sighed and said: 'Was that Nils Laszlo? With Conal?'

He laughed. 'Life's full of surprises, isn't it?'

'Death too,' I said. 'I wish Conal would change that shirt.'

Seth gave me his old lopsided half-grin. 'I think he will, now. Shut up about laundry, woman. I love you.' He kissed me.

It was what I would have sold my soul for, back in Kate's cells: one more kiss. Just as well I hadn't been offered the option. In some ways Kate had a very limited imagination. In others . . .

He felt my shudder. 'What?' he said, drawing his forefinger lightly from my temple to my jaw.

'Nothing. I love you.'

'I love you too. *What?*'

I touched one of the ugly gashes in his flesh. Then another, and another.

I didn't meet his eye. I kept running my fingers over every place where the knife had sawn and twisted in the body I loved more than my own, the body that could give and take so much pleasure, the body they'd all but torn to pieces.

He blocked very well. But when he let his guard slip even for an instant, I could feel how deep the blade had gone. They'd done it with such precision, letting him bleed and beg and *live*. In my head I could feel the echo of his screams and howls like a physical force.

I said, 'Why are you not dead?'

I knew I wouldn't like the answer but I had to ask. I had a responsibility to him. I'd bound myself to him and that meant certain things.

He sighed, closing his fingers round mine. Then he laughed dryly. Oh, he could laugh at anything. I loved him for it and it infuriated me beyond reason.

'Okay,' he said. 'It was that healer of Kate's. Who ought to be struck off, in my opinion.'

I stared at him. I didn't laugh. I was too busy fighting nausea. 'He will be.'

Seth knew what I meant. His thumb caressed my cheekbone and he was silent for a long time, reading my eyes.

'Stay human, Finn.'

'Part of being human,' I said, 'is not letting them get away with it.'

'*Them*.' He tilted his eyebrow. 'The ones who forgot how to be human?'

'Yes. Them. You know as well as I do there's a line.'

'Sure. I worry for you, that's all.'

'After what I did to Kilrevin?'

'After what you had to do.' He took my fingers and kissed them.

'You'll have to keep a close eye on me, then.' I let my thumb brush his lip. 'Don't go wandering off again. Getting in trouble.'

'I don't plan to.' He smiled and wriggled closer, but I shivered as I wrapped my arms round him. He felt it and hugged me tighter. I hadn't meant to shiver; it was only that someone had said those words to me before, and the memory niggled at the back of my skull. *I don't plan to, toots. I don't plan to die.*

'We've seen the worst, haven't we?' I whispered, as his body stirred against me and I stroked his familiar scarred back. Kate had failed spectacularly. I ached for him. I longed for him. I wanted my mind tangled up in his as he moved inside me, but I had to ask first. 'It'll never be so bad again?'

He kissed my lower lip. 'I will never let anything bad happen to you again.'

'You can't promise me *that*.'

'Caorann. Love of my heart.' He ran his hands across my breasts, my ribcage, my hips, my thighs. 'You're mine and you always were. I was with you. You know I was. You were with me.'

I felt hot tears on my face and I didn't care. He was right. Even sorcery and a rowanwood cell couldn't keep us apart, and I should have remembered that all along.

He trailed kisses along my neck, my shoulder. Gently he lifted me to him, and a short while later I lost my mind, or maybe it only got so mixed up in his that we both lost track of ourselves. When we came back to reality, as we had to, he rolled onto his back and pulled me against him, his arms locked tight around me.

~ *Caorann*, he said.

'Oh, God, Seth. I can't exist without you. I can't. It terrifies me. *Murlainn*.'

'Love of my soul.' He pressed his lips to my forehead. 'Forget what happens next.'

'We're mortal. We're so mortal. I could not *stand to lose you*.'

'I know. Sh. Listen, we've lost friends, but we're luckier than they were and we should do them the honour of knowing it.

We're happy, we're safe, we're together. This is the best life can be.' Closing his eye he smiled and held me tighter. 'How long do you think we can make it last?'

We got our answer, two years later to the day.

Finn

Damn, but I loved this room. I felt like I'd loved it all my life, like I'd been Seth's all my life instead of a few short years. I lay watching moon shadows on the machair through the open casement, hearing the distant hiss and tumble of waves on the sand. How many times had I lain and watched that scene, listened to the sounds of our world and our home? And every time it was different. Every time.

Seth's face was pressed to my back: I could feel his breath against my shoulder blade. I reached back to thread my hand into his hair.

'Four hundred years,' he whispered. 'Finn. Why did I have to wait so long for you?'

'Sh. I'm here now, that's all.'

'The gods are unfair.' He kissed my spine.

'You're an atheist,' I reminded him.

'Mm-hm,' he mumbled. 'Four hundred years . . .'

'C'mon,' I laughed softly. 'You haven't been celibate.'

I tried to wriggle round to face him, but he held me still.

'Don't mock me,' he whispered. 'Not tonight.'

I paused, traced his unseen face with my fingers. I frowned at the wall.

'All right.'

'Sleep,' he said.
I did.

I loved waking up before Seth. It didn't happen often: he'd always been an early riser and anyway, since the war two years earlier, his nights were disturbed again. It was getting better. He didn't yell and thrash in his sleep so much; he didn't wake up screaming every night. He fell asleep faster in my arms. He didn't feel he had to lie there clutching me till dawn, terrified some night terror would take me away.

So on the rare occasions when I woke before him, I'd just lie there and look at him and wonder how in heaven's name I'd have gone on existing without him. The damage done by the Wolf hadn't healed so well as his older wounds but it had healed after a fashion. The healer had at least done a professional job: one reason I'd let him impale himself on his own sword. While I watched, obviously.

Sometimes I thought about things like that and wondered what happened to a sixteen-year-old girl who thought that was all she was. I wondered what she'd think of me now. Perhaps she'd walk away in disgust. Perhaps she'd run.

He'd lost some of his appetite for the Captaincy but that was okay, we commanded the clann together. Not that we always agreed: but if it wasn't much fun falling out, it was a lot more fun making up. Seth was more merciful than I was, and that caused a few rows. He said he'd been shown mercy as a traitor; I told him he hadn't, and reminded him how back then he'd never let me hear the end of it, all that stuff about taking it like a Sithe.

Well, between us we dispensed a kind of justice, the fairest we could manage. He'd banned floggings long ago (for all his finger-wagging lectures about tradition), but there were exiles, imprisonments, confiscations of property. Not for ordinary soldiers or captains, of course: fighting for a cause isn't a crime. Other things are, whether done in a cause or not. I won't pretend there weren't executions. War's war. I put a sword through four of them myself, and I made them watch my eyes while I did it. Even Cuthag didn't dare to look away.

As for the healer: well, Seth had begged for death, and the man had ignored him. So the healer had to die instead, but I gave him the honourable choice and he took it. I'd already dealt with the Wolf, of course, but I wish it had taken longer. I wish it had taken the three days he gave Seth. I wish it had taken three years.

Seth's body was damaged but it wasn't broken. It could still fight and run and love; oh, gods, could it love. His face was still beautiful despite the scars and the missing eye, or it was to me. It was calm as I watched him breathing that morning. No bad dreams. He was lying on his back and one arm was still around me, the other flung up above his head. His mutilated left hand: it didn't work well, but hey, he was right-handed.

I stroked his hair back from his face, careful not to wake him. There were strands of it across his forehead as usual, one lock long enough to touch the bridge of his nose. I smiled and lifted it delicately away, smoothing it back above his right ear, the one with the old missing bit at the top.

I blinked in the thin early light and looked harder. Either it had happened in the night or I just hadn't looked properly for a few days. Above that maimed ear, the black hairs were not all black. There were threads of grey, as if they'd been woven there in the night by some spiteful elf.

I stared for a long time, not wanting to see; then I looked at his face. His eye had opened to watch me, but he didn't move for a long time. Neither of us did.

Then his mind brushed against mine, very gently, and I began to cry.

He curled up, and pulled me down into his arms. 'You noticed.'

I didn't answer. Couldn't.

'We still have some time,' he said. 'Don't be unhappy. Not yet.'

'It felt like. Before, I mean. I thought it would be.' Tears blocked my throat. 'It felt like forever.'

'Nobody gets forever, Finn. And you know it happens quickly now.'

He was too calm. He'd been planning what to say to me. His heart had been breaking for days. Had I just not wanted to see?

Why? I thought. He was young. Why would he die? The question everyone's always asked, all through the ages of time. The one you never get an answer for.

'By the way,' he said lightly, 'you've made me happy. Happier than I ever thought I'd get to be. I thought I'd better tell you that. In case I forget later.'

'Oh, okay.' I managed to speak. 'So long as—I mean, I thought for a moment you were going to leave. Now. Today.' I tried to laugh. Failed.

'I don't want you to watch till the end. But I haven't got a battle to go in now.'

'Well, damn.'

'So I'll go to the Selkyr, okay? Like Leonie. So don't be obstreperous about that.'

'Right, okay. Because you'd never do such a thing yourself. Try to stop someone going to the Selk—' My voice caught on the word, but I forced back my tears, because they weren't fair on him. 'Just don't—don't sneak off like she did.'

'I'd never do that. Never.'

And then it hit me, so hard. Maybe the word. Because *never* meant nothing. There wasn't a *never* any more, there wasn't a *for-ever*. There were a few prosaic, countable weeks. Not centuries. Not years. Weeks. Yet for all it meant nothing, *never* was a blade, a physical thing, slicing into my head and my heart. For a moment I couldn't breathe. I could only feel his skin, warm and alive. For perhaps a minute, it was all that kept *me* alive.

And suddenly I understood them, all of them. I understood Leonie, and my mother. I even understood Eili. The grief would cut out your heart and your mind.

'Don't follow,' he said. 'Please.'

'How can I stay? Switch off my heart?'

'Oh gods,' he said. His lips touched my face. 'I've done such a terrible thing.'

'No.'

'Not wrong. Never wrong. But it was a terrible thing, Finn.'

'There. You've said it. Be satisfied. I don't want you to say it again.'

'All right,' he said after a pause. 'If you promise to live.'

I touched his face with the back of my hand, watching his eye through my fingers. 'I don't want to stay.'

'You've got to.'

I stared, felt my heart beat slowly. 'I'll try.'

'Promise.'

'I will not promise forever,' I hissed. 'Nobody gets forever.'

He hesitated, then said sadly, 'All right.'

'I'll live. I promise, for now. But I'm giving you no promise beyond that.'

His breath came out in a great sigh. 'Oh Finn.' He curled into me. 'I want to stay. I don't want to leave you. I want to get old.'

'So do I. Now. With you. And die.'

'It's stopped being about what we want.'

'When was it ever?' I said bitterly.

He didn't scold me. His arms tightened round me. I felt his breath on my skin. I kissed him, to taste him.

'I've heard,' he mumbled. 'Well, they say it's a good way to go. The Selkyr hold you. You're not alone. They stop you panicking, make it easy, help you—breathe. You know? Just breathe in. And then it's over. And it doesn't hurt any more.'

I raised my head, but he had averted his eye.

'How do they know?' I whispered.

'I don't suppose they do, really.' His gaze on the dawn machair was desolate.

Just for a moment, I hated him for the promise he'd forced from me. 'You'd better say goodbye, you bastard.'

'I'll say goodbye.' He pulled my tear-sodden face into his shoulder and stroked my hair. 'But not yet.'

There was nothing defined about our last weeks. Every day, every night melted into the next. I didn't ride my own new horse. If we rode out together it was both of us on the blue roan: me at his back, my face pressed between his shoulder blades to feel his heartbeat, or him behind me, one arm round my waist, clutching me tightly against him as if he could hang on to life that way.

We sat up on the battlement as we always had, his arms round me, staring out at the flowers on the machair, happy not to speak. And we made love: fiercely, desperately, clinging onto each other, as if we could imprint a memory on one another's skin and flesh. Our gazes locked, our minds tangled, our bodies so entwined we must have hoped it might be impossible ever to separate them; as if in one body we could live forever.

'Please stay,' I begged again. 'I don't care if you get old.'

'I'll get old,' he said bitterly. 'For a month? Two? I'll wither in days and hours, and you may not care but I do. Be raddled and

rotten and mad in a month, and then die anyway? Merrydale's
nothing on a Sithe death. You don't know what it's like, Finn,
you've never seen it. I've seen someone refuse the Selkyr.' He shuddered. 'I want to go, Finn. I want to go while I can still run.'

I didn't know what he meant by that. Not then. After all, wasn't
he drumming it into me day after day?

There wasn't any running from it.

He woke me in the early hours, maybe two weeks later. I hadn't
been counting. I'd been desperately not-counting. He took my
hand and we dressed in silence and went barefoot to the stables,
and the roan hooked its head over his shoulder and whickered. I'd
never heard it make such a mournful, human sound. When we
rode out of the dun gate, only the guard saw us go.

The machair was dappled with starlight, but no moon. He'd
seen his last moon. The roan cantered easily, and just for a moment I took one arm from around Seth's waist and laid my hand
against its warm flank, felt the muscles moving. A memory jolted
through me of the first time I'd laid eyes on it, when it tried to eat
me. I knew after tonight I'd never see it again.

The wind was high, blustering my hair across my eyes. The
roan was running with it, so when it plunged down the dunes and
trotted to a halt, I felt the unbroken force of the breeze even
stronger. Seth swung down from the horse, and caught me as I
dismounted. I had a sense he was holding me to stop me looking
at the water's edge, but it would be no more than his protective
instinct. He can't have imagined I wouldn't turn. He can't have
imagined I wouldn't watch the three Selkyr, patient, black-eyed,
their sealskin coats glistening and whipping in the wind. The blue
roan had gone already. Vanished.

Stupidly I wrapped my arms round Seth's neck and hugged him fiercely, refusing to let go. The sea looked so wild, so cold, and I didn't want him to go into it. Just the thought of it hurt my heart. I wished it could be me instead. I wished it could be me as well.

Then realisation broke over me like a wave. No vow I'd given him could trump the one I'd made all those years ago. I didn't have to lose him. He was the love of my heart and the other half of my soul. That was it. That was why this had felt so wrong. I let go of him, laughing.

He frowned, reached out to me, but I'd already turned and shouted to the Selkyr.

'I'm coming too!'

The tallest of them—and that was saying something—examined me with mild interest. Seth seemed stunned. He couldn't do anything, though, because one of the Selkyr had come forward and grasped his arm with its wet clammy hand.

'No,' he said. 'No.'

Well, that confirmed it. He'd said it twice because he *wasn't* certain. Deep down he knew what I knew—well, of course he did—and he wanted this as much as I did. I'd never felt such certainty in my life, or such pure intense happiness.

'I'm coming with you,' I said again.

His eye was bright with shock. Shock, and uncertainty, and ferocious love. Grief too, but too late.

Done deal, my lover.

Until, out of nowhere and nothing, the tallest Selkyr launched itself at me. Its eyes lit like black flame and it opened its mouth wide, screaming with rage, so that I could see nothing but black emptiness. I was so stunned by terror I stumbled back, almost falling, and I cringed as its death's-face screamed into mine.

I'd heard one of these things speak before, and I'd never forgotten its cold liquid voice. This one said the same words, but the sound was altogether different, mad with rage.

'NOT YET!'

I shuffled backwards away from it, frantic. The thing was almost on top of me. Its breath was like cold sea already covering my face, suffocating me, so that I had an inkling of what waited for Seth, and the terror shrank every nerve and vein in my body. Its webbed fingers slapped onto my face, physically shoving me back and down.

'Not while there's life in you!'

I was stunned. I was *lost*. I remembered the time the Selkyr lunged for Jed, just because he'd shown up in the wrong place at the wrong time. I didn't understand: dying, living, sick or well, I thought these things would never fail to take another. It was what they were *for*.

Then Seth was tearing himself from the other Selkyr, flinging himself at me across the sand, dropping to his knees and pulling me up into his arms. His Selkyr grabbed for him but he flailed, batting it away as happiness lit his face.

I held him, hugged him, barely believing I'd been allowed to touch him once more. But didn't he always cheat death? He was famous for it. He was going to stay!

Then I thought: *no, that's impossible*, but he was going to *make them take me*.

I came back to myself and to grim sanity, and he was holding me like he was never going to see me again, and he was laughing and crying all at once.

'Finn! There's life in you!'

For seconds there was only the thud and rush of the sea, the wild howl of the wind. And then I understood.

And then I knew *why*.

'No,' I whimpered. What did I think I was denying?

'Two.' He pressed his scarred cheek to my belly, kissed it. 'One boy.'

'What will I do?' I cried. 'What will I *do*?'

What time did he have to give me a guide for three lives? None.

'Give them names of their own,' he whispered. 'Don't be your mother. Live.'

'Choose,' hissed the Selkyr. It didn't touch him. 'Choose now or we won't wait. Come now or let your lover cut your throat.' It gave a lipless smile. 'Or rot for her.'

Seth pulled away from me very suddenly, as if he had to do this quickly or not at all. He smiled, flipped his eyepatch by way of a wink, and then he'd turned and was running, running with death at his heels, and as the Selkyr howled and keened with anger he kept running towards the sea. They followed, but I knew they weren't hurrying, that they were exasperated more than anything.

The blue roan came out of nowhere, faster even than the Selkyr, overtaking them and galloping abreast of Seth, and my heart almost exploded with the joy of it. He reached for its mane as the Selkyr screamed and raced for him, but he was on its back now and they were flying together into the sea. Great fans of spray went up around the roan's hooves, and the Selkyr burst through it, gaining on the roan at last as it breasted the crashing waves. Seth looked small and hopelessly brave against the fury of the water but at least he wasn't alone any more.

I ran to the water's edge in time to see first one Selkyr, then the other, dive through the water like dolphins and swarm up onto the roan's back and envelop him. And then the roan screamed once and submerged, and they were all gone, and I was alone on the beach as the sea closed over him and rolled on forever.

Finn

Seth had a tiny baby cradled in his arm. One hand held a bottle deftly to its mouth while the other played idle piggies with its toes. He was grinning into its big solemn eyes. I thought it was a twin, but it wasn't. It was me.

If I have a baby, he crooned, it'll look just like you. So I'll practice with you, okay? Is that okay, Fionnuuuuuuala? Can I look after you? I won't walk away, I promise. I won't let anybody treat you like they treated me. Okay?

Gods, I had no idea he could babble like a doting old woman. As if a baby could understand a word. But maybe he was talking more to himself than to the baby.

Anyway, he went on, I'm not going to have a kid for ages, if ever. But if I do? She'll look exactly like you. Exactly like you.

He turned and looked straight at me, at the grown-up Finn, and smiled a smile of breathtaking beauty and trust. My heart twisted achingly. And that was when

I woke up. The paperback was still in my hand but even as my eyes flickered leadenly open it clattered to the floor. I was facing the cot and I could see two small dark eyes staring at me. The other twin, whichever it was, was asleep, its face pressed to its sibling's arm. I had no idea which was which. The one that was awake went on gazing into my eyes. There was something beseeching in its gaze, but nothing judgmental. Fine, fine. I reached down for the paperback and turned away onto my side.

Please. Come. Back. To. Me.

Stupid, eh? He wasn't coming. Not ever.

I stayed for you! I screamed inwardly. *Why couldn't you stay for me?*

'Finn?'

Oh, for God's sake, not again. Nagging time. I looked over the paperback at Grian.

'Don't look at me like that, Grian. I fed them.'

He sat down on the bed beside me and took the paperback out of my hands to study the blurb on the back. 'That's not all there is to it, Finn.'

'I had them, didn't I? What more do you all want of me?'

'It's not about what we want. And Finn?' He stroked my hair out of my eyes. 'It's not even about what you want.'

I slapped his hand away. 'Don't lecture me, Grian. There's been two men I've allowed to lecture me and they're both dead.'

He sighed. 'What now, Finn? There's nothing physically wrong with you.'

'No, there isn't, is there?' I rolled my head round to stare at the wall. 'Actually, Grian, you'll have to bear with me. I didn't think this far ahead. I was kind of assuming I'd die in childbirth.'

'Kind of assuming?' he said. 'Or kind of hoping?'

I looked at him, expressionless.

Grian took a deep breath. 'Finn, there's been no decision. You still have a right to the Captaincy.'

'I don't want it.'

He rubbed his hand across his face. 'You'll have to renounce it in front of witnesses.'

'So arrange it. I never wanted the Captaincy, Grian.' I looked right into his kind eyes. 'I would only ever get it with his death, so why would I want it? He made the mistake of wishing for it. I never did.'

'You'd make a fine Captain, Finn.'

'No, I wouldn't. Not alone. Let Rory take it, and that's my last word.'

He sighed and stood up. 'Can Rory come and see the twins?'

'That's a stupid question, Gri.' I managed to smile at him.

All I wanted to do was sleep. It was the closest I could get to death, after all, so I was asleep again when Rory came. He was there when I woke, a gurgling baby in his arms, and another gazing hopefully up at him from its cot, waiting its turn. He was talking nonsense to the one in his arms, a big stupid grin on his face. Strands of his unruly overlong hair fell forward into his grey eyes. Gods, he was so like his father it hurt. If his hair hadn't been the colour of Conal's, I might have mistaken him . . .

Fiercely I rubbed my eyes. ~ *Rory*, I said.

He looked round at me, happiness lighting his eyes. 'Finn. Oh, Finn. They're so beautiful. My brother and sister. Oh, Finn.'

'Yes,' I said. 'Of course they're beautiful. All babies are beautiful. He was beautiful. QED.'

Rory blinked, puzzled. To fill the awkward silence he laid down one baby and lifted its twin. 'You must be very proud,' he said softly, but he didn't look at me this time.

'Proud?' I shrugged.

'My father would be proud.'

'Yes. He would.'

Rory looked at me again, then down at the baby in his arms. 'What are you going to call him?'

'I don't know. That's the male one, is it? S-Se-uh—your father said they needed names of their own.' I swallowed hard. 'Otherwise I'd have called him Conal. Why don't you think of something?'

'Because *Seth* would want you to choose,' said Rory, a hard edge to his voice. 'That's why not.'

Well, bully for him. He might be able to say the name, but I couldn't. He wasn't bloody judging me on it. 'Well, then. I'll think of something.'

Rory laid the infant down beside its twin, then stood up abruptly. 'You're a Sithe, Finn. You have two kids. Makes you kind of lucky, doesn't it?'

I didn't deign to reply.

'Finn.' He was speaking over tears in his throat. 'You're not the only one who's lost someone. He was my father. Jed was my brother.'

So making me feel worse was his way of helping, was it? I curled into a ball and closed my eyes, and after a moment he walked out and shut the door quietly.

I don't know how long I lay there weeping soundlessly, hating myself even more than I hated those wretched babies. When they began to cry again someone came in and took them both away. Good: better that way. Someone competent could feed them. I wanted to concentrate on the down pillow beneath my face. I breathed in the smell of him, not wanting to exhale, suffocating myself in it. I was terrified and intent because it was months now, and the smell of him was fading; it would fade to nothing and I didn't know what I was going to do when it was gone.

I didn't hear anyone else come into the room, was only aware someone had when a weight sat down beside me and light fingers rubbed my shoulder. I'd long run out of tears by then and I'd failed to smother myself, so I could only stare dry-eyed at the wall.

'Must be awful,' murmured a voice. 'Everybody expecting you to love those infants.'

Oh, bloody hell. *Orach*. The woman who'd loved him through four hundred years of his solitary existence, the friend who'd seen him through crises I could only guess at, the occasional lover who'd only finally dumped him when she saw me coming. They'd loved each other very much, in their own way. I hoped she wasn't going to gloat, because I liked her and I didn't want to have to kill her.

'Sh. It's okay.' She stroked my hair. 'And I'm not going to nag you, I promise. I think I'd hate those little buggers too. Knowing he'll never see them, when he'd have loved them so much. And he wasn't even there to hold your hand when it hurt. And it's supposed to be the two of you. And it isn't.'

'Orach,' I whispered. 'I—'

'Did he say you had to go on living? Did he tell you you had to love them? Yeah, that'd be like him.' Orach squeezed my shoulder. 'What did he know, Finn? You're the one who got left behind. Not him. You.'

I began to cry again. 'That's just a bit of it. That's not—'

'Not all, no. I bet you lie awake and wonder. We're only supposed to get old because we don't breed, aren't we? That's what Eili used to say. Do you worry he spent some of his life fathering them?'

Aching sobs tore out of my throat. Orach wriggled down beside me and put her arms around me.

'Sh. Sh. It isn't true. Okay? Wait till you're thinking straight. Before long you'll know it isn't true. Listen to me. Seth didn't die because he fathered those babies, and in a month or two your brain will be straight again and you'll know it. Seth died because he took too much punishment. He died of Eili, and Kilrevin, and Laszlo's crossbow. He died of his own clann and his own guilt. Most of all he died of the curse he threw at Kate and her people, and *he always knew he would*. He knew that, even as he spoke it. You can't fling such deadly hate and not get caught in the blast yourself. He did it because he had to, they'd have killed him otherwise.'

I remembered him telling me. *They couldn't believe I'd bring such anathema on myself.*

'He didn't do it to save himself, Finn. If he'd died that day, they'd have come after Rory with no-one to stop them. Then you'd have died too, and Jed and Sionnach and Eili. And they'd have had Rory, and then we'd all have died. Seth had no choice. Oh, Finn. Seth died because he was a fighter, not because he was a father.'

I curled into her arms, weeping till I thought I'd never stop. I don't know when I stopped crying, because long before I did, I was asleep. I slept a blank and dreamless sleep for a night and a day, and I know for a fact that Orach didn't leave my side.

~ *I hope you're grateful.*

~ *Grateful?* I told the thing in the dark. ~ *I couldn't keep him. After all that, I couldn't keep him. You call that a promise?*

~ *I never promised you anything of the sort, child of mine.*

I prowled the cavern, running the flat of my palm across smooth black rock. It was vast, but I knew it now, I knew every cranny and every outcrop and every pool that never saw the daylight. I'd visited it often enough. I circled the vast space without the need or desire for light, my bare feet finding familiar dips and ridges, and I trod softly back to the glowing alcove: the place where the child's corpse sat, deaf and blind and mute; and heard and saw everything, and spoke.

~ *Do you know what Kate NicNiven once said to me?* Low gurgling laughter echoed from nowhere and everywhere. ~ *She said: What strong witch wants another to have power over them?*

~ *Yes,* I told it dryly. ~ *That sounds like her.*

~ *And yet here you are.* I felt something enfold me, something cold like a shroud, yet it fitted me snugly. ~ *She was fire. You are ice and stone; you're the deepest heart of the glacier.*

~ *You're full of shit.*

We laughed together.

~ *You're as much part of me as I am part of you, Icefall. You make me proud.*

~ *All right, Soul-Eater,* I said. ~ *Reward me.*

~ *I rewarded you with life. I rewarded you with power. You reached out for me in the darkness and I was there.*

~ *Because,* I told the Darkfall with a smile, ~ *you are everywhere in the darkness. Especially that one.*

The light flickered in the child's cupped hands. Water dripped, slow and steady, somewhere deep in the tunnels that threaded the rock like the paths of monstrous devouring termites. No human had ever walked those tunnels. No human ever would. But I'd dare. I'd dare. If the Darkfall wouldn't give me what I wanted.

~ *Presumptuous. Like the other one.* There was a hint of anger in its voice.

~ *I'm not a bit like the other one,* I said, smiling. ~ *I'm better.*

The breath of the rock whispered across my bare feet, raised gooseflesh on my arms. I didn't rub them.

~ *Perhaps you are,* it said. ~ *We could make a bargain, you and I.*

~ *If our interests coincide.* I closed my eyes and lifted my face to feel its breath. ~ *As with all bargains.*

I thought perhaps it laughed again.

~ *Your lover ended the monarchy, but no god guaranteed him the last word. You can be queen. You can rule and be loved.*

~ *Yes, let's get that offer out of the way, shall we? You know it isn't what I want.*

~ *Very well.* Its coldness enfolded me. ~ *It was worth a try. Ah, Icefall, you're very predictable in your own way, aren't you?*

~ *So are you.* I stepped forward to the corpse of the child, crouched to gaze into its eyeless sockets. I reached out a hand and lowered my palm to the flame, and held it there. So cold. I smiled. ~ *Now let's talk about what I truly want.*

The Darkfall was silent for a long, long time. But I could wait. I had all day and all night. I had forever, if I chose to ask for it.

At last its breath sighed around me, stirring my hair.

~ *You know you can have him back. You know this.*

~ *I know this*, I said. I rose to my feet. ~ *But I won't hand over my soul. Don't ask me to make Kate NicNiven's deal.*

~ *I wouldn't dream of it. Not that I dream.* It chuckled. It had a wicked sense of humour, the Darkfall.

~ *Give me my lover*, I said. ~ *Give him back to me, and I'll give you the Black Veil.*

~ *You want that kind of love, yet you won't hand over your soul? You're arrogant, child.*

~ *I have cause to be.* I smiled for the Darkfall. I knew it was proud of me.

~ *You won't make the NicNiven's deal*, it said thoughtfully. ~ *Yet the agent must be the same.*

~ *I know that too.* I opened my eyes to blackness. ~ *But will that agent want to do as I ask? I doubt it. I doubt he'll follow me with his eyes wide open.*

Something sighed, long and contented, and the last spark in the child's cupped hands guttered and died.

~ *Take the boy by the hand, then. Close his eyes. Lead him.*

Hannah

'Where did you go last night?'

I eyed Finn, but she only focused the blowtorch flame, and leaned into the workbench, and said nothing.

'You know what Grian calls that hour? Devil's Hour.'

'Does he now?'

'Yes,' I told her. 'He says it's when people tend to die.'

She smiled, then gasped in anger, threw down the blowtorch and sucked her scorched finger.

It had taken me long enough to pluck up the courage to ask her where she'd been. I'd used up my nerve and I didn't dare sympathise about the burnt finger. Nobody dared sympathise with Finn, about anything: not even Rory, and he was her Captain. She lived these days on the very edge of cold fury, and a word from either of us now would get our heads bitten off. She got to her feet and stood over the workbench. Under her glare, stones and settings and rejected bits of silver flew scattering onto the floor.

'Sorry,' she muttered after a moment. As she bent to clear up the mess—using her hands this time—I saw tears glint in her eyes.

Rory nibbled his lip. 'Finn, you only just started to do this . . .'

'No,' she snapped. 'I'm no silversmith, I never could do it. Faramach used to sit there beside Leonie and laugh his stupid head off at me. Forget it. I'm going down to the hall to see Sionnach. Rory, I need to die.'

So abrupt, so out of nowhere, it still took my breath away. Every time she said it.

She scared me. She scared us all. But at least I was finally seeing the point of the anthill thing. I wasn't pure-blooded Sithe, thank God, so it wasn't the same for me, but I'd watched them long enough. They didn't love fiercely but ferociously. They lived so terribly long and they weren't faithful, but their link with their bound lovers was for life and for death. They had their teeth and their claws and their hearts in so deep they couldn't let go.

I had to talk to Rory. Tell him to quit nagging Finn. After all, I liked to think I could let go of Rory's ghost, but maybe, if it ever came to that, I'd be just the same. That was the point of the anthills, wasn't it? So the children still had a family when one parent followed the other into oblivion.

'Rory,' said Finn, glancing at me. 'If anything happened to me—'

'Nothing's going to happen, Finn.'

'Yes, but let's suppose it does. You and Hannah. You'd look after them, right? The twins. You'd be better parents than me anyway.'

'Stop it!' barked Rory. 'Stop that! If Dad could hear you!' He sucked in a breath. 'Gods, what if he *can*? Stop it!'

She iced over, I saw it happen, like she'd psyched herself up to demand something and he'd given her the chance she needed. 'You want me to stop, Rory? Do you really?' Her eyes were dead and her smile was chilly. 'Open the Veil for me.'

He looked bewildered. 'You want to go to the otherworld?'

'Gods forbid. No. The other Veil.'

'*What?*'

'You heard.'

He took a step back from her, shaking his head. 'You're out of your mind. Well, of course you are, we all know that,' he spat. 'But I won't do that.'

'I only want to see. I want to see him. One more time.'

'Finn, you're insane. It's too much. How would you know where he'll be?'

'I know where he'll be. He'll be at the Stones. Waiting.'

'No, Finn. No, no, no. He won't be waiting anywhere because he *asked you to live*. He is *not waiting for you*.'

'He is,' said Finn coolly. 'He'll be there because I've asked him to.'

Rory went pale. 'Don't speak to the dead, Finn. Don't.'

'The *dead*? He is your father! He is my lover!'

'He *was* my father. He *was* your lover. Finn, he is *gone*.'

'He is waiting, Rory, and I want to see him. It's the last thing I'll ask of you.'

'And if I can't close it?'

'You'll close it, Rory. You want to know if you can.' She stroked his face gently. I think it was meant to be encouraging. It was something else entirely. 'Now you'll find out. Remember when we heard the horses? We shouldn't have heard them, should we? But the Dark Veil's yours. It speaks to you, it answers you, it *obeys* you.

'The *Sgath Dubh* obeys nobody.'

She twisted her lips thoughtfully. 'It calls out to you, then. That's why we heard the horses.'

'Are you sure it's me that it calls?'

Finn laughed. 'Oh, *Rory*. In the whole of history, since the foremothers, no-one has had the power over the *Sgath Dubh* that you have. And it's getting easier, isn't it? That's why you're so frightening.' She dipped her lashes, letting the flattery sink in. 'That's why you scare me.'

'Look who's talking.'

She smiled again, but there was madness in her face. 'You know you want to open it again. You have a connection, you have the power. You know you *can*.'

Rory hesitated, just half a second too long.

That's when I knew he'd do it.

Bloodstone & Icefall

It was one of their favourite places, he knew that. Rory shivered, eyeing the stones. The ring was so ancient its perfect symmetry had been distorted by weather and time, but the gist of it was there in the stones that were left. Some stood tall, others slumped drunkenly or had fallen flat, half overgrown with grass like forgotten tombstones. Some bore the ghosts of carvings; others were pitted only by rain and storm and wind. It was the stillest place he knew, and the eeriest. Only Finn and Seth had ever felt entirely at peace and happy here. They'd liked the loneliness: if anyone asked why, they called it privacy, and laughed. Most people feared the ghosts. Rory did.

He rubbed his arms in the cold lateness of the day. Finn just stood there, unmoving.

'Finn?'

'What?' She didn't turn.

'Finn? Please don't do this. Please don't ask.'

She ignored him, tilting her head and frowning slightly as if he was disturbing her.

'Finn, I've been thinking about this. He drowned. In the sea.'

'I'm aware of that. And?'

Rory swallowed. 'Remember Conal? How he looked?'

She shrugged. 'Did that bother you?'

'No, but I—Finn, *please* think about it. Who knows what the Selkyr do?'

'You know he's there.' Her voice was eerily, hideously calm as she turned and came closer to him. 'You know as well as I do.'

He raked both hands through his hair. 'I'll do it, Finn, if you want me to. But *please* don't ask me.'

'I'm sorry, Rory.' She stroked his cheek.

He shut his eyes. Bitterly he said, 'Show me, then. Show me where.'

He sat down on the grass on the edge of the circle. As the sun slid down the white sky, the stone shadows grew longer. Finn didn't speak. She stayed motionless.

A heavy chill travelled down his vertebrae. Something touched him, something feather-gentle on his cheekbone. Rory stood up. Shuddered. He walked to her side.

He said, 'He's here.'

Finn said nothing.

Something in the air trembled. It was growing visible, reflecting twilight. Pressure crushed against his eardrums, sang against the membranes.

There you are. Sgath Dubh. We know one another. You'll open for me. You'll close for me.

Dread washed through his body, and so did a violent need. He wanted this. He didn't want it. He'd made a promise, and Finn was raising her hand, placing her palm against something he couldn't see.

He stretched out his own fingers, gripped an unseen thing that coiled round his fist, loving him as much as he loved it. Like silk, like smoke, like mist, like nothing. His muscles tensed and flexed.

My father. One sight. All she wants. Dance to my song, Sgath Dubh.

Finn sighed out a breath.

Clenching his fist, hesitating, Rory turned his head sharply. He no longer couldn't see the thing she touched. There was something. Against her hand, the imprint of another. She was still, absolutely still. She didn't seem to be breathing.

'Finn,' he said, and his voice sounded like a feeble alien thing against the native weight of the Veil. 'Finn?'

She gave a gasp, stepped back, lowered her hand, squeezing it into a fist so tight her nails drew blood. The other hand's imprint was gone. A cold salt breeze shivered through the stones, and the thing that had glimmered in the late light grew still.

'*Finn!*'

'Rory?' She snapped her head to face him. Her eyes were silver and red. 'No. Rory, don't. *Don't.*'

'But . . .'

'I've changed my mind. Don't open it. Please. I've changed my mind.'

'Finn, what do you—'

'*Don't do it.*'

The pressure was gone. His ears popped. He gasped and reeled slightly, and he heard the birds begin to sing again, somewhere on the moor. He hadn't realised they'd ever stopped.

'Finn? *Finn.*'

She sat down on the cropped turf, right in the heart of the circle, hands over her face. Rory wondered for a hopeful moment if she was laughing, till he saw the tears squeezing out between her fingers, unstoppable. He watched her for an age, but the tears didn't stop coming and she kept her hands over her inhuman eyes.

He left her to the twilight and the darkening sky, and set off for the dun at a fast walk, with an awful tearing fear in his heart. He hadn't gone ten paces before he broke into a run.

. . .

He returned with the dawn, nodding to the guard he'd sent up to keep an eye on her. Maybe there had been no need for that, but he didn't think he'd ever shake his nervous constant state of alert, peace or no peace.

Finn was safe here. After what he'd seen her do to the Wolf, he reckoned she'd be safe anywhere, but still . . .

'She's not moved,' remarked the guard, as he set off back to the dun with a palpable air of relief. 'She's never spoken.'

Rory nodded. Walking towards her, he saw quickly that she'd stopped crying, and her hands were no longer over her face. Her eyes were blue and altogether normal. She blinked as he sat at her side, licked her lips. Gently he let his mind touch hers.

'You're like your father,' she murmured into space. 'That felt like your father.'

He didn't know what to say, so he said nothing.

'It doesn't upset me,' she said. 'I don't mean it like that. Don't ever feel you can't do it. Please.'

'No,' he said. 'I know.'

They sat in silence as a hazy sun rose behind them and gilded the sea.

'I've done something evil, Rory.'

He glanced at her sideways. He wasn't entirely confident, but he said, 'I don't believe that.'

'Then let's be kind, and say I almost did. You'd have torn the Black Veil for me, wouldn't you? Because I asked you. Because I loved your father. Because you did too.'

Rory tasted blood, and realised his own teeth had drawn it. 'Yes.'

'And you'd never have closed it again. Would you?'

He wanted to say *I'd have done my best*. But even as the words formed, he knew it wasn't true. His best was always beyond him, beyond everyone, and his almost-best wouldn't have done it.

'The Darkfall played Kate like a puppet, and it nearly played me too. All it's ever wanted is the destruction of its own Veil.' She rested her chin on her arms, melancholy, but for the first time it looked like a sadness that wasn't insanity.

'The *Sgath Dubh*?'

'The *first* Veil. It holds the Darkfall in place. Has done forever. Should do, forever. And all the Darkfall has ever wanted, for the whole of space and time since the Universe exploded, is *out.*'

A coldness beyond the physical flooded his bloodstream.

'Kate failed it, and it had offered her a godhead. All it had to offer me was my lover back.'

'Finn.' He cleared his throat, still nervous of the subject in her company. 'You'll have him back. One day. You know that better than anybody.'

'Yet still I'd have done it. To have him *now.*'

He wanted to say more, but he couldn't think what.

'Don't go talking to the Darkfall, Rory.' She leaned her cheek on her arms and managed to smile at him sideways. 'And don't go talking to the dead.'

He returned her smile. 'No.'

'Oh, and don't go thinking there's anything you can do about the Darkfall. *There are things you can't kill and you mustn't try.*' She made a face. 'So there.'

He laughed. 'Had a go at you, did he?'

'Gods, yes. He knew what I was up to. He warned me. So many times. I think he must have heard it call him, too. But he was too canny to answer.'

'He always was a bossy arse,' said Rory. 'And obviously still is.'

She gave a genuine hoot of laughter. 'And just as well.'

The sea was lightening fast, shimmering with flints of light. It was going to be a beautiful day, he thought. High summer. He could take the twins to the beach.

She said, 'How long has it got, Rory?'

He wanted to say *I don't know what you're talking about.* He wanted to say *How long has what got?*

Instead he said, 'Two or three years, I think. Not much more. Maybe four.'

'Yes.' She sighed.

'How did you know?'

'I realised, that's all. I realised when he touched me. When I felt the other side. The difference in the Veils. What it must have been like, once. What it's like now. I realised then. But I think—you know—I think I've known for a while.'

'Yes,' said Rory. 'Me too.'

'Your father once told Jed there was more to this than Kate's personality.' Finn skimmed a pebble out into the waves as they walked together along the water's edge. 'He was wrong. That's all there's ever been to it.'

'So Uncle Conal was wrong too?'

'Yes. Conal was wrong and Kate was right, but only about the least important thing. And the least important thing was the Veil.'

Hands in his pockets, Rory watched the horizon. The day's promise had darkened in the last hour. The line between sea and sky was obscured by mist, the cloud cover overhead leaked stray droplets of rain, and the wind had an edge of chill. Not a perfect Sithe day after all, and that was just as well. It would have hurt too much, sun and an endless sky and light glittering off blue water, and the sun-burnt scent of whin, and the buck-and-toss of half-wild horses racing the late summer breeze for the pure fun of it.

'Our Veil was doomed from the start, Rory, just like the rest of us. You know better than anyone it was a living thing. All living things die.'

'Especially when you stick a blade in their heart.'

'Ah, Rory. You used our own Veil to close the Black Veil, didn't you? You took all the strength it had left. But Rory, it was dying anyway. This was the last thing it could give us. You had no choice but to take it.'

'Maybe not. But gods, we wasted everything in this war. So many lives, so much time.'

'No. You know what the prophet said? Nothing about you saving the Veil. You'd determine its fate, that's all. Do you know what she told Kate?' Finn halted, staring at the sea. '*Destroy the Veil, and the NicNiven will have all she desires; let it die or survive, and nothing will be hers.* Know why?'

'No, but you're going to tell me.'

'Yes, Captain.' She gave him a rueful smile and a mocking salute. 'Kate couldn't be allowed to wait for the Veil to die, because the Darkfall couldn't wait. The death of our Veil wouldn't affect the death of the *Sgath Dubh*. That's the one it needed you to tear to ribbons. That's why Kate's godhead depended on you, and on you tearing down the Veil. The Darkfall wanted the *Sgath Dubh* destroyed. It needed you for that. It needed you to hone your skills on our poor dying Veil, and then turn your attention to the real one. And so we got a prophecy and a promise of salvation.'

'Prophet! Hah! They should have drowned the old bitch at birth.' Rory managed a dry laugh as he passed a handful of flat pebbles to Finn. 'The trouble she caused.'

Finn couldn't speak. Incapable of looking at him—the opinionated cynicism was right, the face and the voice weren't—she concentrated on her skimming technique for maybe a minute. When the last stone had bounced off a wave, she sighed and wrapped her arms round her thin body.

'The Veil the foremothers made was a pale imitation of the *Sgath Dubh*. The one that was there already, always had been, because it lies between life and death and there'll always be those. How could they make a Veil as strong as that? Gods help us if they could. They cobbled together a shadow of it. They never expected it to survive forever. It's the *Sgath Dubh* that matters. That's the one that survives, the one that'll always be there, if some idiot witch doesn't turn to the Darkfall. That's the Veil we mess with at our peril.'

Rory blew a lock of hair out of his eyes. Finn almost flinched at the mannerism.

'That's why Conal told Dad not to be scared, isn't it? Because he knew what he didn't know before. There was nothing to be frightened *of*.' Rory grinned. 'Well. At least, nothing there's any point being frightened of.'

Finn laughed. He liked the sound. 'Yes. The death of our own Veil was nothing to fear. The other Veil, the Dark one? You watch what you're doing with it, young man.'

'You're the one who—'

'Asked you to do what you never should. I know. I'm sorry. When Kate failed the Darkfall, it tried me. And it came *this close*.' Rubbing her arms, she made a rueful face. 'It was Kate who had to be defeated, Kate who would have destroyed us. That's what it's been about.'

'Not the Veil surviving. Us.'

She shrugged briskly. 'Her prophecy came true. Nothing was indeed hers.'

'Till my dying day, I'll remember her face.' An echo of horror tickled his spine.

'She got a legacy of a sort, then.' Finn smiled at the ocean. 'Well, Conal was right to fight her, even if he didn't know why.

We had to survive Kate, and stay human. Me included, Rory. Up till last night it was a bit of a close-run thing.'

'Kate might still destroy the Sithe, Finn, dead or not. You sure we'll survive without our own Veil?'

'Oh, hell, yes. We're human, Rory. We've a right to live with other humans. We've a duty to live with them, we were *built* to live with them. Jed was always right. That isn't the otherworld, this is. A ghetto. It protected us while we needed it.' She grinned, a little wickedly. 'Besides, who's going to protect the full-mortals from Lammyr and Selkyr and kelpies when the Veil dies? They have no idea what's going to hit them in a few years' time.'

There was such smug satisfaction in her voice, Rory couldn't help his snort of laughter.

Finn slipped her arm through his. 'Well. Now we're all grown up, and maybe the full-mortals are, too. We have to learn to live together. Without killing each other. That's all.' She shrugged. 'What else does it mean to be human?'

Rory sobered, and fell silent for a long moment. 'Can you see Sionnach living without this world?'

She rubbed a hand across her tired face, then said quietly, 'Or me.'

He swallowed. 'Finn—'

'If we can't adapt we'll die, Rory. That's evolution.'

'No, it's natural selection.'

She laughed at the correction. 'Yeah. Is there a better kind?'

'Are you leaving, Finn? Because that isn't what Dad wanted.'

'Not yet.' She stared out at the horizon.

'Let him go, Finn.'

'I have to, don't I?' She rubbed her fist across her nose. 'He told me to, there in the Stones. He said *Let me go.* Because he wants me to live. Damn him.'

'He'll still be there.'

'Yes. The dead are dead, Rory. I've got no right to hang on and hold him down. But I do have the right to go to him. And I won't wait forever.'

'Fair enough.' Clasping her hand, he kissed it. 'Nobody gets forever.'

EPILOGUE

Hannah

'There's something I keep wondering,' I told Rory.

A year later we sat on horseback among the pines at the Loch of the Cailleach. On the spit of beach Finn and Sionnach sat close together, hands linked in the sand as they watched the twins paddle and splash and fall over. Laughing, Finn stood up to rescue one of them, passing him into Sionnach's arms as the other, too, fell onto its backside and began to wail.

Branndair didn't move to help, just watched them contentedly from the rock where he lay half-dozing. Too old for infant rescue missions, was Branndair. There were grey hairs on his muzzle and I expected him to be gone, one morning soon. I was surprised he'd stayed this long, but Seth had told him long ago to keep an eye on Finn. Old habits died hard for Branndair, and besides, I think he was enjoying the holiday of his dotage. He liked to have small children climb on him. He had all the patience he needed: for boisterous twins, and for waiting. He sat among the Stones sometimes, was all.

Each consoling a sodden infant, Sionnach and Finn made wry faces at one another, and Finn pressed her head to Sionnach's arm. He loosed it from Nathair to put it around her shoulder, and she huddled into him.

Finn's night visits to the sea weren't so frequent now. When I

431

woke in the small hours and watched her ride out, I didn't worry so much. Not quite so much. Still, I wouldn't go back to sleep till she rode back, the hem of her coat dripping seawater, her jeans and boots soaked.

Trying it out, said Rory. *Getting up the nerve.*

He would come to my side and put his arm around me and together we'd watch her ride back across the moonlit machair.

What woke you? I'd say, and he'd raise his wrist to show me the cold green stone frosted with condensation.

This, he'd say. *Let me know she was gone. It does that.*

One day we'd wait, and wait, and we wouldn't see her ride back. Finn would go to the Selkyr in the end, and Sionnach would go with her. Rory knew that and so did I. Who were we to stop them?

But I knew they wouldn't go yet, not while the twins were so small. They'd go before the Veil died, but that might not be for a year or two. And in the meantime, they weren't alone. Watching Finn's fingers tighten on Sionnach's, catching her wicked smile aimed only at him, I knew that.

But like her mother, Finn would die one day of her own volition. The oath hadn't killed Stella: we'd worked that out. Stella had willed the thing that killed her into existence, and given in gratefully, because she could no more be parted from Aonghas than Finn could from Seth.

Finn was handling life a little better, though. I thought that and laughed as I watched her nuzzle the squalling Allta into quiet contentment. And I could do that, I thought. I could be a mother, even if I could never have a child with Rory. Nathair and Allta could have us. Anthill stuff.

'What were you wondering?' asked Rory.

'It's stupid.'

'I bet it isn't.'

'My Dad, Jed, Eili. The rest.' I hesitated. 'Why d'you suppose they were armed?'

'That's not stupid.' He grinned at me sheepishly. 'I was wondering that myself.'

'You think Kate's still around?'

'Nah. Nothing left of her.'

I sighed. 'So what would they be fighting?'

'That old legend. The one about the rebel angels?' He scratched his neck. 'Maybe it's not all legend.'

'Oh, yeah? Minions of Satan, and all that?'

'Nah. I'm not sure even proper angels take sides.'

'Who you calling improper?'

He grinned, blew hair off his face. 'Oh, bear with me. You ever wonder why the Lammyr look forward to dying? Why the Selkyr are so damn keen to help us on our way? It's like we're ordinary humans who came from somewhere else in the first place.'

'Aye, right.'

'And maybe—I dunno—there's further to go? Veils beyond veils beyond veils.' He pulled a face, half-smiling, a little awkward. 'More adventures.'

It had an appeal. It had a distinct appeal. Against my will, I gave him a wry smile.

'An awfully big adventure?' I suggested.

A grin split his beautiful face.

'Just that, Lost Girl.'

He linked his fingers with mine, and kissed the back of my hand, and in the late sunlight of a dying world we rode back to the dun together.

THE END

REBEL ANGELS
NOTES

THE TRUE NAMES

I've mentioned before that the Sithe play fast and loose with their Gaelic, and nowhere is this truer than with their names. With one exception, I left out all the graves and acutes that adorn real Gaelic; this makes it less authentic in terms of our own world, but after one attempt to put them all in, I gave up on the grounds that it was more distracting than helpful. Sorry, real Gaelic speakers. Gaelic words also tend to have different spellings, and a multiplicity of meanings depending on pronunciation, but that was another thing I learned to live with. I picked a word and a definition on grounds, usually, of its beauty or its aptness for the character. And some of them, like Sorcha, Luthais, Raonall, and Fearchar, go simply by their birth names (in those particular cases, they are the Gaelic versions of Clare, Lewis, Ranald, and Farquhar).

MURLAINN
Seth's name is one I have only ever found in one Gaelic dictionary—defined as *falcon*—but I didn't let that put me off. It suited him so well, I couldn't resist. A merlin seemed too appropriate to turn down: small, but fast and deadly. Anyway, Seth insisted, and there's no arguing with Sithe names.

Cù Chaorach

Apart from the slight echo of the great Irish hero Cuchulainn, I liked this name for Conal: it means 'hound of the sheep,' or sheep-dog, which suited him down to the ground.

Caorann

I named Finn *Rowan* because that tree is traditionally a protector against bad spirits, and a rowan tree in Scotland is a thing you mess with at your peril. Given Finn's protective role in the clann—not to mention her occasional air of menace—there seemed no more appropriate name for her.

Currac-Sagairt

Hannah's name was a tricky one. She was always going to be *Wolfs-bane,* but the actual Gaelic for that term is *Fuath-a'-mhadaidh,* which is such a mouthful I'm not even going to make a phonetic attempt at the pronunciation. By way of compromise (and taking pity on her friends who had to use it), I decided to go for *Monks-hood,* which is simply a different name for the same poisonous plant.

Other Names, in Alphabetical Order:

Branndair	Gridiron
Braon	Rain, Dew
Broc	Badger
Calman	Dove; Calman Ruadh means 'Red Dove'
Carraig	Rock
Cluaran	Thistle
Cuilean	Young Dog
Cuthag	Cuckoo
Darach	Oak

Diorras	Stubbornness
Easag	Pheasant
Eilid (Eili)	Deer
Eorna	Barley
Faramach	Noisy
Fearna	Alder
Feorag	Squirrel
Fitheach	Raven
Fraoch	Heather
Gealach	Moon
Glanadair	Purifier
Gocaman	Guard, Watcher
Grian	Sun
Griosach	Embers
Gruaman	Sadness, Melancholy
Iolaire	Eagle
Laochan	Young Hero
Leoghar	Brave
Liath	Grey
Lus-nan-Leac	Eyebright
Orach	Golden
Oscarach	Bold
Raineach	Bracken
Reultan	Star
Righil	Reel, Dance
Sgarrag	Ray-fish
Sionnach	Fox
Suil	Eye
Sulaire	Gannet
Taghan	Marten, Polecat
Torc	Boar

| Turlach | Bonfire |
| Udhar | Ulcer (and no wonder Eili was miffed at the name Finn gave her) |

And finally . . .

NATHAIR AND ALLTA

Quite what was going through Finn's mind when she named her twins *Snake* and *Savage*, I don't know. Even though she was on the other side of sane at the time, I'm sure she had her reasons. One day they might turn up in my head again, and tell me.

THE MYTHS

I cherry-picked the myths and legends of Scotland and did what I liked with them, because I firmly believe that's what they're for. No disrespect to the marvellous originals, but myths, legends, and folklore are made to be played with.

THE SITHE

I never wanted to use the term *Sidhe* because it's so closely identified with the Irish faeries. I'd always planned to use the Scottish word *Sith*, but by the time I came to write the books, it had been used by some guy called George Lucas, and I thought I had better differentiate my characters from a dark galactic brotherhood. The word *sith* (pronounced shee) is found in many Scottish place names, such as Glenshee; sithe also means 'peace,' but then the faeries were also known as the 'people of peace,' a fact to which Seth refers rather ironically on several occasions.

Faery traditions survive amazingly strongly, even in modern-day Scotland. There are still those who won't cut down a rowan tree for fear of offending the little people; when my mother-in-law did so, and her house burned to the ground shortly afterwards, her good friend pretty much said 'I told you so.'

There's a seeming contradiction in the relationship of rowans to faeries, in that while the trees are said to be sacred to the faery people, they are also supposed to ward off evil spirits. Given that faeries and evil spirits were considered interchangeable after the Middle Ages, with the rise of devil-phobia and the witch persecutions, that might seem to make no sense; but I chose to make rowanwood a material that naturally blocks my characters' telepathy. So, while it would be of value as a defence, it could also be used against them—as Kate does so effectively in *Icefall*.

There are many local variations of the myth about the faeries being the rebel angels who were thrown out of Heaven, as described in Revelation Chapter 12. The angels who fell on land became the faeries; the ones who remained in the sky, caught on their way to Earth, became the Merry Dancers (the *fir chlis* or Northern Lights); and those that fell in the water became the Blue Men, or seals, or selkies.

There are too many fairy traditions to count, but they include child abduction, the seduction of mortals into the otherworld, and the nasty tendency of time to pass differently in the faery world. A tale is told of Finn MacCool's son Oisin, who lived for many years in Tir nan Og, remaining beautiful and young, until he visited the mortal world; whereupon he slipped from his horse, touched the ground, and became an old and wizened man. (There are surprisingly modern variations on this myth: people who appear, bemused, in the middle of cities, having accepted an invitation from a beautiful stranger only the previous night. These tales usually end with the poor humans dissolving to dust on being told of the actual date and year.) I've used and abused many of these traditions. There's no better collection of them than John Gregorson Campbell's *The*

Gaelic Otherworld (Birlinn Ltd), which is comprehensive, detailed, and, once you open it, almost magically impossible to put down.

In Dunvegan Castle on the Isle of Skye there is a fragile remnant of a flag known as the Fairy Flag (*Am Bratach Sith*). It belongs to the Chieftain of Clan MacLeod, and while many legends are attached to its origins, most involve the mystical banner being given to an early chief as reward for services rendered. It's supposed to have many magical properties that can aid in battle, but it can only be unfurled three times; allegedly it's been unfurled twice in history. There are too many variations on this story to list here—and they're worth looking up—but needless to say, I gave a MacLeod a very special favour to do for the faeries in *Firebrand*. Entirely my own invention, but no less probable than the ones in the legends.

Cold iron has always been said to be harmful to faeries, hence traditions like the nailing of horseshoes to doors for the protection of livestock. It wasn't a practical aversion to give my own Sithe, given the amount of time they spend with swords, daggers, and arrowheads; I've turned this particular tradition around to make 'cold iron' a metaphor they use for the loss of a soul.

THE WOLF OF KILREVIN

It's not just myths that I've maltreated; I've had my wicked way with some historical figures too. The Wolf is *very* loosely inspired by the fourteenth century Earl of Buchan, Alexander Stewart, known as the Wolf of Badenoch for his (alleged) savagery and ruthlessness. His grudge against the Bishop of Moray led him to ride down from his fortress on Lochindorb, sack the town of Elgin and burn its cathedral (the impressive ruins still stand). He was excommunicated for this act, and had to beg forgiveness from the Bishop of St Andrews in the presence of his brother the King of Scotland, but this struck me as exactly the kind of pragmatic and cynical move that my own Alasdair would make. After all, neither his political machinations nor his brutality ended with the Wolf of Badenoch's apology.

Local legend tells that the Wolf of Badenoch met his death after a game of chess with the Devil; his lifeless body was discovered unmarked and unscarred, but the corpses of his men were sprawled outside his fortress, blackened as if by lightning.

KATE NICNIVEN

In some sixteenth century manuscripts, the name Kate McNiven (or NicNiven, or NicNevin, or McNieven, or Nike Neiving) is given to the queen of the Scottish dark witches. (NicNiven may also have been a leader's title in witch cults.)

A witch by that name was said to have been burned at the Knock of Crieff in the sixteenth century. Captured by townsfolk, she was tied to a stake; a local landowner attempted to save her but was rebuffed by the villagers who by that time were no doubt thoroughly wound up to enjoy a good witch fire. Kate McNiven reportedly cursed the town, but bit a moonstone from her necklace and spat it at the more sympathetic laird, saying his house and family would flourish so long as they preserved the stone. According to the tales they did indeed prosper, while the town went into decline. North of the Knock of Crieff there is a standing stone, remnant of a circle, known as Kate McNiven's Stane.

Stuart McHardy tells her story, and many more, in his addictive *On the Trail of Scotland's Myths and Legends* (Luath Press). Brian Froud has a fabulously sinister portrait of "Nicnivin, Elph Queine of the Unseelie Court" in his *Good Faeries/Bad Faeries* (Pavilion).

THE KELPIES

Kelpies and water horses (*each-uisge*) can be entirely different beasts in many legends, being sometimes-humanoid, sometime-equine demon spirits, but I've made mine the war horses of my Sithe. Since the best war horse was always one that was as savage in battle as its rider, this made sense to me. In old legends, a water horse would lurk around rivers and lochs looking available and tame and rather beautiful—until some weary traveller decided to make use of it, whereupon he would find himself unable to dismount. The horse would then undergo a serious personality change, plunge into the water, drown the traveller there and eat him. (Except for the liver, apparently. Anyone who has a cat knows that this rings true.)

THE SELKYR

Selkies in traditional myths tend to be gentle creatures, taking the form of seals. In many stories a human will fall in love with a beautiful man or woman who is discovered basking on a Highland beach (our summers aren't as bad as many people think). The selkie might stay with its human lover for a while, and even give them children, but if the seal-coat isn't found and hidden (for it slipped out of it only for a moment), the selkie will inevitably put it back on, and abandon its family to return to the sea. The stories are often tragic or melancholy. My Selkyr aren't quite like that, which is why I changed their name; but selkies were undoubtedly their inspiration.

THE LAMMYR

I made them up. That's allowed. Though I'm not sure what it says about me.

THANKS

My poor Sithe. I painted them into a nasty old corner at the end of *Wolfsbane*, and if it hadn't been for Elizabeth Garrett and her generosity, I'm not sure they'd ever have found their way out of it. Her beautiful Cliff Cottage is amazingly spacious, and can accommodate an entire clann, their warhorses, their familiars, and their author. I just hope we didn't make too much of a mess. Thank you, Elizabeth, for giving me so much time and space—and, of course, the cliffs.

Many thanks to the Estate of Edwin Muir and to Faber & Faber Limited for their kind permission to reprint lines from 'Love in Time's Despite' (*The Labyrinth*, 1949).

Thank you, Whitney Ross, Amy Stapp, and everyone at Tor—you are such great guys to work with. Seth loves New York!

Lucy Coats is always riding to my rescue, and she did it again with *Icefall* by taking her perfectly honed blade to my overpopulated manuscript, and by asking very incisive questions. There was blood all over the carpet. I'm beyond grateful, and so are Seth and Finn.

Alison Stroak, thank you, thank you for saving me from myself and my giant foot-in-Seth's-mouth blunders. I hope Damien has forgiven me for the tissues. And massive thanks too to Lawrence Mann and Steve Stone, who created beautiful covers and yet more gorgeous images of my imaginary friends.

Graham Watson, Michael Malone, Derek Allsopp, and Keith Charters were burdened with the first draft of this book, but they liked it enough to convince me it could work. I am not sure how I'd have faced a second draft without their faith, so huge thanks go to them.

Chris Curran supported and encouraged me through all four Rebel Angels books, and was a fount of good advice. Catriona Smith was incredibly kind and patient with my floundering attempts at Gaelic, and gave me crucial help, especially with a particular place name. Ross Walker advised me about the world of drugs, and Iris Rooney gave me the Devil's Hour. My Twitterpals were there as always with answers and advice and virtual tequila. And Ian Philip, who doesn't even like fantasy, put up with A LOT of it. I am so very grateful to you all.

Huge thanks to Robert Roth, who donated very generously to the Authors for the Philippines campaign and can now be said to be a Good Guy turned (fictionally!) Bad Guy.

I'm pretty sure the magical island of Colonsay is indifferent to the fleeting gratitude of mortal authors, but I want to thank it anyway, for being a landscape where so much could happen in my head.

Finally, there are certain otherworlds where I am completely lost. So thank you, Jamie Philip and William Lofthus, for letting me sit in on some long Xbox sessions, for correcting gaffes, and for being very tolerant of my complete bewilderment. Equal thanks go to Lucy Philip for selecting and downloading a fabulously motivating soundtrack that did not date from the 1980s. Kids, I'm very, very grateful and I love you. Now go and tidy your rooms.

ABOUT THE AUTHOR

GILLIAN PHILIP was born in Glasgow but has spent much of her life in Aberdeen, Barbados, and a beautiful valley near Dallas (not that one). Before turning to full-time writing, she worked as a barmaid, theatre usherette, record store assistant, radio presenter, typesetter, hotel wrangler, secretary, political assistant, and Celtic-Caribbean singer.

She has been nominated for a Carnegie Medal and a David Gemmell Legend Award and short-listed for many awards, including the Royal Mail Scottish Book Award. Her favourite genres are fantasy and crime (her novels include *Bad Faith, Crossing the Line,* and *The Opposite of Amber*), and she has written as one of the Erin Hunters (Survivors) and as Gabriella Poole (Darke Academy).

She lives in the northeast Highlands of Scotland with husband Ian, twins Jamie and Lucy, Cluny the Labrador, Milo the Papillon, Otto the half-Papillon (guess how that happened), Buffy the Slayer Hamster, psycho cats The Ghost and The Darkness, Mapp and Lucia the chickens, and several nervous fish. She is not getting any more pets. No way.